Praise for _The Changeling Plague_

"A very intriguing read."
— Vernor Vinge, Hugo Award–winning
author of _A Deepness in the Sky_

Praise for _Technogenesis_

"Perhaps the most captivating science fiction read of recent months . . . [a] terse thriller that holds many unexpected twists and turns. An exceptional story."
— _The Bookwatch_

"Hard SF with romantic spice . . . satisfyingly rich . . . a taut and suspenseful read . . . great for fans of writers like Catherine Asaro—the romance structure and high technology setting work well together."
— Science Fiction Weekly

"Imaginative and pleasing . . . a fresh and entertaining tour . . . a suspenseful read that creates some tough problems and then deals with them in some realistically messy ways."
— _Locus_

"Mitchell blends high-tech speculation with high adventure. . . . Quite well done and genuinely creepy."
— _Science Fiction Chronicle_

"An absorbing and creative science fiction tale . . . the protagonist is flawed and weak at times, yet so heroic that she represents the finest qualities inherent in our species. On a scale from one to ten, this novel is an eleven."

"Fun and mind blowin

D0816305

Praise for *Murphy's Gambit*
Winner of the Compton Crook Award

"Mitchell combines first-rate hard-SF storytelling with a strong female protagonist in a fast-paced space adventure." —*Library Journal*

"An enjoyable high-tech space opera . . . a well designed tale . . . readers will line up for book two." —*Midwest Book Review*

"The fast pace and high adventure make for good fun." —*Locus*

"You forget you're reading an author's first book. The future society explored here is fascinating, complex, and fully realized. I was reminded . . . of Robert Heinlein's *The Moon Is a Harsh Mistress*." —Duane Wilkins, *Talebones*

"Pure, unadulterated pleasure. Syne is a born teacher and storyteller. Murphy is as realistic and appealing as any character in science fiction. Talent like Syne Mitchell's is the kind you can't afford to let slip by." —Lisa DuMond, SF Site and MEviews.com

"A fun tale." —*University City Review* (Philadelphia)

"*Murphy's Gambit* is the real thing: adamantine-hard science fiction with heart." —Eric S. Nylund, author of *A Signal Shattered*

THE CHANGELING PLAGUE

Syne Mitchell

A ROC BOOK

ROC
Published by New American Library, a division of
Penguin Putnam Inc., 375 Hudson Street,
New York, New York 10014, U.S.A.
Penguin Books Ltd, 80 Strand,
London WC2R 0RL, England
Penguin Books Australia Ltd, 250 Camberwell Road,
Camberwell, Victoria 3124, Australia
Penguin Books Canada Ltd, 10 Alcorn Avenue,
Toronto, Ontario, Canada M4V 3B2
Penguin Books (N.Z.) Ltd, Cnr Rosedale and Airborne Roads,
Albany, Auckland 1310, New Zealand

Penguin Books Ltd, Registered Offices:
Harmondsworth, Middlesex, England

First published by Roc, an imprint of New American Library,
a division of Penguin Putnam Inc.

First Printing, February 2003
10 9 8 7 6 5 4 3 2 1

Copyright © Syne Mitchell, 2003
All rights reserved

 REGISTERED TRADEMARK—MARCA REGISTRADA

Printed in the United States of America

Without limiting the rights under copyright reserved above, no part of
this publication may be reproduced, stored in or introduced into a
retrieval system, or transmitted, in any form, or by any means (electronic,
mechanical, photocopying, recording, or otherwise), without the prior written
permission of both the copyright owner and the above publisher of this
book.

PUBLISHER'S NOTE
This is a work of fiction. Names, characters, places, and incidents either are
the product of the author's imagination or are used fictitiously, and any
resemblance to actual persons, living or dead, business establishments,
events, or locales is entirely coincidental.

BOOKS ARE AVAILABLE AT QUANTITY DISCOUNTS WHEN USED TO PROMOTE
PRODUCTS OR SERVICES. FOR INFORMATION PLEASE WRITE TO PREMIUM
MARKETING DIVISION, PENGUIN PUTNAM INC., 375 HUDSON STREET, NEW
YORK, NEW YORK 10014.

If you purchased this book without a cover you should be aware that this
book is stolen property. It was reported as "unsold and destroyed"
to the publisher and neither the author nor the publisher has received
any payment for this "stripped book."

For Eric, whose love and encouragement make all the difference

ACKNOWLEDGMENTS

Many talented people generously shared their knowledge and time to help me improve the science and writing in this book. Any mistakes remaining are entirely my own invention.

My "patron saint of genetics," Dr. Peter Byers, took time out of his schedule to answer my many questions about genetics and gave me my first glimpse of a DNA sequencer.

Dr. Ruth Levy and Dr. Maynard Olson gave me a tour of their wondrous genetics lab at the University of Washington.

Andy Blinn shared his life experiences and helped me add verisimilitude to the story.

Tim Allen, David Fleischman, Jane Hawkins, Steve Husak, and Ralph Squillace bravely read an early version of the book and suggested improvements.

Jennifer Heddle's keen editorial insights took the book to a higher level.

And, of course, Eric Nylund was there from the first glimmerings of the idea to the last revision, challenging me to always improve the book.

PROLOGUE

The biohazard suit's bulky gloves made it hard for Dr. Lillith Watkins to program the car's destination. But the Racal suit, with its self-contained oxygen tanks, was necessary in this part of Boston. Muhn's disease had been detected in this, the industrial sector.

Lillith, a junior researcher at the Centers for Disease Control, was here to check the quarantine and disinfection of a computer assembly plant. It had been shut down when ninety-six of its workers were diagnosed with the disease.

Outbreaks of Mahn's had taken the lives of thousands in Moscow, London, Beijing, and Paris. It was Lillith's job to make sure the disease didn't get a foothold in the United States.

The van rounded the corner and the three-story plant loomed into view. It was tented with blue-green plastic, like a house about to be fumigated. Stenciled in white lettering was the name of the company: DAVIS COMPUTERS.

She pulled to a stop in front of the factory and popped open the van's cargo doors.

Drs. George Danvers and Isabetta Schneza, also in biohazard suits, climbed out of the back of the van and unloaded the wipes and the squat air sampler that would detect viral particles.

If the virus was not detected, the owners could petition the CDC to lift the quarantine.

Danvers and Schneza were easy to distinguish, despite the suits. Danvers stood a head taller than the five-foot-two Schneza. Their names were written in large block letters down their arms.

Lillith paused in the unloading and looked at the tented building. How had Dr. Heinrich Mahn felt knowing his name had become synonymous with death? She'd read the CDC bulletins that proved the origin of the pathogen was Mahn's research on a cure for hemophilia. With the best of intentions, Mahn had created a disease that swept across Europe and Asia.

"Come on," Danvers said. "The sooner we start, the sooner we finish."

Lillith kept her eyes on the factory. "Did you see the morning news?"

Danvers hefted another box of sample wipes out of the van. "About Mahn? Yeah. I can't believe they let the shooter get that close. I mean, Mahn was gunned down on the courthouse steps. You'd think there'd be better security at the Hague."

Lillith shook her head. "Such a waste." She helped Schneza attach filters to the air sampler. They rolled it to the front door. Lillith verified the door was locked, then tapped in the alarm deactivation code.

Schneza pushed in the air sampler, and Danvers and Lillith carried in the boxes of wipes. Once they were inside, Lillith checked the building's alarm display.

She frowned. A window was open.

Lillith waved Danvers over. She pointed out the red icon on the display and shouted through the muffling layers of her helmet's faceplate. "There's a window open on the second floor. I'm going to investigate."

Schneza looked up from the sniffer's console. "You want one of us to go with you?"

Lillith shook her head. "It's probably a malfunction, or someone forgot and left it open. I'll stay in radio contact." She pointed to the microphone built into her helmet.

Schneza nodded and resumed programming the sniffer to sample the air.

Lillith lumbered up the stairs, not trusting the elevator. Getting trapped in a level-four biohazard region was not something she wanted to do.

Navigating the stairs was challenging in her Racal biohazard armor. It was built like a space suit, complete with its own air source. It was kept at positive pressure so that, in the event of a leak, air flowed out of instead of into the suit. Safe, but the inflated arms and legs were cumbersome.

As she took another step, Lillith heard a high-pitched sound. She stopped, her foot resting on the next step, mouth open, her whole body listening. There it was again. A high keening, like a baby's cry.

Impossible. Unless . . . there was an open window. But who would break into a factory quarantined with a deadly disease? It must be the wind against the plastic sheeting.

The sound came again.

The back of Lillith's neck prickled. She pressed the radio button on her chest. "I'm hearing a strange sound, a wailing. Going to investigate."

"Wait, what's your loc—"

Lillith cut off the radio. Going on a wild-goose chase was bad enough; taking someone along to witness your embarrassment would be worse.

Lillith emerged from the stairwell into a long hallway with doors on either side. Light filtered in from a window set into the near end of the hall.

She peeked through one of the glass doors and saw a large room. Along the walls were counters strewn with partially constructed computer systems. Boxes of memory, processors, and motherboards were organized on shelves above the workbenches.

Davis Computers specialized in custom machines and repair of antique computers. Each machine was hand-built. It was a niche market. The company employed one hundred and twenty workers, most of them semiskilled assemblers.

The sound came from farther down the hall. Lillith

walked softly, ears pricked. There was little natural light in this interior hallway, so she turned on her chest light. The wide-angle beam lit up her path.

At the end of the hallway was a pair of bathrooms, male and female, separated by a watercooler. She continued past. There were several more workrooms on either side of the hallway before it terminated in a door marked OBSOLETE PARTS.

The sound came from the other side of the door. This close she could hear it rise and fall as if forming words.

Lillith tried the door handle. The noise abruptly stopped.

Her breath caught in her throat. Lillith's hand hovered over the radio. Caution warred with the desire not to look foolish. It could still be the wind, stopping by coincidence at the moment she touched the door.

She tried the handle again and discovered it was locked. Damn.

Sighing, Lillith tapped the radio button on her chest. "I think I've found something. I need to get through a locked interior door to be sure."

"Be careful," said Danvers. "One puncture and you'll be quarantined in the slammer for a month . . . or worse."

There was a palm pad mounted on the wall next to the door. Lillith typed the alarm deactivation code into the panel underneath, but the door stayed locked. The palm pad was useless—it wouldn't recognize Lillith's print, and the point was moot because of her suit's thick gloves.

Lillith knocked on the door and shouted, "Can you open this from the inside? I'm here to help."

Silence.

All of Lillith's senses were alive. She tasted the tang of sweat when she licked her lips. The dim hallway seemed brighter, and each sound made her jump. Was there someone in there, or had she imagined it all?

Danvers radioed, "Where are you?"

Lillith gave him the directions. She looked in one

of the side workrooms for a crowbar or something else she could use to pry open the door. Her eyes fell on an empty server rack. She pulled out one of the slats that held the servers in place. Going back to the hallway, she slid it between the door and the jamb. For an agonizing moment she jostled it up and down without success; then the door's weak interior lock gave way.

Lillith pushed the door open slowly. "Anyone in here?"

The room beyond was dark, lit only by a clerestory window high above. When her eyes adjusted, she saw computer parts piled on the floor. There were cases, motherboards, network cards, all in different heaps.

A whimper from the far corner of the room was cut short. Had a puppy gotten trapped in here? Perhaps one of the workers had left it behind when the building was quarantined. Lillith imagined the poor animal trapped in this dark room without food or water for the past week. The thought twisted her stomach.

"Good boy," she cooed. "It's going to be all right."

She turned the corner around a pile of old CRT monitors. Something flashed in her vision and bounced with a jolt off her helmet's faceplate, scoring the plastic. As it skittered under a shelf, Lillith saw the gray metal housing of a power supply.

Lillith blinked. Her neck ached from snapping sideways with the blow. She checked her suit's display. It was intact. She turned the beam of her light in the direction of her attacker.

Nothing she imagined had prepared her for this. A boy and girl, so alike they could be twins, were manacled to the metal shelving lining the far wall.

They were gaunt and dressed only in the tattered remains of T-shirts advertising motherboards and molecular memory. Five feet away, the shell of an old CRT monitor had been used as a toilet.

The girl lay glassy-eyed on the floor, her face covered with the red boils symptomatic of Mahn's disease.

The boy crouched over her, his face tight with anger

and pain. He grabbed another power supply from the shelf and drew back to throw.

Lillith held up her hands. "Easy. Easy now. I'm here to help." She looked at the girl lying on the floor. "How long has she been sick?"

"What's going on?" Danvers asked over the radio. "I heard something fall."

"Stay back," Lillith answered. "I've found two children."

"Jeezus!"

"They're scared and I think more people would only frighten them. Call for a quarantine ambulance. They're both dehydrated and malnourished. The girl exhibits symptoms of Mahn's."

"How did they—" Danvers began

"Later. Right now I want to get them stabilized."

She backtracked to the water cooler she had seen in the hallway. Lillith filled two disposable paper cups and went back into the room.

When she returned, the boy eyed her warily but licked his lips at the sight of the water.

Lillith knelt and held out one of the cups to him.

The boy took it as if the water were gold; all his being concentrated on not spilling a drop.

He surprised Lillith; instead of drinking, he dipped his finger in and dribbled water onto the lips of his sister. After he repeated this a few times, the girl's cracked tongue licked the drops. Only then did he sip.

Lillith handed him the second cup, and he looked at her with openmouthed surprise.

Tears welled in Lillith's eyes. What had these children endured that a cup of water could generate such raw gratitude?

"I need the medical kit from the van," Lillith radioed. "Can one of you bring it? Just leave it outside the door. I don't want to scare them."

"Will do," Danvers radioed back.

A minute later, the boy tensed. He raised a power supply and glared at the door.

Danvers waited outside the door, holding the medical kit. "The ambulance should be here in thirty minutes; there's an accident blocking I-93. How bad are they?"

Lillith shook her head. "Bad. Their ankles are handcuffed to the shelving. It looks like whoever did that just left them here when the building was closed." She looked away from Danvers's gaze. "I hope the bastard's dead."

Lillith got another cup of water and hefted the medical bag.

While the boy drank, Lillith knelt and examined his sister.

The girl's pupils did not contract when Lillith shone a penlight in either eye. Unable to take a pulse through bulky gloves, Lillith turned up the gain on the electronic stethoscope and listened. The girl's pulse was rapid.

She moaned and writhed when Lillith touched her. The girl's skin had a jaundiced cast, and Lillith saw more of the characteristic boils on the girl's calves.

It was the final stages of the disease. The virus, intended to cure hemophiliacs, caused excessive clotting. The girl's blood was sticking in her veins, piling up under her skin. In the final stages, a clot would reach her brain and cause a stroke, or seize her heart.

"Idy!" the girl called out. "Idy!"

The boy pushed Lillith aside and put his forehead to the girl's. He cooed nonsense syllables until the girl hushed. "Help," he said, looking up at Lillith. His bright blue eyes glittered with tears. "Help her," he sobbed. To his sister, he wailed, "Don't leave me."

The boy's voice was high and pure, like a tenor in a boy's choir. The contrast between the innocence of his eyes and the conditions he'd been subjected to were a knife in Lillith's heart.

The girl began to seize: Her body trembled and her head knocked against the ground.

The boy's eyes widened and he backed away, his mouth working soundlessly.

Lillith pulled the girl's head onto her lap so it

wouldn't pound against the floor. With a clumsy glove she stroked the child's hair. It was pale and fine, like spun gold.

There were no anticonvulsants in the first-aid kit. There was nothing she could do but comfort the girl and ride out the convulsion.

Lillith murmured encouragements. "It'll be all right. Easy now. I'm here." All but the last were lies. Tears flowed down Lillith's face.

The girl had once been beautiful; she shared the startling glacial-blue eyes of her brother, and her pale skin was porcelain fine. High cheekbones in an oval face hinted at Norwegian ancestry.

The boy crept closer and put his cheek against the trembling girl's stomach.

Lillith stroked his head as well. The children looked eight years old, or perhaps ten if privation had stunted their growth. So young to have lived through so much horror.

After long minutes, the seizure stopped. Lillith checked the girl's heartbeat. Silence.

The boy clutched his sister and cried.

Lillith considered CPR, but how could she perform respiration through her suit? The medical bag from the van was only a first-aid kit intended to patch up abrasions and dispense aspirin. It didn't include a defibrillator or a breathless resuscitator.

Lillith considered taking her suit off to administer CPR. But the girl was infected with Mahn's, which had a ninety-eight percent mortality rate. Doing so would be suicide.

Feeling helpless and cowardly, Lillith decided not to try. The girl had at most a few days to live. Why pound her back into life just to have her suffer and die again in a hospital?

The boy touched his sister's chest. He looked up, stricken, into Lillith's face. "Help her!" he screamed.

Lillith shook her head. "There's nothing I can do. She's gone."

The boy's eyes widened. He shook his sister,

clutched her to his chest, and wailed. His howl of anguish rose and fell, sending shivers down Lillith's back. The sound was inhuman.

His whole body shook with crying. "No, no, no," he repeated.

Lillith pulled him into her bulky arms. Through layers of plastic and Kevlar, she hugged him tightly until the quarantine ambulance came and took him away.

The boy, who gave his name as Idaho Davis, was found to be immune to Mahn's disease. He was sent to live in a foster home in Cambridge, Massachusetts. For a few years, Lillith checked on him from time to time through governmental channels. His grades were deplorable, with one bright spot: an aptitude for computer science. But Idaho ran away from his foster home when he was fourteen, and after that there were no further records.

CHAPTER 1

> *... this agreement shall impose a renewable moratorium of five years on viral engineering, as this technology presents a clear and present health hazard. Infraction shall carry a penalty of no less than twenty years' imprisonment and may be a capital offense in some nations.*
>
> —*Beijing Treaty, 2013*

Geoffrey Allen balanced the injector on his palm. Inside it, the deadly AIDS virus had been tamed into a tool of medicine. The virus contained a payload that would alter his DNA and undo the damage nature had wrought when his parents' chromosomes meshed.

Around him, the mansion was silent. Dawn was still hours away. His parents and the house servants slept. The curtains on the open window breathed with the wind off Puget Sound. All was peaceful. Geoffrey should have been dreaming himself, but he had lain awake all night contemplating his choice.

Geoffrey's reflection was distorted on the glass ampoule of the injector. It stretched his thin face, giving it the appearance of a skull—which was what he would be in a few months without the treatment he held in his hands.

The fingers wrapped around the injector were thickened at the tips, an artifact of the genetic anomaly that was destroying his lungs and intestines.

This tiny vial violated the Beijing Treaty. It had cost two hundred million dollars to bribe the lead researcher at Caduceus International to develop the illegal treatment in secret.

Geoffrey coughed to clear the fluid buildup in his lungs. His face reddened with the effort, and his eyes watered. At last he hacked up green mucus into a disposable cup. He threw it into the trash where it landed on top of others.

The ampoule contained the classic choice: the lady or the tiger. Without human trials, there was no way to tell if it would work. It could as easily kill as cure.

But all the other treatments for his cystic fibrosis had failed. Conventional gene therapies faded within months, and he was too weak for a heart-lung transplant. Even with the best medical care, the doctors had given him two months to live, perhaps three.

This uncertain cure was his last chance.

He breathed heavily. What did he have to lose but two months of pain and dwindling life?

Geoffrey closed his eyes, pressed the injector against his chest, and pulled the trigger.

Lillith woke out of a cold sweat. She'd been dreaming about the speech she was to give tomorrow. In the dream, she'd forgotten her notes and stood frozen behind the podium, her mouth gaping like a fish's.

The bedside phone rang again.

"Light," Lillith mumbled. "Phone onscreen."

The ringing stopped and the room brightened. Lillith pulled the covers up to shield her naked body from the camera mounted next to the wall screen.

"Who is it?" The display was a uniform gray. No picture. Was it malfunctioning?

"THIS is IDAHO Blue." The voice was strange, a blending of male and female tones, low and masculine on "this" and "Idaho," high and feminine on "is" and

"Blue." The name was not familiar, but there was something about the voice. . . .

"Do I know you? This is room 1229 at the Hilton. Do you have the right number?"

"Dr. Watkins, it's STARTING AGAIN."

Lillith scrubbed sleep from her eyes and peered again at the screen. It was still blank. "Who are you?"

"You have to STOP THEM."

Scared and a little angry, Lillith said, "I won't do anything until I know who you are—show me your face."

An image resolved onscreen. Two pale Nordic faces merged into one, the left half male, the right half female.

Lillith gasped. It had been ten years since she'd walked into the computer warehouse, six since he had run from foster care . . . but there was no forgetting those glacial-blue eyes.

"Idaho?"

The generated face did not respond to her question. It repeated, "STOP THEM."

"Stop who?" Her mind reeled with questions. How had he found her? And why?

To her alarm, Lillith's laptop whirred to life. She jumped out of bed, wrapping the sheet around her, and flipped open the lid. A file was downloading to the desktop.

"You can't—" She looked up at the screen. The protest died on her lips. The caller had disconnected.

The file contained a log of DNA synthesis. The date and tracking-code fields were blank. The description was equally unhelpful: "Sample four."

The nucleotide components of the DNA were displayed as green, black, red, and yellow dots. She looked at its modification date. The file had been created three months ago.

Why was Idaho sending this to her? She didn't know anything about him other than he had a horrific childhood and a facility with computers. He might still blame her for his sister's death, for not saving the girl named Blue.

If so, this could be a trap. Was a destructive program hidden in the file?

Lillith didn't need this distraction tonight. Not the night before the biggest speech of her life. Lillith pulled out her laptop's wireless chip to disconnect it from the Net and shut it off.

Then, with determination, she turned off the lights and lay back down to sleep.

A warehouse filled with dying children haunted her dreams.

The next morning, Geoffrey woke to the trilling of thrushes. He breathed in and felt a rush of energy. Was it his imagination or was his breathing easier? He took another breath. Either this was one of his good days or the viral treatment was working. Hope bubbled in his chest like carbonation.

The plastic of the oxygen tent obscured his view, bathing the room in a hazy glow. Geoffrey pulled it aside and stood. Pleasure swept through him. The sensation took a minute to pinpoint. It was the release from pain he had lived with all his life, which had hummed through his nerves like background noise, unnoticed until it was gone.

Geoffrey took another deep breath, stretching his arms wide as if to embrace the world.

A light tap on the door. "Señor Allen?" The voice belonged to June, one of the housemaids. "Are you awake?"

"More awake than I've been in years," Geoffrey said. He grinned so hard his face hurt. But he couldn't stop. Living felt so good this morning.

The door to his bedroom opened and June wheeled in a stainless steel cart. She stopped when she saw he was out of bed. She smiled warmly. "It is one of your good days?"

He had never noticed how the reddish brown of June's full lips complemented her olive complexion. Her figure was hidden beneath a starched uniform and apron, but its outline was fit and trim.

Wisps of black hair escaped from her chignon and curled against her cheeks. For an instant, he fantasized about removing her maid's cap and letting the dark locks fall down around her naked body.

Geoffrey climbed back into bed before June could see the effect she was having on him.

Apparently he was too late. June blushed and fumbled with the serving tray. Her smile had become fixed.

She lifted the tray's cover, revealing a breakfast of grapefruit, papaya, hot cereal, and coffee. With practiced movements, she unfolded the legs of the tray and placed it across Geoffrey's lap.

Geoffrey felt himself blushing, too. But he couldn't help himself. The musky scent of her as she leaned over him was intoxicating. He wanted to grab her right there.

June curtsied and scurried out of the room, throwing a last troubled glance over her shoulder.

He looked at the door after she had gone. Life, indeed, had much to offer.

Geoffrey savored the bite of the grapefruit, the warm taste of oatmeal, and the rich perfume of the papaya. The food tasted sharper and richer now that his nose was not congested.

After he'd swigged down the last of his coffee, Geoffrey automatically picked up the enzyme pill from the white cup beside his plate. He had it on his tongue before he realized it might not be necessary.

Then again, his contact at Caduceus had warned him the treatment would take a couple of weeks for full effect. He swallowed the pill.

If he felt this good after one night, how would he feel after the virus had been in his system for a week?

Is this how everyone felt all the time? A pang of jealousy for all the years he had wasted being sick swept through him. No longer.

He climbed out of bed and pulled clothes out of his dresser. There was a world out there he'd never had time or energy to experience. Now he would.

CHAPTER 2

Dr. Lillith Watkins waited offstage in the Senate chamber. She wore a crisply tailored butter-yellow suit that set off her dark skin.

She forced worries about her midnight phone call from her mind. This moment was the culmination of years of hard work; she'd honed her message over weeks of preparation and practice.

Arrayed in the audience were senators from all fifty states. The domed room was paneled in mahogany and reeked of history. In this room, laws had been passed and presidents impeached. In a few minutes it would be her turn to address the Senate.

Visitors to the Senate watched from a balcony overlooking the proceedings. Lillith's eyes wandered over the audience: a group of school-aged children, men and women in dark suits, and a face she recognized, in the front row of the balcony. Lillith froze.

Dr. Julian Fowler. She hadn't seen him since they'd interned together at Caduccus International. Her face heated. She'd had a crush on him once . . . before he'd stolen her research and used it to gain a permanent position with the company.

What the hell was he doing here?

The preceding speaker finished his report on new mutations in staphylococcus bacteria and left the podium.

Lillith worked to control her breathing, to regain the calm she'd need to address the Senate.

The Senate chairman checked his agenda, then said, "Now we welcome Dr. Watkins to the stand. She is a distinguished researcher at the Centers for Disease Control and will speak on the obligation of private corporations to share genetic-mapping data."

Lillith tapped her electronic tablet to refresh the screen, glanced briefly at her notes, and stood up. She took a deep breath to stop her hands from trembling and addressed the crowd.

"Senators, the human genome was fully sequenced over thirty years ago. But until we map genes to their function, the sequence of nucleotides in human DNA is as useless as Egyptian hieroglyphs were before the Rosetta stone. Once we understand the roles these genes play, we'll be able to cure endemic diseases such as heart disease, diabetes, and cancer."

A murmur rippled through the crowd.

Lillith continued, "Public institutions are working on this problem, but much of the funding and research is carried out in the private sector. Private companies are hoarding their findings, hoping to profit from their research."

In the balcony, Fowler tipped an imaginary hat to her.

Lillith pulled her eyes away, focusing on her notes. "This short-sightedness delays our effort to understand the genome, a breakthrough that will save millions of lives. I beg you to pass the proposed legislation. It will ensure that gene-mapping data is freely available to all."

A light went on at one senator's desk, and the chairman pointed his gavel at Frank Avery, the Republican senator from Texas. "The chair recognizes Senator Avery."

Avery was a short man, even in cowboy boots with two-inch heels. A brocade vest strained over his well-fed middle. "While we appreciate Dr. Watkins's testimony, we must also respect that private companies deserve to reap the rewards of their research and development efforts."

Lillith glanced at Fowler. His brown hair was slicked back and he watched the proceedings with amused interest.

Senator Avery wrapped up. "To ask these companies to give away for free the results of their time and money would have a repressive effect on research in the public sector. Wouldn't you agree, Dr. Watkins?"

Lillith straightened her shoulders and met the senator's gaze. "Certainly not. The bill contains language that would allow companies a share of any profit from treatments developed using their data. What would be repressed is profiteering at the expense of public health."

In her peripheral vision, Lillith saw Fowler type something into the keypad of his cell phone.

Senator Avery checked the screen built into his desk and nodded. "But didn't Caduceus, this hoarder of secrets, recently release—without any prodding from the U.S. government—information about the Henly gene cluster on chromosome four, gene-mapping data vital to predicting pancreatic cancer?"

"Yes, but . . ." Lillith paused, stalling for time to think. Caduceus had published the data only last night. Avery would never have seen it without coaching.

In the balcony, the corners of Fowler's lips spread into a smirk.

Lillith hoped the damn banister would break. "Caduceus released that information only in response to this hearing."

"Really?" Senator Avery's eyebrows rose. "Then you are apprised of the company's motivations. You are perhaps on the board of directors?"

A chuckle rippled through the Senate.

"Of course not." Lillith fumbled with her handheld computer to find her place in the notes.

Senator Avery jumped into the pause and addressed the room with a wide, sweeping gesture. "Ladies and gentlemen, our legislation already burdens pharmaceutical companies with thousands of regulations. These businesses are owned and operated by concerned citizens. Caduceus International has demon-strated its willingness and ability to work towards the common good without additional legislation, and you will find similar examples of altruism from the other major pharmaceuticals. It is my opinion that additional legislation is not necessary and would only further complicate an already cumbersome legal code."

Lillith saw heads nodding around the room. She had to change their minds.

"Caduceus International," she said, "showed abso-lutely no interest in data sharing before this meeting was scheduled. If this legislation is not passed, their cooperation will end, setting the field of genetics back years." She narrowed her eyes up at Fowler. "And if Caduceus and the other companies are already com-mitted to sharing data in the public interest, this legis-lation poses no burden."

"Thank you, Dr. Watkins," the chairman said, com-ing up behind her. "That will be all."

"But—" Lillith started to protest. The chairman's hand on her elbow was firm, escorting her away from the podium even as he shook her hand.

Lillith took the hint and walked down from the dais and out into the relative calm of the hallway outside.

Lillith stomped across the floor, her heels clicking a rapid tempo, past the security station and out into the open air of the capital. Her eyes stung with tears of anger . . . at herself, at Senator Avery, at Fowler and that sideswiping stunt he'd pulled.

There were four automatic cabs waiting at the curb and one limousine with a human driver.

Lillith slid into a small two-seater cab and said, "Grand Hyatt Hotel, please."

The cab slid smoothly away from the curb.

Lillith fumed. The Senate had asked her to report before the subcommittee, had acknowledged her techni-cal expertise, but would they act on her recommenda-tions? Not while companies like Caduceus, Nuvogene, and Pharmacopoeia funded their campaigns.

They drove past the mall. Hundreds of milling tourists wandered along Constitution Avenue, between the Smithsonian Museums and the Washington Monument.

The sequencing of the human genome, done in the last decade of the twentieth century, was just the beginning. Until humanity found a Rosetta stone for the function of those genes, the genomic data was nothing more than an interesting wall poster.

Lillith punched the vinyl seat next to her.

"Are you in distress?" the automated cabbie asked.

"No," she assured the synthesized face on the dashboard. The cab changed its human façade to match the gender and ethnicity of its passengers.

The cab's computer now projected a woman with chocolate-brown skin and close-cropped hair. The details of Lillith's face had been averaged with the population to produce an image: the automated cabbie's nose was narrower than hers, its chin less pointed.

Lillith slumped back in her seat. She blew out a breath. Which was worse, her appeal failing, or the fact that she'd been outmaneuvered by *Fowler*? She pressed her hands to her temples and leaned her elbows against her knees.

How could she ever have been attracted to him? The memory of their time together at Caduceus, and how he had used her, made her stomach ache.

She pulled out her vidphone. "Atlanta, CDC headquarters, Dr. Lam." The gray LED screen displayed the blue-and-white logo of the Centers for Disease Control while her call went through.

Dr. Lam answered immediately. His thin brows drew together with concern.

"I assume you were watching C-SPAN?" Lillith said, her lips pursed in self-disgust.

Lam inclined his head. "Senator Avery asked tough questions. I think you did well . . . under the circumstances."

"Not well enough," Lillith said.

"Wait for the vote," said Dr. Lam. "Then we'll know how to proceed."

Lillith nodded, feeling miserable.

"Do not be so hard on yourself," Lam said. "What is done, is done."

"I'll see you on Monday," she said.

"Safe flight." Dr. Lam disconnected.

A few minutes later the cab arrived at the Grand Hyatt Hotel. Lillith stepped out and pressed her thumb against the paypad on the door.

She took the elevator to the twelfth floor. Her thumbprint opened the room door and she tore off her butter-yellow suit and threw it on the bed.

Lillith stepped into the shower and ran it full blast, the hot water scalding her skin. She worked a dime-sized amount of shampoo into her close-cropped skullcap of curls. Then Lillith scrubbed her skin raw with the hand towel, as if abrasion could wash away her failure.

After the shower, she dried herself with three of the skimpy hotel towels.

Lillith moved to the tiny desk and popped open her laptop. She browsed through the mystery file. She felt a measure of safety with her computer disconnected from the Net. Without a connection, Idaho's file couldn't steal information from her laptop or download anything else.

The genetic code was still a mystery. Lillith's eyes flicked down to the list of nucleotide codes. The file used the standard encoding: A for adenine, T for thymine, G for guanine, and C for cytosine.

"CATGATATATAC."

Lillith froze. It was a common enough sequence. In the human genome it was repeated thousands of times in the twenty-three billion base pairs. But the mnemonic "cat got at a tack" was one she and Fowler had used during her summer at Caduceus.

The size of the file was small—15,342 nucleotides long. Something that small must be a DNA fragment . . . or a virus.

Lillith's breath caught in her throat.

At Caduceus, she and Fowler had worked on engineering viruses to accept DNA payloads. By crippling the virus so it couldn't reproduce, you could use it to deliver repaired genes to the patient. The inserted genes cured the disease by restoring functionality that the patient's original DNA didn't contain, such as generating missing proteins.

That was before the disaster of Mahn's disease and the adoption of the Beijing Treaty. Viral engineering was a dead science now, and all their samples had been destroyed.

Why would Idaho send her a copy of research shut down more than a decade ago . . . except the file's properties showed it had been recently modified.

Lillith's hand flew to her mouth. Was this file from Caduceus? Were they conducting research into viral engineering? Why now, after so many years, and in violation of the Beijing Treaty?

If Caduceus could be shown to be engineering viruses in its labs, it would blow things wide open. During the investigation, the company would *have* to expose their files to public scrutiny.

If this was real.

Idaho, a troubled boy she had met once, in extreme circumstances, was hardly a reliable source.

The wall television spoke. "User-programmed event available: C-SPAN network, congressional vote."

Lillith said, "Display."

The screen hanging on the wall came on. Four different video streams showed Congress voting on various measures. Words at the bottom indicated the topic.

"View three."

The other video streams disappeared and the sound came on. The chairman read the text of the bill that Lillith had supported, then called for the vote.

Sixty-two against, thirty-one for, with seven abstentions.

Lillith closed her eyes as waves of anger rolled through her. How could they? It wasn't right to allow companies to hoard information that could save lives. "Television off."

But what, really, had she expected? If the measure

had a chance in hell of passing, Dr. Lam would have presented the argument instead of her, a lesser functionary at the CDC. Lillith realized she had been sent to make the attempt, for form's sake.

She opened the file Idaho had uploaded.

Lillith swiveled in her chair to face the wall screen. "Hotel computer: on. Search for exact wordings: 'Idaho Davis' and 'Idaho Blue.' "

The screen returned only thirty-seven hits. The small number surprised her. There was nothing from the Social Security Administration, no childhood records, no school files, no employment details.

She paged through the abstracts of the hits the search had returned. Half were FBI notices on hackers. The others were anonymous posts to news lists. Idaho appeared to be in the business of selling protected information: patented research, usernames and passwords, home addresses of company executives, and the private vidmail addresses of media celebrities. Warrants for his arrest for industrial espionage were listed by local police, the FBI, and the NSA . . . there were also several anonymous recommendations from satisfied customers.

Even more telling was the absence of any personal data on the Net. Searching on the name of an average citizen returned thousands of hits. His had either never been entered into the Net . . . or had been meticulously erased.

Her cell phone rang.

Lillith dug the phone out of her suitcase and answered it. "Hello?"

"Did you FIND WHAT you were LOOKING FOR?"

Hairs on the back of Lillith's neck stood up. Her eyes slid sideways to the results still displayed on the wall screen. "How did you know to call me?" She walked over and tapped its off button. Then another question occurred to her. "How did you get my personal number?"

"YOU READ the FBI's posts. INFORMATION is MY trade. Did you READ THE FILE?"

"Yes. Where did it come from?"

"CADUCEUS."

"How do I know you're telling me the truth?"

"You want PROOF?"

Lillith cupped her hand over the receiver. If the CDC discovered she had conversed with a suspected criminal without reporting it to the FBI, she would lose her security clearance. If she solicited him to obtain information for her illegally, she could lose her job. She might even be arrested.

Lillith pressed the covered receiver against her forehead. What had Fowler said to her that night? It was all in the timing.

The FBI memos mentioned Idaho Blue as a ghost figure in the Net. Someone they weren't even sure existed outside of legend. That implied he was good at covering his trail.

She wasn't doing this to get back at Fowler. Lillith needed to crack Caduceus open, get their data into the public record. Caduceus's indictment might even tip the scales for Congress to pass a sunshine measure on all genomic pharmaceuticals.

Lillith put the receiver to her mouth and said quietly, "Yes. I want all the research you can recover from . . . that company . . . for the last six months. Anything that will prove they're performing live tests." The instant she said it, she wanted to take the words back. What if the FBI were tapping his phone line? Cell phone conversations traveled through the air, open to anyone with a receiver.

She groaned. "We're talking on my *cell* phone."

"Don't WORRY," Idaho said. "I've ENCRYPTED THE channel. We CAN'T TALK long or THE FEDS will become SUSPICIOUS."

Lillith didn't trust Idaho, but she'd already committed herself. "Well?"

There was a pause. "I CAN do what you ask. But for A PRICE. I want BLUE'S DNA sequenced."

"What? Why?"

Idaho's face remained passive. "THAT IS MY PRICE. Can you MEET IT?"

Lillith shook her head. "I can't add samples to the sequencer schedule without an explanation."

Silence from the other end of the line.

"All right, all right. I'll find a way. You have a suitable sample?"

"You will RECEIVE A PACKAGE from a fictitious COMPANY in Azure, MONTANA."

Lillith pressed her fingers to her temples. She was conspiring with a person wanted by the FBI. This was insane.

"ONE MORE thing . . . buy A BIGGER hard DRIVE." Idaho disconnected.

Lillith turned off the phone and sat on the bed, feeling both exhilarated and sick to her stomach. Finally, she was accomplishing something . . . but if things went wrong, it could destroy her career and might even land her in jail.

CHAPTER 3

Idaho sat in the center of a spider's web of wires that fed into his central nervous system via subcutaneous electrodes. He'd had the needle locations tattooed on his skin, a blue network of constellations. Catheters and IVs supported his body while his mind hunted on the Net. He resented coming back to the physical now that Blue was gone and took steps to delay it as long as possible.

There was nothing in the physical world to inspire him. He lived in a single-wide trailer devoid of any decoration or personal effects. His only furniture was the ergonomic chair that dominated the living room and the shelflike bed built into the trailer's back bedroom.

In the Net, he was endless. When Idaho surfed, it was as if he didn't exist; he was only a jumble of incoming sensations without ego or consciousness. All his mental processing was given over to searching out connections and breaking into secured pathways. There was nothing left of himself to feel sorrow or self-pity. It was his only release.

Lillith had asked for his help. He had known she would. Idaho had recorded her voice from the CNN coverage of the trial and run it through a psychological analysis program he'd downloaded off the Net. She wanted the data from Caduceus. Wanted it bad.

It would be simple to retrieve. He'd started cracking

Caduceus years ago. He had backdoors into the company's personnel database and from there could retrieve access keys for any user. Spoof the system admin and he could go wandering through Caduceus's internal network with godlike privileges.

His curiosity about Dr. Lillith Watkins and the disease that killed his sister had led him to read the research files of several biotech companies. That was how he'd stumbled onto Caduceus's work on viral engineering.

But he had work to do in the physical world now. Idaho disconnected the IV from his arm. Then he plucked the conductive needles out of his nerve centers and dropped them into a mason jar filled with rubbing alcohol.

The trailer contained few possessions. Idaho liked life simple, easy to abandon at a moment's notice.

He crawled out of the ergonomic chair, knelt in the center of the room, and poked at one corner of a linoleum tile that looked like all the others. This one was loose, however, and using his thumbnail he was able to pry it up. Inside lay two nine-millimeter guns, ammunition, and a box made of white gold. Idaho pulled out the box, rubbed dust from its surface, and opened it. Inside lay twelve golden hairs. They were finer and lighter than his own. It was all he had left of Blue. He had found them tangled in his fingers when the paramedics tore him away from her corpse.

He selected three and wrapped them in a coil around his little finger. The others he returned to the box.

Idaho would ask Exeter to bring him packaging materials the next time she resupplied him. Then she could post the parcel to Lillith.

He'd only left the trailer twice in the eighteen months since he'd rented earthmoving equipment and buried the trailer under the Montana soil. A stranger wandering onto the ranch would see only an abandoned farmhouse and barn, and never suspect Idaho's subterranean abode. A necessary precaution; Idaho spent so much time unaware of his body, he didn't dare leave it undefended.

Idaho replaced the box and settled the tile back into place.

Stroking the hairs around his finger, Idaho recalled life in the computer factory. He'd been able to stand the neglect and deprivation, because he'd had *her* to share it with.

Since he'd run away from foster care, he'd sought to understand the trick of genetics that had made him resistant to Mahn's disease. To understand what saved him and killed Blue. Idaho studied microbiology and genetics from the Web. He had downloaded a DNA simulation from Caltech and spent hours modifying the program, customizing it to answer his questions.

Somewhere locked in these three strands of Blue's hair was the secret to all her potential. All she was and all she might have been had she lived.

Idaho carefully coiled the hairs into a glass and placed a plate on top to protect them from dust and wind.

Then he used the bathroom, stretched, crossed to the kitchen, and swigged a Mountain Dew from a can in the fridge. That was enough of the real world.

Idaho reattached the catheters, IV, and conductive needles. He lowered the VR goggles over his face.

Lying back in his ergonomic chair and closing his eyes, Idaho reentered the Net. He dispatched an instant message to inform Exeter he needed mailing supplies.

In his mind, the Net was an endless expanse of data and programs, winding off to infinity in all directions. He activated search programs to hunt for Caduceus's IP6 address.

Clipping bots followed in their wake, obscuring his progress through the Net and hiding his activity from the FBI detection programs.

Idaho connected to Caduceus's security database, conveniently named security_db. He encoded the username and password in an enzyme and sent it out into the Net.

Seconds later the result: access denied.

The Caduceus administrator had changed the system password. Idaho wondered if it was a routine change or whether someone had noticed his previous infiltrations. Either way, it didn't matter. He'd covered his tracks, routing his incoming requests through anonymous servers maintained by the HackThePlanet co-op.

He had the database name and the IP6 address; all he need do now was crack the password. For that attack, he enlisted computers from around the world, spreading out the connection attempts from different IP addresses to make it harder for monitoring equipment to detect. Even once it was recognized as an attack, it would be impossible to hone in on its origin.

Idaho called into a network of computers set up by hackers for this purpose.

Information enthusiasts from all over the world had contributed to the distributed attack engine. Idaho had helped write the code that broke the attack into several streams and load-balanced the work across thousands of computers spread all over the world: Dev8staytor.

It had begun years ago as an adaptation of the code used by the SETI@home project and now was an octopus stretching its tentacles into the login programs of companies and government agencies all over the world.

Idaho uploaded his request to Dev8staytor and, using a backdoor he had left in the system, bumped the priority of his request up to pri-one.

Computers in Albania, Cuba, Argentina, France, and Russia began trying to connect to Caduceus International, using twenty-seven search algorithms that had been honed by generations of hackers.

These computer enthusiasts updated the cracking software regularly with new exploits and workarounds for security patches. The only reward was notoriety among a small community of individuals, but in their minds the respect of equals was the brightest coin.

By day's end, Geoffrey felt he could move mountains with his bare hands. He ran from one end of the family private beach to the other. Each breath filled him with energy like a jolt of adrenaline. Free! He had never felt so exhilarated.

Geoffrey ran back to the house, enjoying the feel of sweat drying on his skin. He tasted it. It was mild; gone was the pungent saltiness characteristic of cystic fibrosis. The cure was real. The engineered virus had been strong enough to propagate throughout his body, healing *all* his cells. This time there would be no regression, no slow slide back into illness.

He had been near death, and now he was cured. Geoffrey whooped with joy and ran through the marble-tiled hallways. He jumped in mid-stride and tapped one of the smaller chandeliers to set it swaying.

June and Maria were pushing the silver cart that held his mother's afternoon tea.

Geoffrey pecked a kiss on June's cheek in passing. He looked back to see June press a hand to the spot. Her eyes were wide with surprise. Maria crossed herself.

He ducked into his bedroom and opened the top drawer of his chest of drawers. Geoffrey began flinging all his medical equipment out of the room. He tossed percussion hammers, inhalers, therapeutic kazoos, steroids, the lung-capacity machine, and his blood pressure cuff.

Geoffrey sprang to the bed and snarled his hand in the plastic sheeting. With one glorious yank, he pulled it down. He gathered it up and flung it out the door.

Then he unchained the oxygen tank from his bedside. He duckwalked it to the hall and kicked it over, not caring whether the nozzle broke off and turned it into a dangerous projectile. He was immortal today.

He had been given weeks to live and now had years. They stretched before him like an eternity.

Geoffrey jumped on the bed. He couldn't stop laughing. With one last leap he fell backwards on the bed and hugged himself. "I'm alive, I'm alive, I'm alive," he chanted.

"Agreed. But it appears you've lost your mind."

Geoffrey propped himself up on his elbow.

His mother stood in the doorway, a pair of gold-rimmed bifocals held loosely in her hand. Behind her, Maria and June goggled at the destruction.

Geoffrey leapt up and grasped his mother's hands. He led her into the room and shut the door on the maids.

When they were seated on the bed, he said in a whisper, "I'm cured this time, Mother. Truly cured."

Her eyes grew sad and pitying. "Geoffrey." She touched his upper arm. "We've been through this before. Gene therapies, miracle drugs, even spring water from Guadalupe. You have to accept . . ." Her eyes filled with tears and she turned away.

Geoffrey grabbed her shoulders and shook her. "No. No, I don't."

His mother pushed away his hands. Her voice hardened. "Then tell me, what have you done now?"

Geoffrey found himself reluctant to speak. She would be on his side, but it was still an illegal act.

Her eyes bored into his as she waited for his reply.

At last he said, "I had a virus engineered to fix my DNA. It's superior to the standard gene therapies because this virus spreads throughout the body, cascading cellular changes. There will be no regression."

His mother's eyes widened. "But Dr. Ambrose told us newly engineered viruses were illegal. We couldn't find a reputable lab to create one."

Geoffrey met his mother's gaze. "I found a researcher who'd lost his retirement funds to bad investments. I was able to . . . persuade him to do this research in secret."

His mother's hands flew to her mouth. "How do you know you can trust this man, or his cures? If he's selling an illegal treatment . . . it can't have been properly tested."

Geoffrey's face darkened. "What did I have to lose, a month of life? Attached to a ventilator? I heard you and Dr. Ambrose discuss moving me to an intensive care unit. I don't want to die tethered to a machine." He stood on the bed and spread his arms wide. "In fact, I don't want to die at all."

His mother captured one of his hands and pulled him off the bed. "Of course, dear. All I'm saying is we should be cautious." She slipped her arm around his shoulders. "You dealt with an unscrupulous man. Before we build a bonfire on the beach to dispose of your medical equipment, let's make sure of this cure. I'll call Dr. Ambrose to evaluate your condition."

Geoffrey's brows knit together. "Why can't you believe this is real? For the first time in my life I'm healthy, cured. And you doubt it?"

Geoffrey's mother squeezed his shoulder. "If what you say is true, no one will be more pleased than I. I'll throw you the biggest celebration the world has ever seen. But"—her eyes were sad—"I want to be sure."

He pushed her hand away. "So call him. I'll prove it to you. To you both."

Dr. Ambrose was a short man with thinning hair and a waistline that testified to his love of port and smoked salmon. His shirt collar was crumpled after the half-hour flight from the mainland, and he dabbed perspiration from his forehead.

Stuffing the handkerchief into his jacket pocket, he extended a hand to Geoffrey. His eyebrows rose with surprise. "You're looking well."

"Dr. Ambrose." Geoffrey's mother used her entertaining voice, bright and relentlessly cheerful. "I'm grateful you could make time for us."

Ambrose bent over the hand Geoffrey's mother offered him and kissed it. "I always have room in my schedule for you and yours, dear lady." The gesture made the old man look foolish, but his mother brightened.

She pushed him playfully away and dropped her tone. "In here, please. For privacy." She led them to Geoffrey's bedroom.

Ambrose paused as he passed the discarded medical equipment in the hallway, now neatly stacked and boxed by June and Maria. "You've been redecorating." His eyes flicked back and forth between Geoffrey and his mother. "What's going on?"

"I want you to examine Geoffrey . . . discreetly," Mrs. Allen said, following him into the room. "There is to be no record of tonight in Geoffrey's medical chart. Then we'll talk."

Ambrose frowned but did not ask any questions. He put his antique leather bag on a side table and pulled out a stethoscope. "As you wish, Mrs. Allen."

Geoffrey, familiar with the procedure from countless previous examinations, raised his shirt so Dr. Ambrose could listen to his chest and back.

Geoffrey breathed into a portable spirometer to test his lung capacity. Ambrose spread conductive jelly on Geoffrey's back and scanned his lungs with a handheld ultrasound generator. "Amazing," Ambrose said, with a rising note of excitement. "Absolutely amazing."

Geoffrey itched with curiosity. "Are my lungs clear?"

"As if you'd never had cystic fibrosis at all." Ambrose shook his head in wonderment. "How is this possible?"

Geoffrey opened his mouth to speak, but his mother silenced him with an upraised hand. "Did you bring the biochips I asked for?"

Ambrose nodded. "But I don't see—"

"Please check his DNA," she told Ambrose.

The doctor pulled a handful of genome chips out of his pocket. The tiny nylon rectangles were composed of microarrays filled with tethered nucleic acids that detected other, target, nucleic acids. The chips were calibrated to screen for the damaged genes that caused Geoffrey's cystic fibrosis.

Donning a set of latex gloves, the doctor pricked Geoffrey's fingertip with a disposable lancet; capillary action sucked a drop of blood into the corner of the biochip. Ambrose shook the rectangle to distribute the blood among the microarrays.

While they waited for the reaction to finish, Geoffrey held his hands in front of him to examine his fingers. They were still clubbed. He wondered if his new genome would eventually be able to effect structural changes.

Ambrose shook the plastic chip again. "This is amazing. Your blood shows no sign of CF. Codon 508 of the CFTR gene on chromosome seven is perfectly normal." He held up another plastic chip. "I want to confirm the results."

Geoffrey nodded and they repeated the procedure.

When he was done, Ambrose sat heavily on the bed. "A new gene therapy. I guess from your secrecy this is different from the publicly available treatments we've already tried. . . ."

"I—" Geoffrey started.

Ambrose shook his head. "I don't want to know. Your mother has asked me to keep this night's work confidential. I don't want to jeopardize that by learning anything I would be obligated to report to the authorities." His gaze fixed on Mrs. Allen.

She inclined her head.

"I would, however," said Ambrose, "like to take tissue samples back to the mainland for further study."

"Of course, Dr. Ambrose," said Geoffrey's mother.

Ambrose took skin core samples, scrapings, and throat cultures. Mrs. Allen had Maria bring some dry ice that had been left by the caterers. Ambrose used it to pack the samples for the trip back to the mainland.

As Ambrose packed his medical bag, Mrs. Allen stopped him with her hand on his arm. "Is this cure lasting?"

Ambrose snapped the brass clasp on the top of the bag shut. "We won't know that until we see how far the genetic changes propagate through his body. The problem with conventional treatment is that only a handful of cells are affected. As cells die before propagating the changes, the effect fades." Ambrose patted Mrs. Allen's hand. "The fact that the change is in his bloodstream is a good sign. I can tell from Geoffrey's condition that his lung tissue has been affected, so it's spreading. How far it will go . . . only time will tell."

"But if a treatment was able to fix most of his cells?"

Ambrose smiled. "If that were possible, he would be as healthy as if he never had CF. But none of the current technologies . . ." He looked at Geoffrey speculatively. "Whatever you did, it's a miracle."

Mrs. Allen closed her eyes and smiled, letting out a sigh that had been pent up since Geoffrey was diagnosed. Then she straightened and met Ambrose's eyes. "What about children?"

Geoffrey blushed to the top of his head. Like most men with CF, he was sterile, his body's thickened mucous acting as a natural vasectomy.

Ambrose chuckled. "Yes, that may be something for him to start worrying about."

"No," Mrs. Allen said, "I understand that. What I mean is, will they carry the CF gene?"

Ambrose paled. "International law forbids modifying germ-line cells, those a person passes to their offspring. Stem cells, which only affect the host, yes, under the right conditions and taking the Beijing Treaty into account." His eyes searched Mrs. Allen's face. "But scientists all over the world have avoided altering germ-line cells. To do so would forever change the gene pool of man. No one can predict the long-term implications for the human race. It's too dangerous to attempt."

"Ah well," Mrs. Allen said with a dismissive wave. "No matter. The important thing is that he can look forward to a long and healthy life. And if he marries a woman who is not a carrier, I can look forward to healthy grandchildren."

Mrs. Allen smiled at Geoffrey. She threw open her arms and pulled him into a tight embrace that took his breath away.

Then, with abandon, she hugged Ambrose. When she let go, Ambrose rocked on his feet, his glasses askew.

Tears trickled from the corner of Mrs. Allen's eyes. "Forgive me." She pulled a lace handkerchief out of her pocket. "This calls for a celebration. Dr. Ambrose, you will come back for the party?"

Dr. Ambrose said, "I wouldn't miss it for the world."

Geoffrey watched the doctor leave. When he was once again alone with his mother, he said, "The treatment I took does not differentiate between stem and germ-line cells. I am cured, Mother, completely cured."

His mother took him into a spontaneous hug. "Oh, Geoffrey. I'm so happy. The mistake your father and I made—the genetic tests that missed my carrier gene—that mistake has all been undone."

Geoffrey patted his mother's back, feeling ambivalence. The mistake she referred to, after all, was him.

CHAPTER 4

Lillith opened the package on her desk. It had been insured for ten thousand dollars. Inside were layers of bubble packing. In the center, wrapped in a clear cellophane acid-free envelope, were three human hairs. Lillith held them up to the light. The follicles were intact on two of them.

The pale gold color reminded her of the warehouse room where she had found Idaho and his sister. The filth and neglect. She imagined Idaho plucking these hairs from his dead sister. Precious cargo indeed.

She suppressed a shiver. What did Idaho hope to accomplish by sequencing his sister's genome? Did he think the secrets of her nature were bound up in her DNA? The amino acids that created a person were nothing but a blueprint for the body. A human being was much more than the sum of her parts.

She would slip the sample in with her next shipment from the Boston study. When the lab realized the sample did not carry the marker for hemophilia, Lillith could claim it was an error. She felt guilty about the patient whose sequencing would be delayed because a new sample would need to be taken. Lillith promised herself to do some digging and pick a patient with mild symptoms.

Lillith set aside the hair samples and turned to the data she'd received from Idaho. The ten-terabyte hard drive she had added to her laptop was filled with Caduceus's mapping data.

She paged through the streams of sequenced DNA. Sections that had been mapped to function were footnoted with the proteins and enzymes the gene generated. Some genes had multiple footnotes, indicating differing expression based on environmental factors or gene interaction.

There was a wealth of information. Too much for her to assimilate herself, and she had no way to sneak it into CDC databases. How could she explain where it had come from? She was like a successful bank robber with a stash of money she couldn't spend.

Lillith considered posing as a disgruntled Caduccus employee and posting it on an anonymous Web site. But the company would pull the information and prosecute any lab that tried to capitalize on it.

This information about the human genome shouldn't be trapped in the hands of one company. She had to find a way.

Three thousand miles away, Idaho looked at the data he had transmitted to Lillith. He'd kept a copy for himself. Idaho read the footnotes: "generates glycophorin," "expresses acetylcholine."

All this random information was useless. He needed a way to put it in context.

He'd begun studying microbiology to understand the tragedy of Blue. Along the way, however, he'd become fascinated by the four-digit encoding of the nucleotides that made up DNA: adenine, cytosine, guanine, and thymine. They were analogous to the ones and zeros of binary computing, but offered many more possibilities.

"I see you are feeling better," June said the next morning as she made his bed. "Perhaps Dr. Ambrose gave you a new treatment?"

Geoffrey sat on his desk in the next room, his legs dangling off the edge. He watched June spreading the new sheets, the play of muscles under her calves. "Something like that."

"It must be good to be well after such a long illness, no?"

Geoffrey hopped down from the desk and danced over to June. He plucked her hands off the sheet and whirled her around the room in an impromptu waltz.

June giggled and pushed his hands away. "Mr. Geoffrey, you are silly today. Let me do my work."

Geoffrey knelt on one knee. He folded his hands together in a plea. "Only if you will come to dinner with me tonight, on the veranda."

June's eyes clouded. "That would not be proper. I work here, Mr. Geoffrey, I—I am a housemaid. Mrs. Allen would not like it."

"Forget Mother." He waved the impediment away with a wide gesture.

June's eyes were downcast.

Geoffrey stood and placed his hands on her shoulders and turned her to face him. "I'll tell you what. I'll have Cook prepare a picnic. We'll meet after dinner. You and I can walk along the beach."

June's expression wavered. "Maybe, if no one knows . . ."

"I'll have Cook make all your favorites," Geoffrey wheedled.

"OK." June pointed a finger at his chest. "But just to talk. I am paid to clean house, nothing more."

Geoffrey held up his hand in a solemn pledge. "I'll be on my best behavior. I promise. A perfect gentleman."

June shook her head. "I do not understand you, Mr. Allen."

"Geoffrey. Call me Geoffrey."

June cast a glance at the door. "Not here." Her eyes lightened. "But maybe tonight."

Geoffrey spun a joyous circle and then ran off to the kitchen, to ask Cook what June's favorites were.

Idaho floated in his DNA simulation as a point observer. He followed an RNA polymerase as it teased apart the double helix of DNA and built a complementary copy of one of the genes. This transcribed RNA streamed like a ribbon from the spiraling DNA. Far below, bulbous ribosomes attached to it and began building proteins.

It was a marvel of engineering. Compared with this, the human invention of binary code was trivial. Ones and zeros paled in significance to the challenge of four base pairs of nucleotides that combined into three-digit codons to write the patterns of life.

A green light flashed in Idaho's peripheral vision. With a twitch of his shoulders, he froze the simulation and opened a window to display video from the hidden camera he'd mounted near the ranch's front gate.

Exeter's battered Miata bounced over the cattle grates. Her coal-black hair fluttered around her face. The antique convertible sports car was unsuited to the Montana dirt roads and the harsh winters. Despite frequent maintenance, it broke down every other week. Half the time, his IV supplies were late because her starter wouldn't turn over or the clutch went out.

Exeter was fiercely loyal to the impractical car despite its faults. A faint smile touched Idaho's lips; it might be a reflection of their relationship.

A key rattled in the deadbolt Idaho had installed in the flimsy trailer door. Exeter backed in, carrying a large box of IV packets.

Idaho didn't bother to disconnect his electrodes; Exeter was a Net runner and understood the call of imaginary worlds.

She was tall and thin. Today she wore a black latex miniskirt over red-and-white stockings. On top was a triangle of silver fabric that left her back bare except for ties at the neck and waist.

Exeter set the box next to his chair and squatted next to him. She snaked a heroin-thin arm around his waist. "Idaho," she purred, "I've brought your supplies."

Idaho resisted the urge to push her away. He'd never gotten used to Exeter's liberties. She didn't respect boundaries, not the security protocols of Defense Department computers nor the bubble of space Idaho kept between himself and the world.

But for all that, she was useful. Without body, there could be no mind, and with Blue dead, Exeter was all that held him together.

He kissed her upturned lips, avoiding the probing tongue that tried to force itself into his mouth. He pushed her away. "Hurts," he said, pointing to the dribbles of blood from induction needles shoved too far in.

Exeter's complexion had been porcelain fine but was ruined by stimulant usage and too little vitamin D. A black bob of hair cupped her heart-shaped face, and the tiny dark blemishes of connection ports were sprinkled like freckles across her nose.

She reached over and plucked a connection needle out of his chest. Idaho grabbed her wrist before she could drop it in the alcohol.

Exeter's face screwed up with hurt and disappointment. "You're not coming out?"

Idaho softened his voice. "Not today. I have an important lead to track down."

Exeter released his lead and let it flop onto the chair. "One day you'll realize I'm important, too." She kicked the box of IV bags across the room. "Only then it'll be too late, and you'll have to find yourself another delivery girl."

"Wait." Idaho held out his hand to her.

Exeter froze with her back to him. "What?"

"I'll come to you tonight, online."

"Ha!" Her retort was as sharp as a gunshot. She stepped through the door and slammed it behind her. The trailer vibrated with the force of it.

Idaho waited. Exeter was the only one who knew where he lived. If she turned against him, he'd have to move. He listened.

Silence. Then the sullen click of the deadbolt as Exeter locked it behind her.

She was still his.

Exeter was better online, softer, more beautiful.

She'd crafted an avatar that looked almost exactly like
Blue. It was one of the things that had first attracted
him to her.

Idaho scheduled a reminder to make it up to her
tonight, then sank back into the DNA simulation.

The moon was quarter-full and waxing. It shimmered on the waves of Puget Sound, a silver line running to the horizon.

Geoffrey carried a basket filled with red wine,
cheeses, and cinnamon-encrusted sopaipillas.

June walked beside him in jeans and a red long-
sleeved shirt that clung to her curves.

He'd never seen her out of uniform before, and the
sight made it hard for him to breathe.

They walked along the beach, far from the prying
eyes of the house.

"How's this?" Geoffrey asked, indicating a spot farther up the bank. It rested in the shade of a Doug-
las fir.

June nodded.

Geoffrey spread the picnic cloth out and set the
basket on the plastic-lined cloth.

When they were settled, he said, "I want to know
everything about you."

June looked down at her hands. "There is not so
much to tell. I go to college, run out of money, come
to work here. When I have enough, I go back, become
a nurse."

Geoffrey pulled the wine out of the basket and
punctured the top with the needle of a corkscrew powered by pressurized CO_2. Within seconds the cork slid
out easily. "A nurse, not a doctor?"

June shrugged. "By the time I earn enough money
for medical school, I am so old, I retire."

Geoffrey put the bottle down. "I could give you the
money for medical school."

June looked up at him sharply. "Why would you
do that?"

Geoffrey realized she'd misinterpreted his offer. "Because I think you would be a good physician. The tuition money . . . I have so much, I would never miss it."

"And what would you expect in return?" Her dark eyes examined him closely.

Geoffrey laughed at her expression. "For you to become a doctor." He tossed her a strawberry from the basket. "Don't look so serious. We came out here to enjoy the evening." He leaned back against the tree, his hands behind his head.

A pretty woman seated by his side and the moon spread out before him like a path to eternity. He drew in the clean salt air and decided life didn't get any better than this.

"Why ask me to this?" June asked. "Why not some rich girl?"

Geoffrey shrugged, still looking at the water. "I don't like any of the rich girls I've met. I like *you*."

After a moment's silence, June scooted next to Geoffrey and laid her head against his chest.

Feeling her warmth against his skin and the scent of her hair, Geoffrey realized he had underestimated the evening.

Two weeks later the estate was awash in candlelight and sequined guests. The women's gowns sparkled like galaxies amid the space-black of the men's tuxedos. Extra help had been brought over from the mainland; an army of servers Geoffrey had never seen before wielded trays and wended among the crowd.

The room was filled with his father's business acquaintances and his mother's social contacts. People had come from all over the world: Senator Mackey from Washington, D.C., Ambassador Uta from Argentina, Chef Cretien from Paris, Lord and Lady Kensington from Wales, and Makito Akane, the star of Japanese ballet—a cross section of the wealthy, the powerful, and the famous.

None of them, however, were his friends. Who really, could he call friend? The house servants? Dr. Ambrose?

Geoffrey had been taught at home by a succession of tutors. The only young people he'd met were children of his parents' friends. They usually ignored Geoffrey to swim in the pool or frolic on the tennis courts. A few attended him with bright artificial interest. He could almost hear their parents' admonition: *Be nice to the sick boy*.

His illness had kept him isolated. But that was going to change. A lot of things were.

Geoffrey's thoughts were interrupted by Senator Mackey, a hearty man with dark hair and an olive complexion. He shook Geoffrey's hand and said, "Geoffrey, I haven't seen you in what, two years? You're looking well. What are your plans for the future?"

Geoffrey returned the handshake. "Travel, sir. I've always wanted to see the world."

"Excellent," Senator Mackey said, clapping Geoffrey on the shoulder. "Travel broadens the mind. Just make sure you come back to Washington. We need more families like the Allens in this state."

Geoffrey's mother smiled at the compliment, but her eyes were on Geoffrey.

"I'm just sorry that your esteemed colleague, Senator Wheeler, couldn't attend," his mother said.

Mackey chuckled, "Well, what do you expect from a Democrat?"

As the evening wore on, Geoffrey endured hearty handshakes from his father's associates and inane chitchat with people he didn't know. When the buzz of conversation and self-congratulation got too much for him, Geoffrey walked out of the ballroom onto the balcony. It was an unusually clear night for September, and the half-moon shimmered on the water. The waves of Puget Sound traveled out into the Pacific Ocean, and from there to Alaska, South America, Russia, Japan, Australia, China, India, and Africa.

Lucky waves. Geoffrey silently vowed that he would, too. He would set foot on every country the Pacific Ocean lapped. When he returned home, he would know the water he watched still touched those places.

Geoffrey's mother coughed delicately behind him.

He turned.

His mother's arm was threaded through that of a slender young woman. The woman's auburn hair was swept up and secured with silver pins that gleamed like stars in the candlelight. A strapless dress of emerald silk crisscrossed her body. The flawless fit suggested it had been made for her.

His mother said, "This is Miss Miriam Harcourt. She cut short a safari in Tanzania to be here tonight." She patted Miriam's hand before releasing it. "My son is interested in travel. I thought you two might have much to talk about."

Geoffrey smiled indulgently at his mother. He'd been cured for less than two weeks and already she was matchmaking.

"If you'll excuse me," his mother said, "I have to check on the champagne. We may need to open another dozen crates." She fluttered away.

Miriam stood with a polite smile on her face, one eyebrow raised in an appraising glance. "If you don't like *me*, your mother has four other candidates in a holding pattern under the chandelier."

Geoffrey exploded with laughter at Miriam's unexpected frankness. He patted the rail near him. "Come here; we might as well put on a good show."

Her hands that grabbed the cedar rail were as small as a child's. Geoffrey studied the delicate features of her face, then asked, "Were you really on safari?"

Miriam grinned. "Oh yes. Don't let the charm school manners fool you. I'm quite a good shot."

Geoffrey recoiled slightly. "You hunt?"

She waved her right hand in the air dismissively. "Only clones created for the purpose. Nothing endangered." She spun so her back rested against the railing and she looked defiantly up at him. "Recently had a love affair go badly. There's nothing for getting over a broken romance so satisfying as killing things."

Geoffrey blinked; he didn't know what to say. Was she serious? "I-I'm sorry to hear that."

"Which? That my romance ended or that I like to hunt?"

"Both."

It was her turn to laugh. "You're not a bad sort."

Geoffrey said seriously, "I think I should warn you, I'm already . . . enamored of someone."

Miriam's eyes lit up. "Good for you." She pushed Geoffrey aside to peer into the ballroom. "Is she in there?"

Geoffrey turned and saw the servants moving between the glittering and formally dressed guests. "Yes."

"That one?" Miriam pointed out a young woman with blond curls cascading down her shoulders. She was laughing with the Argentinean ambassador.

Geoffrey shook his head. "Not my type."

Miriam closed one eye and studied Geoffrey. "Now what would your type be?" She picked out an intelligent-looking woman with a smooth cap of straight black hair. "Her?"

"Close, three women over."

Miriam drew back in protest. "But that's your mother!"

"Behind her. With the serving tray."

June was like a cut rose in a bowl of diamonds. Her brown skin glowed with health among all the painted faces.

"The serving maid." Miriam grinned wickedly. "You *are* a bad boy. Does your mother know?"

Geoffrey's eyes followed June.

His mother caught his glance and waved. There was a hopeful smile on her face.

Geoffrey waved back, saying to Miriam, "Not yet. I haven't found the right time."

"There never will be. Better do it soon, though, before she has the entire debutante fleet mobilized. A random shot off some lovely's bow and you might find yourself the POW of a very respectable, very loveless marriage."

"Won't happen," Geoffrey said. "June is the only woman for me."

Miriam shrugged. "It always seems that way at first, doesn't it?" She raised her champagne glass in salute. "To hopeless romance. May yours end better than mine." She downed the drink and hurled the glass against a boulder in the landscape. The crystal shattered into a thousand fragments.

Geoffrey started at her violent action.

Miriam stared into the darkness. "Don't give your heart to your lover." Her voice was hard and flat. "It hurts too much when they leave."

Geoffrey felt sorry for Miriam. He had been lucky to find June. As soon as he was ready for love, he'd found the perfect woman, close at hand.

He placed a consoling hand on Miriam's shoulder.

She turned towards him, a rueful smile on her face. "Sorry, forgot myself for a moment. Must be charming, else Mum would be disappointed."

Geoffrey smiled. "Don't worry, I won't tell."

Across the ballroom, Geoffrey's mother approached, pulling in her wake the blond woman with the cascade of curls.

Miriam put a hand to her hair. "Looks like my shift is over." She kissed him lightly on the cheek. "Good luck."

Geoffrey endured a series of women his mother introduced to him. None of the others were as frank as Miriam. They fluttered and flirted and professed their delight at his recovery. These same women who, before tonight, had never met him.

When he had shaken off the last of them, Geoffrey saw June hurrying to the kitchen. He took her elbow and pulled her towards him.

"Let me go," June whispered heatedly. "I am working."

"Just for a moment," Geoffrey pleaded. "I miss you." He gazed down at her with soft eyes.

June snorted. "You miss me so much you console yourself talking to beautiful women?"

Geoffrey waved his hand. "They're my mother's attempt at matchmaking. I haven't told her I've already found the perfect woman."

June cast a glance over her shoulder. She pulled away from Geoffrey. "I have to go."

Geoffrey looked up. From across the room he saw his mother watching them. Her lips were pressed tightly together.

The party wound down around three a.m. The attendees slipped out to the Allen guest cottages, or limousines that would carry them to the island's airport or the Rosario Resort, on the other side of Mount Constitution.

Geoffrey retired to his own bed, leaving his tuxedo draped over a chair. It had been a wearying night, playing host, responding to the insincere congratulations of his parents' friends. He hoped the overnight guests would leave in the morning so things would get back to normal and June would have more time to spend with him.

Lillith closed the door to her office and turned on her terminal. The walls were covered with colored printouts of DNA sequences, epidemic maps, and a poster of the full human genome, shown in compressed format.

After she had logged on and answered the more urgent of the emails that had piled up while she was in D.C., Lillith downloaded security software to floppies. On her laptop she ran every computer-virus detection program the CDC had licensed, even including the time-consuming program written by the NSA. All the scans came back clean.

Lillith blew out a sigh of relief. The file Idaho had given her was safe. She hooked up her laptop to the CDC's network and uploaded the "cat got at a tack" file. The one Idaho had sent with the cryptic message, "It's starting again."

Once the file was in the CDC's system, she ran a comparison search against all known viral strains. There was a similarity to HIV, but it was only a thirty-nine percent match.

Lillith chewed on a cuticle. When she'd been at Caduceus, she and Fowler had used HIV. As a retrovirus, it was ideal for altering a patient's DNA. A retrovirus was too small to contain its own replication machinery, so it inserted its RNA into the DNA of its victim and used the victim's own cellular mechanisms to create more of itself.

To turn man's deadliest enemy into a cure, you replaced the portion of its RNA that replicated the virus with a a payload gene.

When the retrovirus inserted itself into the patient's DNA, the cell would express the therapeutic gene.

It had been a promising avenue of treatment . . . until Mahn's disease had swept across the globe.

She and Fowler had been researching the use of a HIV-based gene therapy for Alzheimer's disease. The therapy was especially useful because it could penetrate the blood-brain barrier.

Lillith wished she'd been able to keep a copy of the research she'd done at Caduceus. But the company had required her to sign a nondisclosure agreement that prevented Lillith from taking her research notes when she left. All she had were memories a decade old.

Lillith wrote down what she remembered on a piece of paper. She didn't use a computer, afraid someone in the network might stumble upon her notes.

In the meantime, she imported the mystery file into a simulation program that the CDC had developed with researchers at Caltech. It was light-years beyond the primitive simulations she and Fowler had used when working at Caduceus. Lillith selected the age-damaged DNA of an eighty-three-year-old woman with Alzheimer's disease and applied the viral code to the simulated patient. She set it to run on her local machines instead of the supercomputers in the basement. It would take longer, days even, but the test wouldn't be on the supercomputer logs.

What bothered her most was why Caduceus would be bothering with viral engineering. There was no profit in a treatment they couldn't market. The Beijing Treaty had been ratified by every country on the globe. Who would they sell to?

The morning after the party, Geoffrey woke with a throbbing headache. The birds outside his window sounded like screeching tires. His body ached: too many champagne toasts to his future, too many drinks with the socialites his mother had introduced.

When he buzzed for breakfast, Maria brought him grapefruit, toast, and a carafe of coffee. June must have the morning off after serving hors d'oeuvres all night.

When Maria threw open the curtains, the light split his skull. Geoffrey threw an arm over his face and groaned.

After breakfast he felt better. Geoffrey dressed and went to his mother's rose garden to pluck a flower for June.

He carried it to the servants' quarters, where he found her bed stripped to bare mattress. June's personal effects were gone.

Geoffrey ran from the room. He found Maria in the ballroom, polishing the marble floors. He gestured for her to turn off the buffer.

His chest heaving, Geoffrey put his hands on his knees. "Where is June?"

Maria's eyes flicked left and right. "She go. Early this morning."

"What?" Geoffrey felt a stabbing ache in his chest. Had he done something wrong? He thought June liked him . . . especially after what had happened between them the night before the party. The feel of her body moving under his. It had been his first time . . . had he done something wrong? "Why? Did she say why?"

Maria nodded her head in the direction of his mother's bedchambers. "Ask your *madre*. I do not know."

Geoffrey clenched his fists and stormed towards the wing housing his mother's bedroom.

He burst into his mother's room, throwing the French doors wide. His mother moaned and pulled the duvet over her head.

Geoffrey cast open the drapes. He turned to confront his mother. "Where is June?"

His mother sat up and drew her bed gown around her body. "How dare you speak to me that way?" Her intonation was firm and in control, despite the dark circles under her eyes.

Geoffrey took a step closer to the bed. "June is not in her quarters. Her things are gone. What happened?"

Geoffrey's mother smoothed her hair away from her face and plucked together the lace hems of her bed jacket. "She left for the mainland on an early flight. We spoke about her departure last night, after the guests had begun retiring to their cabins."

Geoffrey's chest ached. "Did she say *why* she was going?"

His mother caught his eyes with a cold blue gaze. "I expect because I dismissed her."

Geoffrey drew back, his face flushed. "What?"

His mother continued as if he had not spoken. "I saw she was becoming rather familiar. Wholly unsuitable. I asked her to leave before things became awkward."

"Awkward?" At his sides, Geoffrey's hands clenched into fists. "Mother, I *love* June."

His mother pulled the bedside cord to summon Maria to bring breakfast. "No, you don't. You became infatuated with the first pretty girl you saw after your recovery. Perfectly natural. I should have seen it coming. But there's no basis for love between you. You and she come from different backgrounds."

Geoffrey felt his mouth twist. "You mean because she's Hispanic?"

"Don't be silly. If you wanted to marry the Argentinean ambassador's niece, I wouldn't think twice. But living as we do, maintaining the family's position in society—your little housemaid could never do that."

Geoffrey raised his fist and for an instant thought he might strike his mother. Then, trembling, he lowered his hand. He stalked to the door. Turning, he spat, "It's about control, isn't it? For the first time in my life, I'm well. I don't need you or your money. I can make my own way in the world, plan a life away from this opulent prison."

His mother's eyes narrowed. "Is this the gratitude I get for looking out for your welfare?"

"Is sending June away your sick idea of protecting me? Protecting me from life?"

"Yes." His mother nodded once. "Do you think she would have been interested in you if you weren't my son, with all of the Allen wealth behind you?"

Geoffrey's face heated. June wasn't like that. She liked him for himself. Why couldn't his mother understand? He shouted, "Just because you live in a loveless marriage, doesn't mean I have to settle for one."

His mother's face paled. She leaned back against the cushions, her mouth tight.

Geoffrey felt dirty. His parents had moved into separate bedrooms shortly after his birth . . . when he'd been diagnosed with CF. "I-I'm sorry."

His mother's eyes were bright with tears, but her expression was hard. "Go," she said in a hoarse voice. "Go and find the pain you deserve."

Her words rang like a curse in his ears as he shut the door behind him. Everything was going wrong. Last night he had been on top of the world, healthy, in love, with his parents' affection and financial support. Curing his CF was supposed to make his life perfect. But now everything had turned to shit.

CHAPTER 5

Another dead end. Idaho ripped off the goggles. He was·tired of looking at packets of useless information. It had been nearly a month since he'd stumbled across proof Caduceus was engaging in viral engineering. It had happened during one of his research forays. He routinely scanned biogenetics companies for network weaknesses and downloaded any exposed information.

The file's existence and recent modification implied a field trial was under consideration or already under way. But it gave no indication of who, where, or when.

Blue had died from a man-made disease. He wouldn't let viral engineers start that kind of tampering again.

Idaho adjusted the drip on his IV feed. He knew he should eat solid food a couple of times a week to keep his digestive tract functioning, but he couldn't be bothered now; he had work to do.

Think. How could he determine who had been working on the virus? The other files he had downloaded from Caduceus had listed the researcher's name. But in this file that field was blank. It had been stored on the central supercomputer, in a hidden directory, with no indication of where it had come from or who had put it there.

Idaho slipped the goggles back on. He had to find out who owned the file. Then he could pressure them to tell him whether human trials had started and, if so, how to shut the program down.

Idaho twitched his fingertips and instigated two programs. One, a watcher, pinged the file every other second. If anyone opened it, the watcher would record the IP address of the machine used to open the file, and alert Idaho.

The other wended its way through Caduceus's network, scanning for copies of the file. It looked everywhere, including deleted directories that had not yet been overwritten. It also checked for evidence of a shredder program.

Shredders were only used by people with secrets to hide.

Geoffrey's limo plowed through the streets of Federal Way like a shark, pushing smaller private cars out of its path. People waiting at a bus stop turned to watch it go by.

June's mother lived on the twenty-third story of one of the new low-income housing projects.

After a sharp turn, Geoffrey resettled the vase of roses in the wine bucket and straightened the collar of his tuxedo. A beautiful red satin gown lay in a box on the seat next to him. He imagined it hugging June's curves. After she accepted him, they would dine at the Space Needle and dance the night away with Seattle slowly revolving beneath them.

The limo parked at the curb and Geoffrey got out. He realized he didn't have an access code to get in the building. He wanted to surprise June, so instead of calling up he waited. After a few minutes, a middle-aged woman leading twin boys walked up and pressed several keys. Geoffrey held the door open for her. The woman stared at his tuxedo in disbelief. Geoffrey waited for her to cross the threshold, then followed her in.

"*¿Es usted una estrella de cine?*" the woman asked as they rode up the elevator together.

"Uh, no *hablo* Spanish," Geoffrey said.

The woman shook her head, muttered *"otro trafi-cante,"* and led her boys out of the elevator at the next stop.

The door to Apartment 2309 was dented, and one of the painted numbers was chipped. Geoffrey pushed the doorbell and, when he heard nothing, knocked.

"¿Quién es él?" a high sweet voice called.

Geoffrey's heart leapt. It was June. He straightened his hair and held the roses upright in front of him.

The peephole darkened, and Geoffrey heard the chain rattle.

June's face appeared. The tip of her nose was red and raw, as if she'd been crying. Her skin was sallow. There were dark circles under her eyes. "What are you doing here?" she whispered, looking up and down the hall.

It wasn't the reception he'd been expecting. He held the roses out to her. "These are for you. Can I come in?"

June looked back over her shoulder into the apartment. "No."

Geoffrey shifted the roses to his left hand. He reached out and touched her face. Where he brushed her hair aside he saw pale blotches. "What's wrong?"

June pushed his touch away with a hand holding a tissue. "It's nothing. The flu. Why are you here?"

Geoffrey swallowed. It was now or never, if she wouldn't let him inside . . . He knelt, ignoring the stained carpeting beneath the knee of his twelve-hundred-dollar tuxedo. He took her hand in his. His throat felt tight. Geoffrey took a breath and said, "June Rosalita Escalante, will you marry me?"

June backed up a step.

From one of the bedrooms in the apartment, a woman's reedy voice asked, *"Quién es?"*

June called back over her shoulder. *"No es impor-tante, Abuelita.* Go back to sleep. *Vaya a dormir."*

June pulled Geoffrey up to a standing position. *"Tu loco?* Are you crazy? What are you thinking?"

Geoffrey was hurt. He'd expected her to be happy, thrilled. Had he done something wrong? He'd brought flowers; there was a two-carat diamond ring in his pocket. "I want to marry you."

June pinched the bridge of her nose, shaking her head. She looked up, anger in her eyes. "I was a *maid* in your mother's house. How can I marry you? What kind of life would we have?"

"I could give you everything, June. I promise we'd be happy."

June wiped her nose with the tissue. "Happy? If you marry me, your parents will disown you. Your mother told me. You've never worked. How do you expect to earn a living? What would we survive on— my hourly pay?"

"You would rather have money than me?"

"I would rather have a *future*. Dreams don't fill bellies."

Geoffrey could barely breathe. The roses fell from his fingers. "But I love you."

June shook her head. "No. You lust after me. Not even me, the woman you think I am. You don't even know how to pronounce my name: Junia."

She barked a short laugh. "I was the first woman you slept with, that's all. You think that feeling was love?" She flipped her hand, dismissively. "Go back to Orcas, sleep with the rich *putas* your mother invited. Then see how badly you want me."

"Is this about the women my mother introduced me to? They mean nothing to me."

"No. This is about you and me coming from different worlds. We have *nada* in common. Nothing."

An old woman with a four-footed cane hobbled down the hallway towards the door. She stopped open-mouthed and stared at Geoffrey. *"Quién es?"*

"Nadie," June told the old woman. *"Lo pierden."* To Geoffrey, she said, "I'm going to put my grandmother back to bed. You have to go."

The door slammed in Geoffrey's face and he heard her bolt all three locks. With a fierce sudden anger, he knew how Miriam had felt. He had the urge to hurt something, anything, as much as he hurt right now. Geoffrey picked up the roses and slammed them against the door until their stems broke and petals rained from them like drops of blood. He left the broken bouquet on June's doorstep.

The chauffeur's eyes widened at the expression on Geoffrey's face as he came out of the building sans bouquet and sans fiancée. He opened the door for Geoffrey and, looking down, asked, "Where to?"

"The airport."

As the limousine pulled away from the building, Geoffrey looked back at the lobby door and the windows of the twenty-third floor, hoping against hope that June had changed her mind and would come running out to him.

Nothing happened. The gray concrete of the tower was as ugly and unyielding as a cliff face.

Geoffrey threw the gown out the window of the limousine as it drove along I-5. Its crimson silk billowed for a second, before being sucked under the wheels of a Mack truck.

He uncorked the champagne and drank straight from the bottle. So much for romance.

Lillith was in the middle of reading a bulletin from the World Health Organization when her computer beeped and presented a pop-up dialog indicating that her simulation of the "cat got at a tack" virus was done. Lillith set a bookmark in the file she had been reading, about an outbreak of an unidentified disease in Argentina, and opened the simulation.

A spiraling DNA helix rotated into the air, projected by the holographic display in her desk.

An RNA polymerase enzyme teased apart the DNA where the retrovirus had inserted itself. It constructed an RNA strand from the message encoded in the virus's DNA. The single strand of RNA floated free of the DNA helix, a ribbon of nucleotide message waiting to be read.

A ribosome, a bundle of proteins shaped like two mismatched balls, attached itself to the viral RNA strand and built three proteins, snipping each free.

The proteins ran along the DNA to a new location. One nicked an opening in the DNA's double helix, and a second inserted a new DNA sequence.

The last protein did something she had never seen before: It looped a section of the DNA after the newly inserted code and excised it, editing the DNA.

Spliceosome proteins routinely edited transcribed RNA, but Lillith knew of nothing that edited the DNA helix itself.

Lillith had the program compare the changes with the original virus. The newly inserted DNA was slightly different than the original.

She fast-forwarded the simulation to display the woman's genome after a week-long interaction with the virus. Lillith selected the chromosome that contained the Alzheimer genes, but there was no insertion there.

"Show deltas," Lillith told the computer. Sections of chromosome seven highlighted. She frowned at the display. The virus had inserted itself just after codon 508. She needed a moment to recall her med school training. That was in the gene most commonly associated with cystic fibrosis. Whoever was working on this virus had switched the targeted disease from Alzheimer's to CF. A chill ran through Lillith's spine. She opened a file drawer and dug through her personal mail. She pulled out a pink card laced with white ribbon. Four years ago, Lillith had received Fowler's wedding announcement. In her hands, postmarked three months ago, was the birth announcement of his first child, a daughter. If the little girl had been born with CF . . . Fowler was too driven a man to let ethics stand in his way. And too arrogant to fear his work might cause an epidemic as Mahn's had done.

If Fowler was doing what she suspected, would she turn him in? Lillith was torn.

On one hand was her responsibility as an agent of

the CDC to report any act that threatened public health or that compromised medical ethics or law. There was also the opportunity to crack Caduceus wide open in order to force the company to publicly release its mapping data.

On the other hand was a father's concern for his ailing daughter. Just because Fowler was a jerk didn't mean she didn't still have feelings for him. In his place, with a sick child and only the law standing between herself and a cure, could Lillith be sure she wouldn't take a similar shortcut?

Viral engineering, done correctly, wasn't any more dangerous than treatments currently legal, those that used domesticated adenoviruses to trigger protein production. It was just bad luck that Mahn's disease had exchanged genes with a wild virus that provided the packaging instructions needed for the disease to replicate and spread.

Even if something like that occurred again, what would be the harm in a virus that cured CF? Most of those who caught it wouldn't have the gene mutation that triggered the virus. Those who were CF carriers would, instead of a disease, catch a cure.

Lillith blew out a breath she hadn't realized she'd been holding. Before she made any decision, she needed more information. She had to talk with Fowler.

Lillith plucked her cell phone out of her leather attaché case. She didn't want this call going out on the CDC's line. Lillith looked up Caduceus's number and dialed. When she got the operator, she asked to be switched to Dr. Julian Fowler's line.

While the phone rang, she swung into place the tiny screen. It swiveled from the handset to rest in front of her right eye like a monocle.

Fowler's brows rose when he came online. "Lillith, what a surprise. I'm sorry about the other day. That was just business; I hope there's no hard feelings."

Lillith shook her head. "This isn't about that. I need to ask you some questions about your research."

Julian's smirk faded. "You know I can't talk about it. Everything I work on is under nondisclosure. The company's R&D is private information."

"Maybe some of it isn't as private as you think." Lillith reached forward and pressed a button on her laptop, transmitting the file Idaho had sent her.

Fowler split his screen to view the incoming file. His face paled and his eyes flicked from the file to Lillith. He smoothed the panicked expression into a bemused smile, but Lillith had already seen under his calm veneer.

"What is this?" he asked.

Lillith stared at his image, unblinking. "It's a viral design . . . based on research you and I did at Caduceus before Mahn's disease broke out."

"Where did you get it?"

"Cut the crap, Julian. This is a direct extrapolation of the work we did at Caduceus. Take a look at the last modification date. Three weeks ago. Someone at your company is working on illegal research." Her lips compressed with anger. "Which I think you know very well."

Fowler sat back in his chair. He tapped his fingertips together once, twice, then rested them on the tabletop. "You're making a serious charge. How did you come by this information?"

Lillith looked away. "I'm not at liberty to reveal my sources."

"If it's someone within the company, they're breaking nondisclosure . . . if the file can even be authenticated. How do you know this isn't a hoax?"

Lillith glared at the screen. "This is based on research you and I did during our internships. Don't you think I'd recognize your work? I'm giving you a chance to explain yourself before I go to the authorities."

"With what? A file you can't verify? If you'd gotten this from a reputable source, we wouldn't be having this conversation; I'd be talking to the attorney general's office." Fowler leaned forward, his fingertips resting lightly on his desk. "No, this is a fishing trip. What do you want?"

Lillith blew out a breath. "I want the truth. Is anyone at Caduceus working on viral engineering?"

Fowler's hazel eyes were wide and unblinking. "I give you my word, as a scientist, absolutely not."

Lillith tapped the split screen. "Then where did this file come from?"

"I suggest you ask your source. And keep in mind, even if the file can be proven to come from our network, it's only a design, not an experimental log. There's nothing illegal about *simulating* viral cures."

"But there's nothing profitable about it either."

Fowler touched his brow in a mocking salute. "Touché, Dr. Watkins, touché." An incoming voice conference flashed on the split screen. "As fascinating as this has been, I have work to do. I suggest you stop wasting taxpayer money chasing research that doesn't exist." Fowler reached forward and tapped a button. The connection closed.

Lillith pounded the table. Damn him. In under five minutes he had managed to impugn her data, wriggle out of her accusations—and worse, now he was forewarned.

Idaho's data was good; she knew it. But it had been illegally obtained. Even if she could get it admitted, Idaho would have to come to court and testify about how he'd obtained it. She couldn't see that happening.

Damn. Damn. Damn. How could she have been so stupid? She'd let sentiment stand in the way of doing what was right, and now her one chance to crack Caduceus open was gone. The genetic simulation was now on top of her display. Angrily, she said, "Close simulation."

A dialog box appeared: SAVE RESULTS?

"Yes."

Lillith looked at the files on her laptop. She had terabytes of priceless data that she couldn't use and proof of wrongdoing that wasn't authenticated or admissible in court. Proof Fowler was probably deleting from Caduceus's network even now.

Lillith jerked open her file drawer. The bottle was gone, of course. She glared at the empty spot it had once occupied. It wouldn't have solved her problems. She rested her elbows on the table and cradled her head in her hands.

What could she do now?

Geoffrey lay on his bed feeling worse than he had when he'd had CF. Then he'd been ill, wanting to live. Now he was well and he wanted to die.

The shades were drawn and the soulful, deep crooning of a dark-synth musician played from dozens of microspeakers embedded in the walls. The song spoke of loss and destruction and the inevitable death that awaited all. The words had never rung so true.

Geoffrey held up his hand. There was a brown rash spreading on his fingers. It was the same olive brown as June's skin. It was as if his body were trying to hold on to her any way it could. Didn't she understand the depth of his feelings for her? This was real; he wouldn't use and discard her. He wanted to make a life with her. Without her, what future did he have?

Geoffrey got up and crawled to the bathroom. The music followed him, jumping from the bedroom to bathroom speakers.

He washed his hands in the sink, but the color did not come off. When Dr. Ambrose had remotely examined them via the Net, he said it looked like a fungus, nothing serious. He had prescribed abrasive scrubbing with an antibacterial soap.

Geoffrey laughed a laugh that was half-sob. Everyone said he and June came from different worlds. Maybe if he turned as brown as June, he could prove them wrong.

He pulled a tissue out of a marble dispenser and blew his nose. Crying left him weak and nauseated.

He tossed it into the bathroom incinerator and went back to bed.

An hour later, Maria pushed a breakfast cart into the bedroom. Her eyes were red and puffy. She sneezed into a handkerchief.

"Feeling better, Mr. Allen?" Maria asked.

Geoffrey propped himself up on his elbow. "Yes, but what's happened to you?"

Maria shrugged, "*El* flu. A sick guest . . . now we are all sick." She lifted the silver cover and displayed cereal, milk, orange juice, and a halved grapefruit. "Even Cook is sick," she said.

Geoffrey frowned. "Everyone?"

"Your mother, father, all the servants." Maria scowled and shook a finger in the air. "That ambassador from Argentina, I heard him sniffle. He maybe give us this." She walked to the door and closed it behind her.

Geoffrey felt uneasy. His eyes fell to the brown patch on his hand. No, that was just a fungal infection. And the servants only had the flu. Nothing more. He would not become neurotic over coincidences.

When Lillith came to work on Wednesday, Danvers jumped up from the microscope station. "Did you see the latest report?" he asked.

Lillith hung her coat on a hook. "No. What's come in?"

"Senator Mackey has a virulent form of liver cancer." Danvers shifted his weight between his feet, nearly hopping from one to the other.

"Tragic." Lillith stowed her lunch in the refrigerator, next to bottles of DNA-sequencing reagents. "But why is that a case for the CDC?"

Danvers picked up an electronic ink printout and waved it in her face. "Two reasons." He pointed at the plastic. "First, Mackey undergoes blood screening for cancer proteins every fall. And last year showed no irregularities. His symptoms started a week ago . . .

and they're severe. They sent us a biopsy sample. It's like his liver is self-destructing. You can watch the nonfunctioning liver cells replicate before your eyes. The growth rate is phenomenal."

Lillith nodded at the microscope behind Danvers. "Is that what you've got on the slide?"

"No." Danvers pointed skyward. "Mackey's samples are upstairs. They're being classified as a level-three biohazard."

Lillith cocked her head. "Are you saying it's a *contagious* cancer?"

"Maybe." Danvers licked his lips. "Six of the people on his staff have the same condition."

"Oh God. When did we send out the health bulletin?"

Danvers shook his head. "We haven't. Lam's holding the news until we collect further information. He doesn't want to cause a panic. This is Washington, D.C., we're talking about."

"Send it," Lillith said. "Now. On my authority. If Lam gives you any trouble about it, I'll talk to him."

Danvers's eyebrows rose. "I'll get right on it."

"Have the cancerous cells been sequenced?"

Danvers tapped a button on the desk and the wall screen displayed the current status of DNA sequencer fourteen. "They're undergoing PCR amplification now."

"Call me as soon as there's any data. And send out that report." She walked out the door to the administrative wing. "I'm going to have words with Dr. Lam."

Dr. Lam was in his office, typing on his upright keyboard. The two pillars of keys looked like twin obelisks.

Dr. Lam was in his fifties, with bright white streaks of silver running through his straight black hair. His face was wide with a square jaw. His hands were like bricks; it amazed Lillith that he could manipulate delicate items such as computer keys and minuscule pipettes.

Lillith loomed over Lam, hands on her hips. "What do you mean by not sending out a health bulletin on the Mackey data?"

Lam finished typing a sentence and looked up. His brown eyes were placid below their epicanthic folds. "Calm down, Dr. Watkins. We're talking about six cases in Washington, D.C. This is not an epidemic."

Lillith threw up her hands. "The first proof of a communicable cancer, one that's reduced its victims to dialysis within a week, and that's not news?"

Dr. Lam placed both hands on the edge of his desk and pushed himself back. "We can't afford to create a panic because of a cancer cluster. Washington, D.C., is a politically sensitive area. This might be something environmental. We're checking out the senator's workplace now."

Lillith shook her head. "If the CDC had kept a lid on Mahn's disease, we might not be here to have this argument. Only the quick response of local health organizations kept it from becoming a major epidemic."

"Your concern for public well-being is admirable." Lam held up his palms in a placating gesture. "But don't let your emotions overrule your intellect. We must provide solid information or we'll lose credibility with the local health organizations."

"The health organizations deserve warning. I had Danvers send out an alert." Her mouth was tight, waiting for Lam's response.

Lam said, "Computer: Track down Danvers and patch through an audio feed."

Seconds later, Danvers's voice came over the line. "Sir?"

"Have you sent out that bulletin about the cancer cluster?"

A pause, then Danvers said, "No. But I was just about to."

Lam looked meaningfully at Lillith. "Cancel that. We're not sending anything out until we know more about the senator's illness."

"But—" Lillith said.

"This isn't your decision, Dr. Watkins, it's mine. We will not release any information until we are sure."

Lillith balled her hands into fists. Dr. Lam was a

conservative, afraid of looking foolish. "You're endangering the lives of health workers in the infected area."

Lam's black eyes narrowed. "You will obey my orders or I will have your resignation. Is that understood?"

Lillith's mouth worked. Finally she looked away. "We should at least move the work to the level-four lab, until we know more."

"Agreed," Dr. Lam said.

Lillith ground her teeth together. Lam's conservative policies were endangering the lives of the public. Why couldn't he see that?

CHAPTER 6

Lillith's computer displayed the progress of the DNA sequencer in the level-four lab. Bands of green, blue, red, and yellow marched upwards across the screen. This was the DNA of Senator Mackey sequenced from the tissue of one of his tumors. Somewhere in there was the key to understanding this new, transmissible form of cancer.

Lillith looked up from the display when Danvers entered her office.

"Bad news," he said.

Lillith's stomach knotted. "Another cancer cluster?"

"Two. But neither is liver cancer. One is lymphoma, the other is brain cancer. Same rapid growth rate. The outbreaks are in a low-income housing tower in Seattle and members of the Japanese National Ballet."

"Strange." Lillith tapped her bottom lip with her finger. "What would an economically disadvantaged person in Seattle have in common with a United States senator three thousand miles away and a ballet dancer halfway across the world?"

Danvers shook his head. "I have no idea. We haven't been able to identify an environmental factor . . . and there's no telling if these three cancer clusters are even related. The only similarity so far is the epidemiology."

"Three variants of the world's first verified contagious form of cancer arise in the same week? That's a heck of a coincidence."

Danvers shrugged. "Stranger things have happened."

Lillith's mind raced, trying to form a connection between the two cases. "Do we have a list of the senator and the ballet dancer's recent travel? Were they anywhere near Seattle in the past month? Perhaps they caught a connection through Seatac? They could have encountered the Seattle patient in the airport."

Danvers pulled a palmtop computer out of his pocket and made a note. "I'll check."

Lillith watched the bands of color march across the screen. "Anything else?"

"A report from Argentina. I don't know whether to believe it. It claims three members of the ambassadorial staff are presenting symptoms of thalassemia."

Lillith looked up. "That's a fairly rare genetic disorder. How did they end up working together? Nepotism, maybe? If they were related—"

"Here's the part that doesn't make sense. None of them had the condition a week ago."

Lillith raised her eyebrows. "Adult-onset thalassemia? That's impossible. People don't develop inherited anomalies later in life. The flaw is either there at conception or it's not."

Danvers held up his hands. "I know. I know."

"Request more data on the Argentinean case. Perhaps it's another condition masquerading as thalassemia." She tapped her forefinger against her lower lip. "Do the people afflicted with the contagious cancers have anything in common?"

"Two-thirds of the cases involve influential or important people: a U.S. senator and a Japanese ballet star."

"Bio-terrorism? Could these be manufactured illnesses?"

"Maybe. We could certainly compare the data, see if there are any similarities."

"Do that. Also, have one of the interns scan the

news, see if any terrorist organizations are claiming credit."

A beeping in Idaho's auditory cortex woke him. His eyes fluttered open, lashes hitting the VR goggles that lay askew on his face. Idaho pushed the goggles back into place and focused on the display.

The watcher he had set on the Caduceus file had triggered. Someone had marked the file for deletion. Idaho stored the IP address of the machine that made the request. Then he used a log file from the Caduceus network to map the IP address to the machine owner: Dr. Julian Fowler.

He grinned in the darkened trailer. "Got you."

Idaho transmitted the information to Lillith in an encrypted email to her home address. He bounced the message off a free server in the Netherlands so it couldn't be traced back to his machine.

Fowler, or someone using his account, had deleted the file. It wasn't conclusive. For that, Idaho needed motive and proof of human trials. The first was easy. Idaho opened the copy of the personnel database he had downloaded from Caduceus, and extracted a list of Fowler's dependents: a wife and three-month-old daughter. He set search programs to probe medical databases for information about their and Fowler's health. There were two reasons a researcher like Fowler would risk his position and reputation: personal sentiment or profit.

Once the health search was initiated, Idaho concentrated on profit.

If the virus had been created for profit, there would be a financial transaction linking the buyer and seller.

How much would it take to make Fowler forget his ethics and risk his high-paying career with Caduccus? A million? Two?

Idaho widened his search parameters to find all transactions over fifty thousand dollars into Fowler's bank accounts during the past three years.

Nerve impulses twitched in his hands and arms,

sending signals through the embedded electrodes.
Software converted his movements to actions in the
Net. He activated a program he had downloaded from
LongTr33, a hacker he occasionally swapped code
with.

The program monitored FinWeb, the encrypted I2
network that banks used to route money. The version
LongTr33 made public allowed the user only to monitor transactions, not alter them. Idaho suspected
LongTr33 had a private version that financed his
"computational research." But that was none of Idaho's business.

LongTr33 provided another public service for his
friends. He maintained a database containing every
transaction his program had recorded in the past year.
Terabytes of compressed data.

Idaho twitched and the computer translated the motion into his password. He began sorting through the
trillions of records in LongTr33's database.

If it took hours, days, weeks, he would find the person who'd incited Fowler to break the law and endan-
ger public health. Find him and stop him. For Blue.

Lillith frowned at the senator's DNA data. She compared the sequences again. It showed the same
anomalies.

Lillith placed a call.

Danvers answered on his palmtop. In the background of the wobbly image, Lillith saw reagent bottles. He must be refilling the sequencer's fluid wells.

"Are you sure the lab in D.C. sent us the right
sample? I'm looking at what's supposed to be the senator's DNA, and it doesn't match what's in his medical record."

Danvers scratched behind his ear. "Anything's possible, but it's hard to believe they'd make a mistake on
something that important. How different are they?"

Lillith checked the comparison display. "I'm seeing
thirty-two variations between the DNA in his medical
file and the recent sample. That's more than can be

accounted for by aging or retroviruses. Especially since the sequence in his medical record is only five months old."

"Where are the differences?" Danvers asked.

Lillith caused the comparison to highlight the changed areas. Chromosome seven had been altered near codon 508. She caught her breath. There were the letters: "CATGATATATAC."

"What is it?" Danvers asked. "What are you seeing?"

Lillith shook her head and tried to remain calm. "I don't know. There are changes on chromosomes seven and eight."

Danvers waited. When Lillith remained silent, he said, "I'll call D.C. and check on the sample."

"Thanks." Lillith closed the connection.

Her eyes roamed over the change in chromosome seven. The "cat got at a tack" sequence was there, but there were other changes downstream on the chromosome. Was it possible that Fowler or someone else at Caduceus had developed a treatment for the senator?

Lillith shook her head. She couldn't allow herself to jump to conclusions. It could be a coincidence.

Lillith pulled up the simulation she'd programmed to apply the "cat got at a tack" virus to an elderly woman.

She compared it with the senator's recent sample. The virus had made only one change in the simulation. There were thirty-two in the senator's DNA. Aside from the CATGATATATAC sequence on chromosome seven, the rest of the inserted sections were different.

The elderly woman simulation had been running for a week and resulted in only one change.

If the senator's latest DNA sample was correct, the virus Idaho had found in Caduceus's files couldn't be responsible for the senator's condition.

So what was?

*   *   *

The data from Argentina was getting stranger by the hour. There were four new cases of adult-onset thalassemia. Lillith suggested the Argentinean doctors compare the current genetic data with childhood scans.

The differential analysis software found changes in the DNA. Science had known for years that a person's genetic structure was not fixed—was, in fact, constantly rewritten by retroviruses and mutagens—but these changes were startling. Unlike classical thalassemia, where a flawed terminator in the DNA prevented production of the enzyme that created hemoglobin, in the Argentinean patients that gene was scrambled. The nucleotides were all wrong.

Lillith checked the childhood scans again. At birth, each of the patients had a functioning gene.

She compared the changes from each patient with the others. They were identical. Lillith whistled. This was like nothing she'd ever heard of. Lillith requested verification of the genetic scan and childhood data. If this was real, it represented a new type of retrovirus. One that not only inserted its genetic structure into human DNA but also *overwrote* a critical gene in the process.

The logical, scientific part of her brain was fascinated. Her emotional part, horrified.

Lillith scanned the nucleotides along the damaged portion of the gene. There it was, in a section of junk DNA near the damaged codon, the CATGATATATAC sequence.

The coincidences were becoming statistically improbable. But if this was the same virus that attacked the senator, why was the damage so different?

Was there more than one version of the virus, or did it react differently to each host's DNA?

Lillith kicked off two new simulations on the supercomputer, high priority. One ran the Caduceus virus over the Argentinean ambassador's healthy DNA, the other over a simulated patient with the most common form of CF.

The results came back in five minutes.

In the case of the CF patient, the CF defect was cured. The virus inserted itself downstream of the repaired DNA in an unused intron section.

The ambassador's simulation generated the error that caused thalassemia. She scanned the downstream introns. There was the retrovirus's starting sequence, but what came next was different.

Lillith continued the simulations, displaying the region of interest onscreen. When another copy of the virus interacted with the CF patient, it hit the inserted intron and detached from the DNA without inserting its payload.

In the case of the Argentinean simulation, the virus attached to the DNA at another site, altering a portion of the patient's DNA and inserting itself, along with part of the altered gene, downstream on the chromosome.

In the case of a CF patient, the virus cured the defect and stored itself and a copy of the edited CF gene in an unused section of DNA. If the simulation was correct, this then acted as a stop for future copies of the virus. Once the repair was made, the virus became nonreactive to the cell.

It was elegant and beautiful.

But in the case of a patient without CF, the virus, unable to find the CF defect, attached to another part of the person's DNA, made the programmed changes to the wrong location, and incorporated a gene at random into its downstream insertion point.

The virus, which cured CF, would cause random genetic damage in anyone without CF, resulting in cancers, thalassemia, and a host of other genetic diseases.

Lillith pinched the bridge of her nose. She had worked with Fowler for three months. His drive for results was so strong he took shortcuts. She could imagine him creating the perfect cure for CF and never considering what it would do in a person without the disorder.

Onscreen, a messenger RNA scooted along the DNA to the intron, and snipped it out of the portion of the DNA to be expressed. The virus, as specified in the file, was unable to reproduce.

The first step in creating a therapeutic virus was to strip the encoding that enabled the virus to be packaged for transmission to other cells.

But mistakes had been made before. If some of the viral sample had retained the ability to reproduce, or it had interacted with a wild virus, as had happened with Mahn's disease . . . then it could have retained or acquired the ability to become infectious.

Lillith forced herself to breathe. This was just a computer simulation. Its programming could be wrong; the results would have to be verified in live trials.

In the meantime, she had to advise medical staff treating these patients to consider this a level-four bio-hazard and to quarantine them separately.

There'd be no covering this up now. Lillith had to go to Lam and show him the Caduceus file. Even though consorting with a hacker would jeopardize her career, it was Lillith's duty to alert health officials. She agreed with Idaho: If this was another Mahn's disease in the making, it must be stopped no matter the cost.

The truth about the virus's origin would out, and whoever had created it would be prosecuted, legally and in the media. Lillith hoped against reason that it wasn't Fowler.

Lillith said, "Computer: request immediate meeting with Dr. Lam. Highest priority. Also invite Dr. Danvers."

They met in Lam's office. It was bigger and had wall screens on three out of the four walls.

Lillith displayed the results of the simulations she'd run and explained her conclusions.

Lam's head swiveled back and forth among the three screens. "Very interesting. But what I don't understand is where this"—he pointed at the middle screen, which contained the simulation of the original virus—"came from. I thought the lab was having trouble isolating a viral particle."

Lillith was grateful her complexion hid the heat of her face. What could she tell her boss? Idaho was an unreliable source, a computer hacker, for God's sake. But on the other hand, the file he had given her matched what they were seeing in the field exactly.

Lam and Danvers stared at her. "Well?" Lam said.

Lillith squared her shoulders. She had to put the health and lives of others before concerns about her career.

"I was warned this epidemic was coming. By a—" She hesitated. If she gave them Idaho's name, they would search for him. Lillith had no doubt the hacker would elude them, but if she betrayed his trust, he would become unavailable to her, and she needed his information.

"By an anonymous source," she finished. "He told me the file came from the internal network of Caduceus International. That someone there was practicing viral engineering. I believe the current crisis is the side effects of that research."

Lam's eyebrows rose to the top of his square face. "That's a very serious allegation. Does your"—he wiggled his fingers in a pantomime of quotes—"anonymous source have proof that Caduceus has actually synthesized this virus?"

"No. Not yet."

Lam stared at the central screen, where the viral DNA spiraled like a corkscrew. He pointed at Danvers and Lillith. "Until we have proof, I don't want either of you mentioning this. Danvers, how close are we to having viral particles isolated?"

Danvers's face pinked. "The virus is nonproliferating, so there aren't many free-floating particles. It appears to attach at the site quickly and—"

"How long?" Lam repeated.

"A—a week, maybe two," Danvers said.

Lillith pursed her lips. "I've prepared a nationwide health bulletin."

Lam shook his head. "Too wide a distribution. Send bulletins only to the impacted regions."

"But this is a level-four contaminant. And appears to be spread by an airborne vector. The health organizations need to know."

Lam met her eyes unblinkingly. "We've been through this before, Dr. Watkins. There are also consequences to igniting a worldwide panic. When you bring me proof, then we'll tell the world. Right now we have only guesses and anonymous tips."

Geoffrey's mother lay on her bed, wheezing. The drapes were closed and the room had a musty smell of phlegm and unwashed bodies.

Geoffrey drew open the drapes. "Mother?"

She coughed into a silk handkerchief.

Geoffrey was alarmed to see red flecks of blood on the white lace. He knelt by the bed and felt her brow. She was burning up. He grabbed her shoulders and shook her. "Mother?"

Her head lolled. "Geoffrey?" Her dilated eyes searched the room. She reached up with a hand and found his cheek. His mother smiled. "Geoffrey. I thought you had gone. It's . . . it's good you're here."

Geoffrey eased her back onto the bed. "I'm going to call Dr. Ambrose."

On the way back to his suite, Geoffrey checked on his father. The older man lay on his bed, barely breathing. He had dark splotches, like those on Geoffrey's hand, covering the left side of his face.

The servants weren't in much better condition. Maria was dressed in her uniform, but sat in a chair in the kitchen, arms folded on the table. Usually, she was a dynamo of action, cleaning from the time she rose until she got off work at six.

When she lifted her head and saw Geoffrey, she

tried to rise. "I just take a rest, Mr. Allen." Her knees wobbled and she sank back into the chair.

Geoffrey patted her shoulder. "Go back to bed. This is more than flu. I'm going to call Dr. Ambrose to come out."

Maria nodded and sighed. "That is good." She began a tottering walk back to the servants' quarters.

Back in his suite, Geoffrey sat down at his desk. A flat screen extruded from the desk top.

"Computer: Call Dr. Ambrose. Highest priority."

The screen showed a connection bar. Geoffrey impatiently watched the stripes of the bar march right. When it completed the connection, a recorded message came onscreen. It was Jill, Ambrose's receptionist. Her pert image, its blond hair twisted in a chignon, said, "The offices of Dr. Ambrose and Dr. Kyley are closed today. For emergencies, please call Evergreen trauma center." It was the automated message the office played on weekends and holidays.

Geoffrey checked the day. It was Wednesday, 10:42 A.M. The office should be open. Even if both Dr. Ambrose and Dr. Kyley were out on house calls with wealthy patients, the office staff should have been there to take a message.

Geoffrey called Ambrose's home number. After twelve rings, Ambrose answered.

His eyes were bloodshot above an unshaven chin, and the tip of his nose was chapped. "Geoffrey." His lips spread in a thin smile. "How ironic. Today you are well and I'm the one who's ill."

"Mother and father are sick. The staff, too." Geoffrey wiped his hand across his chin. "I don't know what it is . . . at first we thought the flu. But it's something more. Something serious. We need you to come right away."

Ambrose snorted. "Physician, heal thyself. Geoffrey, I'm in no condition to travel. Call Kyley."

Geoffrey shook his head. "He's not at the office. The whole place is shut down."

Ambrose's eyes widened. "Then you'd better call an ambulance. This may be more serious than I thought." Ambrose looked down at his hands, then studied Geoffrey's face. "That cure you took . . ."

Geoffrey glanced over his shoulder to make sure the door to his room was closed. "My source assured me the virus couldn't spread. This couldn't be caused by my treatment"—his chest tightened—"could it?"

Ambrose coughed into a paper tissue. "I don't know, my boy. I assume from the effects that it was a genetic therapy?"

"Yes," Geoffrey said. "One with a viral vector."

Ambrose's eyes widened. "If it interacted with a wild virus and mutated . . . that's what caused Mahn's disease. You're too young to remember. But it was horrible, just horrible." Another coughing fit took the old man.

"Do you want me to call an ambulance for you, too?" Geoffrey asked.

Dr. Ambrose shook his head. "No. I can do that myself. See to your parents, Geoffrey." With that, he reached forward and disconnected the call.

Geoffrey called 911 and told the emergency operator that an unidentified illness had struck his family and staff. She took down the list of symptoms he provided and said she'd alert Harborview Medical Center on the mainland.

That done, Geoffrey checked on his parents. His father was asleep, snoring wetly.

His mother had dressed herself and was trying to lace up her shoes.

"Mother, take it easy." He grabbed her shoulders and pushed her back towards the bed. "I've called 911, EMTs should be here within the hour. Just rest."

"I've got to check on your father," she argued, resisting his hands.

"He's asleep. Get back into bed, please?"

She looked up at him with red-rimmed eyes. "This isn't the flu, is it?"

Tears prickled Geoffrey's eyes and he frowned. "No. I don't think so."

His mother let him ease her back under the covers. He stripped off her shoes and set them beside the bed. Geoffrey kissed her sweaty brow. "Hold on, Mother, help is coming."

She nodded, dozing off as her head hit the pillow.

Geoffrey straightened. There was one more call he needed to make before the EMTs arrived. Someone on the mainland had some explaining to do.

Geoffrey crept past his sleeping father into the man's study and closed the door. He sat down at his father's machine and placed a call using the encrypted line his father kept for financial transactions.

"Camera off." The green LED of the embedded camera faded to gray.

"Call Caduceus, extension 49727."

The computer placed the call. A dialog box appeared: CALL REFUSED BY RECIPIENT.

"I bet you don't want to talk to me," Geoffrey muttered. "Redial, highest priority."

After a long pause, the connection was made. Like Geoffrey, the man who answered had his camera off.

"I told you never to call me again," the man said in an angry whisper. "Especially not here. Do you want to spend the rest of your life in jail?"

"People around me are getting sick, I need to know . . . is this because of what I, we, did?"

There was the barest flicker of a pause. "No, of course not. We removed the portion of the virus's RNA that manufactures its lipid packaging. Without that, there's no possibility it can spread."

Geoffrey thought of his mother, coughing blood onto a handkerchief, of his father lying with a mysterious rash and a fever. "Are you sure you didn't make a mistake? Dr. Mahn, after all, thought his research was safe, too."

"You got what you paid for: a cure for CF. Don't come whining to me every time your friends come down with the flu."

"This isn't the flu," Geoffrey said, his voice breaking. "My parents are dying. My mother's spitting up blood, and my father's running a fever of 104. He hasn't gotten out of bed in three days."

Another pause. "That's tragic, but it has nothing to do with my research." The voice lowered until it was barely audible. "We broke laws to give you what you wanted. Talking like this puts us both at risk. My work gave you a future. Unless you want to spend it in jail, never call me again."

The connection ended.

Geoffrey picked up his father's keyboard and hurled it against the wall. Then he let his head fall into his hands and wept.

He didn't believe his contact's assurances.

Geoffrey had wanted to be well. Dr. Fowler had been the tool, but Geoffrey had been the hand that set everything in motion.

Please, God, he prayed silently, *let my family survive and I'll recant everything. I'll go to jail, just don't let them die. Take me instead. It was supposed to be me.*

Lillith read the latest reports from D.C. and Seattle. The infection was spreading rapidly, despite the authorities' attempts to control it. Racal biohazard suits were backordered at the factory, and medical personnel were forced to use flimsy plastic emergency suits. In some areas even those weren't available. Punctures were costing lives that could have been saved with the right equipment.

The losses would have been greater save that Mahn's disease had prepared the medical establishment for such an emergency.

Lillith's thoughts were interrupted by a call from Danvers. He was seated at his desk in the lab. "I verified with D.C. that the samples are correct. They just completed their sequencing and report the same anomalies you found." He pushed a lock of sandy brown hair out of his eyes. "I also got the senator's itinerary for the last month. He was in Seattle two weeks ago, attending a social function on Orcas Island."

"Where?"

Danvers scrolled down the report on his palmtop. "The party was at the Allen estate. Apparently, he stayed overnight in one of their guest cottages. The case in Seattle might have worked at the airport or could have been hired by the Allen family as catering staff."

"Hmm. What do we know about the Allens?" Lillith opened up a search window and typed in "Allen, Orcas Island." She used the manual interface so she could keep talking to Danvers.

The first two hits described the opulent retreat the Allens had created in the San Juan Islands of Puget Sound. There were interviews in *Architectural Digest* and *Vanity Fair*.

The third hit chilled Lillith's blood. She clicked on the link. In it, the Allens were lauded for their generous donation to the Cystic Fibrosis Foundation. It was noted that their son had been diagnosed with CF at birth.

That was it. The missing link. The virus had been bought by the Allens to cure their son. Somehow the senator had become infected when he visited the compound.

"Danvers, find out if the Japanese ballet star and the Argentinean ambassador were at the party."

Danvers nodded.

A high-priority call arrived, blinking red in her inbox.

"Hang on," Lillith said, "something's just come in." She answered the call.

A thin man with a dark brown goatee was on the other end of the connection. He looked to be in his forties. "This is Dr. Cabot with the Puget Sound Health Organization. We've received a call over 911 emergency services, and we're not sure how to respond. The caller describes symptoms similar to those in the latest CDC bulletin about the level-four biohazard in this region. Our stockpile of biohazard suits is already in use at local hospitals, and we don't have additional quarantine gear. Can you advise?"

"What are the symptoms?"

"They're all over the map. Fever, internal hemorrhaging, skin discoloration."

"That doesn't sound like the same infection. How many people are at risk? Is the outbreak in a rural or urban area?"

"Fortunately, the outbreak occurred on one of the San Juan Islands. It's fairly isolated."

Lillith froze. "The San Juans, which one?"

"Orcas Island—"

"Is the outbreak near the Allen estate?"

Cabot cocked his head, "Yes. The call originated from the estate. How did you know?"

Excitement tingled along Lillith's neck. "Do you know if"—she checked the article on the Allens' charity donation—"*Geoffrey* Allen is involved?"

"Yes." The doctor's voice rose with incredulity. "He placed the call."

Lillith's heart skipped a beat. "Good. Don't send any of your people in. This virus is deadly. I'm sending one of our quarantine-ready Boeing 847's to pick up any survivors. We should be there in a little less than seven hours."

Cabot's shoulders relaxed. "Glad to hear it. The quarantine ward in Harborview Medical Center is already full. Is there anything we can do to help?"

"Keep a line open to the Allens. Tell them we're on our way. My office will contact yours when we're in the area." She saved Cabot's email and phone codes and closed the call.

To Danvers, she said, "Did you get that? I want to be on the ground personally in less than seven hours."

"Will do." An excited fervor lit his eyes. "Are you thinking what I'm thinking?"

"Yes. Geoffrey Allen is patient zero."

With the information locked in his DNA, they could test Lillith's theory and perhaps stop this disease before it spread further.

*   *   *

Geoffrey stood on the front steps of the Allen mansion. From here he could see the gatehouse, the skies, and—if he walked around the corner of the house— the docks.

Nothing. It had been six hours since he called, and the EMTs still had not arrived. He listened. Only the sounds of seagulls and waves reached his ears. Even the usual sounds of speedboats in the sound were gone. It was as if the whole region held its breath.

Geoffrey jabbed the keys on his cell phone and redialed 911. "This is Geoffrey Allen, on Orcas Island. I called hours ago and no one's showed up."

"Mr. Allen," the young woman said, "I've put your request into the system. Medical staff will reach you as soon as possible." By now her voice was familiar; Geoffrey had called her twelve times in the past six hours.

"My parents are dying, this is an *emergency*. I need help—now!"

"I understand your concern, but be assured the medical authorities are doing all they can under the circumstances."

"What circumstances?"

Her brows lifted in surprise. "The epidemic on the mainland."

Geoffrey froze. "What's broken out on the mainland?"

"It's not appropriate conversation for this line, Mr. Allen. But it's on all the news."

Geoffrey snapped the phone shut without saying goodbye and went inside to the theatre.

It was a soundproofed room with padded leather chairs arranged in tiers. One wall was a giant screen.

"Theatre on. Satellite input. Find all references to disease in the Pacific Northwest, Seattle, or Puget Sound."

The wall lit up and displayed sixteen cubes, with an arrow indicating there were more selections to choose from. The news was on every channel. A new disease—no one knew what it was—had exploded in a low-income housing project in Federal Way.

They showed a picture of June's building. EMTs in white quarantine suits carried out patients on gurneys fitted with plastic covers.

Geoffrey screamed at the image, a cry drawn from the back of his throat, and folded in two. Not June, too. *Please, God, take everyone else, but not June.*

He should have realized she might be infected. If she hadn't been on the night of the party, he had carried the disease to her with his stupid proposal of marriage. Geoffrey pounded the phone against his forehead: stupid, stupid, stupid.

He told the phone: "Call June's home number."

It dialed, then rang. Geoffrey let it ring twenty-eight times, but no one answered—not June, her mother, or her grandmother.

He had to tell someone what had happened, give them information to help save June. Geoffrey called the Harborview Medical Center, but all lines were busy. He tried the Puget Sound Health Organization offices and got a recorded message saying the current health crisis was being handled by local authorities and that citizens were encouraged to stay home, if possible.

Geoffrey thought he heard a noise and ran outside. He listened, his mouth open. Only the waves and the wind.

Help still had not come.

In the CDC's modified Boeing 847, what would have been the coach passenger area had been converted to a quarantine unit with its own atmosphere and pressurized air system. Lillith and Danvers traveled in the first-class section, just behind the cabin.

It took six hours to fly across the United States. Lillith used the time to send emails ordering a quarantine room prepped in the level-four lab and requesting Geoffrey Allen's medical records.

Like most of the wealthy, he'd had a full DNA screening done at birth. That had been how his CF was detected in infancy. Lillith contacted the CDC's supercomputer and started it running the simulated virus over Geoffrey's DNA.

When they got him in custody and sequenced his DNA, she could compare the results and test her model of the virus.

The 847 couldn't land at the small airport on Orcas Island, so Lillith negotiated with a local medivac team for the use of a helicopter and pilot in exchange for a dozen biohazard suits and four bubble stretchers from the CDC's stores in Atlanta. The local health organizations didn't have the resources to handle the current plague, and quarantine equipment was in short supply.

It was late afternoon by the time they flew across Puget Sound under the chuffing rotors of the medivac helicopter. The day was fine and clear. Brilliant white puffs of clouds drifted across a bright blue sky.

The emerald green of Mount Constitution dominated Orcas Island. There was smoke rising from the center of the island. As they passed over, Lillith saw a Beechcraft plane smoldering. It had crashed into a billboard on the opposite side of the road from the runway.

Lillith called in the accident over the noise of the helicopter. They couldn't afford to delay their recovery of Geoffrey Allen to investigate.

The helicopter skirted around Mount Constitution to the east side of the island.

The Allen estate blended into the forests. It was on the water, with a dock extending out into Puget Sound.

Swinging over the grounds, Lillith saw a swimming pool, tennis courts, and greenhouses.

Looming over it all was a two-story mansion of slate and cedar. The ceilings of each floor had to be twenty feet high. The architecture was at once rustic and elegant, like a hunting lodge built by a Manhattan architect. Cedar timbers rose in polished pillars to support a slate roof. The walls were granite.

On the front steps a man stood, one arm up to shield his face from the helicopter's wind. His smoking jacket buffeted his body. Light brown hair lashed his face.

When the helicopter had finished landing, the man duckwalked under the still whirling blade and approached. Lillith lumbered out of the helicopter, clumsy in her biohazard suit.

The man grabbed Lillith's arm. "Where the hell have you been?"

She felt a moment of fear. If he breached the suit, she might become infected.

He pulled her towards the mansion. "They're in here."

Lillith pointed to the bubble stretchers, hoping the pilot and Danvers would understand her meaning.

Lillith pressed the speaker button on her chest that amplified her voice. "Who are you?"

The man pulled her into a darkened bedchamber. "Geoffrey Allen." He pointed at the bed. "That's my mother." A sob broke his voice. "I think she's dying."

The woman was unresponsive during Lillith's examination. Lillith switched her speaker to automatic. Still bending over his mother, she asked, "How many people are here?"

Geoffrey ticked off people on his fingers. "Fifteen— no, twelve. Some of the servants ran away when everyone started getting sick."

Lillith raised her head in alarm. "Where did they go?"

"One went back to Seattle. The other two are from local families, on the west side of the island. I guess they went home."

Lillith thought of the wreck on the airfield, how there were no fire trucks on the scene, no medics attending the wounded. Depending on how contagious the virus was, the whole island might be contaminated.

"Of the people who were exposed to your parents, how many became sick?"

Geoffrey brushed a lock of hair away from his eyes as he contemplated the question.

The motion exposed a patch of dark skin over his left eyebrow. It hadn't been in the publicity photos for the CF donation.

"All of them," he said at last.

Lillith sucked in a breath. His anecdotal data hinted at a transmission rate nearing one hundred percent. That was unheard of. Some people were always immune, even to diseases such as AIDS, Ebola, and Mahn's.

The woman on the bed moaned and Geoffrey knelt by her side. "You have to help her," he said.

Lillith nodded and directed Danvers and the pilot to load Mrs. Allen into the bubble stretcher they'd brought.

The helicopter could hold only four of the bulky gurneys. If the contagion had spread off the compound, it might be easier to quarantine the whole island.

Lillith told Danvers, "We need to check the other inhabitants." She unsnapped a chest pocket on her quarantine suit and extracted her cell phone.

While Danvers and the pilot loaded Geoffrey's parents and a housemaid into the helicopter, Geoffrey led her into his office and opened the phone program.

Lillith called Dr. Cabot. When he answered, she said, "I need someone on your staff to call every inhabitant of Orcas Island and determine if they've been infected. According to one of the patients, some of the staff left the Allen compound and traveled to the town on the west side of the island. If they're not infected, they need to be evacuated. If they are infected . . . I may have the solution to your lack of quarantine space."

"It's that contagious?" Cabot asked.

"That's what we're trying to find out. I'd make the

calls myself, but"—she gestured at her biohazard suit—"I don't want to scare them."

Cabot nodded. "I'll get someone right on it."

The best way to verify the health of the inhabitants would be through home visits. Lillith asked Danvers, "How much Envirochem do we have on the helicopter?"

"I loaded a couple of liters this morning, for emergencies."

Lillith considered decontaminating the outside of her suit and taking one of the Allen cars. But the spread pattern at the senator's office indicated that the virus might be transmissible via airborne particles. Without enough Envirochem to decontaminate the car, she might spread the virus to the very people she wanted to save.

Lillith's palmtop rang. She pulled it out and answered the call. It was Cabot.

"On an island of forty-five hundred inhabitants, only fourteen people answered the phone. All but one admitted to illness in the family. Eight displayed visible symptoms."

"What geographical location of the island is the most affected?"

Cabot uploaded an image of a map of Orcas Island onto the screen. The eight red dots were spread randomly all over the horseshoe. Lillith waved Danvers over to look at the display.

"That's it. I'm calling it. This island is now under official CDC quarantine. Call the FAA and coast guard and get them to enforce it. No one's to come onto the island or leave it without CDC approval. We need to set up a field hospital on the island." Lillith discussed with Cabot how to requisition materials to implement level-four biohazard protocols for the field hospital.

When she hung up, Danvers said, "Dr. Lam is going to have a fit. Quarantining an entire island will cause a panic."

Lillith transmitted a copy of her phone conversation

with Cabot to Lam, so he'd know the conditions behind her decision. To Danvers she said, "I'd settle for a panic. I have a feeling we may be in for something worse."

Geoffrey walked over to where Lillith and Danvers were talking. "There's a gardener. We can put him in the fourth gurney."

Lillith said, "The fourth gurney's for you."

Geoffrey's brow furrowed. "I thought I'd ride up front."

"No. We don't have any way, other than the gurney, to isolate you. If you rode up front, you'd risk infecting people when we land."

"But . . . what about the others?"

"The local CDC is setting up a field hospital. They're sending out medics even as we speak." An exaggeration, but she had to get Geoffrey in the gurney. As patient zero, he was invaluable. He'd been infected the longest and could provide clues as to the progression of the disease. He seemed to be in a stable state; was that normal or something unique to Geoffrey's body chemistry?

Lillith pointed at the empty bubble stretcher. "If you want to stay with your parents, be there when your mother wakes up, you'll get in that gurney."

Geoffrey bit his upper lip, looked back at the estate. "There are eight people in the servants' quarters. Make sure the medics know that."

Danvers opened the plastic case on the quarantine gurney, and Geoffrey slipped inside. Lillith helped Danvers load the gurney into the helicopter and attach it to the negative pressure system.

Danvers nodded his head at the mansion. "You want me to stay until the medics arrive?"

Lillith's heart contracted. It would be twelve hours, at least, until the local CDC could muster resources to create a field hospital. If she left these people behind without medical help, they might die.

The pain in her chest was the same she'd felt while triaging patients for Mahn's disease. It was the reason she'd gotten away from fieldwork and taken a research position. They needed to understand the disease in order to find a cure. That was the important thing now, not tending people already marked for death. What could Danvers accomplish with a first-aid kit against mutating cancers? No, she needed him more in Atlanta.

"Get in the helicopter," Lillith said.

Relief flickered over Danvers's face as he stepped into the seat beside her.

Geoffrey Allen pounded on the inside of his gurney. He shouted to be heard over the helicopter's rotor as the pilot prepped for takeoff. "I want to go to the same hospital as June Escalante. She should be at Harborview Medical Center."

Lillith shouted back, "We'll see what we can do."

Geoffrey did not look completely satisfied, but he nodded and lay back in the gurney.

Danvers gave Lillith a sharp look at the lie.

Lillith patted his knee. If this disease was anything like Mahn's, a little white lie was nothing compared to what lay ahead.

CHAPTER 7

Idaho closed the connection. Lillith wasn't answering her office phone. Subtle motions of his fingers opened a new call. He'd tried her home number and cell phone. Nothing. Where was she?

His anger caused side effects in his network connection. Tensing muscles opened unwanted windows. He had to get himself under control. Idaho disconnected the computer from his nervous system and breathed from his diaphragm, calming himself.

He had proof: financial records linking rich kid Geoffrey Allen to Fowler at Caduceus. She could warn people now, stop the plague before it spread. Catch Fowler and punish him. Punish him like he deserved. Idaho pressed his hands to either side of his head to stop the memories from flooding back. He'd expunged them from his mind, but they still lingered in his muscles, his bones: the chafing of the handcuffs that bound his ankle to the metal shelving; hunger cramps; stiffness from waking up in a cold, unheated warehouse in the winter.

Idaho thought about the guns. He could get them out and drive to California. He had Fowler's address. He could stop this all, right now. Stop it like someone should have stopped Mahn.

No. It was already too late. The disease was out. Fowler had information. Lillith might be able to use him. Where was she?

For a paranoid second he wondered if she'd joined

forces with Fowler. They had been friends once; Idaho had found traces of their relationship in old backup files of email.

Or maybe Fowler had her eliminated because she was getting too close. If she had told Fowler about Idaho . . . Fowler might send someone to find him. No, Lillith didn't know where the ranch was. No one knew but Exeter. And Exeter was safe, because she cherished secrets more than what they could buy her.

Had to distract himself from the possibilities. Had to wait for Lillith to return.

Idaho reconnected the computer to his nerve impulses and sent search bots into the Net to find any transmissions originating from her cell phone or palmtop. If Lillith made any calls or went online anywhere, he could find her.

Geoffrey's father coded during the helicopter flight. Lillith saw the status indicator change from yellow to red seconds before the alarm sounded.

"What's going on?" Geoffrey pounded the inside of his sealed gurney. "What's going on?"

Lillith ignored his cries and scrambled to remove the portable crash unit from under her seat. "Is everyone still sealed?" she yelled over the noise of the rotors.

She did a quick check of her own suit. Its computer verified there were no punctures.

Danvers and the pilot gave her a thumbs-up.

Lillith popped the top off the gurney and tore open the old man's pajamas. She administered the therapeutic shock, trying to restart his heart.

Geoffrey continued pounding to be let out.

To Danvers she mouthed, "Sedate him." Danvers nodded and pumped a syringe of propofol into the IV port.

While the paddles were recharging, Lillith glanced at their other two patients. The middle-aged maid was asleep. Geoffrey's mother fluttered her eyes once, then drifted back into unconsciousness.

Lillith worked on the father for another ten minutes, then called the code. She resealed the gurney and asked the pilot to tell the ground crew what had happened during the flight. It would ensure they took extra precautions when decontaminating the helicopter.

Local CDC agents met them at the cargo runway at Seatac and helped load Geoffrey Allen into the quarantine chamber built into the modified Boeing 847.

Lillith kept him sedated through the six-hour plane trip back to Atlanta and while he was installed in one of the maximum quarantine units.

They took blood samples from all the patients and started the process of sequencing their DNA.

Lillith and Danvers looked at the blood samples under an electron microscope while they waited for the sequencer to finish.

In Geoffrey's sample, the crescent shapes of sickle-cell anemia were mixed in with normal, round, red blood cells.

"It's just like the thalassemia patients," Danvers said. "He's acquired a mutation in adulthood that's not in his medical record."

Lillith changed the focal point, searching for other abnormalities. "The virus is rewriting his DNA."

When the results from the sequencer were finished, they found that the Orcas Island patients suffered from several abnormalities: inconsistent melanin expression, sickle-cell anemia, mutations of the HEMA gene on the X chromosome, and acid maltase deficiency. But none of them had thalassemia.

"I'm going to recommend transfusions to address the sickle-cell anemia."

Lillith nodded without taking her eyes from the empty search pane. "Of course. We'll need enzyme replacement for the acid maltase deficiency." Lillith looked up. "We should ask the pharmaceutical companies to ramp up production of the enzymes we'll need. If this thing spreads, they won't be able to keep up with demand."

Danvers paused in the doorway. "That could take months."

Lillith looked back at the delicate tracery of DNA base pairs. "They'll have to work faster. This virus won't wait for us to catch up."

"I'm going to get some coffee. You want anything?"

Lillith dug in the slacks under her lab coat and handed him a couple of bucks for a latte. When he had left, she started another search for variations of the intron pattern she had found in Geoffrey. She got back 897 hits. One by one, she began going through them, scanning up and down the DNA around the hits, looking for similarities. As good as the analysis software's pattern-matching routines were, there was still nothing like a trained human brain.

When Danvers returned from the cafeteria, Lillith moved the search results to her palmtop so he could continue sequencing.

When she was only halfway through the list she said, "Gotcha."

Danvers paused in the middle of loading another set of samples. "What?"

"Look at this," she said, handing him the palmtop. "Each site where there's been gene corruption is followed by an intron pattern similar to the one I found in the senator."

Danvers looked at the colored bars of the DNA readout, comparing them with the other onscreen. "Similar but not identical."

Lillith adjusted the display to compare the two introns. She used a stylus to highlight the disparities. "I think this section encodes the gene that's being modified."

Danvers looked skeptical. "That's a stretch."

"I'm going to send this to the bioinformatics team, see if they can figure out what these sequences mean."

The lab door's lock beeped and Dr. Lam strode in, followed by an assistant pushing a motorized cart stacked six feet high with Styrofoam shipping containers.

"What are those?" Lillith asked.

Dr. Lam signed the release pad hanging from the deliveryman's belt. "Blood samples from D.C. and Seattle. They want us to analyze them for the new pathogen."

Lillith looked at the pile of refrigerated boxes in alarm. There were enough containers to house thousands of ten-milliliter blood samples. Every sample potentially represented a victim of a disease that, so far, had a thirty-five percent mortality rate.

It had been nearly seventy-two hours, and Lillith had been able to catch only a couple of hours' sleep on the trip back from Seattle and in her office while the DNA sequencer processed the blood samples.

Her body felt leaden. Lillith decided the messages waiting in her office could wait another day, and called an automated cab to take her back to her apartment. She was in no condition to drive.

When she palmed the lock to her front door, the apartment opened and turned on the lights. It said, "There are forty-eight messages. Shall I play them?"

Lillith stumbled through the living room and collapsed on the couch, sinking into the leather upholstery.

Peekers, her gray tabby cat, leapt onto her stomach and began kneading.

Lillith stroked his head. "Play high-priority messages."

"Thirty-two high-priority messages," the computer said.

Lillith groaned.

Idaho's voice came on the line. "Where are you? Pick up the phone." This same message was repeated thirty-one times in increasing tones of anxiety. All the high-priority calls were from Idaho.

Lillith pulled out her cell phone and turned it on. It held forty messages. What had happened while she was in Seattle?

She pressed the phone against her forehead and lay

back on the couch. She intended to call Idaho back, but before she could lift the phone, sleep dragged her down. The ringing of her phone on her chest sounded far away.

Automatically, Lillith clicked the phone off with her thumb and rolled over. Oblivion claimed her.

Geoffrey woke feeling stiff, with a pounding headache. Something was wrong. The sounds of birds and surf were absent, replaced by a fluorescent hum. He cracked one eye and bright artificial light lanced his skull.

Holding up his palm to ward off the light, Geoffrey sat up. Mistake. His head felt like fragments of bone were being driven into his brain. Nausea filled the back of his throat.

The events of the day before came back to him. The quarantine gurneys, the helicopter ride, his father sick . . . then nothing. Was this Harborview Medical Center? Where was June?

When his head stopped spinning, Geoffrey looked around. The room was like no hospital room he had ever seen. The door was oval, like a submarine bulkhead. Overhead a nest of pipes had multiple silver nozzles, none of which were in use. The walls were white and unbroken. The plug sockets were sealed with clear gel. Along the far wall was a blue curtain that could be pulled around a stainless steel toilet and sink.

A second blue curtain covered the wall opposite the door. Geoffrey crawled out of bed and pulled it aside. The whole wall was glass. The room behind was dim, but in the light from his chamber Geoffrey saw theatre seating, enough for two dozen observers.

His bed was standard hospital issue. Controls on the headboard raised and lowered it. There was a red call button.

Geoffrey pushed the button.

A few minutes later, pulleys along the ceiling opened the curtains covering the wall. On the other side of the glass was a tall man with a mop of light brown hair. It was canted to one side, as if he had just woken up.

"I'm Dr. Danvers," he said.

Geoffrey squinted his eyes at the man. "You were at the estate"—he waved his hands on either side of his head, pantomiming a helmet—"in one of the suits."

Danvers nodded. "That's right." He sank into a chair in the front row. "You called?"

"Where am I?"

Danvers pushed his thumb against his forehead. He sighed. "I'm not at liberty to say. There'll be a briefing with Dr. Watkins and Dr. Lam in the morning. They'll be able to tell you more about the status of your case."

Geoffrey paced in front of the glass. "At least tell me how my parents are doing. Is my mother well?"

Danvers's eyes drifted left. He said, "She's stable."

Pressing his palms against the glass, Geoffrey asked, "And my father?"

Danvers crossed his ankle over his knee. "Really, I think you should wait for the briefing tomorrow."

Geoffrey pressed his head against the glass. It was cold on his forehead. He felt something harden in his chest. "My father's dead . . . isn't he?"

Danvers looked down at his hands. "I'm not supposed to discuss certain issues."

But it was all there, in the droop of the man's mouth, the pitying look in his eyes. Geoffrey sank down onto his heels. *I'm a patricide,* he thought. *I've killed my father.*

Danvers stood up. "Is there anything I can—"

"No." Geoffrey waved the man away. "Just go."

With the whine of small motors, the curtain slid shut. Geoffrey squeezed his eyes against burning tears. His headache was back.

Lillith woke to an insistent ringing in her head. It was her cell phone. Hadn't she turned it off last night?

She picked up the phone and pressed it to her ear, not bothering to swing out the display screen. It was too early, and she was too disheveled, to deal with video.

"Hmm?" she said in way of greeting.

"Lillith! Where HAVE YOU been?" Idaho's mismatched voice was tight with excitement. "Hang on WHILE I ENCRYPT this." A buzz and a click, then his melded voice was back online. "I FOUND it—proof THAT CADUCEUS sold the virus AS A TREATMENT for—"

"Geoffrey Allen, in Seattle," Lillith interrupted. "I know, I've got him in custody."

"You WHAT?" Idaho's voice jumped an octave.

Lillith smirked, glad she could surprise him for once. "Picked him up yesterday. That's where I've been."

"WHAT ABOUT Fowler?"

Lillith sat upright and flipped the screen down.

Idaho's avatar stared back at her, the melded male and female face impassive.

"What *about* Fowler?" she asked.

"IF YOU know Geoffrey Allen was THE RECIPIENT, then you must know FOWLER WAS the source." He cocked his head. "You DIDN'T know, did you?"

"Do you have proof?"

"TWO HUNDRED MILLION dollars, routed through SWITZERLAND from Geoffrey Allen's accounts to a PRIVATE ACCOUNT owned by Fowler." The twinned face grinned. "Do you want A COPY?"

"Yes." Lillith stood and paced in front of her couch. "Are you certain? This is for real?"

"If you don't TRUST ME, subpoena the BANK RECORDS." He lowered his voice. "I'VE GOT TO GO before the FBI's MULTIVORE program finds THIS TRANSMISSION. Get FOWLER off the streets . . . BEFORE I DO."

The line went dead.

Lillith felt more awake than if she'd had a pot of coffee. Her heart pounded against her ribcage. Fowler had lied to her. Of course he had. Breaking international law and releasing a plague on mankind wasn't the sort of thing you admitted to.

She slammed her cell phone against the back of her couch. Fortunately, it was sturdy and survived her rage. Lillith put it up to her ear and said, "Dr. Lam's personal phone, encrypted connection."

Lam answered in pajamas and a robe. "Lillith, what's going on?"

"I need you to contact the Justice Department. I've got proof the virus came from Caduceus and the name of the researcher who manufactured it." She told him the information she'd gotten from Idaho, but not the source.

Lillith heard Lam's wife murmur something to him in the background. He held the phone against his chest and murmured back. When he spoke next to Lillith, he said, "How do you know all this?"

Lillith met his gaze without blinking. "Just ask for the subpoena. The information is good. I'd bet my career on it."

Lam sighed. "That is exactly what you're doing."

The level-four biosafety ward was constructed with reinforced bulkheads and oval-shaped, high-pressure doors. There were biometric identity checks at three points. Lillith showed her badge to the guards on duty outside the quarantine unit, typed in a key code and used her thumbprint at the second set of doors, and exposed her retina for scanning at the third layer.

To the left were the biohazard suit lockers and the gray zone. Lillith turned right into a corridor where multiple plates of glass protected visitors from the quarantine ward without the need to suit up. A set of six rooms were set up in a row. It was like the display at a public aquarium. You could walk from one viewing theatre to another and see all six labs. Up until now they had been used primarily for medical workers who'd had an accident in one of the level-four rooms. Or, occasionally, for researchers who'd been exposed in the field.

Danvers waited for her in front of Room 1, looking as tired and rumpled as Lillith felt.

They walked past empty Rooms 1, 2, and 3. The maid, Maria Sanchez, lay in Room 4.

"What's her condition?" Lillith asked, looking at the woman strung up with IVs and lying unmoving on the bed.

"Critical, but she's stabilized since we put her in isolation."

Lillith read details about the woman's pulse and temperature from her palmtop, then moved on.

Mrs. Allen was moaning in her sleep, her hands raised as if to ward off an attacker.

"Restrain her," Lillith said. "I don't want her pulling out her IV. Not when it takes us six minutes to suit up and get to her."

Danvers made a note on the woman's chart via a pocket computer.

The last room held Geoffrey Allen. Unlike the others, his curtain was closed.

"Status?" Lillith asked.

Danvers looked at his shoes. "Alert and angry. He thinks he's still in Seattle."

Lillith checked her supervisor's schedule on her handheld. He was free for the next hour and a half. Lillith sent a meeting request to Dr. Lam. They needed to discuss how to handle Mr. Allen.

The curtain slid back, startling Geoffrey. He threw his legs over the other side of the bed to face the theatre.

Danvers was there, along with two others. An Asian man in his fifties, stocky, with a wide face. Next to him, a slim woman with brown skin. Her chin was pointed, like that of a fox. Her wide nose had delicately flaring nostrils. But most startling of all were her huge eyes, bright with intelligence; they watched him intently. He'd seen her at the estate, giving orders.

The Asian man said, "I am Dr. Lam of the Centers

for Disease Control. I believe you have already met my associates Dr. Danvers and Dr. Watkins."

Geoffrey stood, uncomfortable being seated when they were on their feet. "What hospital am I in? Where are my parents?"

Lam folded his hands in front of his waist. "You are in the best quarantine facility in the country: the CDC headquarters in Atlanta, Georgia."

Geoffrey's heart skipped a beat. He rushed the glass to look closer at Lam's expression. He'd thought he had been flown to Seattle, but *Atlanta*? "Why did you bring me here? Where is my mother?"

Lam replied, "We relocated you here because this is the best facility to treat your disease. We believe you have a very virulent, very infectious new virus. I apologize for the inconvenience of quarantine, but I assure you it is a necessary precaution." He raised his hand to cut off Geoffrey's interruption. "Your mother is in a similar quarantine unit on this same ward. Her condition is serious but stable."

Geoffrey sat back on his bunk in relief. "Can I see her?"

Lam shook his head. "Not at this time."

Lillith leaned over and whispered something in Lam's ear. He nodded.

Lam said, "We were wondering if you had any ideas about the origin of the virus."

Geoffrey willed his expression to remain calm. He felt a blush creeping up the sides of his face.

Lam continued, "Have you been exposed to any people who were sick? Any new medical procedures?"

Geoffrey licked his lips. He should tell them everything, about Caduceus and bribing Fowler. But . . . to do so would brand him a criminal. Surely they could stop this epidemic without his help. "No," he said. "Nothing."

Lillith glared at him as if she knew he was lying. Geoffrey's eyes drifted from Lam to her intense stare.

"You're sure?" Lam asked. "Your medical record

states you have CF. Surely you required treatment sometime in the last six months. Perhaps you tried a new therapy? You seem very healthy for a man who was diagnosed with only three months to live."

Geoffrey looked down at his blotched hands. "I've had remissions before."

Lam and Lillith exchanged a meaningful look.

"We will discuss this later, when we have more data." Lam spoke to Geoffrey, but his eyes were on Lillith.

The woman's lips compressed into a tight line. She nodded.

The doctors turned to leave.

Geoffrey pressed his hands against the glass. "Wait!"

Lam and the others turned.

Geoffrey pointed at the television in his room. It was set into the wall behind a glass shield. "This TV doesn't have uplink capabilities. I want a computer, a video phone, something I can use to connect with the outside world."

Lam looked down at his hands. "I'm afraid CDC policy is to restrict two-way communications for patients in level-four quarantine. This is a stressful time. Let's concentrate on stabilizing your condition. Then we can consider how to manage communications."

Geoffrey pounded on the glass, but Lam and the others filed out.

Lillith was the last to leave. She looked back at Geoffrey, her eyes appraising.

Lillith relieved Danvers from duty, then checked the video feeds from quarantine rooms. All three patients were resting quietly; heart and lung monitors were stable. Lillith recorded the time and went upstairs to the waldo room.

Refinements in robotic technology made it possible to replace work that had once been done in biohazard suits with robotic manipulation. The robot was in the center of the level-four laboratories, but Lillith manipulated it from a special workstation one floor above. Her hands slid into gauntlets that controlled the robot's arms and three-fingered pincers. A pair of goggles displayed the robot's environment in a three-dimensional view.

Earlier in the day, she had taken blood samples from the patients. Now she pipetted a drop from each sample into wells of a plastic manifold that would fit into the automated DNA sequencer.

Once the manifold was in place and the sequencer had begun the PCR process, Lillith hit the STERILIZE button. Ultraviolet lamps and hot bleach bathed the robot.

New techniques meant that a person's entire DNA could be sequenced in hours instead of days. Lillith walked back downstairs to observe Geoffrey while she waited.

She was tempted to go back to her office and call Fowler, to confront him with what she knew, but that would only give him advance warning. She wouldn't make that mistake again. He might flee the country. It would be better for him to be taken into custody, where they could use his information to learn more about the virus.

The bulletin she had sent to local health organizations had been leaked to the public. There were already Web site headlines announcing, UNKNOWN CANCER PLAGUE HITS SENATE. On the cab ride in, Lillith had listened to a radio announcer blaming the health crisis on South American terrorists. As always, propaganda and fear overshadowed the truth.

Lillith went back to the on-call room of the level-four quarantine area and checked on her patients. The women showed no change. She watched Geoffrey on the closed-circuit camera that monitored his room. He was lying on the bed, pretending to do postural drainage.

Her mouth tasted sour. Whom did he think he was fooling?

Lam had forbidden her to speak to Geoffrey about

the case, on the grounds that it might scare Geoffrey and prevent him from reporting his symptoms accurately. But Geoffrey might have information that would help them stop the spread of the disease. And cut off from communications as he was, whom could he tell?

Lillith went back to the viewing theatre.

Geoffrey was hanging off the side of his bed when she approached. He sat up, coughing into his fist.

Lillith looked at him a long moment before she spoke. "I know what you did."

Geoffrey paled visibly; even the dark patches on his face faded. "What?"

"I know about Caduceus, Fowler, all of it."

Geoffrey's eyes slid to the side. "I don't know what you're talking about."

Lillith pounded on the glass. When he looked over his shoulder, she said, "I think you do. I'd feel pretty low if my trafficking in illegal viruses killed my father."

Geoffrey looked at the floor.

Lillith continued, "Eight people on Senator Mackey's staff are dead. Fourteen more are ill in Japan. Hundreds in Argentina. Nearly a thousand in Seattle. Your denials won't save you from prosecution—we've traced the money you wired to Dr. Fowler. But your information may help us stop this thing . . . before it becomes another plague like Mahn's."

Geoffrey pressed his knuckles into his forehead and squeezed his eyes shut. "I want to know what happened to June Escalante."

Lillith's brow wrinkled in confusion. "Who?"

"She was a maid in my mother's house. I want to know if she's," he swallowed and continued in a whisper, "still alive."

Lillith thought of the outbreak in the low-income housing. "I'll find out for you, I promise. Will you help me?"

Geoffrey took in a long shuddering breath. When he blew it out, he seemed calmer. He wiped his eyes with the front of his hospital gown. "What do you want to know?"

Lillith pulled her palmtop out of her lab coat's pocket and flipped it open. She tried to hide her rising excitement. "When did you take the treatment?"

"A month ago."

Longer than she had expected. The senator's and ambassador's symptoms were apparent after only eight days. Was the virus accelerating? "What was it supposed to do?"

He looked at her as if she were stupid. "Cure my CF. That was all."

"Nothing else? You don't have any idea why it's making people sick?"

Geoffrey sat on the edge of the bed. "No. I don't. If I had known all this was going to happen"—he looked at his hands—"I never would have taken it."

Lillith led him through the previous month, step by step, every symptom, each sensation, his rising health, the subsequent illness of himself and his family.

After half an hour of her probing, Geoffrey exploded: "I don't know why this is happening. Ask Dr. Fowler, he's the doctor who developed the damn thing. He's the scientist, not me. Ask *him*!"

Lillith closed her palmtop and nodded. "I intend to."

Two days later, Lillith gave a report of their preliminary findings to the directors of the CDC, World Health Organization representatives, the attorney general, several high-ranking military officers from the United States Army's Medical Research Institute of Infectious Diseases, and medical officials from Argentina and Japan. All one hundred and twenty seats of the CDC's conference room were filled, and a dozen people stood up against the back wall.

Lillith rubbed her palms on her woolen skirt. This time would be different, she told herself. This time her audience *wanted* to hear her message.

"Ladies and gentlemen. Dr. Lam has already

briefed you on the history and epidemiology of the disease we are calling Acquired Human Mutagenic Syndrome, or AHMS. I am here to describe what Dr. Danvers"—she nodded at Danvers in the front row—"and I have discovered in our investigation of the patients recovered from Orcas Island."

Members of the audience leaned forward in their seats, listening closely.

"To understand the disease, we began by analyzing and comparing DNA fragments from the patients." Lillith tapped a button and the wall screen displayed six sections of DNA. "These are samplings from Geoffrey Allen. The first is a childhood identity scan that shows his DNA at birth. These intermediate ones are from gene therapy in his teens. Nothing significant or lasting; his CF was not cured." She enlarged the last three sections. They appeared in the display as a pair of color-coded strands. Green, blue, yellow, and red represented the four base nucleotides that compose DNA: adenine, cytosine, guanine, and thymine.

"This is his scan after he injected an experimental treatment. Notice that the CF gene has been repaired." She highlighted a long section of the DNA following the repaired gene. "But here's something we missed back then. It's located in an intron region, junk DNA discarded by spliceosomes during expression." She flipped to another strand. "This is a sample from one of the Orcas Island patients. Here you can see degradation of the encoding domain for the beta-globin gene. And here"—she scrolled down the DNA—"is what we missed on first analysis."

She repositioned the senator's DNA under Geoffrey Allen's. The sequence of the introns matched. It was a long sequence and its purpose unknown.

"We believe this to be DNA inserted by the AHMS retrovirus. Records show that Geoffrey Allen's DNA has the same markers as found in the DNA of Senator Mackey and in the outbreaks in Argentina and Japan. I believe all of these outbreaks have the same source: an illegally engineered therapeutic virus developed in the laboratories of Caduceus International. We have evidence implicating Dr. Julian Fowler as the researcher who manufactured this treatment."

Dr. Lam interrupted, "Mr. Attorney General, you see why Caduceus must hand over their records. It's vital to public health."

The attorney general said, "Yes, of course," and mumbled a note into a pen-sized recorder.

Lillith continued, "After we recovered Mr. Allen from Orcas Island, we found several other changes." Another click of the remote and fourteen other sections of Geoffrey's genome were highlighted. "What's interesting is that subsequent analysis of Mr. Allen's DNA indicates that it is still changing. Each changed sequence is followed by the same pattern the virus inserts in the intron region."

Lillith saw the doctors in the audience nodding. It had perplexed her and Danvers when they kept getting different readings from Geoffrey and the other patients.

"Environmental mutagens can cause changes in DNA, and such errors contribute to the aging process. The rapidity and severity of *these* changes, however, are unnatural."

She touched the remote, and Geoffrey's DNA was replaced by the colored bands encoding the virus. "This same pattern was found in the DNA of both the Argentinean and Japanese patients. We believe this pattern can be used as a diagnostic when testing for the presence of this new pathogen."

From the audience, she heard more notes scribbled on tablet PCs and mumbled into recorders.

"This first change is found in the Seattle strain of the disease. It causes a rewriting of the genes that express melanin. This change seems benign and is what gives rise to the mottled skin." She clicked the remote and a slide of Geoffrey's arm and shoulder appeared. "It is one of the more easily recognizable symptoms. What's frustrating is this disease constantly mutates. The varieties in Argentina and Washington,

D.C., are different. All have similar viral DNA, but with subtle differences. Part of the virus's behavior is to continuously rewrite itself. Each new host acts as a catalyst, creating new variants of the virus.

"Once we isolate the patients, the virus stabilizes. We have not found any new mutations since Mr. Allen was quarantined."

When Lillith had finished presenting her findings, she opened the floor to questions.

Dr. Evanson, a researcher from the army institue, asked, "What are you doing to treat these patients?"

"Right now we can only offer symptomatic treatment," said Lillith. "We use enzyme and hormone replacement as well as conventional genetic therapies to reverse the viral transcription errors. It's a deadly game of catch-up, trying to find and fix the mutations caused by the virus before the patient dies. For some defects, we can use preexisting gene therapies. For others"—Lillith shrugged—"we've dedicated all the resources we can to this problem. We'd be happy to share treatments we develop with your governments and hope you will do the same."

The surgeon general asked, "What health care policy do you recommend in the current crisis?"

Lillith swallowed. "It is not my place to make policy, but I think a reasonable first step would be to quarantine regions containing infected individuals. Patients should be kept in separate, self-contained atmospheres. We are working on a test to detect the presence of AHMS. Until that is ready, all suspicious cases should be quarantined."

After a few more questions, Dr. Lam rose to his feet. "Thank you Dr. Watkins." He nodded to Lillith. "Now we'd like Dr. Danvers to present his report on the infection and mortality rates of the disease."

Lillith walked down from the raised platform and took a seat in the front row.

Danvers was saying, ". . . the mortality rate is fifty-seven percent and continues to rise as we receive more data."

Lillith wondered what the final number would be. So far no one had displayed immunity or recovered from AHMS. As far as anyone knew, the final mortality rate might be one hundred percent.

Dr. Lam met with Lillith and Danvers after the meeting ended. "Thank you. I think that went well."

Danvers asked, "Will we get the funding we need?"

"Given the deadly nature of this crisis . . . yes, I believe we will get full cooperation."

"How many cases so far?" Lillith asked.

Dr. Lam looked at his palms. "Worldwide or in the United States?"

"Both," said Lillith.

"The numbers are still coming in, but we've had thirty-two hundred verified cases in New York and Seattle. Worldwide, five thousand."

Lillith's mouth fell open. "In less than a week?" She swallowed.

Dr. Lam's eyes were ringed with dark circles. "Yes. We must stop this virus. Or it will stop us."

Idaho was in the shower when Exeter arrived. He heard her grunt, and then the whole trailer shuddered as she dropped in something heavy from the tunnel outside.

Idaho wrapped a towel around his waist and grabbed the gun on the bathroom counter. He opened the door and peeked around the corner to the living room.

"It's me," Exeter called.

Idaho nodded to himself. Of course it was. She was the only other person who knew where he lived and had a key to his deadbolt. Still, it never hurt to be cautious. As a hacker, Idaho knew how easily security could be compromised. He tucked the gun into a drawer under the sink and picked up a second towel to dry his hair. In the weeks he'd been online it had grown long enough to get in his eyes.

When he entered the living room, Exeter broke open a box and tossed him a tube of Neosporin. "You need to come down more often. You're starting to get bedsores."

Idaho smoothed ointment into the raw spots on his butt and shoulder blades.

Exeter left the trailer and came back with another box. It was half again as wide as she was and barely fit through the trailer door. She grunted as she tossed it in. Then she wrestled an armored biohazard suit through the door. Dropping it in a heap, she leaned against the doorframe, breathing hard.

"I've got two more of these in the car. Why do you need all this crap?"

Idaho riffled through the contents of the first box: IV packs, nutrient bars, bottled water, extra batteries for his portables. "The plague."

Exeter lounged against the doorframe, one hip jutting out. "That crap on the news is why you're packing in the supplies? Because there's a new killer disease? Wake up. There are ten billion people on the planet. Viruses and bacteria are multiplying and swapping DNA. An evolutionary meltdown is inevitable." She examined her left hand critically and pulled off a chip of broken fingernail.

Exeter was dressed in a tight latex skirt and a red lace shirt that showed her belly. Her lean body reminded him of other needs he'd denied himself. Idaho adjusted his towel.

Exeter hefted in two more suits and several gallons of Envirochem disinfectant. "That's the last of it. Why do you need *three* suits?"

Idaho pursed his lips. "One's for you. How do you like the color?"

Exeter held the bulky black armor against her body, cocking her head to look down at herself. "Kinky."

Idaho grabbed her wrist and pulled her over to him. He placed her arms around his waist. "Stay," he said.

Exeter plucked the towel away from his body and grinned, then kissed him hard.

He led her into the trailer's tiny bedroom, away from the servers and network equipment.

Exeter was a voracious lover, and twice Idaho had to pull her nails away from the raw spots on his back.

Afterwards, Idaho used the crumpled bedsheet to wipe red lipstick off his chest.

Exeter was in the bathroom, reapplying her makeup and artfully mussing her hair.

"Stay," Idaho said.

Exeter poked her head out of the bathroom and blew him a kiss. "Gotta meet a man about a horse."

Idaho felt his brow pucker in distaste. "You should quit using. It makes you unreliable."

Exeter twirled her finger in the air. "And you should stop wasting away on the Net. We've all got our escapes, Idy."

"Stay here. I don't want you sick." Not like Blue . . .

Exeter blotted her lipstick on a piece of toilet paper. "I'm not planning any trips to Seattle. Don't worry. This will all blow over in a month or two. You'll see."

Idaho eyed a roll of duct tape in the living room. He could keep her here, with him. Protect her from the coming plague.

Exeter smacked his cheek, leaving another lipstick wound, and danced out the front door. She slammed it behind her.

Idaho heard the deadbolt slide home. Next time. He'd save her next time.

Within days, the National Guard was mobilized to establish quarantine borders around infected towns and regions.

Lillith saw the news when she was riding into work. Tanks rolled across cornfields in Nebraska, through the streets of Seattle and Washington, D.C.

Protestors in Seattle marched the streets, demanding an explanation for the mysterious illness sweeping the area. A reporter interviewed one of the protestors. The man's ruddy face filled the screen. He was unshaven and his mouth contorted in anger. "It's a government conspiracy." He shook his fist at the camera. "They're lying to us. This disease is going to kill everyone."

When she got to work and checked her messages, there was one from Dr. Lam asking her to drop by his office.

His wall screen replayed the news story she had watched on the way in.

"I know," she said, dropping into one of his guest chairs. "I saw it already."

"We have to make an announcement, quell the public's fears."

Lillith smiled blandly, biting back "I told you so."

"I want you to make that announcement," Lam said.

Lillith cocked her head. "Me? I thought, after the Senate—"

"You did nothing wrong at the Senate meeting. You were merely outmaneuvered. You handled the briefing well. As the head researcher on this project, and the person who discovered how the virus works, you are ideal to handle the press conference."

Lillith smoothed the thighs of her slacks. "Thank you."

The corners of Lam's lips twitched up. "You wouldn't say that if you'd given a press conference before."

The lights of the reporters were blinding. Lillith squinted as she stepped up to the podium. She read from a TelePrompTer.

"The Centers for Disease Control has uncovered evidence linking Caduceus International to a recent viral outbreak. It is believed that a researcher within the company developed, in violation of the Beijing Treaty, a virus engineered to treat cystic fibrosis. Errors in the design of this treatment enabled the virus to replicate and mutate outside the lab."

The reporters yelled questions: "How deadly is the new virus?" "Who was the researcher?" "Will there be a trial?" "What precautions should people take?" "Will this be as deadly as Mahn's disease?"

Lillith pointed to a red-haired woman who had pressed her way to the front of the crowd. She repeated, "What precautions should people take?"

"At this point we recommend only that people monitor their own health. If they experience any of the symptoms listed in our health bulletin or on our Web site, they should contact their doctor."

Lillith acknowledged a tall reporter with a mustache. He asked, "How deadly is this new virus?"

Behind the podium, Lillith shifted her weight. "Mortality rates currently hover at sixty-five percent."

A murmur ran through the crowd. The high piping voice of Ellie Peterson, the CNN health correspondent, broke through the noise. "How does the virus work?"

Lillith ran a hand over her cap of curls. "We are still investigating. At present, all we know is the virus introduces errors in the host's DNA. This can cause cells in the body to malfunction, mimicking cancer—"

At the mention of the word "cancer," there was an intake of breath. The red-haired woman blurted out, "Are you saying the virus is a contagious form of cancer?"

Lillith shook her head. "No. That is only one of the symptoms the virus presents—"

Lam stepped up to the podium next to Lillith and gently shouldered her aside. "What Dr. Watkins means is that in the early stages of the virus the symptoms are similar to those in cancer patients. That's why it's important that everyone who is feeling unwell check with his or her physician. The CDC is working with Biochip International to develop a quick and easy test that physicians can use to test for the presence of the virus."

Lillith's face heated at Lam's intervention. She suppressed a glare.

"How long will the quarantine remain in place?" a lanky black man asked.

"The National Guard is working with the CDC to contain the spread of the disease. As soon as people in the infected areas are tested and found to be disease-free, they will be allowed to leave."

A tall bearded man asked, "Is it true that Dr. Julian Fowler was the researcher who engineered the virus?"

"The authorities are taking the responsible parties into custody even as we speak. You can expect an announcement from the Justice Department in a few hours. We'd prefer to focus on questions of a technical nature."

"What about rumors the virus is based on Dr. Watkins's work while she was an intern at Caduceus?"

Lam glanced at Lillith uneasily. "Our investigation into the virus is still ongoing."

Lillith felt idiotic standing on the stage with nothing to do, nothing to say. She could kill Lam for interrupting her and effectively declaring her incompetent to talk to the press on live television. If he didn't trust her, why give her this assignment? She straightened her shoulders and stalked off the stage.

Ten minutes later, Lam finished delivering platitudes about how the CDC was making great progress against the disease. He stepped away from the podium and joined Lillith offstage.

Lillith grabbed his arm. "Why did you interrupt me out there? You made me look like a fool."

Lam brushed off her grip and glared at her. "You lost control of the questioning. This is a sensitive time for the CDC. People are already nervous. We don't want to cause a panic. Besides, with your work history at Caduceus, you are politically vulnerable. I should have realized that before."

Lillith took a step back. "Does the Justice Department hold me liable? I worked there more than a decade ago. I had no idea—"

Lam patted her shoulder. "I know, I know. We're not talking about reality here, we're talking about the appearance of impropriety." He sighed. "I think, with the current political environment, it would be best if you stayed out of the public eye for a while. Your history with Caduceus, with Fowler."

Lillith's eyes flashed. "You're demoting me?"

Lam looked over his shoulder to where the reporters were packing up their gear. "No, no," he said in a low voice. "I just think your talents would be best utilized in the lab. You're a brilliant researcher. I want you working full time on the medical aspects of this infection. From now on, Danvers and I will handle public relations."

No matter what sugar coating Lam tried to put on it, this was a demotion. Lillith closed her eyes and counted to ten. Her first reaction was to throw it back in Lam's face, to leave the CDC. A gallows grin crossed her face. There were enough reporters left in the next room that she could make the evening news with her resignation.

She sighed. That wouldn't stop the disease, wouldn't prevent lives from being lost. When Fowler was imprisoned, she'd be the only researcher who'd spent months working on the original virus. She was humanity's best hope against this disease.

Lillith squared her shoulders. She'd find a way to stop the virus—then she'd quit. "I'll be in the lab," she said coldly, and stalked away.

Lillith had just gotten dressed for bed when the phone rang. "On screen," she said.

Lam's face was sober. "I wanted to give you the news . . . before you heard it on CNN."

Lillith sank onto her couch. "What? Is Julian in custody?"

Lam shook his head. "No . . . he committed suicide as the SWAT team was breaking into his office. Shot himself in the head. He was dead when they reached his side."

Lillith jammed her fist against her mouth. "No," she whispered.

Sighing, Lam said, "It's not your fault. You did what had to be done. Dr. Fowler was a disturbed man. The FBI is confiscating his records. I was hoping to have him on the investigation team with us . . ." At her expression, he said, "I'm sorry, Lillith." He closed the connection.

Lillith stared at the empty screen, hot tears streaming down her face. She punched the couch cushions. "Coward," she shouted, though Julian was beyond all hearing. "You damn coward! How could you leave me to clean up your mess?"

She'd wanted to punish Fowler for perverting her work, for endangering people for profit. But not like this. She'd never meant for him to . . . oh God.

Her house computer chimed, indicating another incoming call.

"Computer: Identify caller."

"Dr. Julian Fowler," the machine said in a neutral tone.

Lillith froze. "On screen."

Fowler filled the wall opposite the couch. His hand was trembling and a gun rested on the desk in front of him. The date stamp in the lower right-hand corner was three hours previous. It was a recorded message.

"Lillith, I wanted to make sure you got the attached files. I . . . I'm sorry I won't be able to help you with this one." He smiled, and there were tears in his eyes. "We always did good work together. Even if we weren't so good together in other ways. I—I can't face what's coming. The virus is based on the work we did on an Alzheimer's cure, before the treaty. You understand it best. That's why I'm sending this to you. I messed up in synthesizing the virus, removing the lipid encoding. You were always better at that than I."

In the background, Lillith heard pounding on Fowler's office door. Masculine voices shouted for him to come out.

Fowler picked up the gun with trembling hands. "I've got to go. Tell Melissa I love her. She'll know what to say to . . ." His voice broke. "To Kaitlen."

The screen went blank. The sound of a gunshot reverberated in Lillith's imagination.

Attached to the message were two gigabytes of data. Lillith saved them to her personal files and then forwarded a copy to her work computer as backup.

"You son of a bitch," she told the blank screen. "First you steal my research, then you screw it up, and now you leave me to make excuses to your wife."

CHAPTER 8

Lillith sat in her office, her head propped on her fists. She'd finished reading the reports from Seattle.

Since quarantining Orcas Island, the CDC had taken samples from the air, water, and local animal population. There were no incidents of disease in the indigenous mammals.

Her PDA beeped, informing Lillith it was time to make her rounds.

Lillith sighed and stretched, then walked up the stairs to the biohazard lab.

Maria Sanchez's quarantine unit was empty. Lillith checked the log. The night physician reported that Maria had suffered a massive heart attack during the night. She had not responded to resuscitation attempts. Her body was currently being held in the level-four lab for autopsy.

Lillith sighed. Death was the worst part of working with patients. She preferred research, where failure meant loss of a tissue culture, not a life. Someone would have to contact the woman's family. She made a note in her PDA.

Mrs. Allen was on a morphine drip. She had metastasizing bone cancer. Over the last four days the cancer had grown at an unbelievable rate. The cancer-suppressing drugs had no effect. She was already too weak for chemotherapy.

Lillith felt a weight in her chest, her clinical detachment weakened by her years in the lab. She checked

the morphine levels and prescribed another dose of
the cancer-fighting drugs. It was hopeless. Lillith suspected Mrs. Allen would be dead in a few days.

Geoffrey, by comparison, seemed almost healthy.
He had trouble digesting food due to a virus-induced
enzyme deficiency, and his blood was still clotting due
to sickle-cell anemia, but both symptoms could be
treated with current drug therapies. Otherwise, he was
fine. The melanin instability that caused patches of
darker skin to migrate across his face seemed benign.

"How's my mother?" he asked, looking away from
a CNN report of unrest in an Argentinean quarantine camp.

Lillith licked her lips. "She's not improving. The
cancer is spreading."

"She's going to die, isn't she?" Geoffrey's blue eyes
were wide and red-rimmed.

It was too raw an expression to lie to. "Probably."

"When?"

"We can't know for sure . . . but if I had to guess,
perhaps sometime in the next few days."

"Can I see her . . . to say goodbye?"

The request tore at Lillith's heart. "We can't let you
leave quarantine. It's too dangerous."

He spread his hands in a pleading gesture. "What
if I wore a biohazard suit like you do?"

"No. Those are positively pressurized, so that any
leak flows outward. They're designed to keep viruses
out, not in."

"My mother's dying in the next room and I can't
see her?" Geoffrey asked, his voice cracking.

Lillith pressed the heel of her palm against her forehead, rubbing away the stress. "I might be able to
arrange a closed-circuit video feed. It'd be bending
the regulations, but I think I could get approval."

"I want to be with her, to hold her hand one last
time."

Lillith shook her head. "That's not possible."

Geoffrey hung his head. Two tears fell on the lap
of his paper gown. When he raised his face, his eyes

were bright with anger. "I want this virus stopped. Call Fowler, tell him to undo the damage he's done."

Lillith said, "Fowler's dead."

Geoffrey's eyes widened. "I didn't know. How did he die?"

Lillith sighed. "Yesterday, as the SWAT team was coming to arrest him, he committed suicide."

Geoffrey looked down at his hands. He nodded slowly. "I can understand that."

Lillith made a mental note to have Geoffrey's surveillance tapes monitored more closely. He might be a suicide risk.

"When can we set up the network to my mother's room?" he asked.

"I'll see if we can arrange it for this afternoon."

"Thank you, Dr. Watkins." Geoffrey's face was set in a determined expression. "If there is ever anything I can do for you, just ask."

Lillith locked eyes with Geoffrey, her dark brown gaze burning into him. "Stay alive. Help me fight this thing."

Geoffrey sighed a long, shuddering sigh. "I'll try."

Henry J. Poulson, Esquire, had been the family lawyer for longer than Geoffrey had been alive. The old man was tall and rawboned, looking more like an aging gunfighter than a lawyer. But his bright black eyes betrayed an intelligence that had destroyed many an argument on the stand.

"Geoffrey," the lawyer said by way of greeting. He half-raised his hand to shake, but the layers of glass between them prevented that, so Poulson let his hand fall and inclined his head.

"Hello, Henry," said Geoffrey, standing up from his bunk and coming to the front window. "This is a real mess I've gotten myself into, isn't it?"

Poulson scrubbed a hand across his forehead. "That's an understatement."

Geoffrey checked the video camera in the corner. In the interest of client-lawyer confidentiality, it had been turned off for this meeting. The green LED on the top of the unit was dark.

"First," Poulson said, "let me tell you how sorry I am to hear of your parents' passing. The loss of your mother leaves the world a darker place."

Geoffrey nodded, swallowing against the lump that formed in his throat at the mention of her. "Were you able to find out anything about June Escalante?"

Poulson sucked his teeth. "Using the patient number Dr. Watkins supplied, I was able to learn that the young lady was treated at the University of Washington Medical Center. Unfortunately, she succumbed to the same ailment that claimed your mother."

"Bone cancer?"

Poulson nodded.

Images of June, wasted and in constant pain, as his mother had been, flashed through Geoffrey's mind. He bit his lower lip. He would not break down in front of Poulson. "I presume you brought the will?"

Poulson nodded and pulled a notarized printout out of a soft-sided leather briefcase. "I won't bore you with a verbatim reading. It's quite simple. Aside from your mother's ten million dollar bequest to the Seattle Opera, the remainder of the estate belongs to you."

Geoffrey nodded. It was what he had expected.

"Your parents appointed me executor. Seeing that you will be . . . detained for an indeterminate amount of time, I am more than willing to handle the financial transfer."

"Yes, of course."

Poulson nodded at the television mounted in the corner of Geoffrey's room. "Does that work?"

Geoffrey nodded. "I've seen the CNN coverage. Fowler's dead."

"The executives of Caduceus International are denying any knowledge of Fowler's research. They're still liable, but the corporation will probably declare bankruptcy soon. Which will leave the government only one person in its sights: you."

Geoffrey's body ached all over. "Have charges been filed yet?"

Poulson shook his head. "I haven't received anything official, though I have been in contact with the attorney general. He tells me the investigation is still under way at Caduceus." Poulson blew out a breath that flipped the whiskers of his mustache. "Son, they're trying to decide whether, in addition to breaking federal law, you committed treason."

Treason was the only offense in the United States that still carried the death penalty. Geoffrey chuckled darkly. It was unlikely he'd live long enough to be executed, and he was already in prison. "What can we do?"

Poulson pulled a palmtop out of his briefcase. "I'd like you to tell me everything that happened. Hold nothing back, then we can discuss how best to proceed." He held up the palmtop. "May I record this?"

Geoffrey nodded. He told Poulson his story. How he'd been dropped from the organ transplant list because his body was too frail. His desperation at Dr. Ambrose's prediction he had only two months left of life. The way he'd located Dr. Fowler, a man who'd lost his retirement savings on bad investments, and convinced him to engineer a cure for Geoffrey in exchange for two hundred million dollars.

At the end Poulson whistled. "Not good. I understand your motivations, my boy. But it doesn't make my job any easier. Can they directly link you to Dr. Fowler? Perhaps you contracted the virus after the fact and are just another victim."

Geoffrey shook his head. "One of the CDC doctors told me they'd traced the money I wired to Fowler's Swiss bank account. I don't know how; I was careful to use anonymous transfers."

"Let me think about this. There's always the insanity defense. You were dying, in extremis . . . a jury might be sympathetic to that."

Geoffrey had seen the rioters on the streets. Since

Dr. Watkins's press announcement, protestors in Seattle and D.C. had waved signs calling for Caduceus's immediate dissolution and the imprisonment of its executives. He held no illusions that the public, in fear of a deadly new plague, would be sympathetic to his motivations. The world needed a scapegoat, and Dr. Fowler had neatly abdicated that role to Geoffrey.

Poulson tapped on the glass wall, snapping Geoffrey back to reality. "I'm going to press Dr. Lam to allow you a laptop so we can discuss your defense online." His hard gaze softened at Geoffrey's expression. "Don't worry, I'll come up with something."

Geoffrey managed a wan smile. "If anyone can get me out of this, Henry, it's you."

Lillith went home to her Eastside condominium. She had been too busy to clean during the past week, and dishes were piled up around the sink. She swept the cellulose plates into the apartment complex's compost chute.

Peekers, her gray tabby cat, danced around his food bowl, complaining loudly.

It had been over a week since she'd called her grandmother, the social obligation forgotten in the flurry of work at the lab. This was the first night in days that she'd gotten home before eleven.

Sighing, Lillith picked the dirty clothes off her couch and tossed them into the bedroom. The living room was where the biggest wall screen was, and she didn't want her grandmother to see what a slob she'd become.

Lillith checked her face in the hallway mirror, plucked a few gray hairs from her head, and said, "Computer: call my grandmother Jenkins."

The phone rang twice before an elderly woman answered the phone. The image was small and grainy, produced by a tabletop model.

Lillith sighed, "Grandma, you should let me buy you a new wall screen."

The old woman grinned wide. "I don't need one of

those newfangled things." She patted the old phone and said, "I like my technology small and controllable. If I let you buy me a wall screen, where would it end? You'd have my whole house automated"—she flapped her arms—"robots chasing me around the house. At my age, I don't need the aggravation." She squinted at the screen. "How've you been, girl? You look tired."

Lillith scrubbed her face. "Things are busy at the lab."

Grandma Jenkins nodded. "I've seen the news about the killer virus y'all been fighting. But I tell the neighbors not to worry, my granddaughter is on the case and she is smarter than any germ."

Smiling wanly, Lillith said, "Thank you, Grandma. But it might be a good idea to avoid travel for the next few months."

The old woman's smile faded. "You *are* worried, aren't you? Is that why you called? To warn the family?"

"No. I wanted to talk to you; it's been too long. But . . . be careful. We don't know how far this thing will spread. It hasn't hit the Southeast yet but . . ."

"Don't you worry." The old woman nodded. "I'll put the word out. We've survived hard times before, and we'll get through this." She crooked her finger at the screen. "Our family are survivors. We made it through the last man-made plague, and we can make it through this."

"Yes, ma'am." Lillith prayed she could stop the spread of the infection before it threatened her kin. In the past week, the World Health Organization's private network had reported five thousand new cases in Seattle that were overwhelming the city's ability to quarantine all of the patients. There were eight thousand new cases in Argentina and twelve hundred more in Japan. The infection rate was alarming.

Grandma Jenkins winked at the phone. "Did you hear your mother got a new man?"

"No." Lillith's eyebrows rose. "This one black or white?"

"White." Her grandmother's lips twitched down in disapproval. "The girl has absolutely no resistance against a pair of blue eyes. But he's a nice boy for all that."

"Well, I hope he makes her happy," Lillith said. "Daddy's been dead for six years; it's time she started dating again."

Grandma Jenkins nodded and leaned closer to the phone. "How about you? Anyone new on the horizon?"

Lillith shook her head, used to her grandmother's hopeful prying. "No. Work keeps me too busy for a social life."

"Life is *all* social. One day you'll wake up old and alone and wish you'd made the time."

Lillith's temper flared. The world was threatened by a new virus, one based on her early research, and her grandmother wanted her to take time off to date?

Her grandmother folded her arms on her chest. "You found a church up there yet?"

Lillith rolled her eyes. Grandma Jenkins was apparently going to hit all the old favorites this call. She muttered, "No Grandma, I just dance naked in the woods when I want to feel close to God."

Her grandmother's eyes bugged out. "What? What did you say?"

Lillith suppressed a chuckle. "If you let me buy you a proper video system, you could hear what I say. I'll find a church and start dating after I save the world from this latest health crisis, okay?"

Grandma Jenkins looked dubiously at the screen. "Yes, well. We all just want the best for you."

"I've got to get some sleep," Lillith said. "I have to be at the lab by six tomorrow. Give my love to Mother when you see her."

"Take care of yourself," Grandma Jenkins said. "You're my favorite granddaughter."

"I'm your *only* granddaughter," Lillith laughed, in their customary goodbye.

Lillith kicked the pile of clothes out of her bedroom

doorway, undressed, and fell into her four-poster bed and slept. Her dreams were filled with visions: corpses piled into bonfires and infected blood running down the streets.

CHAPTER 9

Lillith logged on to the database created by the World Health Organization to track the variations of the plague. The changes were organized by chromosome. She selected chromosome six to track the spread of one of Geoffrey Allen's variants, entered as WA6-16. It was one of the most widespread mutations, as it caused only minor DNA irregularities and did not immediately kill its host.

The search icon blinked and returned 12,925 hits. It had been five weeks since Senator Mackey's illness was reported.

Lillith's stomach hurt. "Database: Number of distinct variations reported."

The number blinked malignantly: 22,987.

Lillith inhaled sharply. And those were just the ones recorded and reported by medical science. Who knew how many others were out there? At this rate, there was no way medical researchers could devise treatments for each variation. Even if they just focused on the lethal varieties, it was hopeless.

Danvers poked his head in her office. "I was going for some coffee, you want some?" He saw the database program open on her wall screen and looked away. "Ah, maybe another time."

"Computer: Lock system." Lillith stood. "Now is as good a time as any. I could use a break."

Danvers waited for her to exit, then fell into step

beside her. "I try not to look at it any more than necessary."

Lillith didn't say anything.

"Do you think we'll come out of this alive?"

She looked up at him. "We work in one of the most advanced medical facilities in the country—"

"No." Danvers didn't look up. "I meant the human race."

Lillith patted Danvers's shoulder. "Why don't we talk about something else. How's your son doing in preschool?"

Danvers made a sound between a laugh and a groan. "They canceled classes, too great a risk of infection." He shook his head. "There's no escaping the plague." He stopped in front of the automated latte machine. "Even the brand of coffee we get has been affected."

Lillith looked at the machine. The words "One hundred percent Colombian Coffee" had been covered by a piece of white poster board. Written on it in Magic Marker was the word "Jamaican."

Geoffrey stuck his arm into the blood sampler. It was bolted to the wall and looked a lot like a blood pressure cuff. He waited patiently while the IR laser located his vein. There was a cool sensation as the unit spritzed the crook of his elbow with alcohol, and then the sting of the needle.

He looked up and met the eyes of Dr. Watkins. She was watching him from the theatre. Today her normally erect posture was slumped and the corners of her lips were turned down.

"What's wrong?" Geoffrey asked. "You look depressed for a vampire."

"What?" Her eyes focused on him.

Geoffrey gestured at the machine. "A joke."

"Oh," she sighed. "I'd forgotten about jokes."

"I see things on the news. It's pretty grim on the outside, isn't it?"

Lillith nodded. "How's the pain in your joints?"

Geoffrey flexed his legs. "Gone. The sickle-cell treatment is working."

The blood unit retracted the needle and beeped. Geoffrey put on a cotton ball and Band-Aid and applied pressure to the spot.

"Good." Lillith stood.

"Wait," Geoffrey said, his arm outstretched.

The black woman turned on him, raising one eyebrow. "Was there something else?"

Face reddening, Geoffrey said, "You never answered my question. What's it like in the outside world?"

Lillith nodded at the television. "As bad as they say. And getting worse." She moved towards the door.

She and Danvers were the only human contact Geoffrey got all day. He was desperate to keep her here a few minutes longer. "I want to know how the research on the virus is going."

Lillith turned. "Mr. Allen, I am very busy."

"Two minutes." He held up his fingers. "You can time me. Just two minutes to tell me what they're leaving out of the news." Geoffrey's brow creased. "Please, I created this mess. I need to know what's happening in the world."

Lillith stalked back to the glass window. "You want to know what's going on? We've got an airborne virus. Each victim creates a new variant of the disease. Right now there are more than twenty-three thousand variants in the WHO database. That's twenty-three thousand people who are going to die because of you.

"We don't have the resources to devise new treatments for each variant. And even if we did, half the people with the new variant will die because by the time we recognize it, it takes months to design a treatment."

Her chest heaved. "We don't have the information to predict new variants because ninety-eight percent of the world's population still can't afford a full diagnostic genetic sequencing." Her face was inches away from the barrier. "Does that explain why I don't have time to handhold a spoiled little rich boy?"

Geoffrey's face felt as if he had been slapped. In a slow, deliberate voice, he asked, "What do you need to make your work easier?"

Lillith rolled her eyes. She ticked items off her fingers. "The DNA sequence of every human on the planet. An infinite staff of molecular biologists designing treatments faster than the virus mutates, and, oh yes, a cure would be nice." She looked past him, searching the room. "Do you have any of those in there?"

Geoffrey looked down at the stainless steel floor. In a quiet voice, he said, "No."

Lillith checked that the blood samples made it to the sequencing lab and returned to her office.

She shouldn't have blown up at Geoffrey Allen. Getting emotional and assigning blame wouldn't help cure AHMS.

She checked the time on the watch woven into her cuff. It was 4:35. She'd been working for twenty-six hours straight. Perhaps a couple hours of sleep would restore her equilibrium. She went back to her office and shrugged into her leather blazer. There was nothing more she could do tonight.

Her body drooped with exhaustion as she headed to the parking garage elevator. She'd better sleep; new samples were arriving from Brazil in the morning, and she'd need to analyze them immediately.

The cool concrete smell of the parking garage reminded her of a cave. How nice it would be to retreat into a dark underground world. Lillith drove home on an expressway that was less congested than usual. The quarantines in New York and D.C. had the public spooked. Everyone who could worked from home. Had she been smart, Lillith thought, she would have invested in telecommunications stock.

She parked in the garage and stumbled into her

dark apartment. Peekers met her at the door, stretching and clawing at the carpet in his joy. Lillith went into the kitchen and poured kibble into his bowl. Then she opened the top cabinet and fished in the back until she found the bottle of Dewar's she kept for special occasions.

Discovering that the work she had done as an intern had contributed to a planetwide catastrophe. What could be more special than that?

She poured four fingers of Scotch into an iced tea glass and took both glass and bottle with her into the bedroom.

Lillith's wall phone rang. "Computer: Answer."

The merged faces of Idaho and his sister, Blue, filled her living room wall. The merged face scowled. "WHAT IS going on at THE CDC?" the twinned voice asked. "I want to KNOW what PROGRESS you've MADE."

Lillith sat down heavily on the bed. She took another swig of the Scotch in her hand. The burn in her throat helped focus the pain on something physical.

"I'm tired, Idaho. I need sleep."

"I need TO KNOW." His blue eyes glowed neon in the dim light. "I THINK YOU understand why."

Lillith, buoyed by drink, told him everything: the problems of coming up with a reliable test for a plague that constantly changed, the politics of working with health organizations all over the country, and the impossibility of predicting new variations in time to develop treatments for them.

"Is THAT all?" asked the twinned voice of Idaho Blue.

"All?" Lillith flung her empty glass at the wall screen. "Humanity is going down the toilet. Aren't you concerned?"

The face on the screen didn't flinch. "I can HELP. I HAVE ACCESS to a network of VOLUNTEER PROGRAMMERS. Give us access to the GENETICS INFORMATION in the WHO database and we'll predict ALL POSSIBLE VARIATIONS of the virus. Show us how to DESIGN

TREATMENTS for the variations and we will do that AS WELL."

"Hackers?" Lillith scrubbed her forehead in an attempt to clear her mind. "You want me to give access to the most important database in the world to hackers?"

The twinned face relaxed into an ironic smile. "I PREFER the term 'computer ENTHUSIAST.' We WILL DO this work REGARDLESS of whether you GIVE US your password. Having your LOGIN INFORMATION will simply give us MORE TIME to CONCENTRATE on the medical side OF THE PROBLEM."

This was insane even to contemplate. But at this point the medical community was overwhelmed . . . Could she turn down any offer of assistance? "How can I be sure the data they upload is valid . . . and not intentionally or unintentionally harmful?"

Idaho's avatar blinked. The female half of his face looked sad, the male half thoughtful. "I will test EACH RESULT in my SIMULATION before posting it TO THE DATABASE. Please, LET ME HELP."

In his last words Lillith heard the echo of the boy in the computer parts warehouse. "All right," she said and gave him her password.

The connection closed.

Staring at her wall screen's default image—a Hawaiian waterfall—Lillith wondered whether her decision to accept Idaho's help had improved or reduced humanity's chances.

Idaho made a copy of the WHO database on the Internet and spent several hours wandering its data architecture, studying the format and types of data required.

Then he posted his challenge to HackThePlanet .com. He described the problem, what types of computation the CDC needed, and how to format results. Every valid variation not already present in the WHO database would earn the first person to post it a point on Idaho's Web nexus. At the end of each month, the person with the most points would win a Racal biohazard suit. He had enough spares to fund six months of research, bought in twos and threes from medical supply houses when the epidemic first started to spread.

These days, biohazard suits were going for hundreds of thousands of dollars on the black market, when they could be had at all.

Immediately, requests for additional information began flooding in. Idaho programmed a simulated personality to answer the most common replies and began figuring out how to devise treatments for the different variations.

A table in the database cross-referenced links from variants to Web sites describing the applicable treatment. Most involved drugs to replace missing proteins and enzymes. Some, Idaho noticed, used gene therapy to repair the damage done by the virus. The Web sites contained three-dimensional animations that showed how the gene therapy used existing therapeutic viruses to modify the cellular structure of targeted cells.

As far as Idaho could tell from the sites, the difference between these preexisting therapeutic viruses and AHMS was the scope of the changes. The existing gene therapies targeted only a subset of the patient's cells and did not proliferate in the body. As those cells died, the treatment faded, requiring another session of gene therapy.

Idaho, fascinated by the tiny engines of life, had dabbled in microbiology and genetics for years. But these medical sites contained information he didn't understand. Were increased levels of L-tryptophan good or bad? Did 5-hydroxyindole acetic acid levels of 1.2 ng/ml indicate disease or healthy functioning?

More illuminating was the site that displayed a time-lapse comparison of Geoffrey Allen's DNA. As Idaho watched, the tiny colored bars shifted as the data of sequencing at the bottom of the page changed.

Like everyone on the planet, he'd heard the virus

introduced mutations. But seeing it happen in slow motion was chilling. Before his eyes, a man was devolving into chaos.

Retroviruses, such as AHMS and AIDS, inserted themselves into your DNA and used your own body to reproduce themselves. The image of the virus as a tiny hacker subverting a human's DNA made him smile.

"Primordial. We are everywhere."

He didn't know what the affected genes did or whether the changes were harmful. To him, they were just bands of color on the screen. But he could learn. What was DNA but a program for creating life? And programming was something he understood.

He'd dabbled in microbiology . . . now it was time to get serious. Idaho hacked into Caltech's online courseware and found a class labeled "Advanced Microbiology and Genetics." He stayed up until dawn, reading.

There were protestors outside the CDC headquarters in the morning when Lillith came to work.

Twenty people milled around outside the gates of the office park, shouting, "Give us Allen! Justice! Justice! Give us Allen!" The signs in their hands had slogans like SURRENDER ALLEN; MY FAMILY DIED, SO SHOULD HE; NO ALLEN, NO PLAGUE; ALLEN = DEATH.

They rushed Lillith's single-person automobile, and for a frightening moment she thought the minicar would be overturned. Fortunately, the machine's anticollision program took over and jogged the car away from the screaming protestors. They tried to follow the car in through the gates, but the guard shouted at them and they subsided.

Lillith's heart was still racing when she got inside the building. Danvers was by the coffeepot. He poured a cup and handed it to her. "Looks like you could use this."

"Did you see the protestors at the gate?" Lillith asked.

Danvers nodded. "Dr. Lam's called the National

Guard for help with security. Even so, I wouldn't want to be in Geoffrey Allen's shoes."

"The signs are idiotic," Lillith said. "If we handed Geoffrey over, he would only infect them. Don't they realize the man is already serving a life sentence?"

"Not even that if we don't get his sickle-cell under control," Danvers said.

Lillith nodded in agreement and followed Danvers to the lab.

When they broke for lunch, they went up to the third floor, where there was a lounge overlooking the front gate. The crowd had swelled. People stood on top of their cars, shouting and pumping their fists at the CDC building.

Lillith sucked in a breath. "Where is the National Guard? There must be nearly a hundred people out there."

"Aren't they afraid of the plague?" Danvers asked.

"They're afraid," Lillith said, her eyes on the drama unfolding outside the gates. "That's why they're out there."

Suddenly a flame arced from the gathering. It soared high through the air and landed on a low boxwood hedge inside the gate. Someone had thrown a lit bottle of gasoline. The dry landscaping bark under the hedge caught fire, and soon the whole row of bushes was aflame.

The sudden staccato of gunfire made Lillith and Danvers drop behind the couch. Glass shattered on one of the floors below.

Danvers's face was white against the gray carpet. "Don't they realize we're trying to save them?"

Lillith peeked out the window. The protest had turned into a riot as people stormed the gate. The gatekeeper, a man in his late forties, tried to draw his weapon and was knocked to the ground.

"I think they've given up hope of being saved," Lillith said. "Now they want to get even. We better get over to the quarantine lab. Lock it up. If they break in there . . ." She couldn't finish the thought aloud. From the horror reflected in Danvers's expression, she didn't need to.

They ran down stairs, not trusting the elevators, and locked the doors leading into the quarantine ward. To bolster the doors, they pushed lab tables in front of them.

"Our computers," Danvers said, looking at the barricaded doors.

Lillith thought of the files on her machine that hadn't been backed up to the central network. "Too late," she said. "Either security will prevent the rioters from reaching our offices or they won't. We can't go out there."

The sounds of shouting were drawing nearer, as were occasional gunshots.

Lillith went to check on Geoffrey. He was the last of the Orcas Island patients they had left.

Geoffrey was pacing in his room. "What's going on? I heard something." He paused, listened intently. "There it is again. It sounds like . . . gunfire?"

"Stay down. There was a protest outside that got a little out of hand. Security should have things contained momentarily."

"They're coming for me, aren't they?" His blue eyes were sad. "I've seen the protests on television. They want me to pay for my crime." Geoffrey looked at the plastic wall that separated them. "And you stayed to protect me." He touched the clear barrier. "If they break the quarantine, you could be infected . . . but you stayed." There was surprise in his voice.

"No one's getting through security." Lillith looked at the door, hoping her words were true. "And I couldn't let anything happen to you . . . you're too valuable a research subject."

Geoffrey's smile was wan. "Yes, of course. Still, I admire your courage."

A gunshot in the hall outside silenced them both, and they crouched in silence.

Danvers crawled through the door on his hands and

knees. "I heard someone giving orders outside the door. I think the protest is under control."

Half an hour later, a man in a camouflage uniform knocked on the door and informed them the protestors had been removed from the building. He carried an assault rifle.

Lillith stepped out into the hall. Glass windows in doors had been shattered, and someone had written in Magic Marker DEATH TO ALLEN.

The lobby was in worse shape. Bullet holes riddled the wall behind the receptionist's desk. There was no blood, thank God. Adam, who manned the phones for the building, was nowhere in sight. Lillith hoped he was unharmed and had simply gone home early.

National Guard tanks were parked on the lawn. They looked surreal nestled between a weeping willow tree and beds of blooming azaleas.

Dr. Lam was talking to a man in a National Guard uniform. Lam looked up and saw Lillith and Danvers; he waved them over.

He gestured to the National Guardsman. "This is Sergeant Cole. He and his company are protecting the building from another riot. He will ensure your safety." Lam compressed his lips in a frown, then said, "I think it will be advisable if you stayed the night. The activists might target you at home."

"What about our families?" Danvers asked.

Lam raised his voice so the other researchers who had drifted into the lobby could hear. "Sergeant Cole has offered the protection of the National Guard for your families as well. They will be taken into protective custody at the Oglethorpe Armory in Ellenwood. He recommends that you spend the evening here. We have a supply of blankets for people who choose to sleep in their offices."

Within an hour, the CDC complex had the feel of a refugee camp. Outside, armored tanks circled the CDC grounds and kept the protestors at bay. The evening wind carried shouts of retribution and anger.

This plague had infected more than bodies; it had infected a nation's soul.

Lillith went back to her office and retrieved her video messages from home. Two were solicitations: one for a bulky face mask that claimed to screen harmful viruses from the air, and the other for good-health novena candles.

Neither would provide the purchaser anything but hope.

The third message was from her grandmother; the time stamp was eleven in the morning. "Computer: Play message, closed captioning."

The characteristically fuzzy image from her grandmother's outdated equipment came online. "Lill, honey, this is your grandma Jenkins." The old woman's voice shook with emotion. "I wanted—I thought you should know, your cousin Elwood has the sickness. He's in treatment at County General in Fairbanks, but if there's anything you can do for him, any treatment the doctors up there might not know about . . . your aunt Marla's beside herself."

It was the last straw. Lillith had borne it all without a crack in her façade, but her grandmother's pleading voice broke down her last reserve of strength. Lillith closed the door to her office, crawled under her desk, hugged her knees to her chest, and cried. There was nothing she could do to stop this virus. It would take them all.

A mental image of everyone she loved, dying in agony like the Allens had, flashed through her mind. Her mother, the twins, Grandma Jenkins.

What was the good of all her studies, her training, if she couldn't stop this damn plague? It was built on top of her work—hers. She should have insight that would point the way to a cure.

She pounded her fists against the side of her head. It was as empty of solutions as Fowler's, rotting in his grave.

CHAPTER 10

Days later, California closed its borders to interstate travel. Australia, the only populated continent to have avoided the plague, turned away international flights, not even letting the planes land to refuel. Above the Earth's surface, space stations took extra precautions to decontaminate supply shipments.

In the U.S., grocery stores were emptied of supplies and industry ground to a halt as people refused to leave their homes.

The plague was only six weeks old and had already claimed eighty thousand lives around the world. Another fifty thousand people lay infected in quarantine wards. Medical personnel were the hardest hit. The CDC loaned out as many biohazard suits as it could spare; still doctors and nurses contracted the plague in droves.

There had been twenty-seven disease-related murders in the U.S., and there were reports of entire towns torched in Argentina.

CNN showed smoke rising over a hospital in Atlanta. National Guard members in armored biohazard suits and tanks were rounding up rioters. It looked like something out of Tiananmen Square.

Geoffrey shut off the television, unable to watch further. He felt weak and achy. The sickle-cell anemia was back. No matter how many transfusions the doctors gave him, the new cells wouldn't take. He was scheduled for another tomorrow and was not looking forward to it. Blood reserves, even synthetics, were dangerously low. What would happen when they ran out? All the money in the world was useless if there were no supplies to buy.

Geoffrey pulled aside the green curtain and looked at the empty theatre. Grief choked his throat as he remembered that, except for his lawyer, there was no one in the world for him to call. No one waiting anxiously for him to be released. Mother and Father were dead, as were June, Maria, all the servants he had grown up with. He was left alone in a world that was unraveling—and he was the one who had picked apart the knot that held everything together.

Geoffrey pounded his fist against the glass. There had to be something he could do. After fighting so long for health, he would not accept that this was how he would spend the rest of his life, in isolation, enduring blood transfusions until he died of illness or old age. The world could not end this way, as the victim of a medical accident. Not after surviving the twin threats of nuclear and environmental holocaust. Not when cloning was restoring plant and animal species on the brink of extinction.

Geoffrey vowed to his reflection that he would do whatever it took to help fight this thing. His blood, his wealth. All to the cause. He would go down fighting.

He picked up the computer Dr. Lam had allowed in order for him to plan his legal defense. "Computer: Call Henry Poulson."

Henry came on the line within seconds, his brows lowered in concern. "Has there been a new development? The government file charges?"

Geoffrey shook his head. "No. Not yet." He licked his lips. "I need to know how one sets up a nonprofit organization."

Emergency rooms flooded the CDC with AHMS blood samples, asking for confirmation of the AHMS diagnosis and sequencing of its variants.

The hospital quarantine wards were full, and new cases were constantly coming in. The CDC had begun annexing sites for temporary camps to house plague victims. The justification was that CDC medical personnel could provide specialized care for those suffering from AHMS, but Lillith had been in the room when Dr. Lam proposed the idea. In reality, the camps were a desperate attempt to slow the plague by reducing the number of infected in major metropolitan areas. No one had a cure, or any treatment beyond replacing proteins the body could no longer create because of genetic corruption.

Congress mobilized the National Guard, both to protect the camps from violence, such as the riots that had broken out in Georgia, and to keep victims of the plague from escaping.

Lillith had seen plans for one of the camps. A cluster of barracks surrounded by two concentric fences spaced thirty feet apart, both topped with razor wire. It was not a hospital, but a jail for the infected, a holding place until they died.

Lillith was alarmed when she received an instant message at work from "AzureMontana." She'd told Idaho never to contact her at work. It was too dangerous. The CDC's information technology department scanned for intruders and information leaks. And these days they were on high alert with the attacks against the compound and the media constantly hounding researchers for information.

"What?" she asked.

Idaho asked, "Can A VIRUS that targets a gene ON ONE CHROMOSOME jump to ANOTHER chromosome?"

Lillith was disconcerted and lifted the eyepiece of her wearable to better focus on the chat screen projected by her desktop computer. "I don't see why not." Her brow furrowed. "Why do you ask?"

"RESEARCH. Thanks." The connection closed.

Lillith stared at the empty chat window for a long moment. What was Idaho up to?

*   *   *

Geoffrey placed his arm in the blood sampler. Lillith watched him from the other side of the glass wall.

He felt weak. The melanin imbalances were traveling over his body, giving his skin the mottled appearance of rotting fruit. "Any progress towards a cure?"

Lillith shook her head. "Geoffrey, is there any other information you can give us about the virus? Anything Fowler might have said in passing. Anything at all?"

He shook his head. "I've told you all I know."

"How are you feeling?" Lillith asked.

Geoffrey shrugged. "Weak. There's pain in my stomach."

Lillith said, "I'll increase the dosage of digestive enzymes."

Geoffrey met her eyes. "I've seen the news. It can't go on like this. The world needs a cure."

"Medical personnel are working around the clock trying to beat this thing. Believe me. I want this over as much as you."

"I doubt that. You didn't cause this plague. All those corpses I see on TV." His voice caught. "I killed those people. Me and my ambitions for a cure."

Lillith watched him with sympathetic eyes, and it was almost more than he could bear.

"Don't," she said, placing a hand on the glass that separated them. "Guilt won't make anything better."

He met her eyes. They were like chips of coal. There was a message in her face he couldn't decipher.

Idaho jumped when a hand touched his shoulder. His motion drove the needles in his stomach against the table in front of him.

"Wha—" He snatched off his goggles. He breathed heavily, his heart pounding.

Exeter stood, hand on her hip. "What? Outside camera down?" She shook her finger at him. "Tsk-tsk, such lax security in these troubled times."

Idaho concentrated on his breathing, willing it to slow. He put his goggles back on. His sudden motion had locked up the DNA simulation. Enzymes jittered back and forth on the DNA strand. "I was concentrating on something important."

He'd almost seen it, a way to treat the plague. Answers hovered at the edge of consciousness. Idaho tried to pick up the threads of thought, but they had been scattered by Exeter's intrusion.

"Damn." He slammed his hand against the table. "It's gone."

"So disconnect," Exeter said. "You'll have to come out anyway. I couldn't get more IV bags. It's too dangerous near the hospitals, and all the mail-order places are backlogged. Crazy times call for desperate measures." She plopped a pizza box on top of Idaho's flatscreen monitor. "Real live food."

Idaho's stomach rebelled at the thought. He hadn't eaten solid food in weeks. But sacrifices must be made.

Exeter leaned across him, picked up the goggles, and placed them on her face. "What's so important, anyway?"

Idaho turned off the retinal projector and began the laborious task of plucking free the subdermal connections.

"You've seen the Web nexus. I'm working on treatments for AHMS for Dr. Watkins."

"Oh." Exeter pursed her lips. "Your little doctor friend."

"She's not my friend," Idaho said, gingerly pulling out the pins shoved too far into his stomach. Drops of blood welled from the ports.

"You do her a lot of favors." Exeter pouted, plucking the hair-thin wires from his shoulders.

"She helped Blue. Tried to save her."

Exeter rolled her eyes. She mouthed the word, "Blu-ue," making it two sarcastic syllables.

Idaho slapped her hard across the face.

Exeter sucked her teeth and snarled, "She's dead, Idy. Your beloved incestuous fucking sister is *dead*."

Idaho slapped her other cheek, raising an angry red palm mark on the sallow skin.

Exeter had taken worse. Tears of pain welled in her eyes but did not fall. "Did that make you feel better?" she asked in a poisonous tone. "Did that make you feel strong?"

Idaho's palm stung from the force of hitting her, and he sank onto his heels. "No." Hitting Exeter wouldn't bring Blue back. It only made him more like the monster who had locked them in the warehouse. Remorse flooded him and he dragged Exeter to his chest, not worrying about the needles that still remained.

They clung to each other, damned souls consigned to the same hell.

"Why do you put up with me?" Idaho wondered aloud when he could speak again. He tasted his own tears with the words.

"Hell," said Exeter, "I've fucked worse."

The pizza was cold and congealed by the time they finished digging the needles out of Idaho and salving the worst punctures.

"You look like a pincushion," Exeter said. "You ought to get one of the new magnetic induction rigs."

"Too slow." Idaho forced a piece of pizza into his mouth and chewed meticulously. If he ground it fine enough, perhaps the cramps wouldn't be too bad.

"Want to help me sim-test a treatment?" he asked when the pizza was gone. "We can do it on VR goggles."

Exeter stroked down his bare chest with her finger. "I can think of better things to do."

Idaho grabbed her wrist. She scowled until he kissed her palm. "Don't you worry about the plague? Don't you want to help stop it?"

She shrugged. "We're all dying all the time. Just nobody thinks of it that way. What's one more way to go?"

He placed her hand on his chest, over his heart. "Help with this, please."

"Then what?"

"Then . . . we'll see."

Exeter stood up, towering over him. "You know, I'm not so ugly that I got to put up with your shit. There's lots of guys who would jump at the chance to get with me."

It was true. Exeter was attractive in a stark way: large dark eyes, wide gash of a red mouth. Her body was lean and wasted, but her tiny breasts were pert and responsive.

"So, why are you here?"

She cocked her head and gave him a look. "Damned if I know."

He loaned her a pair of gloves and goggles that he kept as backup. They met online to run Idaho's latest engineered treatment through the simulator.

Exeter appeared as an electric blue point of light in the cellular fluid. Idaho's avatar here was a messenger RNA. He clung to the DNA strand, waiting.

A viral particle attached itself to the DNA, snipped out a gene at random, traveled along the strand, and inserted itself along with a portion of the gene it had removed.

Idaho was about to apply his treatment to the simulation when he heard Exeter's voice in the physical world. "Neat. It edits the DNA and then inserts a stop sequence. It's a lot like a tunneling worm I wrote once to get into DARPA."

Idaho froze. "That's not the cure. That's the virus."

"Yeah?" The blue point of light bounced over the edited DNA. "Looks like a heck of a way to edit damaged genes to me."

Idaho's brain raced with possibilities. Of course, the virus had been created as a cure; why not use it as one? Researchers had been working so hard to keep up with the virus's inherent mutations that they hadn't considered engineering their own.

He could finish Fowler's work, create a version of the virus that activated only when the gene structure it was designed to fix was present, and whose lipid coating had been fully removed so it couldn't proliferate.

It wouldn't remove AHMS from the body—the person would still be infected—but the damage wrought by the disease could be undone, mutation by mutation.

"Exeter, you're brilliant."

"No shit?"

In one voice, they said, "The virus is the cure."

It warmed Idaho's heart. For a split second it was as if Blue were alive again.

Lillith answered her office phone on the third ring. It was four a.m. and she'd been asleep. Her neck was stiff from sleeping hunched over her desk. "What?" she asked blearily, rubbing her eyes.

"The virus is the cure."

A jolt of adrenaline shot through Lillith's system at the sound of Idaho's twinned voice. "You can't keep calling here," she whispered, reaching forward to close the connection.

"Wait!" Idaho shouted. "I know how to cure the damage done by the virus."

Lillith froze. "Wha—How?"

"Engineer variants of AHMS to undo the damage caused by the wild variants."

Her sleep-deprived mind had to play the words back before they coalesced and made sense. She looked up at the wall screen. "How could you stabilize the engineered versions? You might just accelerate the fragmentation of the disease."

Idaho's grin lost wattage. "I don't know . . . yet. But stabilizing the virus is essentially a programming problem, and I'm good at those." He closed the connection.

A dialog box popped up onscreen: "Network monitor detected an encrypted communication originating outside the CDC network. Please indicate whether this was a valid connection."

"Computer: Yes," Lillith said automatically. Her mind was still whirring with Idaho's suggestion of using the virus as a tool. It would go against the Beijing Treaty, but if it could save lives, halt the progression of the plague, it wouldn't matter. No country in the world would forgo any treatment that might save them from AHMS.

Idaho's idea was brilliant or insane . . . perhaps both.

Lillith instant-messaged Danvers. He had just finished changing out of surgical scrubs. "Come up to my office. I've got something to show you."

Danvers's face looked tired, even in the miniature image displayed by his wrist computer. "Can't it wait until morning?"

Lillith bit her lip. "Just give me two minutes."

Danvers sighed. A few minutes later, he appeared in her doorway. He looked tired, his brown hair stuck up at random angles, and he wore three days' growth of beard.

Lillith repeated Idaho's idea.

He looked at her as if she were insane. "You want to infect people with a new version of the virus . . . as a cure?"

Lillith's voice quavered with excitement. "If we finish the work that Fowler started—create a nonmutating version of the virus, one that wasn't infectious. It might work."

"If it's such a great idea, why have none of the other researchers thought of it?"

"Because viral engineering is illegal. We've spent so much time trying to stop this outbreak, we never considered how to *use* it." And she added silently to herself, it had taken the viewpoint of someone who lived outside the law to see that their greatest liability was also their biggest asset.

Danvers shook his head. "I don't know. It's a dangerous idea."

Lillith pulled her fists towards her chest. "Just help me with the simulation. We'll put something together tonight and show it to Lam and the others in the morning."

Danvers looked at the watch woven into the fibers of his sleeve.

"Come on, Danvers, it's only sleep," Lillith pleaded. "This might be the breakthrough we've been waiting for. How could you rest knowing that?"

Shoulders slumped in defeat, Danvers said, "Tell me what you want me to do."

At five-thirty a.m., the first draft of the simulation was done. It was primitive, and there were still mutations in some of the genomes they'd tested it against. But when run against all of the Orcas Island patients' DNA, it repaired the sickle-cell defect.

Danvers pushed his chair back and stretched. "I haven't been this sleep-deprived since Joey was an infant." He yawned with the back of his fist covering his mouth.

He bid her good night and left for his office. He and Lillith had been camped in their offices like refugees since the CDC decided that all essential researchers should be restricted to the compound and the others put on leave for the duration of the crisis. Only supply vehicles moved in and out of the CDC's armored camp.

Lillith stood up and stretched her lower back. She walked to the end of the hallway, where there was a window. Gray twilight filtered in. Outside, the first rays of dawn glistened off a barrier of razor wire the army had erected.

When she had been restricted to the CDC grounds, Lillith had begged Mrs. Kowalski, who lived next door, to take Peekers in and feed him. Lillith had spent an hour assuring the old woman that cats didn't carry the disease. She suspected it was her musings about whether mice might be spreading the infection that cinched the deal.

Lillith went back to her office and curled up under the desk for a nap. She was asleep before her head hit the lab coat she used as a pillow.

She woke several hours later, panting from a nightmare: DNA strands had broken apart and people devolved before her eyes into single-celled animals.

Shivering, Lillith checked the time on her desktop

computer. Seven o'clock. She'd been asleep for just one and a half hours.

She checked Lam's office, but the lights were out and the blinds on the window were closed. He was still asleep.

Exhausted but unwilling to give herself back over to nightmares, Lillith stumbled her way to the rest room and then to the coffeemaker.

Cradling a steaming cup of black coffee, she decided to call her grandmother. The old family farm in central Florida was in the same time zone, and her grandmother would have been up for hours by now.

She closed her office door for privacy. Personal calls were prohibited during the lockdown, but nobody adhered to the restriction. What were they going to do, fire her? Every hand and mind was needed on the task. She placed the call.

"Lillith?" Her grandmother's face was pinched with worry. "You all right?"

"Yes, Grandma. How's the family?"

"They're with me on the farm. Things are better out here." Her smile was determinedly cheerful. "The tomatoes in my garden are as big as your fist."

"And cousin Elwood?"

Her grandmother's smile faded. "He passed, bless him."

Faces crowded around Grandma Jenkins. Among them, Lillith saw her younger brothers and her mother.

Lillith always found it disconcerting to see her mother's face. It was like looking in a mirror time-shifted to eighteen years in the future. But the face was still pretty; only a few worry lines creased her mother's brow.

"Child." The word was tentative, as if she half-expected Lillith to deny the claim.

"Mama," Lillith replied in a firm voice. "How are you?"

Grandma Jenkins waved her hands as if to shoo chickens. "Let the girl talk to her mama."

Her mother's eyes cut left, waiting until the others were out of earshot. "How much longer will this disease last?" she whispered. "Despite what Mama says, we're running out of food. And . . . there was a man shot dead in town last night, for walking too close to someone."

Lillith scrubbed her face. "I don't know, Mama. I just don't know." Her grandmother's enforced cheerfulness and her mother's fright wore her down like sandpaper on sponge cake.

There was an awkward pause.

"I've got to go," Lillith said after a few seconds. "I've got to get back to work."

Lillith said goodbye to her mother, grandmother, brothers, and all the cousins. She promised to let them know as soon as she heard anything, and they promised to be careful.

Lillith disconnected. She hoped Idaho's suggestion was the first step towards a cure. Time was running out.

The curtain slid back on the viewing theatre, and Geoffrey sat up on his cot.

It was Dr. Watkins. Her eyes were bloodshot and her lab coat was wrinkled. She leaned against one of the chairs; from the way her body slumped, she looked as if she would have fallen down without its support.

"You all right?" he asked.

Her lips twitched in a ghost of a smile. "I thought I was supposed to ask you that." She straightened the lapel of her lab coat. "Late night, that's all. How are you? Any recurrence of the muscular weakness?"

"No. Any news on a cure? I don't want to live the rest of my life in a plastic box." He tried to smile, turn it into a joke, but felt himself fail.

Lillith licked her lips. "Actually, there is news. It might be premature, but we've a new idea about how to design treatments for the virus." She looked left and right. "Can you keep a secret?"

Geoffrey gestured to the empty room. "Who am I going to tell?"

"The latest thinking is to design treatments that use the virus itself."

Geoffrey's eyes widened.

Lillith held up a restraining hand. "It hasn't been fully run through the simulator, and it doesn't have approval for human testing yet. It's all very preliminary. I just thought you should know."

Geoffrey was surprised. "Thank you. I thought . . . you didn't like me much."

A sigh, as if the weight of the world pressed down on her. "Recriminations won't cure the plague. You've suffered as much as anyone, more than some. Or maybe you just caught me at a weak moment."

"Do you need human test subjects?" Geoffrey stepped closer to the glass wall. "I volunteer. I'd like to do something to help."

One corner of Lillith's mouth crooked up in a half smile. "I'll let you know. What we really need is more DNA sequences to simulate treatments against."

"What about childhood identity records? Everyone's DNA-fingerprinted at birth."

Lillith sighed. "To keep costs low. The Social Security Administration stores only fragments. Few people can afford full sequencing. Those who can represent a fraction of the population of the United States. Each person is a chance for the virus to mutate. We have . . ."—Lillith cleared her throat—"several computer enthusiasts running simulations to predict new variants that might arise, but without complete coverage they can only predict a fraction of what we find in the wild. Same thing for this proposed cure. Without sufficient DNA samples to model the cure against, we risk launching another cascade of viral mutations."

"Why don't you ask every uninfected person in the United States to donate a genetic sample? Everyone should join in the fight against this disease."

Lillith shook her head. "People are scared. They

won't venture out of their houses. The disease is concentrated in the hospitals; no one's going there
voluntarily."

Geoffrey pounded his fist into his palm. "Then we
should mail them at-home kits. Explain the need, give
them a way to take samples themselves and mail them
back without risk. Hell, pay them if we have to."

"That would cost money. And all the funding we
have is already allocated to research. There's nothing
left for outreach or advertising. What you're proposing
would cost at least a billion dollars. With a 'b'—
billion."

"Apply for a grant from the Open Genome Project.
Its purpose is to fund projects that fight the spread of
AHMS and promote research for a cure."

Lillith looked at Geoffrey as if he'd lost his mind.
"What are you talking about? There is no Open Genome Project."

He opened his laptop and clicked a few buttons,
then turned it so Lillith could see. One half of the
screen itemized his inheritance and totaled his new
net worth. The other half displayed an application
form for a nonprofit organization. Geoffrey said,
"There is now."

Geoffrey felt a surge of adrenaline. This was what
he was meant to do with his family's fortune. It felt
right. He couldn't undo the damage he had done. But
maybe his wealth could help.

He continued, "We'll fund grants to small colleges
so they can help with the research. Every medical doctor, graduate student, undergraduate, anyone who can
help the fight against AHMS, will be eligible. I don't
want any avenue abandoned due to lack of money."

"How will you make funding decisions?"

"With the help of my directors." He met her gaze
and held it. "Will you serve on the board?"

Lillith's eyebrows lifted in surprise. "Me?"

Geoffrey's hand circled in the air as he searched for
the right words. "You care more about finding a cure
for AHMS than anyone else. The others fight out of

duty, out of fear. But you . . . you seem to take this disease personally."

Lillith swallowed. "How much money are we talking about?"

"All twenty-three billion dollars. Will that buy me a cure?"

Lillith blew out a breath. "If not, it's one hell of a down payment."

CHAPTER 11

"**Y**ou're being ripped off." Lillith's face appeared in a small window on Geoffrey's laptop. The rest of the display was filled with a spreadsheet.

The remote collaboration software was a convenient way for Geoffrey to go over the Open Genome Project figures with Lillith. It saved her the trouble of signing in and out of the level-four quarantine ward every time they wanted to talk.

A square on the laptop highlighted as Lillith moused over the per unit price. "This is *four times* what a sterile DNA collection unit should cost, even factoring in the custom printed materials."

Geoffrey sighed. "I know, but the Open Genome Project was launched three weeks ago, and it's taken me that long to find a company that could handle the order. All the companies in the U.S. are short-staffed and backlogged. This company promised delivery in six weeks. It's in southern Mexico, where the plague hasn't penetrated . . . yet."

Lillith's sigh was audible over the tiny speaker embedded in the laptop frame. "All right. But it's criminal the way they're profiteering on disease."

"I agree, but these are desperate times." Geoffrey switched to the company's Web site and ordered three hundred million units.

When he was done, Lillith said, "If we get any significant response rate, the CDC staff won't be able to sequence them all. We're strung thin as it is keeping on top of treatments for new mutations and developing a reliable test for the presence of the virus."

"I've already thought of that," Geoffrey said. He opened a list of contacts: private labs, colleges, and hospitals. "I've gotten commitments from these groups to process the kits and transmit the data to central CDC databases."

Lillith looked at the list. "Saint Leo University doesn't have a DNA sequencer."

"They do now. Some of these groups I'm paying a per unit fee, others I'm supplying equipment in return for their assistance."

"That will cost millions. Genomic Biosystems has doubled their prices on genetics equipment and supplies in the last month."

Geoffrey shrugged. "Dr. Watkins, money is an artificial construct. It has no value outside of what it can buy."

On the screen of Geoffrey's laptop, Lillith shook her head. "Only someone born rich could say that."

"Well, the money won't do any good sitting in a bank vault while everyone dies, will it? I say we fund anyone who's willing to work on this project. If they need equipment, let's buy equipment."

"What will you do once the money's gone?" Lillith asked.

Geoffrey had avoided thinking about that question. He raised his arms to indicate the tiny quarantine cell around him. "The CDC isn't charging me rent." He let his hands drop. "Do you really think I'll ever get out of here?"

Lillith's gaze fell. She said quietly, "I don't know."

After Lillith left, Geoffrey logged on to his investment accounts.

The markets were down, but there were still places capital could grow. He researched companies that would be helped by the plague and its aftermath: medical equipment manufacturers, biohazard suit developers, telecommunications and shipping companies.

He placed a market order for shares in a start-up

called SafeHouse that developed hermetically sealed living quarters. It saddened him to profiteer on disease, but the Open Genome Project needed the money.

Lillith said, "Database: Display total number of records."

Onscreen, numbers flashed as the size was tallied. The result: 75,527,172 entries.

Lam's eyebrows rose. "Impressive."

Danvers nodded. "We've had an amazing twenty-six percent return rate on the at-home DNA sample kits we sent out, and more are still trickling in."

Lillith said, "Not only will this help us track the spread of the disease, but it gives us a genetic baseline for the entire country. We have a large enough sample to finish the testing simulations and start human trials."

"Good work, doctors," said Lam, pumping Lillith's and Danvers's hands.

Lillith said, "The DNA testing was Geoffrey's idea. I just mentioned the problem. He provided the funding."

Dr. Lam released her hand. "Yes. He is to be commended. But the data would not be half as valuable without your brilliant inspiration to use the virus as a cure."

Lillith felt uneasy taking the credit for Idaho's idea, but it was better for both of them. Her career could use bolstering, and she guessed that Idaho wouldn't appreciate the notoriety his discovery would bring.

Idaho Blue was deep into a simulation of AHMS. He froze the program, changed some of the base nucleotides of the viral DNA, and then restarted the simulation to see how the new version of the virus edited the host's DNA. Idaho had altered the AHMS virus to prevent it from reproducing and had changed its payload to a sequence that repaired the genetic defect that caused sickle-cell anemia, one of AHMS's more common variants. The current simulation tested it over a patient without thalassemia. Idaho wouldn't repeat Fowler's mistakes. He had to be sure his version of the virus didn't mutate in the null case.

If this theory worked, if he could convince Lillith and the other CDC researchers his designed virus was safe, this could be the key to stopping the plague.

The virus was the perfect microbiological tool for editing DNA; all he had to do was control its instability. And Idaho was starting to get a feel for protein programming.

He was rearranging molecular bonds when an instant message buzzed in his ear. Idaho twitched his head and the electrodes implanted under his skin signaled the computer to open his videophone program.

It was Dweezer, self-proclaimed god of IP6 hacking. A skinny Hispanic man in his early twenties, he looked more nervous than usual. The room behind him was littered with unwashed clothes and pizza delivery boxes.

"I got to get out of here," he said in a low whine. "I heard rumors about where you live. That you've got some sort of ranch. No people. No fucking plague."

Idaho raised an eyebrow—he'd automatically switched avatars when he'd answered the phone—Bluc's delicate brow lifted. Idaho took pains to ensure that none of his associates, aside from Exeter, knew where his physicality was located. Exeter wouldn't betray him, not without a good reason. Perhaps there was some other breach. The blind trust he had set up in the name Bela Houdi, an anagram of Idaho Blue, might have been tracked. Unlikely, but it was a possibility.

Dweezer's voice jerked Idaho back from his musings. "Come on, man. You got to help me out."

"What do you want?"

Dweezer rocked back and forth, cradling his arm in unconscious parody of a junkie. "I want to come stay with you."

"Indeed."

"Don't give me that fucking Mr. Spock shit. It's bad out here. Me and the others—you don't know what we've had to do to stay clean."

Idaho picked out the most relevant word. "How MANY others?"

"Just Nate and Gordon. That's all. We helped you out when you had a tough run and needed backup. Come on. A freakin' corner of your place is all we're asking."

Idaho thought about the abandoned farmhouse that had come with the ranch. He preferred the privacy and protection of his underground trailer. When Idaho had bought the ranch, he'd rented a bulldozer to dig a subterranean foundation and put in gravel to manage drainage. He'd buried the trailer so trespassers wouldn't be able to find him as he slept.

The farmhouse was too large, too exposed for Idaho's taste, but it would do for the others. It would be good to have the house occupied, to discourage squatters. He'd already had to trigger the security system to fire rubber bullets at two groups who'd tried to break in through the front gates. People were fleeing the cities, looking for safety in the low population density of rural farms.

Dweezer and the others were smart, if unimaginative. They could also help him with his current project.

"Bring your COMPUTER EQUIPMENT. I'll need DNA samples FROM ALL OF YOU, to verify you're PLAGUE-FREE. While you're HERE, you work FOR ME. Understood?"

Dweezer nodded like a plastic dog's head on a spring. "Yeah, anything."

"One OTHER THING."

"What is it?"

"You don't try to FIND WHERE I LIVE. YOU STAY on the ranch. In a HOUSE. But you DON'T TRY TO FIND my body."

Dweezer hesitated a second, taking the directive in. Denying information to a hacker was like throwing a juicy steak in front of a starving dog and telling him not to eat. After a moment where cogs turned visibly within Dweezer's head, he said, "I can promise I won't go there. I can't promise not to figure it out."

"But you WILL NOT actively try."

Dweezer nodded emphatically. "Sure thing."

Idaho Blue, after one last moment of indecision, transmitted the GPS location of his ranch. He also fired off an email to Lillith saying he'd be sending her three samples to be tested for traces of the plague.

He wanted to get inside the plague. He did not want it inside of him.

Later that week, Dweezer, Nate, and Gordon moved into the white farmhouse, repairing the roof enough so the rain wouldn't threaten their electronics.

Idaho kept Exeter away from them. He arranged it so her visits to his trailer occurred when the others had put on biohazard suits and gone out on a food run. He wasn't sure whether this was to protect her from them or them from her. Idaho just knew he wanted to keep the two halves of his life separate.

"Ah man, what is this crap?" Dweezer's avatar was a bald man with a bodybuilder's physique. The bulky body cocked its head at the virus simulation. "Base pairs, DNA. What has this got to do with us?"

Idaho Blue said, in his twinned voice, the amalgam of his and his dead sister's, "The plague IS THE ULTI-MATE hack. Forget COMPUTERS, this microscopic Trojan HIJACKS HUMAN CELLS, rewriting them according to ITS OWN INTERNAL PROGRAM. YOU CAN'T TELL ME that's not interesting."

"Sorta, but I ain't no doctor."

"You're no TRAINED PROGRAMMER EITHER. But that never STOPPED YOU. Of course, if this is TOO HARD for you to APPREHEND—"

"You calling me stupid?"

"No. YOU were DOING THAT."

Dweezer's mouth opened and shut like a carp's. "Shut up. Just shut up and send me the damn files."

Idaho chuckled and transmitted the course work on molecular biology to his houseguests.

Despite their initial reluctance, Dweezer, Nate, and Gordon were quick learners and were soon writing extensions to his object model. Over the next month, they worked covertly with Lillith to devise viral patches that reversed the damage caused by AHMS. It was slow going; each new variation required a different cure. And new variations cropped up daily. Even with a theoretical treatment in hand, it still took days to synthesize treatments. Treatments that sometimes came too late.

Geoffrey was watching CNN when the curtain parted. All three doctors were there: Lillith, Danvers, and Lam. Lillith's and Danvers's faces were lit up. Lam was more subdued.

"What is it?" Geoffrey asked, shutting off the wall screen and rotating sideways on his bed to face them.

Danvers shot a look at Lam.

Before Lam could speak, Lillith blurted, "We might have a way to correct your sickle-cell anemia."

Geoffrey's eyebrows rose. "That's wonderful."

Lam frowned, "Perhaps. It is untested and potentially . . . dangerous. Dr. Watkins's proposed cure involves treating the patient with a modified version of the AHMS virus. We risk repeating the mistakes Dr. Fowler made in his original version. Instead of a cure, it might accelerate the disease."

Geoffrey glanced at Lillith. Her face wore a neutral expression. "You need someone to test the cure," he said.

"Rodent trials have been very promising," Lillith said. "Normally, we would spend years researching the treatment before we'd even consider human trials. But with the current progression of the plague . . ."

Geoffrey nodded. The mortality rates were still rising. So far there'd been no person found to be immune to the plague. Some reporters were asking whether this was a species-threatening plague.

"I want to try it." He raised his chin and tried to look as brave as his words sounded.

Dr. Lam looked at Lillith. He did not look happy.

Lillith breathed out a sigh. "Perfect. You're the ideal candidate. We know more about your genome and the progression of your disease than any other patient's." Her eyes locked with his. "I promise to do all I can to ensure your safety."

Geoffrey watched the doctors file out. The medical establishment must be frightened if it was relaxing the FDA regulations on human trials.

Geoffrey turned the television back on and watched plague statistics scroll across the screen. He was frightened, too.

Two months later, the news on the television was even more grim. The experimental treatments were still being tested, and while the world waited for a cure, the plague took more lives.

Geoffrey had seen that look on Dr. Watkins's face before. "The death rates are rising, aren't they?"

She nodded, checking the readouts of the wireless microphones that monitored Geoffrey's pulse and lung function. They were round flat patches, their beige showing up starkly against the mottled tan and brown of his chest.

Sweat beaded on his upper lip. "What's the current mortality rate?"

Lillith looked up from his chest. "Why ask? They're just statistics. Each case is different. What's relevant to your case is the progression of your symptoms."

Geoffrey swallowed around a sudden tightness in his throat. "The number. Please. I need to know."

Lillith blew out a breath. "The official number is ninety-six percent. But that's just an est—"

"I'm going to die, aren't I?"

Lillith shook her head. "There's no way to be certain, but in my estimation, no. You were fortunate. You contracted only a few variations before you were quarantined here. And the new treatment seems to be reversing the worst damage. Speaking of which, how do you feel this morning?"

"No more fatigue from sickle-cell, and the digestive problems are gone. I feel almost cured. Except for . . ." Geoffrey held up his hands and looked at the mottled skin.

Lillith pulled a needle out of one of her pockets and twisted off the protective cap. "The melanin instability is purely a cosmetic issue. We haven't time to work on those sorts of problems."

"Of course," Geoffrey said. The discoloration was strange and wandered around his body, but it was in no way painful.

Lillith looked up from the display on her handheld. "As long as you remain away from other people, and don't catch any new variants, you should live a long time."

Geoffrey looked at the small room he'd been living in for the past four months. Sterile white walls, ceilings with air nozzles to supply biohazard suits, the mechanized robots that serviced him, the viewing amphitheatre. Except for his laptop, requests for his personal effects had been denied. It was as dehumanizing as the day he'd moved in.

Was living in a cage really better than dying in one?

He quashed the rise of self-pity and tried a smile. "Thank you, Doctor. That's good news." And at least part of it was; he'd have time to see his money well spent towards a cure.

"I can't come over," said Exeter's avatar. Her computer-generated image was a lanky blonde. It lounged against the doorway of the portal to her Web nexus: black-painted walls with neon-light squiggles in electric pink, blue, and green.

Idaho gazed at the image so like his sister. "Why?" With Exeter, he didn't feel so alone. His avatar with her was himself, as it had always been between him and Blue.

A pause. Her Nordic features were inscrutable. Exeter said flatly, "I've got the fucking plague. You'll have to find another delivery girl."

Idaho felt like he'd been suddenly disconnected.

Not Exeter. She went out into the world, yes, but she took precautions. Hadn't he given her a military-grade biohazard armor? "How? Weren't you wearing your suit?"

Exeter's black eyes flashed. "Not while I was asleep." Her voice broke. "They broke into my fucking apartment, okay?" The tilt of her chin warned him not to press further.

Idaho forced himself to breathe. "Are you going to the hospital?"

Exeter waved her hand in a jagged circle around her ear. Her gestures were completely her own. There was nothing of Blue's grace in them.

Exeter said, "You crazy? That's where all the variations are. I'm better off at home."

Idaho took Exeter's virtual hand. "You're sure it's the plague?"

She pulled it away and turned her back to him. "No, I want to break it off with you and this is the best excuse I could think of. Yeah, I'm sure—I used one of those new at-home tests."

Her sarcasm in the face of death made him proud of her. He placed his avatar's hands on her shoulders. "I'm coming to get you."

"No way. You haven't left your trailer in six months."

"I'll be there in an hour. Is your biohazard suit intact?"

"Yeah, for all the good it did me."

"Put it on." Idaho broke the connection, his heart pounding. He wasn't going to lose another. He'd loved only two people in his entire life, and he'd be damned if he would watch them both die. If he couldn't save Ex, he might as well contract the plague and go with her. There was something comforting in knowing that they'd be exchanging genes, killing each other by merging into one chaos.

As he began the tedious practice of disconnecting the subcutaneous needles, Idaho thought about how he would treat Exeter. Quarantine was key. He had to isolate her from other people.

Perhaps Lillith could sequence Ex's DNA and provide treatments. No—that would take too long. Mail was slow these days with all the decontamination and other precautions the postal service imposed. And even at the best of times, overnight between Atlanta and rural Montana would take one to two days . . . time Exeter didn't have to waste.

Lillith could admit her to the CDC's quarantine. Exeter would get the best treatment there. He plucked needles from his arm and cast them into a pickle jar filled with alcohol solution. No, Exeter would never submit to a government agency. And the CDC had a policy of denying patients network access.

He wanted her near him, not locked in a cage in Atlanta. How could he make this work?

He and the others developed theoretical cures. If only they had the training and equipment to develop them for real.

He winced as he pulled a needle out of his eyebrow. Staring at the tiny speck of blood, it suddenly occurred to him. Why not?

How hard could it be to sequence and fabricate DNA? Modern sequencers and synthesizers were automated and run entirely by computer. And Idaho was very good with computers.

"You want what?" Lillith kept her voice low. He was calling on her personal cell phone, but with the heightened security in the building, the IT department might be scanning cell frequencies. Getting caught talking to a computer criminal would invalidate her security clearance.

She sensed it was important, though; Idaho wasn't masking with an avatar. It was the first time she'd seen him as an adult. The childish softness she remembered had lengthened and hardened into a lean, hawk-like face.

His pale face was drawn, and there were dark circles

under his glacial-blue eyes. He repeated, "A DNA sequencer and synthesizer, centrifuge, autoclave, reagents, restriction enzymes, and other lab supplies."

Lillith sat down heavily in her chair, still not believing. "You're not trained to use that equipment."

Idaho didn't blink. "The new systems are automated. I've downloaded Genomic Biosystems' training videos; the process is quite straightforward. I've learned a lot about molecular biology by simulating treatments for your patients. Now I want to move into practical application. Don't worry, I'll continue to share my designs."

"What you're asking costs hundreds of thousands of dollars. A high-performance DNA sequencer and synthesizer alone is a quarter million."

"That's why I'm applying to the Open Genome Project for a grant. Geoffrey Allen has fourteen billion dollars left in his coffers. He can spare the money."

Lillith didn't ask how Idaho had obtained OGP's financials. "Are you infected?"

"No."

She peered at the three-inch image, trying to read his expression. Irritation or fear warred with exhaustion in his eyes.

Idaho continued, "Someone close to me is."

Lillith was alarmed. If Idaho became infected the fight against AHMS would lose a valuable resource and she'd lose . . . a friend?

"He should go to a hospital."

"Hospitals are just holding sites for the dying. You know that. This equipment will give her a chance."

Lillith's eyes rose at the pronoun. She hadn't seen Idaho care about anyone since his sister died. "There's no convincing you to bring her here? She'd be well cared for."

"No." Idaho's lips compressed with irritation. "If it wasn't for me, you wouldn't have known the plague was coming, you wouldn't have known Fowler created it, and you damn well wouldn't have thought to use the virus as a treatment. I've done a lot for you. Now

I need your help." His blue eyes were deadly serious. "Don't deny me this."

Lillith sighed. "I'll talk to Geoffrey."

"Do that." Idaho disconnected and left Lillith staring at a blank screen.

Idaho's car was a faded blue Ford Econoline van. It was covered with dust and parked next to the farmhouse. It had taken Nate and Gordon the better part of an afternoon and new spark plugs to get the motor to turn over. Now they used it for food runs.

Idaho didn't like being around other people. He skulked towards the farmhouse, feeling vaguely like he was stealing his own car.

Dweezer lounged on the front steps of the house, smoking a clove cigarette.

When he caught sight of Idaho, he stood up. Started to say something. Ran down the few steps and stared after Idaho. He watched Idaho get in. "Holy shit, you're a guy." Dweezer ran up to the driver's side. "We all figured you for a girl, or maybe some kind of hermaphrodite, with that wack avatar you use."

"Clean out the barn," said Idaho. "And run ninety amps of power to it. I'll be getting some new equipment."

Dweezer pulled the cigarette out of the corner of his mouth and waved it at the eighteenth-century barn. The structure was intact, but the roof was missing shingles and had caved in at the center. "That thing?"

"And a quarantine room. We'll need to construct one."

Dweezer's brown eyes widened and he took a step back. "What the hell's going on here. Have you got the plague?"

"No. But I'm going to pick up someone who does."

Dweezer's skin faded to a pale yellow. "No way, man. He'll kill us all."

"She," said Idaho. "And no, she won't. Not if you construct the quarantine room adequately."

"We'll all die!" Dweezer's voice was panicked. The two other hackers, Nate and Gordon, came running out of the house.

"What is it?" Gordon asked. A faded Jimmi and the Hendrix T-shirt strained over the bulk of his stomach. His black hair had been pulled into a ponytail and trailed down his back like a rope.

Dweezer pointed an accusing finger at Idaho. "He's going to bring a plague packet here. Set her up in the barn."

Nate's blond hair was short. Freckles covered his face and shoulders. He looked like an Iowa farm boy except for the plugs that pierced both sides of his nose and curled around his nostrils like a boar's tusks. He screwed up his face at Dweezer's announcement. "Someone with the plague. Here?"

"Anyone who does not agree with me may leave." Idaho pointed at the front gate of the fence that surrounded the property. "Take your chances out in the world. Those who stay will help me with Exeter. She is sick and I intend to heal her."

"You crazy, man?" Dweezer said. "We ain't doctors. We write code. The cures we develop aren't real."

"They will be. Fix up the barn and create a quarantine room. I'll be back in three hours." Idaho put the car in gear and drove off, kicking up dust on the dirt road. In the rearview mirror he saw the three men standing in front of the house, arguing.

Idaho walked down the hall of Exeter's apartment building; peepholes darkened as inhabitants looked out. No stranger, these days, passed by unexamined.

Idaho was dressed in Racal bioarmor that made walking awkward. Unlike the thin-walled models medical staff used, this suit had hard joints and a self-contained oxygen supply that could last for hours—longer if he changed tanks. It was top-of-the-line military-issue field equipment from the black market.

He rapped once on Exeter's door. She opened it immediately. Exeter was dressed in identical bio-armor. She looked tired and worried.

"Coming here is sweet, Idy. I know you hate leaving your ranch. But you shouldn't be here. There's nothing you can do. It's my time." She pointed at the drug paraphernalia on the coffee table. A set of needles and several vials of morphine were spread out on a clean towel. "I've been saving up. When things get bad, I'll snuff it."

"No," Idaho said and reached out his hand to her.

Exter took it; when they touched, their hard plastic gauntlets clinked softly.

Idaho said, "I'm going to cure you."

"You're no doctor, Idy."

"I'll become one." Tears ran down his face. Behind the faceplate, there was nothing he could do but let them run. "Let me *try*."

Exeter shook her head. "I might kill you."

He smiled a painful smile. "I take that risk every time we meet."

Exeter pulled her hand away. "Damn it, Idy. Caring whether you live or die is the closest I come to loving anything. Don't fuck that up." Her gloved hand bounced off her faceplate as she tried to wipe away her own tears.

Idaho touched her shoulders and then turned her around to face him. "Please. Let me try."

Exeter shook her head angrily. "You are so messed up. You know that?"

"Thank you," he said, reading defeat in the slump of her shoulders.

Exeter threw her drug gear and a palmtop device into a bag shaped like a daisy and followed him out. She left the door open and painted a clumsy red "X" on it in lipstick.

Idaho cocked his head at the last.

"Only fair to let the looters know what they're up against," Exeter said.

*   *   *

Lillith brought up the video feed from Geoffrey's room. He was seated cross-legged on the bed, laptop in his lap, researching stock prices.

Lillith sent an instant text message to Geoffrey requesting a chat. He tried to switch to video, but she refused the new connection.

"Private," she sent back. "Turn the laptop away from the camera."

In the video, Geoffrey shuffled around on the bed until the screen of his laptop was hidden from view. He typed a reply: "Done. What is this all about?"

"We've gotten a funding request from someone unconventional," Lillith typed. "He's brilliant, but doesn't have any medical training. He wants to set up a private genetics lab."

"Who is he? Is he associated with a university?"

"Not really," Lillith typed. "He's a private individual specializing in computer-science research. Self-taught."

"Hackers?" He pulled away from the laptop and looked up at the camera.

"They've been building computer models of the virus. Your treatments are the result of their work. But I don't think—"

"Buy it for them." Geoffrey typed. "I've been unimpressed by the results of the medical establishment. Give the amateurs a shot."

CHAPTER 12

Idaho drove back to the ranch on nearly deserted roads. With the plague, no one left their homes unless it was absolutely necessary. Exeter huddled in the passenger seat, shivering. Unable to touch her through her suit, Idaho couldn't tell if she had a fever.

"You okay?" What a stupid question. He cursed the words as they came out of his mouth.

Exeter glared at him, then looked away.

As the van approached the ranch, sensors on the front gate scanned the license plate and verified it against the list of approved vehicles. Finding the van, the gate slid open. Idaho crested the hill and in the distance saw the white farmhouse, and something new: a battered Winnebago sat in the middle of an old pasture, five hundred feet from the barn. Idaho drove the quarter mile into his ranch and saw a pair of sawhorses set across the road with a sign that pointed to the camper. It read QUARANTINE.

Idaho parked the van and flipped open his cell phone.

Dweezer answered on the first ring. He smiled broadly on the small screen. "What do you think? Brilliant, eh?"

Idaho looked out the window at the dusty Winnebago. Its dented body might have survived a demolition derby. "Where did you get it?"

"Better that you don't know. But don't worry, man, no one's going to come looking for it."

"I told you to set up quarters in the *barn*."

"This is better. The barn is drafty. There's no kitchen, no toilet. Your lady ain't no animal to be living in a barn. She'll be cozier in the camper."

The Winnebago stood like an abandoned sentinel in the middle of the pasture. "It's also another thousand feet from the house. It's your cowardice, not altruism, motivating you."

Dweezer shrugged in the tiny palmtop screen. "Maybe. But I'm a real *live* coward. We can't cure her if we come down with the plague. This is best for everybody, man. We fixed it up real nice."

Exeter said, "I need to puke."

Idaho put the van into gear and swung it in the direction of the camper. When he got closer he noticed the windows were sealed shut with epoxy and that a plastic solar shower hung like a dying jellyfish over the door. The shower's reservoir was filled with greenish liquid, and someone had written the words DECON FLUID on it in black marker and below that, in red paint, BUG KILLA.

Idaho got out of the van and helped Exeter walk to the camper. He opened the door to her new quarters.

Tattered quilts from the farmhouse decorated the camper's tiny bed and built-in couch. A glass of wildflowers stood on the tiny counter next to the kitchen sink. There was barely enough room for two people to turn around, but Idaho found that comforting. He and Blue had spent most of their childhood locked in a storeroom. Open spaces made him nervous.

They stepped inside and Idaho pulled the door shut behind him. Exeter ran to the back of the van, pulled off her helmet, and knelt in front of the bathroom closet. She vomited into the toilet bowl.

While Exeter was in the bathroom, Idaho pulled his cell phone out of the chest pocket of his biohazard suit and turned off the camera. Using voice only, he called Lillith at the CDC.

Lillith answered his call, looking distracted. Her attention jumped between Idaho's call and something

offscreen that Idaho couldn't see. Her eyes were
bright and she looked excited.

"What is it?" she asked without preamble. She
turned her head and typed on a keyboard attached to
another computer.

Idaho felt prickles of curiosity. He'd have to check
her CDC email when he was attached to his rig. There
was no easy way to access her account using the limited protocol of his cell phone. He said, "Did my grant
go through?"

Lillith looked back at him. "Yes, everything you
asked for. The equipment should be there tomorrow
by special courier."

A knot in Idaho's stomach loosened. "Thank you."

A gleam of triumph lit Lillith's dark eyes. She
opened her mouth to speak, then closed it with a snap.
She said, "Watch the news. Tokyo might make an
announcement soon."

Exeter groaned and fell sideways onto the floor of
the camper's tiny hallway.

"I have to go." Idaho clicked the palmtop closed.
He knelt next to Exeter. "You all right?"

Her face was pale and sweating. "Water."

Idaho stepped into the kitchen and tried the tap. A
brownish fluid came out. He let it run until the water
became clear, then filled a jam jar from the cupboard
and brought it to Exeter.

The equipment would be here tomorrow. But he
still had to get her through the night.

When Exeter finished the water, Idaho helped her
up and wiped her face with a damp towel. There was
a dark patch of flesh under her chin. He rubbed at it.

Exeter took the cloth from his hand. "It's the
plague, Idy."

Idaho felt his chest constrict at this tangible proof
of her infection. It was happening again—this time he
wouldn't let disease take her. No matter what the cost.

He tucked Exeter into the bed built into the back
of the camper, piling three quilts on top of her.

Idaho retrieved her flowered bag from the other

room, pulled out her palmtop, and set it on the floor next to the bed. "Call me if you need anything. I have to go prepare the lab."

Exeter groaned and snuggled deeper into the blankets. "Just leave my stuff near the bed, okay?"

Idaho poured the contents out onto the bed, plucked up the plastic vials of multicolored capsules, the balloons of heroin, a strand of silicon tubing, and the needle, and tucked them into the outer pocket of his biohazard suit.

Exeter sat up in bed and grabbed for the Velcro closure on his suit. "Hey! Those are mine!"

He pushed her hand away. "Later, when you're well." Idaho looked at Exeter, trying to burn his next words into her soul. "I don't want you giving up on me."

Exeter rolled into the bed and pulled the covers over her head. "Fuck you" came out, muffled through layers of blankets.

Idaho looked around the camper. It was filled with sharp objects, cords, any number of things that could be turned to suicidal purpose. "Just give me a week. If things aren't better by then, I'll give them back."

Exeter responded only by burrowing deeper into the covers.

Idaho sighed. It was as much of an agreement as he would get.

He left the camper and sluiced disinfectant over his suit. The van needed to be cleaned out as well. Idaho dragged the hose over, opened all the doors, and soaked the interior of the van. Satisfied that he'd covered all the surfaces, he got in and drove to the farmhouse.

Dweezer, Nate, and Gordon met him outside dressed in clear plastic biohazard suits. Dweezer pointed to another solar shower.

"I already decontaminated."

"Take off your suit and do it again," said Dweezer. "We got to do this right or we could all die."

Idaho couldn't argue with their reasoning. He

stripped naked. Gooseflesh rose immediately on his arms and legs in the cool autumn evening. He stepped under the plastic bag and opened the valve. He directed the hose over his bare skin. The disinfectant felt like shards of ice lancing into his body. It smelled of bleach and stung.

Dweezer watched as Idaho soaked every inch of his body. He handed Idaho a threadbare towel. He nodded his head towards the house. "Come in and warm up inside. Then we'll show you the barn."

The kitchen held a round Formica-topped table and four mismatched chairs. The living room beyond was furnished with three sagging couches, arranged around the perimeter of the room. Server boxes were stacked in one corner, and there was a pile of VR goggles and gloves on the coffee table.

Nate loaned Idaho one of his many pairs of ripped jeans, and Gordon handed him a T-shirt with the logo of a video-band, the Dread Roberts, emblazoned on it. The T-shirt hung past Idaho's knees.

"How's is she?" asked Nate.

Idaho didn't feel like talking. He wanted to be safe in his trailer, reviewing online manuals and making plans for tomorrow. But he needed help to run the lab equipment. "She's all right. I think I got to her before she developed too many variations. If we keep her isolated, we might be able to stabilize her."

Nate and Gordon nodded, but Dweezer looked worried. His eyes kept flickering to the back of the house as if he could see through walls and into Exeter's camper.

Idaho sat at the kitchen table and drank a cup of hot coffee. When Idaho stopped shivering, they took him on a tour of the barn.

Dweezer pointed at the power cable running from the farmhouse's main junction box to the barn. It lay on top of the ground like a thick black snake. "Not exactly to code, man, but you'll have enough juice to do anything you need."

They stepped into the barn. It had been built in the 1800s and was huge. The hayloft alone was sixty feet from floor to ceiling, and the lower floor had had dozens of stalls.

"We knocked the stalls down to open it up." Dweezer waved his hands in a pushing motion. The floor was swept clean of moldering hay and dung. Dweezer pointed up. Plastic garbage bags were stapled to the ceiling. "That's to keep out the rain. The roof upstairs is wrecked."

"A good start," Idaho said. He picked a farrier's hook off the wall and scratched in the dirt floor of the barn. "I want the DNA sequencer here," he said, scribing a square. He drew lines for counters and indicated where each piece of equipment would go, double-checking power requirements and making sure the site was ready. He worked late into the night, planning his lab. At last, after everyone else had gone back to the farmhouse, Idaho snuck back to his underground trailer to sleep.

The next day, a Genomic Biosystems delivery truck pulled up to the ranch gates and honked for entrance. Idaho approved the vehicle and told the driver to wait for him outside the barn.

Then Idaho put on his biohazard suit and walked there from the trailer. Dweezer and the others were nowhere to be seen. Hiding, no doubt, in case the driver brought the plague in on his truck.

The driver wore a self-contained biohazard suit. He jumped down from the cab and had Idaho sign for it with a stylus. Then he unloaded the truck with a pneumatic dolly. The equipment was sealed in plastic marked with red tags that read TESTED AHMS FREE.

Dweezer and the others stayed in the house during the unloading. When the truck left, they emerged in gear and hosed down the outside of the equipment and the road where the truck had been parked.

Geoffrey Allen's foundation had shipped them an automated DNA sequencer and synthesizer, refrigerator, centrifuge, bottles of nucleotide solution packed in dry ice, more decontaminant, an autoclave, and a negative-pressure glove box.

Idaho downloaded the assembly instructions to Dweezer's handheld. "Could you finish setting this up? I need to take a blood sample from Exeter."

Idaho went to the farmhouse kitchen and arranged oatmeal, coffee, and orange juice on a plate for Exeter. Then he suited up and placed a syringe in his outer pocket.

Exeter had discovered the padlock Idaho had put on the front door of the camper. She pounded and cursed so the whole aluminum frame shook.

Idaho smiled. That much energy meant she was feeling better.

Idaho opened the door to the camper.

Exeter lay on her stomach on the bench-sized couch. Her eyes were hidden behind VR goggles, and her muscles twitched in sympathetic movement to whatever world she was experiencing. She wore white underwear and a matching tank top that clung to her chest.

The camper creaked and rocked as Idaho stepped inside.

Exeter whipped off her goggles and looked at him. Her eyes fell to the needle in his hand and she smiled. "Come around to my way of thinking?" She held out her hand. It was so narrow and fragile looking that Idaho wanted to wrap his hand around hers and protect it. But they couldn't touch, not with him in his biohazard suit.

"No," he said. "I've come to draw blood. We need a genetic baseline."

Exeter's smile soured. "A lot of good that'll do. If the plague could be cured, don't you think all those scientists would have done it by now? What makes you think you can succeed where they fail? You're going to put me and you through a lot of pain. For what? Nothing."

"I have to try," he said.

Exeter blew a black lock of hair out of her eyes. With a jerk she thrust out her arm, the crook of her elbow outstretched. "Go on, then."

Idaho wrapped the silicon tubing from Exeter's drug kit around her upper arm as a tourniquet.

She pumped her hand into a fist to raise the vein.

Idaho removed the green plastic sheath that protected the needle. Her veins stood out like blue road maps on the inner crook of her arm. Nubs of scar tissue lined the veins like speed bumps.

He hovered above her arm, not wanting to hurt her, unsure how to hit the vein and not drive past it.

"Oh, for God's sake." Exeter yanked the syringe out of his hand and, with practiced ease, slid the needle into her arm. She pulled back on the plunger slowly until the cylinder filled with bluckish-red blood. She detached the needle and handed Idaho the full syringe. "Some researcher you are." She applied pressure to the puncture with her thumb and untied the tubing with her teeth.

Her words stung. Idaho felt a moment of panic. What if he failed? What if she was right and all he did was extend their misery? He wanted to be away from her scornful eyes, to go to the lab and prove her wrong.

Idaho tucked the vial into an outer pocket of his suit and stepped outside, repadlocking the door behind him.

After decontamination, Idaho took the sample to the lab to analyze. Dweezer and the others were setting up the DNA synthesizer, arguing over the online manual's instructions and debating the orientation of the water pipes for the autoclave. They stopped when they saw the vial of blood Idaho took out of his pocket.

"Hey, man, the biological hood's ready." Dweezer jerked a thumb at the glass-fronted box with rubber glove inserts.

Idaho flipped a switch and a pump came on, converting the box to negative pressure.

Gordon and Nate edged towards the door. "Pizza sounds good right now," said Gordon. "Anyone else hungry?"

Dweezer agreed and ran to catch up with them. With a last look over his shoulder, he followed them out the barn door and shut it firmly behind him.

Idaho was left alone with Exeter's contaminated blood. He placed the vial into the glovebox and, using the rubber gloves, slipped it into a small centrifuge.

The machine spun at three thousand r.p.m. and separated the blood by density into red blood cells, white blood cells, and plasma. Using a tiny pipette, Idaho sucked up white blood cells. He picked up one of the sequencer's manifolds. It was a white block of plastic with ninety-six wells drilled into it. The manifold fit into the sequencer. Idaho transferred the fluid to one of the wells and sealed the top with aluminum tape.

Idaho spritzed the outside of the manifold with Envirochem and removed it from the glove box. Handling this should have been done in a level-four biohazard lab, but he didn't have the facilities or the time to build one. Exeter was dying and needed treatment now. Idaho slid the manifold into place inside the automated sequencer.

The machine included a polymerase chain reaction engine that would duplicate the region of Exeter's DNA he wanted to study. To fuel the enzymic reaction, he poured a solution into the engine's reserve tank. This solution contained engineered DNA terminators seventeen to twenty nucleotides long. There were two types of fragments: one that matched the beginning of the DNA section where the AHMS virus attached, and another that matched the end. The solution also contained enzymes that constructed DNA and the free-floating adenine, cytosine, guanine, and thymine base nucleotides they used as building blocks.

The engine heated and cooled the DNA in succession. When the DNA warmed to ninety-five degrees Celsius, the strands of the double helix melted apart. The engine's temperature then slowly cooled to seventy degrees, enabling the enzymes to zip along the separated strands and rebuild their complement from the terminators.

This cycle would repeat about thirty-five times in as many minutes. Melting and rebuilding, until it contained billions of copies of the AHMS-related DNA segment.

Sequencing Exeter's entire genome would take hours. This process let him amplify and focus in on a smaller region that could be completed in less than an hour.

While the PCR engine worked, Idaho finished setting up the automated DNA synthesizer. The machine could be used to create new DNA terminators as well as construct genetic patches to cure her symptoms.

Thirty-five minutes later, the PCR engine finished and the automated sequencer's internal robotic arm injected samples into four vials containing special versions of the base nucleotides. Each of these nucleotides had an extra oxygen bound to one end to prevent builder enzymes from continuing the strand. They were color-coded by type.

When the reaction finished, the robot arm moved an intake needle into the solutions. Capillary action sucked the DNA-rich fluid into a polymer-acrylomide tube that led to the heart of the sequencer. The rough walls of the tiny tube slowed the larger fragments and let smaller fragments pass through more quickly, organizing them by length.

While the DNA progressed through the tube, shortest ends first, the sequencer read off the color markers bonded to the ends of the fragments. It displayed the colored bands on the screen as the fragments came through the capillary tube.

Idaho stood mesmerized in front of the sequencer, watching the bars creep down the computer monitor. Externally, it was an unprepossessing machine. It looked like a beige refrigerator lying on its side. But inside, tiny tubes and enzymes pried apart Exeter's secrets and decoded her body's encryption.

Cracking life's most basic program. What a rush.

Idaho's chest swelled with power. For an instant he almost welcomed the plague. Without it, he wouldn't have had access to this equipment. He stroked the enameled surface of the sequencer, feeling it hum under his hand.

But Idaho wanted to do more than crack life's codes. He wanted to write his own biological programs. He turned back to setting up the DNA synthesizer and left the sequencer to its work.

Two days after the equipment arrived, Idaho stood on an endless virtual plain with Exeter and watched long segments of her DNA turn in a spiral. The four base nucleotides were color-coded: green for adenine, red for thymine, yellow for guanine, and blue for cytosine.

He touched the spiral, and four sections blinked. "We've found the viral signature in these locations so far. We don't have a baseline, however, so we don't know what your genome looked like before the virus made modifications. Did you send in a sample to the Open Genome Project?"

"No." Exeter shook her head. "I didn't want the cops to be able to track me."

"No childhood scans?"

She looked up at him through a fringe of virtual blond bangs. "My parents barely knew I was around. They didn't worry about my being kidnapped, except maybe to hope someone would."

"All right. I'll compare your DNA against an uninfected person's to figure out what changes to make." He clapped his hands and a second spiral appeared on the plain. It writhed in time with Exeter's.

"Whose is that?" Exeter asked, peering at the linked pairs of nucleotides as if she could recognize them.

Idaho stared at the twisting spiral a moment before he found the courage to answer her. "Blue's."

Exeter twisted her mouth into a lopsided smile.

"How sweet. We'll be like brother and sister." Her avatar's face, blond and Nordic, mocked him with its similarity to Blue.

Idaho caught his breath. In his trailer, his whole body lay tense and rigid, waiting for the next blow. With Exeter, he knew it would fall.

"That's what you want, isn't it? Another twin sister? That's the real reason you won't let me die."

In the physical world, Idaho's face flushed. He prevented it from showing up on his avatar. He said quietly, "Did it ever occur that I might care for you?"

Exeter met his gaze. "Don't lie, Idy." Her words were as sharp as shards of ice. "I can take anything from you but lies." Her voice softened, became a hateful singsong. "I won't mind. Really. I never liked being myself."

Idaho yanked the needles out of his scalp, disconnecting. He slapped needles from his skin like they were biting flies. The crowded mess of his trailer comforted him. He worked to bring his breathing under control.

Exeter's words echoed in his head. The others would never know. They didn't understand the genetic programs they were developing, not like he did. They simply took his orders and ran the machines. By the time what he was doing became obvious, it would be too late.

Exeter had made the suggestion. She knew him well enough not to make the offer unless she meant it. She was many things, but no tease.

He wrapped his arms over his head. God, to have Blue back. Reborn through Exeter's body. It was insane. Idaho tightened into a ball.

One mistake and he might kill her. The changes might trigger a lethal cancer. But if he could pull it off, if he could really do this—he would have everything he had ever loved, restored to him, locked together in one woman.

Exeter's changes were slow, evidencing themselves over a month as old cells died and were replaced by the newly encoded ones. In the past week, Exeter's skin had become paler and the discoloration under her chin had faded. Her irises paled from black to midnight blue, then the electric blue of Idaho's own eyes.

When Idaho caught sight of her out of his peripheral vision, for an instant he would think he had seen Blue.

"How do you feel?" he asked.

"Better." Exeter stretched on tiptoe, raising her clasped hands far above her head. "How do I look?"

Like a blend of the old and the new, his sister and his lover together in one delicate, firm package. Idaho's mouth was dry. "Beautiful," he whispered.

Exeter's black hair was growing out in the pale gold shade Idaho had shared with his sister. The structural changes—the shape of her face, the slope of her shoulders—would take longer. Bone cells lived longer and were replaced more slowly than skin and hair follicles.

Exeter danced lightly over to Idaho, displaying grace she hadn't possessed before the change. She ran her fingertips along the sleeve of the biohazard armor. Leaned down and peered in his helmet faceplate. "Do I make you happy?"

"Yes," he groaned. He reached out with a gloved hand and fondled her hair. Imagining how it would feel under his fingers: silky, soft. "You should cut off the black."

Exeter pulled back for a second and turned away, her spine stiff. That was pure Exeter. Then she sighed and turned back, a manipulating smile on her face. "If I do, will you bring me my drugs?"

A chill closed in on his heart. "I thought we were past that. You're going to live. I'm making you . . . better."

Exeter flopped into the driver's chair. She pleaded with her hands. "I need something to get me through the day. This place, not being able to go anywhere, to touch anyone. You may be able to hibernate on the

Net for weeks at a time, but not me. I need people. I'm going crazy in this fishbowl."

"I'm here," Idaho said, reaching out to her.

Exeter pushed his armored arms away. "I don't want to hug a robot."

"Ex." Her rejections hurt more now that she looked like Blue.

Exeter's eyes glittered. "Stay with me tonight. Take off that armor and stay. If you can keep me well, you can cure yourself."

Idaho took a step back.

"What's the matter?" Exeter's face screwed up. "Is the cure good enough for me, but not precious Idaho? Scared to put your life on the line? A minute ago, you told me I would live—was that a lie?"

"The machines—I need to be able to maintain them."

"Let Dweezer and the others do that. Write the programs from here, or I can move into your trailer. Please." She walked up to him and placed her hands on his shoulders. "Don't leave me here alone . . . waiting to die."

The catch in her voice resonated in his own chest. He'd felt that way when Blue had died. "Don't leave me," he had cried, tears rolling down his cheeks. His lungs burned with remembered emotion. "Blue," he whispered.

Exeter's head was down and she didn't see the name he mouthed.

Idaho closed his eyes, feeling the pain of his sister's death streak like jolts of electricity emanating from his heart. It was crazy to deliberately infect yourself with an incurable disease, but . . . there were a thousand sharp things in the camper. A thousand ways for Exeter to end her life. He'd seen panic and desperation in her eyes. She was right: He couldn't keep her caged like an animal . . . alone.

Idaho rocked on his heels. He couldn't bear to lose her again, to have Exeter die and take the blossoming vestiges of Blue with her. To lose them both. It would be better to die in her arms.

And maybe he could save himself as he'd saved her. As long as they kept ahead of the lethal changes. They could touch. Was it worth the risk?

Idaho opened his eyes.

Exeter's head was still lowered, and tears fell from her eyes. "I don't know how much longer I can live like this," she whispered.

They were the words Blue had spoken the night before she died. His heart raced and adrenaline shot through his veins. No. No. Anything but that. Idaho ripped off his helmet, tearing the seals in his haste.

He encircled Exeter-Blue in his armored body. "I'll keep you safe," he whispered into her neck. "We'll never be alone again."

They spent the night together. Idaho shaved Exeter's head, until only the golden hairs remained. She ran her hands over every part of his body, touching him, tasting him, loving him. At dawn, exhausted, Exeter fell asleep, curled into the crook of Idaho's body.

Idaho lay awake, watching the darkness fade from the sky. He was infected now. The knowledge weighed heavily on him. His skills with genetic modification were good, but his own life hadn't depended on them before now. If he got sick, how could he cure himself?

He would teach Dweezer and the others, but how could he control them when he was trapped inside the quarantine camper? What was there to prevent them towing the camper to the side of the road and leaving him and Exeter to rot? Or worse. Images of flames consuming the camper played in his mind. They were deathly afraid of the plague. Would they go that far? They owed Idaho their lives for taking them in. But how far would that loyalty go? Idaho had learned early in life not to rely on other people's sentiment.

Whatever happened, he must protect Exeter-Blue. If it came down to a choice, he'd sacrifice Dweezer and the others to ensure her safety. The thought of killing left him hollow and cold inside. But he would not—could not—let anything harm the ones he loved again.

And then it came to him, in a flash of simplicity. He needed Dweezer and his friends' help, their loyalty. What better way than to make them dependent on the ranch's cures, too? He would simply put his biohazard suit back on and go outside. They wouldn't know he was infected until they too had contracted the plague.

Then it would be too late to leave. They would need him and his cures. They'd be trapped together, like family, dependent on the cures the ranch produced and unable to leave for fear of being caught and forcibly quarantined.

Idaho left Exeter sleeping in the van. He put his helmet back on, tucking the torn seal into the collar. There were lights on in the house, but the barn was dark.

Idaho slipped into the makeshift lab and took a sample of his own blood. He dropped it in the sequencer. Two hours later, he had his result. It verified that he had the plague. He would have to sequence his own samples when the others weren't around and order additional supplies to cover those he'd use for his own cures. The others must not suspect. Not until it was too late. He would need their help in the weeks to come.

Shouts outside his room startled Geoffrey Allen from a review of his investments. His first reaction was fear. Had the complex been overrun again by rioters? Hospitals had been torched in Europe and Las Vegas. Why not here?

He fumbled with his palmtop to contact Lillith. There was no response. He tried Dr. Danvers. Nothing. None of the physicians who treated him were at their desks.

The door to the amphitheatre flew open, and Geoffrey pressed himself against the wall. The curtain slid back. Lillith stood breathless on the other side of the glass, her face wide in a jubilant smile. "They've done it. The Japanese trials—" She put her palms on her knees to catch her breath.

"What? What?" Geoffrey asked.

"The Japanese have released the results of their vaccine trials. Inoculated health workers have been protected from the disease for a month. It's still in the early stages so there's no press release yet, but finally we have a weapon to stop the spread of AHMS."

Geoffrey sagged back on the bed. "That's great news."

Lillith cocked her head at him. "You're not excited?"

"I am, only . . ." Geoffrey gestured at the walls that enclosed him. "A vaccine doesn't do much for those already infected."

Lillith touched her fingertips to the glass separating them. "Don't worry. If we can develop a vaccine, a cure can't be far off. Think of all the medical resources we'll be able to shift towards treating the disease, finding a cure."

Geoffrey looked down at his parti-colored palms, thinking about the economics of supply and demand. When only a small percentage of the population was infected, would the drug companies still research new therapies? "I hope you're right."

Idaho was in the barn, checking the sequencing progress of his latest samples when Dweezer danced in, jubilant.

"Did you hear, man? There's a fucking vaccine! Gordon pulled it off a private CDC transmission from Japan." Dweezer hugged himself with joy. "The FDA's still testing it for release, but hell, man, if we can get the formula off the Net"—he grinned from ear to ear—"and you know we can get *anything* off the Net. We've got this sweet biolab right *here*—we can manufacture our own." He punched Idaho on the arm. "Think of how we can clean up with a black market version."

Cold irony swept through Idaho's body. How like the world to find a vaccine the night after he'd contracted AHMS.

"No." He looked up from the sequencer. "Fixing Exeter's DNA is our priority. We can't waste time on a vaccine until she's cured."

Dweezer's heavy brows drew together. "It's all the same thing. If we're protected from the plague, we can help her without worrying about getting sick."

"And if you waste time and supplies on developing a vaccine, we might not have enough for Exeter's cure or it might come too late. I won't have you jeopardizing her health with an outside project."

"Hey, man, we'll buy our own supplies, do the work on our own time."

"While Exeter is still sick, you don't have your own time. You work for me, 24/7. If you don't like that, you and your friends can leave. I didn't ask you to come here."

Dweezer shook his head in disbelief. "Man, are you *loco*? This thing could kill us. You should let us manufacture the vaccine."

"After Exeter is cured."

Dweezer looked at Idaho as if he were insane.

And why not, Idaho thought. By their standards, perhaps he was. He bent back to the sequencer and listened to the hum as the robot arm positioned the intake needle into a new sample. There was no time on the equipment for side projects; a side project was already under way.

He would have to work quickly. Idaho had exposed them all to AHMS at breakfast, but there was no telling if they were infected. If they became vaccinated before catching the plague, he'd have no hold over them. And now he needed them more than ever.

That night Idaho searched the lab for evidence Dweezer was working on a vaccine. He found nothing. The refrigerator contained only Blue's treatments and samples. He'd labeled them himself and knew them all by heart. Sixteen treatments, four samples, including yesterday's. He'd looked at the Japanese formula when it had been posted to the Web. It was an unstable compound and needed to be refrigerated.

Idaho swiveled his head in the direction of the farmhouse. The kitchen. They were all in this together, Nate and Gordon and Dweezer. But of course they would be.

Idaho walked across the yard to the farmhouse, up the back steps and into the kitchen. He opened the fridge. It was filled with beer, sodas, and old pizza boxes. He opened the meat drawer. Nothing but a package of lunch meat, turning green inside its Ziploc container.

The salad crisper held a head of lettuce melting into blackish ooze. Idaho felt around it to the back of the drawer.

His hand encountered glass vials.

"Whatcha doing?" Dweezer asked from behind him.

Idaho controlled his startle reflex and eased the drawer shut. He pulled a can of Mountain Dew free from its box and held it up when he turned around. "I wanted a soda."

Dweezer's eyes flicked to the salad drawer. Then he smiled. It was a brittle expression. Even if he hadn't found Dweezer's secret, Idaho would have known he was hiding something.

"How's Exeter?" Dweezer asked.

"Good," Idaho said. "The corrections to her serotonin deficiency are taking."

"Glad to hear it." Dweezer slid past Idaho, grabbed a beer, and shut the refrigerator. Positioning his body between it and Idaho.

Idaho tipped the drink in a salute to Dweezer. "Going to turn in," he said. "How about you?"

Dweezer shrugged. "Nate and Gordon want me to join them in the latest online game, it's a team shooter."

Idaho left the farmhouse and snuck around a circuitous path to his trailer. He felt exhausted. Was this a symptom of the plague? He didn't know. Dweezer's work worried him. If the others had already taken the vaccine, his plans to keep them here, to help him maintain his condition, would fail.

Idaho locked the trailer door behind him. Then he stripped down to his underwear and began inserting the dozens of needles that would connect him to the Net.

It took him two hours to find Dweezer's research. He was working on reproducing the vaccine. Human trials were set for tonight, after Idaho had gone to his trailer.

Idaho snuck back to the farmhouse, creeping along the floorboards so they wouldn't creak. He heard booms and crashes from the twelve surround-sound speakers in the living room. Dweezer, Nate, and Gordon wore full-immersion VR helmets. As long as he didn't trip across them, they'd never know he was there.

Idaho opened the refrigerator slowly, depressing the light button with his thumb to keep the interior light from coming on.

One by one he dumped out the three vials of vaccine and replaced them with saline solution.

Then he went back to the barn and opened the encrypted file he had started on himself. So far, the only error showing up in his genome was what Lillith and the other scientists called galactosemia, a flaw in the enzyme that breaks down certain carbohydrates. It was one of the first variants of the plague identified. An easy fix.

Idaho took a sip of Mountain Dew. As the carbonated drink burned down the back of his throat, he thought about Dweezer and the others. He was worried about what they would do when they discovered his betrayal. Dweezer, at least, carried a knife. In a fury, he might attack Idaho. Do something they would all regret.

Idaho had a cache of guns in his trailer, hidden under a floor panel. But guns were only useful if you had them with you. And he hadn't cleaned or fired them in years.

Dweezer was a small man. Idaho might be able to subdue him alone, but not with Nate and Gordon backing him up.

Idaho pressed his thumbs at the pressure point where his eyebrows began and sucked in a breath. If only he were stronger, he could protect Exeter from them. If he'd been able to defend himself as a child, he could have saved Blue from the imprisonment that had starved her and ultimately had ended her life.

He pounded his fist against the metal table and the monitor shook. The vibration made the colored lines of his DNA dance, suggesting a solution.

Why not? If he asked Exeter to change into Blue, why shouldn't he redesign himself as her protector?

Looked at one way, the plague was a deadly disease. But the very attributes that made it such a tenacious killer—its mutability and ability to rewrite DNA—also made it the perfect vehicle for change. Idaho took another sip of his soda. Hadn't that been Fowler's original intent? If the lipid packaging had been properly removed, the virus—instead of a deadly plague—would have been the ultimate tool for human expression and improvement.

CHAPTER 13

The Japanese released an official report about the vaccine. The news spread on emergency bulletins, through broadcast emails, and by people calling each other, crying and shouting the news over the airwaves. The phone networks shut down for hours at a time, overloaded with traffic.

The day was an instant worldwide holiday. People who had hidden for months in their houses wept for joy. They had survived. Bottles of hoarded liquor were broken out and families toasted one another. Cheering could be heard in the still empty streets.

After the CDC employees had been vaccinated, they traveled to Atlanta's suburbs, injecting people.

Lillith and Danvers rode in the vans with the medical technicians. Every hand was needed to spread the vaccine as swiftly as possible. And this was a moment in history Lillith wouldn't have missed for the world.

They no longer wore quarantine suits, and Lillith reveled in the crisp fall air on her face. The slowdown of industry had cleaned the atmosphere, and she inhaled deeply the scent of wood smoke and Virginia pines.

People welcomed Lillith and Danvers into their homes, offering the best of their dwindling reserves of food, crying with joy as children were injected. Despite the CDC's warning that the vaccine would take a week to reach full effectiveness, some people ran out into the street, shouting at the top of their lungs and dancing on cars in their happiness and relief.

On November 12 the world came back from the dead.

Three months later, Geoffrey sat cross-legged on the bed, managing his investments, when the door to his chamber opened.

"Time for another blood sample?" he asked without looking up. He'd been pricked so often they were having to draw blood from new places—the back of his hand, the underside of his knee—to find unscarred skin.

"No," Danvers said. He entered carrying a quarantine suit.

Geoffrey looked up. "What's that for?"

"It's for you." Danvers laid the suit next to Geoffrey. "You're being transferred."

"Where?"

"A containment camp at the Fort Stewart army base." Danvers looked unhappy. "It's not my idea. Congress has passed the AHMS Containment Act— all infected persons must be contained in special facilities."

Geoffrey gazed around the sterile quarantine chamber with its clean-room oxygen ports, sprinklers filled with Envirochem, and ultraviolet sterilizers. "This doesn't qualify?"

Danvers spread his hands in a gesture of supplication. "It's not my call."

Geoffrey set aside his laptop and swung his legs over the side of the bed. "Doesn't the CDC need samples of my blood to research a cure?"

Danvers looked at the ground. "Our research team has been re-purposed. The top priority now is finding more efficient ways to synthesize the vaccine."

Geoffrey's hands tightened into fists. "And while you work on the vaccine, anyone currently infected is herded into camps to *die*?"

Danvers sighed. He said, "Congress has decided to

focus on the welfare of the billions who are not yet infected. It may be years before we find a cure. Or decades." His shoulders slumped. "Or never. We can't risk public health on quixotic hopes."

Geoffrey shoved the suit off the bed. "And if I refuse to put this on?"

Danvers bent to retrieve the suit and held it out to Geoffrey. "If you refuse, you'll be sedated. One way or the other, you are going to Fort Stewart."

CDC researchers loaded Geoffrey into a quarantine van. There were four other passengers huddled inside. It was his first real human contact in six months, but instead of being glad, Geoffrey was scared. He had survived the plague this long because of his isolation from other infected patients and their variations of AHMS. Now that protection was gone.

The others in the van were an old man, his eyes yellow with jaundice or some other ailment, who lay on the floor of the van in a fetal position; a red-haired woman with milk-white skin who clasped a flaccid toddler to her chest; and the last person was so thin that Geoffrey couldn't tell if it was a man or woman. Lanky brown hair covered the face, and the person sat tucked into a ball in the corner of the van, arms wrapped around its legs.

No one spoke during the five-hour drive to Fort Stewart. The only sounds were the hum of the road and the moans of the old man. The van stank of sweat and desperation.

When the van stopped, the back doors were thrown open and orderlies in white uniforms helped Geoffrey and the others out. The orderlies were not wearing biohazard suits. Geoffrey guessed the camp staff had been vaccinated and was safe from contracting AHMS.

Two other vans were unloading patients. The compound beyond the parking lot was composed of squat cinderblock buildings and surrounded by a fence topped with razor wire. A faded sign near the front still read ENLISTED BARRACKS A1. At intervals along the fence, towers had been erected and were patrolled by guards carrying assault rifles.

This can't be happening, thought Geoffrey, clutching his laptop to his chest. *Not in the United States of America.*

One of the guards prodded him forward with the butt of his rifle. Geoffrey stumbled after the young mother and the skinny person.

Twenty infected people stood or sat on the asphalt of a basketball court. Some, like Geoffrey, were piebald. There were others with oozing rashes or hacking coughs; some were bleeding from the nose and eyes. Their symptoms were different, but their faces wore the same expression: despair.

When the last of the vans was unloaded, a man wearing the uniform of an army captain addressed them. His voice was amplified by a clip-on microphone. "Welcome to the United States Army Quarantine Hospital at Fort Stewart. Our staff is here to serve you and treat your symptoms. The accommodations are not posh, but they will suffice. The guards"—he pointed up at the towers—"are here to protect you and to turn back any confused individuals who try to wander off the compound. Do you understand?"

There was a chorus of moans and assents from the crowd. Geoffrey frowned.

"Are there any questions?"

Geoffrey raised his hand.

The captain narrowed his eyes on Geoffrey and pointed.

Geoffrey said in a strong, clear voice, "Why are all these patients confined together? That will only create new variations of the plague. We should be quarantined separately."

A ripple of concern spread through the crowd. Heads turned back to the captain.

He pointed at Geoffrey and conferred quietly with an aide, then turned back. "Are you a doctor?"

"No, but—"

"Then do not prescribe treatment. We have qualified medical personnel who have planned the treatment and recovery of our patients." He waved his arms. The guards herded the crowd towards the central mess hall and told them to form a line.

Just inside the door was a folding table; behind it sat a gray-haired woman in her fifties. She wore a no-nonsense expression and the uniform of an army nurse. When Geoffrey's turn came, she pointed to the palm-shaped reader. Geoffrey pressed his right hand on it.

The woman read from the laptop screen in front of her. "Geoffrey Preston Allen." Her eyebrows rose. "How the mighty have fallen. Have a seat."

Geoffrey took the proffered orange plastic chair.

The woman scrubbed Geoffrey's middle finger with an alcohol pad. Then she pricked it with a spring-loaded lancet. She dropped the lancet into a sharps container and squeezed a drop of Geoffrey's blood into a capillary tube. When the tube was full, she capped the ends and scanned the tiny bar code on its side.

"What's that for?" Geoffrey asked, as the woman cleaned his left finger with an alcohol pad.

"Genetic baseline," she said.

"But the CDC already has extensive records of my genome. It's been completely sequenced."

The woman snorted. "You may have been something special out in the real world, but in here you're just another case." She picked up a silver cylinder. "Hand, please."

Geoffrey put his left hand in hers, feeling uneasy.

The nurse sterilized the skin between his thumb and forefinger with another pad and then pressed it against one end of the cylinder. She pressed a button on top.

Geoffrey's hand stung like fire and he tried to draw back, but the woman held his wrist tightly. When she released him, he rubbed the spot between his fingers and felt a hard knot like a grain of sand. "What was that?"

"Identichip," she said, tapping an entry into the computer.

Geoffrey was outraged. "But you already had my palm print on file. What gives you the right—"

She held up a palm, cutting off his protest. "Standard procedure." Her voice was matter-of-fact. "The plague changes everything: face, retina, fingerprints. It's the only way to verify identity." She called to the line of people behind Geoffrey, "Next."

The guards prodded Geoffrey along, and she pricked the finger of the toddler, who was too weak to cry.

The next station gave him a bar of soap with an acrid smell.

Geoffrey looked up, his nose wrinkled in distaste.

"Kills lice," the man said.

"We haven't done anything wrong," Geoffrey said. "You're treating us like prisoners." Geoffrey had never been so rudely handled before in his life. It was outrageous. "I want to talk to my lawyer."

"Later." The man's face was impassive. "Move along."

The guards herded the men and women together into the showers and told them to strip. Women sobbed and Geoffrey spent the entire humiliating time staring at his feet. This couldn't be happening. It was unreal, like a bad dream.

Lillith went to check on Geoffrey Allen and found his quarantine room empty. The bedding had been stripped, and the floor gleamed with decontamination fluid.

Her heart fluttered. Had he died during Danvers's shift? His condition was stable—she would have been contacted if something happened. Lillith marched out of the observation theatre to Dr. Lam's office. "Where's Geoffrey Allen?"

Dr. Lam removed his VR goggles and sat up in his chair. "Lillith, hello. Mr. Allen has been transferred to a containment camp."

His last two words stopped Lillith in her tracks. "A

containment camp? But all those variations . . . and when the other patients find out who he is—that he caused the plague—they'll kill him."

Lam's eyes were hard. "Your concern for Mr. Allen is admirable, but the Containment Act requires his transfer."

"That act was passed months ago. Why move him now? Is it because his funding for the Open Genome Project has run out? Is that what this is all about—money?"

"Don't be insulting. I have shielded you—both of you—from certain political realities. That is over. He must go to a camp."

Lillith ground her teeth to keep from shouting her next words. She took a deep breath, exhaled. "Herding the infected together as if they were cattle—it's criminally negligent."

Dr. Lam pinched the skin between his brows. "What would you have us do? This is a research facility, not a hospital. When there is plague, people will die. It is unavoidable."

Lillith jabbed her finger in the direction of the labs. "Geoffrey Allen spent billions to fund research for a cure. Half the equipment used by the Japanese to develop the vaccine was bought with Allen funds. We're going to reward that by dumping him in a containment camp?"

The corners of Dr. Lam's mouth pulled down in sympathy. "I agree with you in principle, but it's not politically feasible." He raised his palms, pleading with her. "It is a tragedy, but we may be able to do nothing for the millions who are already infected. We should focus our efforts on protecting the billions who are still healthy."

"I can't accept that—I won't!"

Dr. Lam shook his head. "What will you do? Travel to the containment camp? Treat the infected with cold compresses and painkillers? Would that be the most effective use of your talents? Is that what Geoffrey would want you to do?"

Lillith remembered Geoffrey's sad blue eyes, his muted reaction when she told him about the vaccine. Had he suspected this was coming?

"Or would Geoffrey," Dr. Lam said, "want you to do whatever you could to stop this plague, to make the vaccine one hundred percent effective and help wipe this scourge off the face of the earth?"

Tears of frustration burned in Lillith's eyes.

"We need your mind and experience here, Lillith, to continue the fight against the virus."

She couldn't convince him to bring Geoffrey back to the CDC quarantine unit. Even if Dr. Lam had agreed with her, the decision had been made at a higher level.

As much as she wanted to go, Lam was right. She couldn't help Geoffrey without the resources of the CDC.

Lillith was the link connecting Idaho's unconventional research with the mainstream medical authorities. She had to stay and keep those lines of communication open.

As if from a distance, Lillith heard her own voice: "You're right, I'll stay," and felt another piece of her soul chip away.

When Geoffrey came out of the shower, his clothes and bag were gone. A placid-looking army private handed him a fluorescent orange jumpsuit with a numbered patch above the left pocket. It looked like a convict's uniform.

"Where are my clothes; where's my bag?" Geoffrey asked.

The guard, whose name tag read ADAMS, said, "They've been stored in a locker for you. There isn't room on the ward for personal possessions."

"A locker where?"

"Later. It's a few minutes to lights out."

He wanted to place a call to his lawyer, anyone who could help him get transferred out of this place. "I just need a minute with—"

Adams, gently but firmly, pushed Geoffrey through the door. He showed Geoffrey his bunk, 57C; it was the top of three bunks. "We put the healthy ones on top," he explained, "since they can manage the ladders."

Geoffrey crawled up to the top bunk, the worn springs of the bed sagging alarmingly. The man below him coughed wetly.

"You all right?" Geoffrey asked, looking down at the man over the edge.

The man, in his mid-thirties with prematurely graying hair plastered to his head by sweat, looked glassy-eyed up at Geoffrey. "Are any of us?" he croaked, and coughed again.

Adams left and a few minutes later the lights went out. The darkened ward was filled with coughs, snuffling, low-pitched moans, and the sobs of a woman. It smelled of urine and the pasty, sweet scent of sick people. Geoffrey rolled onto his stomach and lay awake a long time before sleep claimed him.

Coughing woke Geoffrey. For a drowsy minute, he thought his cystic fibrosis had returned. Many nights he had woken up gagging, unable to breathe. But it was the man in the bunk below him. The chrome poles rattled with the force of his coughing.

Geoffrey leaned over and whispered, "Can I get you anything?"

"Water," the man croaked between coughs. "Water."

Geoffrey climbed down. He threaded his way through the rows of bunks and headed down the corridor that led to the mess hall.

Adams, a pistol strapped to his hip, blocked his way. "Back to bed." He gestured at the darkened barracks.

"I need water," Geoffrey whispered.

Adams pointed at a nearby fountain.

"Not for myself, for one of the others. I need a glass."

Adams shook his head. "The mess hall doesn't open until seven a.m."

Geoffrey cocked his head to look up at the guard.

"You'd begrudge a dying man a sip of water because the mess hall isn't open?"

Adams looked out across the ward, his face wrinkling with dismay. Then he shook his head. "I'm sorry. It's against regulations."

Geoffrey had been hearing that a lot lately. He tried to cup water in his hands, but it leaked from his fingers before he could take three steps. Geoffrey looked at the spilled water, then up at Adams. "Where's the doctor on call?"

The guard pointed at a small table set up in the opposite corner of the barracks. A tired, thin man sat hunched over in a pool of light.

"I need a glass of water for one of the patients," Geoffrey said. "He can't stop coughing."

The man was in his late twenties, with army-cropped brown hair. The label on his lab coat read DR. C. J. ANDERSON. He passed Geoffrey a plastic cup used to dispense pills. He was only a few years older than Geoffrey. "I haven't seen you around before." His vowels were softened by a Southern accent.

Geoffrey took the cup. "I was transferred from Atlanta. Could you come take a look at my bunkmate? He's been coughing all night."

Dr. Anderson grabbed a medical kit and followed Geoffrey to the bunk.

When they got there, the man had stopped breathing. Geoffrey's numb hand lost its hold on the cup of water and the plastic bounced on the floor, spilling his good intentions on the unyielding concrete.

The doctor felt the man's throat for a pulse and put his head to the man's chest. "Damn." He dragged the man out of his bunk and onto the floor. Dr. Anderson rifled through his bag and pulled out a portable defibrillator. He broke open a foil packet and smeared gel on the man's chest and, when the paddles were charged, shocked him. There was no response.

Dr. Anderson repeated the process five more times, then checked the man's chest with a stethoscope and shook his head. "He's gone."

The man had died alone in a room full of people.

Dr. Anderson wiped his brow. "If this were a real hospital"—he glowered at his medical bag—"if I had a trauma unit, I might've been able to save him."

He reached into his bag and pulled out something that looked like a money clip. He slipped it over the flesh between the man's thumb and fingers, reading the implanted identichip. He placed a call with his palmtop. "Another one. ID number 53746. He's on the floor. No response to the defibrillator." A pause as he listened to the person on the other end of the line. "I don't care. When someone codes on my watch, I attempt resuscitation."

The doctor folded his palmtop back into his kit. He patted Geoffrey on the shoulder. "I'm sorry, Mr. Allen, but we have hundreds of terminally ill people packed together; we lose several each night."

A pair of guards with a stretcher came to retrieve the body. They wore headlamps to navigate the darkened room. When they were gone, Geoffrey crawled back into his bunk. He was alone among hundreds of other patients in identical beds. Those who had been here for more than a day didn't even look at the guards or what they were doing; they simply rolled over to avoid the light and went back to sleep.

Geoffrey felt small, insignificant. His billions were gone, spent in a fight against an invisible enemy. If he'd had funds, he would have turned the camps into hospitals, paid for quarantine rooms where people wouldn't cross-infect each other. This camp was more than a waiting place to die; it was a breeding ground for new strains of the virus.

With hundreds of these disease camps set up around the world, breeding new strains of AHMS, the vaccine wouldn't work forever. A new, resistant strain was inevitable. The fight wasn't won until everyone was cured. Why didn't the government understand that?

Geoffrey remembered the man's hacking cough and wondered if he'd just picked up a new variation.

In the darkness, a voice hissed out of a row of bunks

beside him. "I heard the intake officer called you 'Geoffrey Preston Allen.' Then the night doctor calls you 'Mr. Allen.' You the man that started this plague?"

Geoffrey froze. Was it his imagination or had the barracks suddenly become very quiet? He felt as if every patient in the room were listening for his reply.

"I'm here to be treated for AHMS, just like you." He coughed and rolled over on his side.

The man's voice was bitter as acid. "That isn't what I asked. Did you start this damn plague?"

Whispered voices from all around him repeated, "Did you?"

Geoffrey didn't reply. If he ran, could he make it to the guards before the others caught him?

A hand grabbed Geoffrey's arm and hauled him half off the top bunk.

Geoffrey pushed at the fingers, trying to break the man's grip. "It wasn't my fault!" he yelled. "I didn't know."

The man dragged him off the bunk and threw him to the concrete floor.

Stars flared in Geoffrey's vision and the air was knocked from his lungs. He gasped, unable to breathe.

"I lost my wife and son to this damn disease," the man said. A fist connected with Geoffrey's cheek.

Pain shot across his head, and Geoffrey held up his forearms to shield his face. He heard the rustling of bedclothes and the squeak of springs as other patients crawled out of their bunks.

"Geoffrey Allen," they whispered. But in their mouths it was a curse. It became a chant, in time with the blows that rained down from all sides.

These zombies who had resigned themselves to death found, in his punishment, a new animation.

Geoffrey curled into a ball as kicks rained down on him from all sides.

He tasted blood and knew this time he would die.

*   *   *

A week after Idaho had discovered the vaccine in the kitchen, Dweezer, Nate, and Gordon came down with the flu. Or, at least, what they thought was the flu.

While they lay groaning on couches in the living room of the farmhouse, Idaho had the lab to himself. He took advantage of the privacy, running the machines 24/7 to accelerate the changes to Exeter and himself.

He also synthesized medicines for Dweezer and his friends to counteract the protein imbalances the plague wreaked on their systems. It was easy to learn what variants they carried; he just sequenced his own blood as they cross-contaminated each other.

When the treatment was done, Idaho took it back to the farmhouse and mixed it into canned chicken soup and served it to them. He kept his movements deliberately slow, to prevent them from noticing the changes he'd made to his nervous system.

"How do you feel?" Idaho asked, handing them each a bowl.

Gordon wrinkled his nose at the food. "Got any pizza?"

"Drink it," Idaho said. "It will help."

Dweezer sneezed into his sleeve. "Man, the rest of the world catches the plague and we get the flu. How stupid is that?"

"How do you know it's not the plague?" Idaho asked.

Nate and Gordon exchanged a look with Dweezer.

Dweezer shrugged. "Come on, man, we've been taking precautions. And if it were the plague, you'd be sick too. And you look fine." He cocked his head and studied Idaho. "You been working out?"

"I've done some self-improvement." Idaho jerked his thumb towards the door. "I'll be in the lab. Working on new designs for the CDC."

"Hey, why you doing all that work for them? What did they ever do for you?"

Idaho thought of Lillith and how she'd eased Blue's pain at the end. "They financed the lab," he said, and left the room.

Geoffrey woke to a bright light overhead. There were words, but they were fuzzy and indistinct in his blood-filled ears. His left eye was swollen shut.

"Are you all right?" the guard asked.

Geoffrey tried to laugh, but it came out as a series of spasming coughs. His tongue was thick and he tasted blood. He shook his head in answer and stars lit in his brain, burning through his skull.

"Let me see him," said Dr. Anderson. Geoffrey forced himself through the implications. He was still alive; nothing dead could be in this much pain. Not much time had elapsed, because this same doctor was on call.

Geoffrey was loaded onto a gurney and escorted to an examination room.

"Dear God," Dr. Anderson said when he examined Geoffrey. Then he began murmuring words into his palmtop: "Concussion, possible fractured ulna, multiple contusions . . ."

Geoffrey let the words detailing his injuries wash over him. He tried to pick out different melodies in his symphony of pain. His head pounded like a bass drum, setting the rhythm for the lesser aches in his muscles and bones. His arm and face played counterpoint, warring for his attention. The rest of his body filled in pinpricks and aches to round out the chorus.

Dr. Anderson palpated Geoffrey's arm and wrapped it tightly with an Ace bandage. "Whoever sent you here was an idiot," he muttered as he swabbed antiseptic on the cuts on Geoffrey's face. "I'm going to get you transferred out of here."

Geoffrey tried to nod, but the motion reawakened the crescendo in his head. "Yes," he groaned through thick lips, "out of here."

During his CDC quarantine, he'd heard that Orcas

Island had been annexed by the army for use as a containment facility.

Geoffrey clawed at the lapel of Dr. Anderson's white coat. "Home. Want to go home."

CHAPTER 14

The early morning sunshine lit up the ranch, sparkling off dewdrops on the grass. Idaho strode across the driveway to the house. He felt stronger than ever. His latest batches of changes had been successful.

The farmhouse lights were off, Dweezer and the others still asleep in the living room. They still thought they had the flu. Soon Idaho would make them well, once he had perfected himself to the point where they were no longer a threat to him or Exeter.

Inside the barn, Idaho clicked on the lights. The yellow beams shone through airborne dust motes. He closed the door behind him and picked up five of the white plastic manifolds used in the sequencer. With a last look over his shoulder to make sure the barn door was closed, Idaho tossed all five into the air. They arced high, diverging to different quadrants of the barn as they fell towards earth.

Not one hit the ground.

Idaho caught the last one behind his back, smiling. The reflex tuning had worked beautifully.

He had strength and speed. Now he needed a weapon. Something Dweezer couldn't disarm.

Idaho punctured his finger to get a blood sample for the sequencer. He popped Exeter's latest sample and his own into the automated machine. Each morning he checked their genomes, to make sure the virus hadn't mutated, hadn't added a harmful variation. One wrong encoding of a critical enzyme and either one of them could die within days. The price of genetic freedom was constant vigilance.

The reagent wells in the base of the machine were low; hadn't he refilled them last night? Idaho poured more reagent from the amber-colored glass bottles, then started the sequencing cycle.

While the machine began the PCR cycle, Idaho researched the genomes of venomous snakes.

"Idaho, what's wrong?" Exeter's face swam in his vision. She was somewhere floating above him in yellowish haze.

A cold hand touched his forehead. Idaho realized he was sweating. The thin mattress beneath him was soaked. "Water," he croaked. "Wat-er."

His eyes rolled around the room. Exeter's camper. He'd begun sleeping there most nights, sneaking in when Dweezer, Gordon, and Nate had gone to bed or were occupied online.

Idaho couldn't breathe. His throat was swollen nearly shut.

Exeter brought him a plastic cup.

He sipped from it and gagged. Stomach cramps doubled him over. Idaho pressed his face into the bed and moaned. He hadn't felt this bad since the beatings.

"What is it? What's going on?" Exeter's hands fluttered around him, wanting to help, afraid to touch him. She picked up her cell phone. "Should I call Dweezer?"

"No." Idaho grabbed the machine away from her and held it while another cramp gripped his body. Then he pulled up a search engine and entered "rattlesnake bite."

The symptoms scrolled by: vomiting, swelling, respiratory distress, necrosis, and permanent tissue damage.

He'd done something wrong; his body was poisoning itself. "The lab . . . get me to the lab."

If he'd been honest with Dweezer, Gordon, and Nate, he could have gone to them for help. But not now, not weakened as he was. He needed to be strong to face them when they found out.

He would have to heal himself.

Exeter put her shoulder under his armpit and hauled Idaho to his feet. Together they lurched through the camper.

At the door, Idaho grabbed the doorframe. "No. You can't go out there. Too risky. If they see . . ."

Exeter smoothed a lock of hair out of his eyes. Doing that, she looked more like Blue than ever. "You idiot. You'll never make it there alive. If they find out tonight, they find out. They'll need you alive to make cures for them."

"Must be strong . . . to face them."

"Hold on." Exeter transferred Idaho's weight to the doorframe. She took two steps to the kitchen and came back a second later, a sheathed butcher knife tucked into her waistband. "Tonight I'll be strong enough for the both of us."

She helped him down the metal steps and across the courtyard. The night was dark and clear; stars twinkled down on them from billions of miles away.

Inside, the barn was black and cold. Idaho shivered uncontrollably.

Exeter turned on the lights and helped him into a chair. Then she wandered around the lab, touching the glove box, the sequencer, the racks of manifolds and bottles of nucleic acids.

Idaho rolled his chair to the nearest computer. He logged on and opened the encrypted files containing his changes. The characters onscreen wouldn't stay still. They jittered in his vision so he could barely read them. Idaho pressed his palms into his eyes until he saw sparks. When he looked up, his vision was clearer.

Simple. Nothing fancy. Reverse the change that had added poison-producing DNA. Idaho opened his most recent file. Found the change. Reversing it was simple using the helper applications he had written. He specified the payload gene as his original intron, and the gene that produced the toxin as the one to modify.

There was no time to simulate the changes in his model of his DNA, to test for side effects or unexpected reactions. He needed a cure as soon as possible. Idaho transmitted the file to the DNA sequencer, canceling and flushing its current job and replacing it with his cure.

The display on the front of the machine indicated that it had begun the cleaning and sterilization cycle.

Idaho slumped in his chair. "Antivenin," he croaked. "Snakebite kit in the trailer."

Exeter ran out of the barn and came back minutes later with a needle and vial. With expert ease, she slid the needle into his vein and injected him.

Idaho's forehead was slick with sweat and he was shaking.

"What do we do now?" she asked.

"We wait." Either the antivenin would counteract the venom his body was producing long enough for the cure to take effect—or it wouldn't. He reached out his hand to Exeter and she grasped it.

Together, they waited for the machine to finish.

Geoffrey was transferred to Orcas Island three days later. He felt both relieved and anxious. Relieved because he left behind the people who had so brutally beaten him. Anxious because he didn't know what kind of reception waited for him on Orcas Island.

He wore a quarantine suit for his transfer. They flew him to the naval base on Whidbey Island; from there he traveled by ferry to Orcas Island. It was a passenger-only ferry, commandeered by the CDC to transport the infected.

The day was fine. Fluffy white clouds drifted in a clear blue sky, and the waters of Puget Sound were calm. Two coast guard speedboats escorted the ferry, warning away fishing boats and pleasure craft.

Orcas Island's remote location made it the perfect quarantine site. There were no bridges. The only way onto the island was by boat or plane. The other San Juan Islands were too far away for infected people to reach by swimming.

The island had been abandoned when the plague

broke out. Emanating from the Allen compound, the disease had killed all of the original inhabitants. The once exclusive Rosario Resort was now home to the lowest of untouchables and their keepers.

As the ferry approached the dock, a pair of seagulls wheeled over Puget Sound, dipping into the sea to catch minnows. In the background rose the lush green forests of Mount Constitution. How could there be sickness among such beauty?

The passengers were herded into two vans: one bound for Rosario Resort, the other for the Allen compound. These, the two largest estates on the island, had been converted into army hospitals.

Geoffrey's van wound around the roads leading to the east side of the island. He watched trees and orchards roll by. It was an uneasy homecoming. No one walked the streets of downtown or rode bicycles along country roads. Orcas Island was deserted except for the sick and their keepers.

The van crested a hill and Geoffrey saw the iron fence encircling the Allen estate had been reinforced and topped with razor wire. A guard, armed with an assault rifle, stood on duty in the gatehouse.

Geoffrey remembered José, the old man who had manned it while his parents were alive. Like the rest of the servants—like Geoffrey's parents—he was dead. A knot of grief tightened in Geoffrey's chest. This island was where he had grown up, and like him it had changed. Perhaps it was a mistake to come here. When he was at Fort Stewart, he could imagine his family was still alive, his home still a beautiful and welcoming place. Now he had no illusions.

The guard waved the van on. The ornamental cherry trees lining the drive had been cut down; their ruined stumps stuck out of the lawn. Trails of mud were torn in the sod by heavy army trucks and the marching of booted feet.

Piotr, their Russian gardener, never would have allowed such abuse. Not while he was alive.

Geoffrey and half a dozen other sick people stumbled out of the quarantine van and into the light. A guard scanned the chips in their hands to check their identities, then led them up the front steps—Florentine marble streaked with mud—and into the entryway.

They marched through to the back of the house. The delicate antique furniture was gone, replaced by utilitarian gray-enameled metal: cubicle partitions and desks in the library, medical cabinets and operating tables in the dining room, and in the ballroom rows upon rows of bunk beds stacked two high.

The wall decorations and fixtures, however, were untouched. Oil paintings of Allen and Bosworth ancestors graced the walls, interspersed with works by Henri Matisse, Rembrandt, and Johannes Vermeer. A seven-tiered crystal chandelier hung from the ceiling of the ballroom, throwing light and flashes of color over the huddled patients who moaned and writhed on steel-framed bunk beds. It was a surreal combination.

Geoffrey's mother would have wept at the state of her teak ballroom floor. It was gouged and scraped where the soldiers had dragged in bunk beds and medical equipment. Several spots were stained with urine and blood.

The guard escorting them assigned Geoffrey the top bunk of bed 117 and showed him the matching locker where he could store his personal belongings. Geoffrey pushed his laptop and his few clothes into the locker.

His luggage stowed, Geoffrey looked around. Though the army had requisitioned the estate for use as a quarantine camp, it was all still his: the house, the paintings, the grounds. But he didn't say anything. His safety depended on keeping the secret of his identity.

He noticed the other patients all looked eerily alike. It must be a side effect of the plague's gene swapping. Seattle was predominantly a blend of Norwegian, Asian, East Indian, and Hispanic, with other races sprinkled in like spices.

Unlike the early plague victims with their mottled

skin, the people who had been here longest had skin the light brown of a Starbucks latte. Pale Norwegian blue eyes stared out from eyes tilted slightly at the corners, with a hint of an Asian epicanthic fold.

Interesting. Each camp, as treatments enabled the patients to live longer and longer, must develop its own characteristic look, an amalgam of all the people brought there.

He was also curious about how the house had changed. What had happened to his family's personal possessions? When the nurse left him to tend to other patients, Geoffrey ducked into an alcove and opened a seam in the paneling. Servants had used the concealed door during dances to discreetly bring refreshments from the kitchen. The army had either not found the door or had not bothered to lock it. Geoffrey slipped through the kitchen and out into the hallway of the west wing.

He walked past his parents' room. It had been converted into office space for the doctors. Several whitecoated men and women sat in cubicles, looking up diagnoses or typing in reports.

The enormous circular walk-in closet his parents had shared was a storage area for medical supplies. IV bags hung from the rods that had once held his mother's glittering evening gowns. Packs of sterile bandages and medicines filled the shelves.

He kept walking lest anyone notice him and send him back to the ballroom barracks. His bedroom door was closed. Geoffrey hesitated a moment, his hand resting on the handle. Then curiosity overpowered caution and he opened the door.

His bedroom was another office. A man in a captain's uniform worked at the desk that had been Geoffrey's, using the VR equipment Geoffrey's father had bought for him last year.

The man removed the goggles. He looked sixty, with short-cropped white hair and a face weathered by time and experience. "Mr. Allen. I was told you would be joining our camp. But I didn't expect to see you so soon." His voice twanged with a Texan accent. He stood and offered a square-shaped hand. "I'm Captain Morgenson, in command of this facility."

Geoffrey shook the man's hand. It was hard with calluses. "You know who I am?" Geoffrey asked.

Captain Morgenson indicated a chair in front of his desk. "Yes, they told me you would be on today's ferry. They also told me you'd had some"—he examined Geoffrey's battered face—"trouble at the last camp."

Geoffrey took a seat and studied his shoes. "I don't blame them for being angry. I'd feel the same way, in their place."

"That's all well and good, but part of my job is to keep the people under my care alive. Aside from me and the head doctor—who needed access to your medical records—everyone thinks you're Geoffrey Jones, an investment banker from Seattle." Morgenson's eyes twinkled. "It would make my job a whole lot easier if you'd go along with our deception."

Geoffrey touched his swollen eye and winced. "I have no desire to repeat the events in Fort Stewart."

"Good."

"Sir." Geoffrey looked around the room, taking stock. "May I ask what happened to my family's belongings?"

"They've been inventoried and are stored in the garage. The cars are outside, under tarps. All reasonable precautions were taken."

"Thank you." Geoffrey looked out the window at the unchanging Pacific Ocean. "I don't want to cause trouble, Captain, but you must understand how strange this is for me."

"Yes." Captain Morgenson smiled ruefully. "I'd be put out if the army descended on my home. Don't worry, as soon as this bug is licked, we'll be out of here pronto and leave you to it."

"Thank you. I hope AHMS is cured soon, for all our sakes." Geoffrey turned back to the captain. "Could I meet the head doctor? I was at the CDC before the vaccine came out and have been following their research. I want to know if there are any new developments."

"Of course." Captain Morgenson stood up from the leather chair and led Geoffrey down the hall towards his parents' room.

A dark-haired man was removing latex gloves in an examining room. He was tall, six foot one, and looked more like a rugby player than a physician until you met his sharp brown eyes. They glinted with uncompromising intelligence.

Captain Morgenson indicated Geoffrey with his hand. "Dr. Takawari, this is the man we talked about . . . His family owned this estate before the army moved in." He crooked his fingers in the air. " 'Geoffrey Jones.' " To Geoffrey he said, "Dr. Takawari is the head physician. He's in charge of keeping everyone on the ward healthy."

"I don't have time for introductions." Dr. Takawari held up an invoice and slapped it with his free hand. "Have you seen the latest shipment, Captain? AHMS is constantly mutating, and what do they give me to cure patients?" He held up a fistful of individual packets. "Aspirin. Would you fight a war with water pistols? This hospital might as well be a funeral home. Our patients would be better served."

The captain cleared his throat. "Perhaps I should show you—" He started to shoulder Geoffrey back out the door.

Geoffrey planted his feet. "Sell the furniture. Decontaminate it and contact a representative of Christie's to pick it up in Seattle. I'll make the arrangements. Dr. Takawari, provide me a list of the supplies you need and I'll purchase them with the proceeds."

Dr. Takawari's eyes widened. "You're serious?"

"A Louis XIV chair does no one any good moldering in a garage. The money it brings might."

It would hurt, seeing the collection his mother had built over her lifetime broken up and sold at auction.

But she was gone, his fortune was gone, and the furnishings of this house and the land itself were all he had left to offer.

Dr. Takawari shook Geoffrey's hand. "Your generosity will save many lives."

"I hope so," Geoffrey said. He had much to atone for.

Captain Morgenson took off his cap and scratched his white fuzz. "Well, don't that beat all. I thought you'd be mad about us tearing up the place. Instead you're doing your part. You're a good man." He clapped Geoffrey on the back, causing Geoffrey to stumble forward a few steps.

Geoffrey said, "I won't rest until the plague is beaten."

Idaho stepped into the barn before he realized what was wrong: The lights were already on.

Dweezer, Gordon, and Nate were clustered around the sequencer's display. They turned as Idaho entered.

Dweezer's nostrils flared and angry red patches appeared on his cheeks. "What the fuck is going on, man?"

He pointed behind him to the screen. "I got scared that somehow your *puta* had infected us. Given us the plague despite all our precautions. So I ran the test." Dweezer stepped across the room until he was nose to nose with Idaho. "We've got the plague. All of us." He shoved Idaho. "And you knew it."

Idaho caught himself. Cold anger ran down his arms and legs. This was the confrontation he had feared. He had to keep his wits, manage them just right, so they would become allies, not enemies. "Why do you say that?"

"Because you've been curing us. Your fingerprints are all over our DNA."

Idaho said nothing.

Gordon and Nate watched, wide-eyed.

Dweezer shoved Idaho again. He was the same

height and weight as Idaho, dark to Idaho's light. It looked like an even match. Idaho hoped Dweezer wasn't carrying his knife.

Another shove. "We found your biohazard suit. The neck seal's torn. What happened, couldn't keep it in your pants? She so good you just had to fuck her? You didn't care if it killed us all?"

Idaho grabbed Dweezer's right hand and bent his wrist backwards. "Don't talk about Exeter that way."

Dweezer winced in pain and dropped to one knee. "When were you going to tell us?" he yelled, his voice tight with pain. "When?"

"Let him go," Gordon told Idaho. His low voice boomed across the barn. He'd picked up a pitchfork from a rack on the wall. Nate held a farrier's hook.

Idaho heard a snick as Dweezer opened his switchblade with his left hand.

Dweezer swung at Idaho's stomach. But he might as well have been moving in slow motion.

Idaho sidestepped the knife and broke Dweezer's wrist with a sideways snap.

Gordon rushed him with the pitchfork, his head low like a charging bull.

Idaho snatched the weapon from his hand and snapped the shaft in half. Gordon was jerked off-balance when Idaho grabbed the fork and slid sideways across the dirt floor.

Nate swung the farrier's hook down at Idaho. His pale face was red with exertion.

Idaho snatched the weapon and tossed it aside. He grabbed the back of Nate's neck with his left hand and pointed his right index finger at the tender skin at the side of his throat. A needle-thin fang slid out from under his fingernail; a drop of venom gleamed at its tip.

"Freeze," Idaho said, "or I'll kill him."

Gordon looked up at Idaho, a stupefied expression on his wide face. Nate was still, like a rabbit hiding from a predator.

Dweezer clutched his broken wrist to his chest. "What are you, man?"

Idaho held out his right hand; out of cartilage sheaths under his fingernails, he extruded all five fangs. Deadly jeweled drops formed on the ends. "Anything I want to be."

"You moved so fast I couldn't see your hands," Nate said. Idaho could feel the man's throat vibrate under his hand. "And you're stronger. How?"

"The plague is more than a disease." He brought his fist together. "It's an opportunity. Left to its own devices, it will rewrite your DNA with random mutations. But directed"—he flexed his hand and the fangs slid back into their sheaths beneath his fingernails— "it can rebuild you in any way you desire."

Dweezer's eyes teared with pain. "You're *loco*, man, *loco*."

Idaho released Nate, and the younger man backed away.

"I'm sorry you were infected," Idaho said, "but think of the opportunities."

Still on the floor, Gordon shook his head. "What I don't understand is why didn't the vac—"

"Shut up!" Dweezer yelled. "I don't care about no opportunities. We're going to die. One day a mutation will hit us too fast to correct. We'll die of this thing."

"So help me," Idaho said. He reached out his hand to help Dweezer up. "Together we can tame this disease, use it to improve ourselves."

Dweezer stared at Idaho's hand in horror. He scooted backwards on his butt, his feet kicking the dirt. "Who do you think you are—God?"

Idaho let his hand fall to his side. His eyes bored into Dweezer's. "If I recreate myself in my own image. Yes."

Dweezer scuttled to the wall and used it to push himself to his feet. He cradled his broken wrist in his other hand. "You're crazy. I'm leaving." He called to the others, "Gordon. Nate." They followed him towards the door.

When Dweezer was in the doorway, Idaho said, "Where will you go?"

Dweezer whirled, hate hot in his eyes.

"If you leave the ranch," Idaho continued, "they'll put you in a containment camp. Without my treatments, you'll die."

Nate whispered, "He's right, Dweez."

"We could kill you," Dweezer said. "Some night when you're sleeping in that *bruja*'s arms. Kill you both."

Idaho licked his lips. He had to bring them around. "But then who would design the repairs for your DNA?"

Dweezer nodded at Gordon and Nate. "We would. We don't need you."

"You don't understand molecular biology. Not like I do. I've been designing the cures for the CDC's patients. You just run the machines."

"We could learn," Dweezer said. His chin was streaked with tears of pain, but he held it at a defiant angle.

Idaho's voice was soft, almost gentle. "But could you learn fast enough, *mi amigo*? Could you learn before your marrow rotted in your bones and you died screaming on the floor?"

Dweezer's mouth worked, but no sound came out.

"You need me," Idaho said. "You don't have to admit it, but it's the truth."

Dweezer turned and stormed through the door. Gordon followed on his heels.

Nate lingered a moment, looking back at Idaho. Something gleamed in his cornflower-blue eyes. Admiration?

Idaho was vigilant that night. He moved Exeter out of the camper and into his hidden, subterranean trailer. He worried that Dweezer might try to find him. He'd wounded the other man's pride along with his wrist, and that made him dangerous.

The night passed without incident. He left before Exeter woke, leaving a note on the door for her to stay inside, not to give their hiding place away.

Idaho approached the farmhouse with trepidation. He jumped at every shadow. The house seemed dark, but Dweezer's car was still parked beside it, next to Idaho's van.

The barn was dark. Idaho crept inside and turned on only the table lamp. He wanted to give Dweezer as much time as possible to cool down.

Idaho was putting his and Exeter's latest blood samples into a manifold when the barn door creaked behind him. Idaho whirled.

Nate stood in the doorway. His blond hair was tousled and stuck up in random tufts all over his head. "You moved so fast last night I couldn't believe it."

"How is Dweezer?"

Nate's lips tightened under his silicon tusks. "We set his wrist the best we could without an X-ray." He took a step into the room. "Gave him some bong hits for the pain. He's pissed as hell."

"You don't seem angry."

Nate shrugged. "You didn't tell us we were infected . . . but you did cure us. That counts for something." His eyes dropped to Idaho's hands. "Can I see them again? I was a bit . . . distracted, the first time."

Idaho held out his right hand and extruded the fang on his ring finger.

Nate grinned. "That's so cool. Can you do them separately?"

Idaho rippled the muscles in the back of his hand and the fangs slid in and out in sequence. The modification had nearly killed him before he'd learned to restrict the venom gene's expression to his fingers and out of other parts of his body, such as his bloodstream. As a precaution, he had also placed an order for a large supply of antivenin.

Nate's eyes lit up like a kid's at Christmas. "Could you do me?" He touched the tusks on his face and raised his shirt to display a ridge of horn-shaped bumps running along his breastbone. "I've got these, but they're just implants. I want something real."

Idaho looked up into Nate's face. His wide-set eyes and freckles made him look friendly and honest. Like the prototypical Indiana farm boy. Yet he had altered his body and delighted in Idaho's deadly modifications. Idaho wondered what dark things lurked in the mind behind that innocent face.

Would he change Nate? Idaho considered. He was proud of the work he'd done on himself and Exeter. It was a new form of programming, tinkering with the stuff of life. But he was limited in his raw materials. He could paint only a few of his inspirations on a canvas of two. The intellectual challenge of creating new modifications intrigued him.

He met Nate's enthusiastic gaze. "What did you have in mind?"

Three weeks later—after a lengthy disinfection process—the Allen collection was auctioned by Christie's. Dr. Takawari called Geoffrey into his office when he got the statement from the hospital's bank.

"Sixty-three million dollars." He beamed, his brown eyes shining. "I never dreamed it would be so much."

"It is a fraction of the collection's value." Geoffrey looked down at his shoes. "But it's the most I could raise in these uncertain times. I hope it will help."

"It will. I have already backordered replacement enzymes for the SGLT1 genetic defect that came in with the last batch of patients. I only wish more labs were developing new therapies. Almost everyone is converting over to producing the vaccine." His smile became sardonic. "There is more profit in protecting the healthy than curing the sick." ·

"Unfortunately." Geoffrey rose and shook Dr. Takawari's hand. He left the mansion for a walk around the grounds.

Geoffrey brooded over the shortages of treatments for the infected as he walked around his mother's rose garden. It was one of the few areas of landscaping the army hadn't ruined. Captain Morgenson's mother had been an enthusiastic rosarian and, in her memory, the captain had protected this part of the garden. It was early December and the Peace roses were still blooming. Their pink and yellow blooms mocked his dark mood.

Another three patients had died last night. Smoke marred the western sky over the island's incinerator. Their remains would be returned to the families after they were burned and the ashes sealed in decontaminated packages.

Geoffrey wondered how much longer he would survive. So far, he had avoided catching any of the dangerous strains. The most lethal forms of AHMS killed quickly, before the patient could infect too many others. Whether it was because the virus had been designed for his genome, or the effect of gene tampering the CDC had done during his confinement, Geoffrey felt relatively healthy . . . as long as he stayed away from mirrors. His skin was still changing. No one worried about cosmetic defects while patients were still dying. He understood, but it still distressed him to see a stranger's face in the mirror. He was beginning to look more like the other people in the camp as the virus mixed their genes.

His eyes were no longer blue but a muddy brown, and patches of dark and light skin moved across his face on a weekly basis. There was a crease at the inner corner of his left eye that looked like an epicanthic fold.

The plague was far from beaten. Something more had to be done. But what? Geoffrey was, for the first time in his life, penniless. All that remained of his fortune was the house and the land on which it stood. And the army had commandeered those for the duration of the disease.

How did you fight without money? Before, he had always bought his way out of trouble. An easy solution that was now impossible.

If only he could get help from the outside. But that was unlikely. The news rarely mentioned the containment camps anymore. Calls to patients had declined over the six long months of confinement. It was as if they were becoming invisible. People on the outside were willing to forget the infected, to preserve the illusion that the plague had been eradicated by the vaccine.

If only there were a way to get word out that people were still suffering and unable to get treatment because the drug companies had abandoned them. If he could generate enough public outrage, perhaps Congress would force the corporations to develop new treatments.

His plans were interrupted by a tentative voice. "Mr. Allen? Mr. Allen, sir, is that you?"

Geoffrey froze. He turned and saw a man in his late twenties. For a moment, he didn't recognize him behind the mottled skin. Then the man's bone structure triggered a memory. Raoul, the gatekeeper's son.

"It's me," Raoul said, touching his fingers to his chest. "Raoul. Don't you recognize me?" Then he touched his face. "Maybe not, with all the changes."

Geoffrey didn't know what to say. As ashamed as he was to admit it, he feared exposure. He didn't want another beating, didn't want to be hounded for his crimes any longer.

"You must have me confused with someone else," Geoffrey said, his stomach churning with the lie.

"Oh." Raoul's face fell. "Sorry. It's just been so long since I saw someone I knew from before . . . you know." He raised a hand in farewell. "Sorry."

Geoffrey felt like a coward as he watched Raoul walk away. But he was also relieved, glad the disease disguised his features so even Raoul, who had grown up on the Allen estate, couldn't identify him as the man who had once been Geoffrey Allen.

The next morning, Geoffrey placed a call to Lillith at the CDC.

Her eyes widened as she picked up the phone, and she expanded the message screen to get a better look at his face. "Geoffrey? Is that you?"

Geoffrey knew why she was gawking. Half his hair had gone red, the other half was patched blond and black, growing straight in the blond patches and curling tightly in the black. He should shave it again.

"It's me." He touched the calico hair tentatively. "The plague's made a few changes."

"How are you? I didn't hear about the transfer until it was too late. I came to take a blood sample and you were gone."

Geoffrey took a deep breath. "I need your help, Dr. Watkins. People in the camps are dying because labs have focused their research on the vaccine. There are only three facilities in the United States that are still producing gene therapies for the changed. Even if we can raise funding to buy treatments, there's none available."

Lillith's brow wrinkled with consternation. "I know. It's criminal."

"Can you help us?"

"Not personally." Lillith chewed her lower lip. "Dr. Lam is monitoring my work closely. To cure the hundreds of thousands in the camps, you'd need a network of manufacturers." She tapped her lips with a finger.

Geoffrey sighed. Another dead end. "Ah, I see. Thank you for your time." He reached forward to disconnect.

"Wait." Lillith held up her hand. Inner turmoil played across her face in a confusing mélange of expressions. "I said it was difficult . . . not impossible. I know someone who may be able to help."

Idaho swam in a black sea lit only by the fluorescent strands of DNA that wound around him. His virtual hands moved up and down the chain of nucleotides, organizing them to suit his purpose.

A beeping sound alerted him to an incoming call.

Idaho lost his grip on the nucleotide chain. Only Lillith and Exeter had his private number. Idaho morphed into his bisexual metaphor and accepted the incoming call.

He didn't recognize the man on the other end. It was one of the changed, or someone using a changed avatar. Its hair grew in patches of blond, red, and black. His skin was mottled.

"Who THE HELL are YOU?" Idaho asked.

The man's voice lowered to a barely audible whisper. "Geoffrey Preston Allen. I need—"

Geoffrey Allen? Idaho's heart pounded. Why was *Geoffrey Allen* calling him? Did he want the lab equipment back? If Geoffrey had his private number, did he know where the ranch was?

"How DID YOU get this NUMBER?" he demanded.

Geoffrey took a step back, holding his hands up in placation. "Easy. I've come to ask a favor. Dr. Watkins said you might help."

Idaho looked Geoffrey up and down, scanning his avatar for sticky code or other signs of attack. "What DO YOU want?"

"She tells me you've designed cures for variants of the plague. Now I need your help manufacturing them."

Geoffrey held out his multicolored hands. The skin was a mix of races: brown, black, white. "The government is cutting back production on new treatments; they're falling behind the disease's mutations. I think they'd rather we all quietly died off."

"WHAT MAKES you think I will HELP?"

"I bought you the equipment to build a genetics lab, without which someone close to you would have died."

Idaho cut off his connection to his avatar, not wanting to expose the emotions that roiled under his skin: resentment, fear, hatred, and sympathy. When he'd regained control of himself, Idaho reconnected and said, "ONE LAB can only SYNTHESIZE so much."

Geoffrey nodded, his face set in somber lines.

"Whatever you can produce would be appreciated. The more the better, but I'll take what I can get."

Idaho thought of the people dying in the camps, their genome perverted by disease, medically abandoned by the government that had imprisoned them together. It reminded him of him and Blue, abandoned to Mahn's disease more than a decade ago. Somewhere in those camps, a boy and girl might be suffering as he and Blue had. Could Idaho live with himself if he let them die without trying to help?

"LET ME CONSIDER the problem. I'LL CALL YOU." Idaho closed the call and immediately changed his personal phone number.

Idaho pulled the induction pins from his skin and blinked in the dim light of his trailer.

He rubbed his forehead. Synthesizing and delivering enough cures to make a difference to the camps would be a huge undertaking. Much more complicated than uploading and downloading simulated cures for variants.

To move from design to manufacture would require an entire network of people, unfunded and unlicensed pharmacists, collaborating in secret.

Even if he enlisted LongTr33's help in acquiring funds, where would he get the people?

Idaho's thoughts were interrupted by Exeter. She lounged in the doorway from the bedroom, waiting for him to notice her.

Catching her out of the corner of his eye made him think it was Blue—just for an instant—long enough to make his heart flutter with recognition. The inevitable stab of disappointment was a small price to pay for those seconds when he believed his sister was still alive.

Exeter's modifications were almost complete and she was glorious. She had Blue's shimmering eyes, her pale golden hair, the white-gold skin. His work was perfect. Only the deeper manipulations of bone structure remained.

"Who were you talking to?" she asked, toying with her bottom lip with a forefinger. "I felt your pulse rate jump on the Net, and I wasn't in the room." She looked at him from the bottom of her eyes. "Should I be jealous?"

He ignored the question. She knew he was hers, body and soul. The minute she had let him alter her, Exeter had taken control. She looked so much like Blue now, he could deny her nothing.

Idaho asked, "If you wanted to cure all of the changed in the camps, how would you do it?"

Exeter shrugged, a gesture that started in her toes and curled up her body. "Aside from a firebomb?"

The sight of her made Idaho's chest hurt so he could hardly breathe. "Yes."

"Let the changed cure themselves. They're the ones that care about it, aren't they?"

It was so obvious. Why hadn't he thought of it? Idaho could use the same leverage he had on Dweezer, Gordon, and Nate. Once you were infected, voluntarily or not, you needed constant treatments to prevent your genome from mutating further.

Nate had pleaded with Idaho for self-modification the day after he'd seen Idaho's changes. There must be others on the outside, people who hadn't taken the vaccine or who'd avoided the camps. If he could organize them, give them the technology they needed . . . in exchange for their help.

Idaho called Nate on his cell phone and arranged to meet him in the barn.

Nate stood up when Idaho entered the barn. The bone stimulation had worked. Nate looked down at Idaho from his new height of six foot five. "Yes?"

Idaho asked, "You said you knew people, on the outside, who wanted to change. People who haven't taken the vaccine."

Nate's eyes lit up. "Are you going to do them?"

"Perhaps. What I need are people interested in setting up their own labs."

Nate's jaw hung open. When he could speak, he was nearly shouting. "Oh my God. I know Robin would be so psyched, I've told—" He stopped and blushed.

"You told others." Idaho's voice was cold. "Exposing our secret is dangerous."

Nate flushed. "Only a few people who can be trusted, friends from the body-mod crowd: the man who did the septum piercing for my tusks, a woman who designs silicon subcutaneous implants. They all want to become changelings, like me."

"Changelings?"

Nate looked at his fingertips. "That's what I call it. You take away the normal, boring self and replace it with something . . . wilder."

"There would be a price for the equipment and my designs."

"Anything. They'd do anything. They're already infected. I've been sneaking them treatments. . . ." Nate broke off and kicked the dirt floor with his toe.

Idaho raised one eyebrow. "So that's why our reagent supplies have been dwindling."

"I just thought—"

Idaho cut Nate off with a gesture. "It's not important. Are these people intelligent enough to run automated machines like these?"

Nate's head bobbed up and down. "Totally. Jen's the smartest woman I know."

Idaho let the comment lie. "In exchange for my designs, I'll expect them to work for me, to create treatments for the infected inside the containment camps. They will each have a weekly quota. After they fill it, any leftover machine time is their own."

Nate grinned. "Wow. That'll be so great. Jen will be thrilled." He blushed again. Then his brow wrinkled. "But why do you care about the infected in the camps?"

Idaho turned back to the DNA synthesizer and examined its progress. "I have my reasons."

All five of Nate's contacts leapt at the chance to set up their own labs. They flooded Idaho's inbox with requests for equipment and training.

To equip them all would take money. He'd stolen enough from rounding errors in bank software to provide a comfortable living, but his needs now were an order of magnitude greater.

Nate's friends wouldn't be the only infected who had avoided the camps. There must be others on the outside, rich enough to avoid quarantine but without access to private physicians who could synthesize treatments.

All he need do was find them and start charging for black market cures.

CHAPTER 15

Two weeks later, Dr. Takawari called Geoffrey into his office. Takawari sat on the edge of his desk, next to a package labeled UPS OVERNIGHT. He didn't wait for Geoffrey to take a seat; he reached into the box, withdrew a sheet of paper, and thrust it in Geoffrey's face. "What do you know about this?"

Geoffrey unfolded the paper. The return address was a post office box in Seattle. The letter stated that Good Works International was a nondenominational organization devoted to improving public health and helping victims of the plague.

Geoffrey stood and looked inside the box. He removed the Styrofoam inserts. Beneath the packets of dry ice were hundreds of tiny vials of clear fluid. He wiggled one of the vials out of its packaging. There was a bar code on the side.

Takawari folded his arms. "Those match patient ID codes, which are only used by government health organizations. Good Works International is definitely *not* a government organization."

Geoffrey smiled. Lillith and Idaho had come through. He said, "Looks like that miracle you were hoping for."

"Hmmph." Dr. Takawari took the vial from Geoffrey and looked into the fluid as if he could read its DNA directly.

"The letter looks legitimate. Why don't you analyze the serum?"

"I sequenced it an hour ago," Dr. Takawari said. "It appears identical to the gene therapy we receive from the CDC to repair the FBN1 gene on chromosome fifteen." He replaced the vial in the packaging. "What I want to know is how Good Works International knew which treatments we needed."

Geoffrey studied the fingertips of his left hand. "If they knew that one patient in the camp had the variation of AHMS that causes Marfan's syndrome, it would be a safe bet that the other patients would catch that variation and need the same treatment."

Dr. Takawari's eyes narrowed in suspicion. "I see, and how might GWI have found out the medical details of one of my patients?"

Geoffrey shrugged. "Perhaps he sent them the information."

"Hmm. An interesting theory." Dr. Takawari leaned forward, hands on knees. "I checked the Washington State records. GWI was incorporated only last week."

Geoffrey said nothing. He'd had to pull strings with the governor to get the incorporation through so quickly. GWI consisted of a Web page, a post office box, and a nonprofit business license.

Dr. Takawari picked up the box in his large, nimble hands. "I've received a package—from a company that's only existed for a week—that appears to have treatments we desperately need. It might be from a philanthropic organization. Or it might be from a psychotic who wants to poison my patients. Letter bombs have been mailed to the camps in Des Moines and Poughkeepsie. Before I use this, I need to be sure it's safe, and we don't have the facilities here to do a full toxicology screening." He looked at Geoffrey over the top of the box. "What would you suggest?"

Geoffrey met his eyes levelly. "I assure you, GWI is exactly what it claims to be. I have friends on the outside who are . . . unorthodox, but they do good work. You can test the treatments on me, if you wish."

Dr. Takawari's suspicious expression slowly relaxed into a grin. "I see."

"You might also consider sending GWI a list of the treatments you need, for future shipments."

Dr. Takawari took the letter from Geoffrey. He reread it and shook his head. "I don't know how you did it, but thank you."

Geoffrey stood and shook the doctor's hand. "You do good work. I want you to have all the tools you need." He exited the office, smiling as he closed the door behind him.

Idaho crawled out of bed, leaving Exeter-Blue curled up on her side like a cat. It was four a.m. He washed his face and the pockmarked connection ports that covered his body. While his skin dried, he popped open a Mountain Dew and ate a few handfuls of Doritos.

The first few needles slid in painfully. They were thin, like acupuncture needles, ending in a threadlike antenna. Idaho rolled them as he punctured the tattooed dots on his body, aiming for nerve clusters.

The needles were inconvenient and took half an hour to insert and calibrate.

Perhaps he should look into modifying himself to make tiny receptors for the needles: enlarged hair follicles, or he could grow a new cluster of nerve cells on the back of his neck and have only one port to mess with.

When he was able to sink into his connection, Idaho checked his email. The encrypted account he'd set up to manage the network of hackers and changelings had one hundred and sixty-three new emails. One was from Lillith, describing new variations of AHMS that had been isolated in Brussels. Nine were invoices from shipments his remote labs had sent to containment camps. Two more were requests for new laboratories. Twenty were hackers sending in proposed treatments for Idaho's review. The others were special design requests. He dealt quickly with the administrative letters.

Idaho enjoyed creating new DNA structures. It challenged his programming skills.

Idaho opened a message from a man in California. It was hard to tell whether the image was real or an avatar. The man was covered completely in tattoos. His face was a tapestry of flowers and snakes and skulls.

The recorded image said, "I want a ring of horns, right here." He placed his fists against his forehead. "Can you do that? I heard you could do anything." The man glanced behind him, displaying a length of neck in which a coral snake wound up his jugular vein and whispered in his ear. When he looked back at the camera, he held a fan of thousand-dollar bills. "I'll pay anything you want."

Idaho's eyebrow rose. Interesting. His network of labs could use money, and the technical challenge of creating a human variant that produced bovine horns was intriguing. He would have to prevent allergic reactions as well as carefully encode the horn placement, or the man might have them erupt anywhere on his artfully decorated skin.

An intriguing challenge.

Most of his patients requested only treatments for health problems caused by the plague, or invisible changes such as mood-altering enhancements that enabled the host to produce its own heroin highs throughout the day.

But there was a minority who saw past the limitations of their own bodies. People like him and Exeter and Nate who saw their flesh as a canvas for their fantasies.

The requests of these changelings pushed the spectrum of humanity further than it had gone in nature. And made it more and more likely that his genetic alterations would be discovered.

Idaho twitched a muscle in his chin, opening an encrypted connection to return the man's call.

The man answered on the third ring. When he saw Idaho's avatar his eyes widened and he burst into a grin. "Can you do it?"

"YES," Idaho's twinned voice said. "BUT there is DANGER."

The man's chest puffed up. The motion caused flowers to bloom wider and snakes to inhale. "I'm not afraid."

"Danger TO US ALL. What if YOUR CHANGES are QUESTIONED?"

The man blinked. "I'll say they're subdermal implants. I don't take blood tests, so they won't know otherwise."

Idaho said nothing, merely studied the man for emotional cues.

Sweat broke out on his painted brow. "Did you see the money? There's more where that came from."

"GOOD." This man was stupid, but no more so than average. Idaho pulled up a map of Los Angeles. "WAIT at the corner of SUNSET AND La Brea."

The man's brow puckered. "When?"

"Until THEY COME."

"How will I recognize them?" His eyes widened. "Are you going to be there?"

"THEY will recognize YOU."

The man nodded, his whole body rocking with the motion. "How much money should I bring?"

Idaho smiled. "ALL of it." He closed the connection.

Public health campaigns during the early days of the plague had encouraged people to register their DNA with local health departments. So modifications to repair or duplicate human DNA was just brute-force hacking to break into those databases and find what he needed for the simple modifications.

Common cures had been posted to the Net by humanitarian hackers who believed that medical knowledge should not be hoarded by private companies or government organizations.

For similar reasons, Idaho had anonymously posted

his tools for designing new gene therapies, creating a new generation of gene hackers.

But the real challenge lay in requests like this, which asked for forms of humanity that couldn't exist without his technology. In this area, Idaho was still the best gene hacker in the world.

Idaho's research spiders now crept into university microbiology systems, returning with DNA sequences for insects, small mammals, fish, and birds. They scoured the records of agricultural firms and livestock breeders. Pet cloning had been a thriving business for decades. All that genetic data was available for anyone who knew how to get at it.

These extreme changes made it inevitable that one day the world would know about his work.

With that in mind, Idaho made sure that none of the labs he worked with had his location or the location of any of the others. He encouraged them to screen their clients and meet them in public places to exchange samples and treatments.

What amazed Idaho was that the secret had not gotten out before now.

In the United States there were at least five thousand people who had become infected and avoided the camps, and Idaho's network discovered more every day. Some had become infected before the vaccine was available and had, through luck or self-quarantine, survived for months without medical treatment. Others had avoided the public vaccinations, fearing a government conspiracy, or by not understanding English well enough to know it wasn't the INS, or because they were too knocked out on drugs to care.

Word of black market treatments were whispered in pool halls, opium dens, back alleys, fish markets, college dormitories. Cures that could make you stronger than before you got sick.

Idaho opened the next email. The sender wanted gills. Another complicated change. First he'd have to analyze raw genetic data from the fish hatcheries and finish the computer-intensive work of matching genes to expressed traits. Biologists had sequenced the DNA of a snail darter nearly fifty years ago, but that was no use until they figured what the genes did. They'd begun the work by cloning fish with various genes missing. But their work was primitive compared with Idaho's modeling.

All over the world hundreds of supercomputers, in the basements of universities, government agencies, and commercial labs, generated endless simulations of DNA at Idaho's instruction, piping the results back to a central mainframe hidden in an armored compound in Colombia.

Idaho smiled at the challenge and added this request to the problem set of his simulations.

The next email he opened started, "I've taken the vaccine, but I want to change, can you help me?" Idaho felt a pang of regret. He moved the email into a folder with hundreds of others.

Should he create a version of AHMS resistant to the vaccine? Idaho twitched the muscle of his left shoulder and opened a file he had created shortly after creating the first nine labs.

Inside were several thousand base pairs. The beginning of a vaccine-resistant virus. Idaho rotated the DNA spiral, taking in the elegance and beauty of nature's design. It wasn't finished. He sighed and closed the file. The world wasn't ready.

Not yet.

Over the next few months, Dr. Takawari contacted physicians he knew at other camps and told them about GWI. It offered free treatments in exchange for blood samples.

Coming at a time when Congress had slashed funding for the camps, it was too good an offer to refuse. With Dr. Takawari's assurances the treatments were legitimate, every clinic signed on.

Geoffrey didn't know how Idaho raised the money to buy new equipment and supplies, and he didn't ask.

It was enough to see the people in the camp around him improve. Raoul recovered from jaundice. A toddler who had nearly died from thalassemia lived to celebrate her third birthday. The death rate dropped to two percent a month.

Despite the improvements caused by Idaho's treatments, life in the camps was still hard. Geoffrey and the other three hundred people barracked in his parents' house shared the ballroom. Portajohns had been brought in to supplement the mansion's bathrooms, and the pool house was converted into a shower room.

Too many sick people, in too small a space, with no staff dedicated to cleaning the facilities, took its toll on the opulent house. Those well enough to work were organized in shifts to clean the rooms, do laundry, and look after other light maintenance, but it wasn't enough. Geoffrey was glad his mother couldn't see the ruin of her clean, orderly home.

Everywhere people were coughing, vomiting, and having night sweats. When one patient broke out in a rash, the others contracted it within days. All it would take was one person with a fatal variation, and the whole camp would die. It had happened in Indiana. The majority of the inmates were despondent.

The government had stockpiled them like nuclear waste, waiting for their half-lives to expire in obscurity.

"I go! Must go!" a reedy voice said.

Geoffrey looked up from the news channel he was watching on his laptop.

Across the ballroom, a man in his seventies struggled with a guard a third his age. His lilting accent hinted that he had once been Asian. Now he had the same blended DNA as everyone else in the camp, sharing their tan mottled skin and dark brown hair. Tears streamed down his face. "My wife is die of cancer. All alone in hospital. No family except me. Must go!"

The guard, wearing close-cropped brown hair and an expression of pity on his square-jawed face, pushed the old man back towards the bunk beds. "No one who is sick can leave. You'll make other people sick if you go."

"Wife dying. She no care if sick. Please. Wife thirty-five years. Good wife. Not let die alone."

The story reminded Geoffrey of his mother's death, when he'd been unable to go to her. His heart ached for the old man. Geoffrey climbed down from his bunk and crossed the room.

"What's going on here?" Geoffrey asked.

The old man looked at Geoffrey. His rheumy eyes were bloodshot from crying. "Please help. You speak good. Guards listen to you. Must go."

Geoffrey patted the old man's shoulder. "Yes, I heard." To the guard he said, "Why can't he visit his wife?"

"Orders. This is a quarantine facility. No one infected with AHMS leaves."

"Surely everyone on the outside has been inoculated against the virus by now. Why can't he travel?"

"You'll have to speak with the captain on that," the guard said. "I've got my orders."

"Yes," Geoffrey said, "I will." To the old man, he asked, "What's your name?"

The old man bobbed his head in greeting. "Yi Yong-Jin. In this country, I called Mr. Yi."

Geoffrey returned the gesture. "Mr. Yi, I think we should talk to the captain." He led the old man out of the ballroom and down the hall.

Captain Morgenson was in his office, reviewing reports online. He looked up when Geoffrey and Mr. Yi entered.

"Mr. Yi has a request," Geoffrey said without preamble. He nodded for the old man to go on.

"Please, Captain, sir." Mr. Yi bowed low. "Wife dying. I must go. No other family. Thirty-five years wife. Bury two sons. Only me left. I go, sit by bed, hold hand. Please?"

Captain Morgenson blew out a breath. "Geoffrey, you know I can't."

"Why? The vaccine's been publicly available for five months. In the past three, we've had only two new cases of disease, and both of those were illegal immigrants who avoided the community health vans. Who could he infect?"

"If I apply for a pass for Mr. Yi, my commanding officer will refuse."

Geoffrey gestured at Mr. Yi with an open hand. "Isn't thirty-five years of marriage worth a little inconvenience?"

Captain Morgenson looked at Mr. Yi and back at Geoffrey. "You're not making this easy."

"It isn't easy for Mr. Yi. Why should it be easy for us?"

Captain Morgenson threw up his hands. "All right. All right. Prepare the paperwork and I'll forward it up the chain of command."

Geoffrey went back to the bunk room and helped Mr. Yi draft his request. When they were done, they emailed the letter to the captain.

"Thank you, thank you much," Mr. Yi said. "It so hard in this country, not speaking English much. In Korea, I work as electrical engineer. Design molecular microchip." His hands jumped from one knee to the other, pantomiming a trip across the Pacific. "Come here. No speak good, no one hire. I open own store, fix computers. Make good living, bring wife over. Then . . ." Mr. Yi sighed and held up his disease-mottled hands. "This."

Geoffrey winced internally, wondering whether Mr. Yi recognized him. He had changed so much in the last few weeks, he hoped the old man didn't connect him with the irresponsible rich boy who'd started the plague.

Idaho was interrupted during his review of gene therapies designed by a twelve-year-old girl in Zambia. They were quite good, and the beeping of an incoming call annoyed him.

The message was from Lillith, high priority. With a sigh, he closed the file, opened an encrypted channel, and answered.

Lillith's brows were drawn together and her black eyes flashed. "What's going on? We're twenty units short at the Cincinnati camp."

"Twenty units SHORT OF WHAT?" Idaho asked.

"Everything across the board: sickle-cell, lymphoma, galactosemia."

By concentrating on the muscles of his neck, Idaho brought up a spreadsheet showing the supplies recently shipped to Cincinnati. He read numbers off to Lillith.

She compressed her lips. "Well, that's not what arrived."

Cincinnati was not a camp Idaho supplied directly. He shipped treatments to camps in Montana, Idaho, and Washington. "I'll make SOME calls. ANY CHANCE a guard is STEALING THEM?"

"That's absurd. Why would anyone . . ." Lillith's eyes widened. "People infected with the plague who are hiding from the camps?"

Idaho cocked his hand into a gun shape and fired at her. "Part of our funding efforts comes from black market cures. I think someone's found a way to cut out the middleman."

"But that's unconscionable, stealing cures from the camps."

Idaho shrugged. "I'll LOOK INTO it."

Three days later, Captain Morgenson summoned Geoffrey and Mr. Yi to his office. Captain Morgenson handed Geoffrey a tablet PC.

Geoffrey held the screen so Mr. Yi could read it. On the screen was their emailed request, and the response: DENIED. The colonel quoted from the AHMS Containment Act and said that although he sympathized with Mr. Yi's situation, he could not permit such travel at this time.

Mr. Yi deflated and sank heavily into a chair. "Must go," he said in a broken voice. "Good wife. Should not die alone." His eyes turned to Geoffrey, pleading.

It felt like a punch in the stomach. Geoffrey sat down heavily in the guest chair.

"I know you're disappointed, but I warned you." Morgenson tapped the tablet PC. "There is some good news. I made arrangements with the hospital where Mrs. Yi is being treated. They've agreed to set up a live video feed from her bedside. I've had a tablet PC configured for Mr. Yi. The connection is live, twenty-four hours a day. They can talk all night if they want."

Geoffrey felt a burning in the back of his throat as he thought of Mrs. Yi, dying alone, with no hand to comfort her, no gentle touch to brush the hair from her brow. "It's not the same, Morgenson. And you know it."

"I'm sorry, Geoffrey. Federal law states the changed must remain in quarantine, no exceptions."

Geoffrey stood. His hand clenched into a fist. "Then we have to change the law."

Dweezer stroked the soul patch he had grown to complement his new, flawless face. "You ain't going to believe who I've found, man." His hazel eyes were bright with triumph. "You wanted rich people with the plague who were hiding out from the camps? I hit the jackpot, man!"

Idaho looked up from the DNA synthesizer. "Who?"

Dweezer leaned forward. "Lacey Johnstone." He laughed at Idaho's surprised expression.

"The president's daughter?"

"No shit." Dweezer shined his fingernails on the front of his tank top. "She ran away from Daddy and all that first daughter crap. Developed a little substance abuse problem like your girlfriend." Dweezer pantomimed injecting a needle into the crook of his arm.

Idaho frowned. "Go on."

"One of her pushers gave her the plague. Poor little Lacey can't go home without causing a national incident. You want me to make contact?"

Idaho sucked his teeth. The president's only child. "Yes, she would be useful. Invite her to stay with us on the farm. Tell her I've got a modification she'll enjoy."

Dweezer's mouth broke into a grin. "The joy juice, eh? I should try that one some day. Gordon says it's like having a morphine factory in your skull."

Idaho had designed the modification to the brain's pleasure center to help Exeter kick her heroin addiction. When your own brain chemistry produced bliss at regular intervals during the day, who needed drugs?

The next morning, Geoffrey took his laptop to the rose garden. It was one of the few places in the compound where he could be alone.

He sat on a stone bench, opened his laptop, and called Ewan Wheeler, the United States senator who had been unable to attend his homecoming party. It gave Geoffrey a pang to realize it was the last party that his mother had thrown.

Wheeler's secretary put Geoffrey on hold for a second before transferring him.

Senator Wheeler's receding hair was swept back into a stylish pompadour. His eyes widened when he came on screen. Geoffrey felt a pang of rejection. He was getting used to people's reaction to his appearance.

The senator suppressed his surprise. "Geoffrey, how good to hear from you." His voice was serious but compassionate. "I was so sorry to hear about your illness and your parents' passing. These are hard times."

Geoffrey nodded. "Thank you, Senator, for taking my call."

"Geoffrey, I've known your family for forty years. Please, call me Ewan."

A good sign. Perhaps the senator would be willing to help him after all. "All right, Ewan. I've got a situation and could use your assistance."

Wheeler spread his hands magnanimously. "Name it. If it's within my power to grant, it's yours."

"It's about the law restricting people infected with AHMS to the containment camps. There's an old man here whose wife is dying of cancer. He wants to be with her in her last days, and his request for travel has been denied."

"Ah." Wheeler steepled his fingers. "Well, I might be able to work out an exception in his case. I'll talk to a General friend of mine, see if we can be flexible in this matter."

"Thank you, but I was wondering . . . why not repeal the law? The vaccine's been out for months. There's no danger to the public if victims of the plague are allowed to go home."

Wheeler's smile disappeared. "Well, now, I don't know about that. I'm on the Health and Education Committee, and our advisers from the NIH, CDC, and WHO say it's too early to tell whether the vaccine is one hundred percent effective."

"How long?"

"What?"

"It's been five months and there have been only three reports—worldwide—of vaccine failures. And those are suspect, due to lack of record keeping by the local health care authorities. Three out of six billion. That sounds like one hundred percent to me."

Wheeler glanced at his watch. "It's a complicated issue. There's also the question of infrastructure. It's easier to provide treatment to patients when they're centralized. What you're suggesting might result in new cases of the plague or in the unnecessary suffering of the infected. Neither of which is in the best interest of the public."

Geoffrey shook his head in disbelief. "Some of these people have been imprisoned against their will for nearly a year. Is that in their best interest?"

Wheeler's face grew somber. "It's unfortunate, but it would be irresponsible—"

Geoffrey's voice rose. "What's *irresponsible* is herding together people infected with AHMS. The disease is unstable—each new host creates new mutations, new variations. When patients are housed in close proximity, they accelerate the evolution of the disease."

"I want to help you with this," the senator said, looking again at his watch. "But I have a meeting in five minutes. Let's talk more about this later."

Geoffrey sighed. "All right. Thank you for your time."

When the senator disconnected, Geoffrey closed his laptop and looked around the rose garden. Without Piotr's regular sprays and fertilizers, the leaves were mottled with yellow and black. Powdery mold had killed the Peace rose on the far right, and aphids sucked the life out of any new buds, leaving them to die without blooming, shriveled on the branch.

He hoped the federal government's neglect wouldn't have the same effect on the patients in the camps.

It was late at night when an anonymous call came through. Idaho blinked his eyes behind the VR goggles. He'd been on for eighteen hours and had started to disconnect when the high-priority call came in.

What was interesting was that the call was stripped of header information. It had bounced through servers in Zurich, New Zealand, and San Francisco, but the place of origin had been removed.

Nice work. He wondered if it was another hacker auditioning to design modifications. Idaho started a tracer worm to find the signal's origin.

He brought up his avatar and answered, "Ye-ES?"

A man in his early sixties squinted at the screen and asked someone off camera, "What's with the fag? You said this was a smart guy."

Idaho froze. It wasn't the first time his avatar had been misinterpreted. "FUCK YOU, too," he said and began the disconnect protocol.

"Wait, wait!" The older man shrugged. "I'm sorry. This whole virtual shit, it takes getting used to." As he shrugged, the white line of shirt at his collar gaped open, revealing a patch of mismatched skin.

Idaho relaxed. The caller needed what he could provide. It changed the dynamic of the conversation in his favor. "Two seconds to EXPLAIN YOURSELF or I DISCONNECT."

The old man's eyes widened as if he wasn't used to being spoken to in that tone. Then he said, "I want you should design some work for me and the boys."

"Gene WORK?"

"Yeah. I heard you make cures for the plague."

Idaho twitched a muscle in his neck and started a backwards trace on the connection. "I treat SYMPTOMS. There is NO CURE."

"Whatever. I need medicine and I ain't going to no death camp."

The worm Idaho had set loose traveled the signal towards its source. San Francisco, New Zealand, Zaire . . . Chicago. Idaho's eyes flicked to the readout. An address in Little Italy. Without changing his avatar's expression, Idaho asked, "What do YOU OFFER in return?"

The old man sucked his teeth. "Distribution. I got people all over the country who can move the stuff."

"Why should I SELL to YOU?"

"Money. Everybody wants it, everybody needs it. You telling me you supply these camps for free?"

Idaho said nothing.

The old man's eyes widened. "Well, consider this an opportunity to expand. The money you make from this, you can fund good works all over the globe."

Idaho's lips twitched at the characterization of himself as a selfless philanthropist.

"My pushers used to sell smack, horse, poison. Now they can sell cures. If you don't help me on this . . . I'll find someone who will. Only maybe they won't have your skill. People will buy hope at any price. If you come in on this, maybe they can buy a real cure."

"You'd SELL fake TREATMENTS?"

"What am I, a doctor? How should I know what's fake?"

"Why ME? THERE ARE OTHERS you could contact. People more AVAILABLE."

The old man touched his chest and spread his arms in an embracing gesture. "Because I hear you're the best. When Antonio wants someone to work on his body," he said, pulling back his sleeve to reveal the marks of AHMS, "he wants the best."

Idaho recalled Lillith's call about disappearing shipments. "I could USE YOUR help in OHIO. Some of our shipments have GONE MISSING."

Antonio chuckled. "Consider it solved. Do we have a deal?"

Idaho knew the man was desperate. He'd felt the same fear when he'd caught the plague from Exeter, when he'd been unsure he could stay ahead of the variations.

"I don't know. Medical supplies are hard to get, even with money. We sometimes can't buy what we need."

Antonio licked his lips. "I can help you there, too. But for this, you give extra. I hear you do more than cures, that you make . . . improvements. Fix up me and my boys, and a couple of cases of whatever you need falls off a truck in Jersey. My friends can help your friends."

The old man's brown eyes glittered with greed. "Do we have a deal?"

"Of course, DON ANTONIO MORETTI. Always A PLEASURE to do business with CHICAGO."

The old man's mouth gaped open. "How did you—"

Idaho cut the connection, smiling to himself. It was good to keep the upper hand when dealing with dangerous men. Two problems solved: Ohio and supplies. He would sleep well tonight.

Geoffrey called Senator Wheeler every day for the next week. Each time he was told by his secretary that the senator was in a meeting.

That Thursday, Mr. Yi's wife died with only the image and voice of her husband for comfort.

When Geoffrey heard the news his chest seized up. If he hadn't pushed Wheeler to rescind the law, the senator might have pulled strings for an exemption for Mr. Yi. Geoffrey had thrown away the old man's last chance to be with his wife.

He lay on his bunk facedown in the pillow. It was hopeless. As long as 99.9 percent of the voters lived outside of the camps and were afraid of the infected, the changed would stay imprisoned.

If only there was a way to convince the public that the vaccine would protect them, to show them how unjust it was to separate people like Mr. Yi from their families. If he could get the voters on his side, the politicians might come around.

He needed publicity, a way to get the message out to millions of people. But he didn't have money for a public relations campaign; he couldn't even afford a newspaper ad.

Geoffrey flipped over on his back and propped his laptop on his stomach. It was tuned to CNN. He watched images of villages burning in Mozambique where the plague had struck. Russia was deporting foreign nationals with the disease, dumping them at the border without transportation or food.

A blond woman in Chicago stood in front of a housing project where a man had been killed because his neighbors suspected he'd contracted the plague. He'd been tossed out of an eleven-story window.

She wore a crisp pink suit and spoke passionately. "This is the fourth death on the South Side in the last month. Which leads this correspondent to question which is the greater disease, the plague or our own paranoia."

Geoffrey checked her name on the screen: Ellie Peterson, CNN health correspondent.

Ellie was clean-cut, opinionated, and articulate. He went to the CNN Web site and pulled up a list of stories she'd worked on in the last year. Ellie had traveled to the scene of inner-city riots, filmed guerrilla action in Costa Rica, and visited hospices that cared for patients with Vratsa. She was no figurehead for the camera, but a reporter willing to put herself in harm's way for an exclusive.

She was ideal. Geoffrey picked up his cell phone and placed a call.

Ellie Peterson was an athletic twenty-eight, with a shining cap of blond hair and a winning smile. When Geoffrey first saw her in person, however, she walked hunched over like an old woman, her hair was uncombed and dirty, her face bare of makeup, and she wore a faded pair of lavender sweats. She looked perfect.

Ellie stepped off the ferry with the other passengers from the mainland: a scruffy man dressed in boots, jeans, and a plaid flannel work shirt, a homeless woman who muttered to the space above her left shoulder, and two men who spoke Spanish to each other in low fearful tones.

New infections had dwindled to a handful of people a month who either had missed the publicity blitz about vaccination or who avoided government agencies for reasons of their own.

Geoffrey had arranged for her to come to the Allen compound instead of Rosario Resorts by telling Captain Morgenson she was his second cousin, Eleanor Willis, and should be housed on the family estate. Morgenson had agreed with ill grace. His attitude towards Geoffrey had changed since the incident with Mr. Yi.

"Eleanor!" Geoffrey called, waving.

Ellie returned his wave with a timid gesture. She stepped off the gangplank and joined him.

They exchanged a polite hug. "Is everything in place?" she whispered.

"Yes. You have your, uh, equipment?"

Ellie tapped a hearing aid in her left ear and pulled a pair of wire-rimmed glasses out of her sweatshirt

pocket. "Not the most fashionable," she said, placing
them on her nose, "but they get the job done." She
scanned the ferry, the dock, the army trucks and their
drivers, the guards on the pier holding assault rifles.
Geoffrey wondered which of the shots would make it
into her story.

A guard checked Ellie's fake ID and waved her and
Geoffrey onto the truck bound for the Allen estate.

At Ellie's intake examination, Dr. Takawari surprised the duty nurse by offering to perform the procedure himself. When the nurse left, Ellie asked, "Can
we talk now?"

Dr. Takawari shook his head. He leaned close while
examining her ear with an otoscope and whispered,
"This evening I'm on call. Fake a seizure and I'll take
you into one of the private examination rooms."

A guard escorted Ellie to her bunk. It was in the
row beside Geoffrey's, three columns down. Dr. Takawari had arranged it so she would be close to
Geoffrey.

When the guard left, Geoffrey led Ellie outside and
told her to wait at the tennis courts.

Then he went to the ballroom to find Mr. Yi. He
was lying in bed. It was where Mr. Yi spent most of
his time since his wife's death. Geoffrey knelt down
by the old man and said, "Mr. Yi, come outside. I
know a young lady who would like to interview you."

"No want talk with anyone," Mr. Yi said and
rolled over.

"Please," Geoffrey whispered. "It's a reporter; she
wants to talk to you. Maybe if enough people know
what happened, they'll let us go home to our
families."

Mr. Yi grunted into his pillow, "My family dead.
Nowhere to go."

"Yes, but don't you want to help the others?"

Mr. Yi sat up. "Why you speak soft?"

Geoffrey looked over his shoulder. It was lunchtime, and the other inmates were in the dining hall.

"I don't want the captain to find out what we're doing."

Mr. Yi's black eyes glittered. "I talk, bad for captain?"

Geoffrey paused. Mr. Yi was such a soft-spoken man that his vengeful intensity startled Geoffrey. "Yes," he whispered, "it would upset the captain and his commander greatly if they knew what we were doing."

Mr. Yi leapt out of bed. "I go."

Ellie waited for them on the tennis courts. They were indoors, and on rainy days patients ran laps on the green asphalt, but the sky was clear today and the courts were deserted.

"This is Mr. Yi," Geoffrey said, "the man I told you about." To Mr. Yi, he said, "Ellie Peterson, a reporter for CNN. She's going to ask you some questions about your wife."

Mr. Yi's expression fell at the mention of his dead wife, but he straightened his back and said, "Ask."

Ellie took Mr. Yi's shoulders and turned him so his face was in the light. When he was in position, she said, "Mr. Lee, how long have you been at the Orcas Island camp?"

Mr. Yi looked at Geoffrey, who nodded for him to continue. "Eighteen month."

"During that time has your family visited you?"

Mr. Yi shook his head. "No, no can visit. Not allowed."

"Have you been able to call them?"

"Yes." Mr. Yi raised his index finger. "Can call one time a month. Half hour."

Ellie's voice became sympathetic. "I hear your wife of thirty-five years recently passed away from cancer. Were you able to visit her in the hospital?"

Mr. Lee's brave expression crumpled. "No. Not allowed. She die without me, much pain." He hid his face in his palms. "I wish I join her soon. Too much pain here. Miss her. Miss her very much."

Ellie took a step back, her eyes scanning Mr. Yi for the best shot. "Families estranged, loved ones unable to reach a dying partner's bedside. How far are we willing to go to protect ourselves from the plague? Are the camps even effective? To answer these questions, let's talk next to the camp's head physician." Ellie snapped off her glasses and tucked them into her sweatshirt pocket. "That was great."

Geoffrey wrapped his arms around the still crying Mr. Yi. "Yeah," he said tonelessly. "Just wonderful."

He felt despicable for using the old man. But maybe Mr. Yi's pain would move people outside the camps.

While they waited for nightfall, Geoffrey took Ellie around the camp. He showed her the overflowing portajohns, the rows of sick and dying stacked in bunk beds. Ellie wore her glasses, recording a man coughing blood into a handkerchief, the listless expression of a woman with jaundice, a child's bleeding sores, and Geoffrey with his mismatched hair and skin—all material for the story she would edit when she returned to the mainland.

When they were in a quiet corner of the rose garden, Ellie said, "I'm here with Geoffrey Allen, patient zero of AHMS, and the man who first got the plague—"

Geoffrey held his hand up to block the camera embedded in her glasses. "Do we have to use my real name?"

Ellie cocked her head and put her hand on her hip. "Yes. It's not a compelling story without *the* Geoffrey Allen. You're famous."

"Infamous." Geoffrey showed Ellie a pink scar that bisected his left eyebrow. "A boot did this. When I was in the last camp, they found out who I was."

Ellie blew out a breath. "Look, I heard about the attack. I know you've been through a lot. But"—she spread her hands—"we can't get this on the air without you. I mean, all I have so far is a sad old man and an angry doctor. You're the man everyone wants to hear."

Geoffrey bit his lower lip. He wanted to help the changed, to undo some of the damage he'd caused. "All right," he said, squaring his shoulders. "Continue."

Ellie grinned and adjusted her glasses. "Geoffrey Allen, you've been accused of creating the disease. What do you say to that?"

"I—" Geoffrey's voice choked in his throat. "I don't know what caused the disease, whether Dr. Fowler made a mistake engineering the virus or it exchanged genes with a wild virus. We may never know. What's important is to focus on those people living with the disease and do everything we can to make their lives better."

Ellie moved closer, tightening the focus on Geoffrey. "Tell me, Geoffrey, what's the worst thing about having the disease?"

Geoffrey flipped the hair out of his eyes. "You mean other than waiting to die?" He stared up at the sky, looking for inspiration. Then he met Ellie's eyes, staring right into the camera. "The worst thing is the dehumanization. The Orcas Island camp is better than others, but even here we aren't allowed more than an overnight bag's worth of personal gear." He plucked at the orange jumpsuit he wore. "We're forced to wear these. The orange makes it hard to escape. Look at this." He flicked the numbered label. "Not even a name tag—just a number. We're not allowed to leave. As if having a terminal disease wasn't bad enough, we're cut off from our families and treated like prisoners."

After the dinner meal, four guards led the changed to the barracks, allowed half an hour to get ready for bed, and then turned out the lights.

Ellie waited an hour, until the ward was quiet and the patients were asleep. Then she began thrashing in her bunk. Her faked seizure was so violent that the bed frame shuddered and its feet screeched on the floor.

Geoffrey climbed down from his bunk and ran to

her side. He dragged her out of the bottom bunk and, with one of the guards' help, half-carried her through the maze of beds to Dr. Takawari's office. The doctor had arranged to be the physician on call that night.

"In here," Dr. Takawari said, leading them into a guest bedroom that had been turned into an examination room.

Inside the room, Dr. Takawari dismissed the guard with a peremptory wave of his hand. "I can handle it from here."

When the door closed behind the guard, Ellie stopped thrashing and smoothed her hair back. She waited, listening to the door, until the guard's footsteps had receded.

With her thumb and forefingers, she tried out camera angles. "Over here," she told Dr. Takawari, patting the end of the examination table. She had him sit on the table, with his ankle crossed over his knee. A defibrillator cart and heart monitor stood in the background. Ellie put on her glasses and checked the shot. "Good."

She took a step back and asked, "Dr. Takawari, can you tell me some of the health risks associated with the camps?"

Dr. Takawari nodded, his expression somber. "The worst is the overcrowding and cross-contamination. AHMS is a very unstable virus. Each new genome it encounters creates new variations. When infected people are crowded together, they cross-contaminate, accelerating both the evolution of the disease and their own deterioration."

Ellie slowly crept in on Dr. Takawari, creating a zoom effect. "Are there any implications for the rest of us?"

"Yes." Dr. Takawari pulled his fingers together, drawing a shrinking circle. "By collecting the infected together, we will create more virulent versions of AHMS. A mutation will inevitably arise that is immune to the vaccine."

Ellie froze, and rotated the frame of one of her

lenses. In a low, ominous voice, she asked, "In your estimation, how likely is that?"

Dr. Takawari didn't blink. His voice was confident and final. "As I said, it is inevitable."

Ellie pulled off her glasses and looked at Dr. Takawari. "Off the record, how much danger am I in here?"

Dr. Takawari shrugged. "I can't say. We've had no substantiated cases of a vaccinated person contracting AHMS, but there is always a first time."

Ellie swallowed and put the glasses back on. "Are the CDC and NIH aware of your concerns?"

"Yes, cross-contamination and its implications for breeding viral mutations resistant to the vaccine were addressed in the NIH's last report. They recommended separate quarantine for patients." Dr. Takawari turned his hands palm up in a gesture of surrender. "As you've seen, we don't have the facilities for that. I think in-home care would be the logical alternative."

"Is that a possibility?"

"Not with the current law. It confines patients to the containment camps. Before there was a vaccine, quarantine was necessary. Now it's dangerous. The NIH and CDC have stated that patients should be released when the vaccine is proven effective. But they don't provide any clear criteria for making that determination."

"Do you believe these health organizations are stonewalling the release of AHMS patients for political reasons?"

It was a dangerous question for an army physician to answer publicly. Dr. Takawari squared his shoulders. "Yes, yes, I do. There is no scientific basis for imprisoning these people."

Ellie asked a few more questions, clarifying some of the terms Dr. Takawari had used and expanding on the technical side of his argument for patient release. When she was done, she tucked the glasses into her sweatshirt pocket.

"Given that patients aren't allowed to leave, how are you going to get me off the island?"

"Simple," said Dr. Takawari. "I'll say you're a fully vaccinated schizophrenic whose records were filed under the wrong number. Even in this electronic age, mistakes happen. Your corrected case number shows a current vaccination for AHMS."

Geoffrey escorted Ellie back to her bunk. He wondered what story she would weave out of the material she'd gathered.

The story came out two days after Ellie returned to the mainland. Geoffrey had watched CNN constantly since she left, to make sure he wouldn't miss it. When the segment came on, Geoffrey waved Mr. Yi over to view it.

A voice-over described the statistics and history of the plague while Ellie's camera wandered through the barracks, showing gaunt bodies, a woman vomiting into a bucket, a five-year-old girl crying in her bunk, alone, her parents not allowed to join her at the camp. Mr. Yi came onscreen and told about his wife.

Ellie panned over the doctors' station at the front of the ballroom and explained that just five doctors managed the care for more than three hundred terminally ill patients. She played Takawari's interview.

A cleaned-up Ellie in a peach-colored suit brought the segment to a close. She looked intently into the camera and said, "Overcrowding, inadequate staffing. Are we shipping our most desperately ill citizens off to die? And what are the implications for the rest of us, should these breeding grounds produce a mutation of AHMS immune to the vaccine? From Chicago, this is Ellie Peterson."

The story had painted a dark picture of despair and medical mismanagement by the current administration. It was chilling. Perfect.

Mr. Yi tapped the screen when the report was over. His face screwed up with a hurt expression. "She say you Geoffrey Allen. Not Jones—Allen?"

There was a bellow from Captain Morgenson's office. "Geoffrey, Yi, Takawari, get in here!"

Geoffrey and Mr. Yi caught up with Dr. Takawari in the hallway. The three exchanged worried looks.

Inside Morgenson's office, the wall television replayed Ellie's report. Her expression was somber as she interviewed Dr. Takawari.

"What *the hell* is that?" Morgenson shouted, pointing at the screen. Geoffrey and Mr. Yi sat in the twin guest chairs. Dr. Takawari leaned against the wall.

Morgenson pointed an accusing finger at Takawari. "You are gone. Start packing. If I have my way, you'll be thrown out of the army."

"I can explain—" Geoffrey started.

Morgenson rounded on him. "And you! I gave you liberties. Kept your identity secret so the other patients wouldn't abuse you. This is how you repay me? This makes me look like an incompetent idiot."

"Sir," Geoffrey said, "we didn't bring you into this because we wanted you to have deniability."

"I've got deniability all right. From here on out, consider any requests you make denied."

The phone on Morgenson's desk rang. He glanced at the caller ID. He waved his arm at them. "Go! I've got damage control to do." He slammed the door behind them. Geoffrey heard him say, "Yes, General, I saw the story."

Geoffrey walked down the hall that led from the officers' wing to the barracks.

In the big room he heard whispering. The other patients followed him with hazel-brown eyes like his own.

"Is it true?" one man called. "Are you Geoffrey Allen?"

Geoffrey turned to face him. All of the patients had exchanged so much DNA, it was like looking in a mirror.

Geoffrey faced the crowd. This was the risk he'd accepted to get his message out. "Yes. Yes, I am."

"Then this was once your house," the man said. He was flanked by three other men. The speaker climbed up a set of bunks and tore down one of the chandeliers that lit the ballroom turned barracks.

The crystal bounced off the metal bed frames on the way down and smashed to fragments on the hardwood floor.

The man looked down at the broken fixture. "My lover used to love crystal. But now he's dead."

A woman in the crowd shouted, "They're all dead—because of you!"

The crowd began tearing into the walls, ripping down the curtains, stomping on paintings, tearing the frames apart and throwing the pieces at Geoffrey.

Geoffrey watched, frozen, as the mob gutted the room his mother had loved. If the CDC was to be believed, this was the very room where the epidemic had begun. Just outside those French doors he had spoken with Miriam on the balcony . . . in another lifetime.

Dr. Takawari burst out of the hallway that led to Morgenson's office. He shoved the two men closest to him, bowling them over with his rugby player's physique.

"What are you doing? Are you insane?"

A man, Geoffrey wasn't sure if it was his first interrogator, pointed his way. "He's Geoffrey Allen. He caused the plague."

Takawari shook one of the men by the shoulder. "Look at him." He turned the man in Geoffrey's direction. "Look. He's one of you. He bears the same marks of disease. He suffers the same ailments and hangs on to life just as tentatively. He's lost his entire family to the plague, everything he ever cared about. His home has been confiscated by the government. He deserves your pity, not your wrath."

The man squirmed in Takawari's grip and wailed, "He killed my family."

The crowd watched, their eyes flitting between the doctor and Geoffrey.

"No," Takawari said, "a virus did that. No one

knows how Geoffrey's treatment became a plague, but he has lost as much—or more—than any of you. You want to punish him? Then leave him alive, in the ruins of his family home, haunted each day by memories of the people he loved."

Geoffrey felt his eyes sting with tears. He was afraid. He still bore the scars of the beating at Fort Stewart. A wrong move from him could incite the mob into frenzy.

In his peripheral vision, Geoffrey saw the guards circle the mob.

Takawari said, "He came here under a false name because he was attacked at the last camp. He was nearly beaten to death. But still he gave that interview to CNN—knowing what might happen if you found out. He did that because he's trying to make things better, not just for himself, but all victims of AHMS."

Takawari let the man he was holding go, and the man slumped to his knees.

"He gave away his wealth to fund research into the plague. And after a vaccine was developed, he sold his family's antiques to pay for the daily treatments that keep you alive. Destroy this house and you destroy yourselves. How many doses could that"—he pointed to the destroyed chandelier—"have bought? How many lives are you willing to sacrifice to your anger?"

Tears streamed down Geoffrey's face. He had been hated for so long. To hear Takawari speak in his defense was worth almost getting killed.

"Think about that. He's given everything he has to help you. What have you done to help yourselves?"

The guards closed in and drove everyone outside so the janitoral staff could clear the mess.

Takawari clasped Geoffrey's shoulder. "You all right?"

Geoffrey nodded and dashed away the tears with the back of his fist. "I'll live." But he wasn't sure if that was a blessing or a curse.

*   *   *

Three days later, Morgenson's retribution for the CNN story came through: Dr. Takawari was demoted and transferred to a camp in southern California.

When Geoffrey heard, he went to Dr. Takawari's office.

Takawari packed his personal possessions into a cardboard box: a phalaenopsis orchid, a picture of his daughter in a Stanford University sweatshirt.

Geoffrey stopped in the doorway. "I'm sorry to see you go. I never meant for this to happen."

Takawari smiled a brave smile. "I knew what I was doing. A response was inevitable. When you lance a boil, there's a mess. The truth needed to be told. I wouldn't take back a word."

The doctor the army brought in to replace Takawari was Dr. Samuel Richardson. He was a lean African-American with a close-cropped beard and a spine as straight as a plumb line.

Dr. Richardson's first act as head physician was to review the medical records and processes used by the other doctors and lay down new guidelines. Geoffrey knew the first time he saw the new head physician march by with a gaggle of doctors flying in his wake, that he would find no ally in Dr. Richardson.

CHAPTER 16

Lillith stopped her Lexus at a traffic light, feeling conspicuous. Her new car stood out in this low-income neighborhood.

Abandoned warehouses with cracked windowpanes lined the street. Garbage piled up in alleyways and spilled out of cans. A two-foot-long rat ambled under a Dumpster as her car eased along the street. Lillith suppressed a wave of nausea when she saw three children chasing it. She was tempted to stop the car right there and march them to the nearest elementary school. But there was no time. Even with the air conditioner on full blast, the dry ice she'd used for the samples would last only an hour in this heat.

She'd gotten Idaho's email about this drop last night. "Good news," he had written, "I've got a new associate in Atlanta. You won't have to forward blood samples to Miami anymore."

It had sounded like a good idea at the time. The GWI samples could be sequenced faster if done locally. But now, driving through backstreets, Lillith had second thoughts.

She checked her GPS to make sure she hadn't taken a wrong turn. No, this was definitely the right section of southeast Eighth Street.

Idaho had instructed Lillith to take the samples to "Louie" at the Cut-Right barbershop. From the greasy windows and grimy barber pole outside, "Cut-Rate" would have been more appropriate. Two young men in torn jeans and leather vests panhandled Lillith as she walked by. With their clean faces and well-fed bodies, their pleas for money seemed more sport than need. She ignored them and stepped through the door.

Inside, an ancient man said, "Sorry, don't do ladies." He scratched the nap of white hair that barely covered his dark scalp. "Not even lesbos."

Lillith wondered if this last was offered as general information, or if he'd made an assumption about her personal life.

"Are you Louie?"

The man grinned, exposing four teeth and an expanse of speckled gum. "Me? Naw. That's a good one. Louie's my grandson." He pointed through the plate glass. "One of those no 'counts outside."

The two teenagers who had panhandled her were leaning over her car, pointing at something inside.

Lillith hurried outside. "Louie?"

The lighter-skinned one smiled; there was a resemblance to his grandfather in the way his eyes crinkled. Gold flashed on his right incisor. He had blue eyes. Not the gray green she'd seen on some light-skinned blacks, but brilliant blue, almost turquoise. They must be contacts.

"I've got a delivery for you," she said.

Louie looked around and pressed his hands at her in a shushing gesture. He placed his arm on her shoulder and drew her into a huddle. "Not here. I'll meet you around back."

He straightened and said loudly, "Drive that hair tonic to the alley, and I'll unload it for you."

Who was the show for? Lillith didn't see anyone on the street except a crumpled heap of rags that might have been a homeless man. She nodded and got into the car, drove it around back, and parked in the alley.

Louie and his companion took the two Styrofoam boxes from her passenger seat and carried them through the barbershop's back door. Stairs led to an apartment above the shop. It didn't look big enough to house a genetics lab, so she guessed this was another drop point.

"See you next week," Louie said. He wasn't play-acting anymore; there was a furtive seriousness to his face.

Lillith understood from his tone that she was being dismissed. She nodded and backtracked down the stairs to the alley. The two young men followed.

Louie's companion smiled as Lillith backed the car out of the alley. His teeth stood out against the nearly blue-black gloss of his skin; the canines were nearly an inch long. She looked back. It must have been a trick of the light.

Louie and the other youth waved: normal, healthy boys who should have been in college instead of standing on street corners.

Lillith locked her doors and drove slowly out of the neighborhood.

When Lillith got back to her apartment, she called Geoffrey and described what had happened. "I don't like it," she told Geoffrey when he came online. "Something's going on with Idaho's associates."

Geoffrey shrugged. "Contacts and teeth implants. So they're into body modification. Who did you expect Idaho to recruit, the Salvation Army?"

Lillith paced the length of her bedroom. "Did you ever wonder what hold Idaho has on these people? They're not philanthropists. They wouldn't help him unless they got something out of it . . . or Idaho had threatened them.

"What's more, there's talk at the CDC of burglaries targeting medical supply houses in Chicago, Seattle, New York. All the major companies have been hit. The stolen goods include anhydrous acetonitrile, DNA-grade tetrazole, capping reagents A and B, restriction enzymes, and oligo purification cartridges—all supplies used in gene sequencing and synthesis. I think Idaho's people are involved."

Geoffrey pinched the bridge of his nose. "Is there any proof linking Idaho's group to the burglaries?"

"No. But it's too much of a coincidence to ignore."

"These are desperate times, Dr. Watkins. Isn't a little theft worth the thousands of lives they'll save?"

Lillith shook her head. "Yes, but it's not fair to turn young people into criminals."

"This disease isn't fair," Geoffrey said. "We have to fight it however we can."

What Geoffrey told Lillith about using every weapon at their disposal was true. But there was one card he hadn't yet played. His stomach tightened up into a knot when he contemplated it, but this was no time for pride. Geoffrey placed a call to Henry J. Poulson, Esquire.

Poulson answered on the third ring. He reclined in a leather high-backed chair, smoking a Havana cigar. His expression flickered with dismay when Geoffrey's face came on screen. Poulson took the cigar out of his mouth and leaned forward. "Geoffrey. How are you doing?"

Geoffrey swallowed. He had to get this out before he lost his nerve. "Henry, my family has been good to you, have they not?"

"Of course. I numbered your parents among my closest friends."

"I hate to ask, Henry . . . but I've no choice. I want to challenge the law that restricts the infected to the camps. Did you see my interview?"

"The whole world saw."

"Then you know the containment camps are medically dangerous as well as a violation of our constitutional rights. I want to file a suit to overturn the law but . . ."

Henry Poulson took the cigar from his mouth and pointed it at the screen. "You haven't any money."

"Correct." Geoffrey looked at his blue-slippered feet. "I'm willing to give you a mortgage on the family estate." Geoffrey swallowed. "You wouldn't be able to collect, however, until the army disbands the camp and moves off the property and I sell the property."

Henry tucked the cigar back into his mouth and chewed on the end. "No. I couldn't accept that."

Geoffrey's chest constricted. Henry Poulson was the best of the best. Without a high-powered lawyer, the legal attack would fail. "I understand. Thank you for—"

"No. I don't think you do. Your mother was the finest lady I ever had the pleasure to meet. They don't make them like her anymore. If you think I could offend her memory by forcing her son to sell his home, you've got another think coming." He tapped cigar ash into a tray. "I'll fight this one to the Supreme Court on sheer cussedness."

Geoffrey was ashamed to have misjudged his old friend. "Henry," he choked, "thank you."

"Don't despair, boy. I intend to win."

Ellie's newscast aroused public interest. Geoffrey received emails from patients in other camps, thanking him for speaking out, asking what they could do to help convince Congress to repeal the law.

There were condolences about his condition from friendly acquaintances and his aunt in Boston. Senator Wheeler sent a letter promising to bring the issue up in committee.

But Congress chose not to review the law.

Slowly the messages from the outside world trickled from hundreds, to dozens, to just a few each day. Without additional stimulus, nothing would change. The public would move on to the next story of the week. Geoffrey needed some way to pressure Congress to reconsider the issue, some way to show how strongly he and the other patients felt.

But what could he do? Captain Morgenson would never let another reporter on the island. The IDs of all incoming patients were now checked and double-checked.

Geoffrey looked at the guards patrolling the perimeter. Why should he and the other patients be treated like prisoners? They'd committed no crime. They weren't enemy agents captured in wartime.

Or were they? Geoffrey mulled over the concept: He and the others were like prisoners in the war against AHMS. Geoffrey recalled the old movies he'd watched as a child, the scenes of soldiers shot down and suffering in crowded camps.

A frequent refrain in those movies had been that the first duty of any prisoner was to escape. What would happen, he mused, if all the ambulatory patients in the hospitals simply stood up and walked away from the camps? Would the guards shoot? Would Congress send tanks against them? Images of Tiananmen Square and Gandhi's protests against British colonialism flashed in his mind.

It would take more than one person. One patient climbing over a wall was an escape attempt. Hundreds fleeing the camps was a movement. It would remind people the infected still existed and were being held against their will.

Portraying the patients as prisoners in the war against AHMS would make them more sympathetic to the public, perhaps sway popular opinion. Let Henry Poulson fight the legal battles. Geoffrey would wage a war of images and semantics.

But he'd need allies. Geoffrey opened his laptop and started an encryption program. He emailed patients in other camps: the ones who'd contacted him after the CNN interview, who seemed sincere and frustrated by their incarceration, ready for action. He asked them to meet him online at 9 P.M.

The day dragged as he waited for the arranged time. At 8:50 P.M., he opened the first connection.

The encryption software scrambled the messages en route so anyone intercepting them or monitoring his communications would be unable to read them.

A man with the medium brown skin of the Leland camp in Jackson, Mississippi, appeared onscreen.

Other figures appeared, their features a blending

of the ethnic groups that populated their region of the country.

It surprised Geoffrey how much they all looked alike. From the Mississippi Delta to Boston to Southern California, the blended faces were more similar than different.

When they had all assembled, Geoffrey said, "The Constitution guarantees each of us personal liberty, which includes the right to move freely. The law that keeps us imprisoned in these camps is therefore unconstitutional." He tapped his fingers against the laptop's touchpad. "Those of you who saw Dr. Takawari's interview know it is medically irresponsible as well. Now that there is a vaccine, there is no reason why we should have to remain in these camps and every reason to set us free."

"What can we do?" a woman from the California camp asked, spreading her hands.

"I've got a lawyer filing a suit to have the courts overturn the law." He dismissed the lawsuit with a wave. "But that may take years to filter through the courts. Years some of us don't have. I propose we stage a protest. If we can get popular opinion on our side, we can force Congress to rescind the law."

"What sort of protest?" asked the Mississippi man.

"We try to escape."

"But there are guards," said a man from Boston. "With machine guns. There's no way we could make it."

"The point," said Geoffrey, "is not to escape, but to raise awareness about our cause. If suddenly hundreds of prisoners—from camps all over the country—are climbing over the walls, it'll make national news. We can use that as a platform to state our case." He raised a warning forefinger. "But you're right. There are risks involved. I don't think the guards will fire on us if we try to escape in a peaceful and orderly manner. But there's always the chance something will go wrong. The guards may panic. I won't lie to you: There are risks."

"I don't care," said the man from Mississippi. "It's been eleven months since I've seen my kids. My wife wouldn't even put them on the phone last time I called. She told me it was better they believed I was dead. My only chance to see my sons is to get out of this damn camp. I'm going over that wall and, if I make it, I'm not giving any press conference. I'll grab my kids and you'll never see me again."

"Fair enough," Geoffrey said. "Who else wants in?"

Everyone did. They agreed to coordinate their escapes for the same night. On April 19, patients from camps in Mississippi, Massachusetts, Texas, California, Georgia, Wisconsin, Nevada, and Washington would go over the wall.

"We need to recruit others," Geoffrey said. "The more attempting to escape, the better. But be careful not to speak to anyone who might, deliberately or otherwise, reveal our plan."

They would need outside help. He thought of Lillith. No, he needed her to continue her work for the CDC. He couldn't ask her to do something illegal. But there was someone else. Geoffrey placed a call to Ellie Peterson. He explained the reasoning behind the escape attempt and bargained for transportation off Orcas Island in exchange for an exclusive interview afterwards.

Idaho used a double-blind encryption scheme to talk to his New York contact. It piggybacked a compressed signal on top of a music stream. The real data was ASCII text, no images, no sound. Triple-DES encoded with a 2,048-character key. Nearly unbreakable.

"I need the locations of major suppliers," said Idaho. His voice was translated into luminous lime-green characters that scrolled across the screen: "Lock combinations, current inventories, security guard schedules."

His contact's reply printed beneath Idaho's request. "I can do that. You providing the muscle?"

"If you've got local talent, I'll cut them in for a fourth."

"Consider it done."

"Good. When I get the supplies, your group is next in line for a sequencer."

"I can barely wait." The contact's words glowed a second and then faded. The connection unraveled itself, reducing any traces on the Net that the conversation had ever existed.

A message icon flashed in Idaho's peripheral vision. Idaho changed the focus of his goggles. It was a trace log he had attached to Geoffrey Allen's virtual address. He'd begun recording all of Geoffrey's communications after his call about collaborating on treatments for the camps. Geoffrey had surprised Idaho once, and Idaho intended for that never to happen again.

His trace program wrote a log containing the transcript of the interaction, as well as a legend listing the speakers' names, locations, IP addresses, and other relevant information.

Idaho replayed the conversation. When it was over he leaned back and tapped his fingertips together.

Geoffrey Allen, never a dull moment. But what could you expect from the man who had unleashed genetic fire upon the world?

He forwarded the transcript to Lillith.

That done, Idaho reviewed today's requests for changes. They came from all over the world. He highlighted six and moved them to his contacts folder. They would be useful when the time came.

As Lillith read the email from AzureMontana, her blood pressure rose. What an idiotic plan. What did Geoffrey hope to accomplish with this useless grandstanding?

She loaded encryption software and called Geoffrey. He answered after two rings. His face was slightly grainy from the low-resolution camera built into his laptop, but even through the pixelation Lillith saw dark circles under his eyes.

"Are you insane?" she asked.

"Hello to you, too," Geoffrey said. "Did you call just to check my mental status?"

"I know about April 19. Do you have any idea what kind of chaos that stunt will cause?"

"How did—" His brow furrowed.

"Our friend in Idaho is watching you. You can't do this. It's too dangerous. If guards start shooting, it'll be a bloodbath."

"The federal court dismissed my lawsuit." Geoffrey balled his hands into fists. "There's no other way. People won't listen unless we make them. Passive resistance is the only tool we have."

"Give me three months. I'll find a better way."

"Some of the people in these camps don't have three months. It's been nearly a year since the camps were set up, eight months since the vaccine was developed. If they don't release us now, when? I'm through waiting for a solution."

Lillith shook her head at the Web camera mounted at the top of her wall screen. "Fight the system, but not this way."

"Peaceful solutions don't work." Geoffrey's avatar pulled away. "I've been trying to find a 'peaceful' solution for *eight months*. And what have I accomplished?" He scrunched his brows together in a glower. "Nothing. No one cares about the infected. The time for talk is over. We must use action."

"Violence isn't the answer."

Geoffrey cocked his head. "How could you possibly understand what we're going through? You're not sick. You haven't been warehoused with dying people, waiting for your turn in the incinerator. You're safe in a secure government job. Follow the rules, research what they tell you to. You're a pawn of the system."

Lillith's face grew hot. "I'm a pawn? Me?" She jabbed her finger at the screen. "Who helped you find a contact to synthesize cures? Who fought Lam to keep you in the CDC quarantine? Who risked death from infection to pick you up from Orcas? I have put my career and my life on the line for you. How *dare* you call me a pawn?"

"All right then, help us. You must have contacts—"

Lillith shook her head. "No. What you're doing is wrong. Even if the guards remain calm, there will be a backlash of public opinion. Patients breaking out of facilities in major population centers, in Boston, Dallas, and San Diego? People will panic."

Geoffrey threw up his hands. "The public's been vaccinated. There won't be any threat. That's the point we're trying to make. There's no medical reason to keep us in quarantine."

Lillith narrowed her eyes. "That's not relevant. People respond to threats emotionally, not logically. Not everyone believes the vaccine will protect them. You'll set the release movement back to prevaccination days."

Geoffrey pounded his fist into his palm. "I've got to do something. They've left me no other options. I have to get the public's attention any way I can."

"Not this way, Geoffrey. I won't let you."

Geoffrey's face paled. "Will you tell the authorities?"

Lillith raised her chin. "If I have to. What you're planning is wrong. People could get hurt."

Geoffrey grabbed the sides of his laptop. His face loomed large onscreen. "People already are. I thought I could depend on your support. Apparently I was wrong." With a punch of his finger, he broke the connection.

Lillith threw an empty carton of Chinese food at the screen. Damn him anyway. Where did he get off calling her a pawn of the system?

"Computer: Redial last connection."

The wall screen froze, then returned a dialog box: RECIPIENT REFUSES CONNECTION.

"Computer: Raise priority. Try again."

The same dialog box appeared.

Damn it. She had to stop him; otherwise all hell would break loose.

CHAPTER 17

The night of April 19 was cold and clear. A full moon lit the landscape. Geoffrey crept out of bed and tiptoed past rows of bunk beds.

A small figure blocked his path. In the dim light, Geoffrey couldn't see who it was until he was right on top of the old man.

"I go too," Mr. Yi whispered.

Geoffrey froze. Mr. Yi hadn't been in on the escape planning. Maybe Geoffrey had misinterpreted Mr. Yi's request. He asked, "Do you need help getting to the bathroom?"

Mr. Yi made an impatient *tsk* sound. "Mr. Yi old. No one sees Mr. Yi. I stand by wall. I see everything, hear everything. You escape; I go too."

Geoffrey shook his head, amazed by the old man's perceptiveness. "Your offer is brave. But this is dangerous."

"I not afraid." He thumped his bantam chest. "What have to live for, besides fight?"

Geoffrey put his hand on the old man's thin shoulder. "Let me fight this battle for you. Go back to bed and rest."

Mr. Yi knocked Geoffrey's hand away. "I go." His eyes were hot with determination.

Geoffrey sighed. "Is there no discouraging you?"

"I go. Your duty to take me."

"What?"

"We family now." Mr. Yi pointed at his own face, then Geoffrey's. "You have my eyes."

Geoffrey had seen what he meant this morning in his shaving mirror. Slight epicanthic folds creased at the corners of his eyes. The old man was right, in a way; all of the changed in a camp were family, sharing a single pool of genes.

Geoffrey's expression softened as he looked at the old man who had no other family. Geoffrey knew how lonely that was. "All right, you can go. We're meeting at the portajohns at eleven forty-five."

The old man nodded his white-topped head and walked off muttering, "Eleven forty-five."

By ones and twos, Geoffrey and the others snuck to the chemical toilets. They spaced out their trips in fifteen-minute intervals to prevent the guards from realizing how many people were leaving.

The toilets were the perfect rendezvous spot. Because of the smell, they were situated far from the house, along the western gate. For the same reason, they were poorly guarded. No one stood downwind of them any longer than they had to. And if a few patients snuck away to the toilets in the middle of the night, who would notice?

Geoffrey sheltered between two portajohns. "Is everybody here?" he whispered to the darkness.

Mr. Yi and the twelve other patients silently crept out of their hiding places inside and behind the toilets and congregated in the shadows around Geoffrey.

Geoffrey held his finger to his lips for silence. Guards patrolled the grounds at night, and Geoffrey didn't want to risk alerting them with voices. Silently, he counted heads to make sure the entire group had arrived.

He peeked out between the toilets. No guards were near; the yard was empty. He waved the others to follow him to the fence.

Geoffrey had played around and on the venerable iron fence surrounding the Allen estate all his life. He knew its strengths and weaknesses. Although it was now topped with razor wire, the fence itself was old and brittle. It had stood for forty years in the salt-air environment and was quite rusty.

Geoffrey pushed against one of the solder joins between the uprights. The metal groaned. "Help me," he grunted.

The other prisoners rushed against the fence, pushing with Geoffrey. The fence twisted like a tormented snake. It groaned and creaked.

Geoffrey worried that the sound or motion would bring guards. They had to get through the fence—now. He shoved harder at the weakened metal.

A weld broke free at the bottom. Geoffrey and the other patients pushed the base away from them, creating a triangular hole they could crawl through.

Geoffrey held open the hole and waved through the mother who wanted to reach her children.

A voice from the teak decking that surrounded the mansion shouted, "Stop or I'll shoot!"

"Quickly," Geoffrey said, waving the others through after her. He hoped Ellie had been able to keep her part of the bargain. She had promised to have a speedboat waiting at a pier half a mile west of the Allen compound. If she hadn't been able to sneak the boat up to Orcas, this escape was doomed to fail.

Shots rang out overhead. Geoffrey felt something slice across his upper arm. It stung like a branding iron. "Shit," he hissed. His good arm trembled from the pain, but he kept the way open for the others. Hot blood soaked through his sleeve and trickled down his other arm.

Six guards ran towards them, heavy-booted feet pounding the sod. They scattered the patients like wolves charging a flock of sheep. One plucked Mr. Yi out of the opening and threw him to the wet grass. The others fanned out to encircle the escapees.

Some patients threw up their hands, screaming in fear. Others scrambled to crawl under the fence.

"Freeze!" the leader of the guards shouted. "Stand away from the fence—hands above your head."

The man about to escape backed out of the fence opening and raised his hands.

For an instant his movement shielded Geoffrey from the guard's view. Geoffrey ducked through and ran. His heart pounded in his chest; every moment could be his last. The skin on his back prickled, waiting for a bullet.

Suddenly, bright lights flooded the area, blinding Geoffrey. Ellie Peterson stepped from the line of trees surrounding the Allen estate and rushed forward like a storm trooper in a peach-colored Diaggio suit.

She gestured at the fracas and spoke towards the microphone on the video recorder. "This is Ellie Peterson with CNN. I'm standing near a quarantine camp in the Pacific Northwest. Twenty-two patients have just escaped over the fence. Reports coming in from other camps indicate similar breakouts are occurring all over the United States."

Geoffrey stared at Ellie in shock. What was she doing near the camp? She was supposed to remain hidden, help them get off the island. Geoffrey ran past her and into the woods beyond the gate

Two guards rushed after Geoffrey. One tackled him around the knees and Geoffrey went down, his wounded shoulder slamming into the ground. The pain brought tears to his eyes, blurring his vision.

Rough hands jerked his hands behind his back and lashed his wrists together with cable ties. The guard yanked Geoffrey to his feet.

Geoffrey blinked to clear his eyes. All around him, patients were being rounded up and handcuffed. Mr. Yi struggled near the fence in the grip of a man twice his size.

Ellie's cameraman filmed the action, panning across the unfolding scene.

The escape had failed, but perhaps something could be salvaged. Geoffrey jumped straight up. "Over here!" he called to Ellie.

The camera swung his way.

Before the guard leading him could react, Geoffrey shouted, "The infected are being held against our will and in violation of our constitutional rights. We want our *freedom*!"

The guard shoved Geoffrey through the fence. With a jerk of his thumb he indicated the reporters. To the guard who held Mr. Yi, he said, "Get the recording."

Geoffrey watched over his shoulder. The burly man approached the reporter. The cameraman made as if to run, but Ellie restrained him with a hand on his arm.

"Drop the cameras!" said the guard.

Ellie's cameraman unbuckled a shoulder strap and lowered his equipment to the ground. Ellie held up her hands passively.

The guard pointed to the camera. "Give me the disk!"

The cameraman looked at Ellie.

She smiled, knelt down, and opened the back of the camera. There was no DVD. Standing up, she brushed the skirt of her Diaggio suit. "Disk? What a primitive concept. We were transmitting live."

The guards escorted Geoffrey and the other prisoners to the mansion's eight-car garage and forced them to kneel on the concrete floor.

"Knees hurt," Mr. Yi said as he was pushed down. The guards ignored him.

The door to the mansion banged open and Captain Morgenson strode in. His face was puffed and red with anger.

"What *the hell* were you trying to prove?" His Texan accent was pronounced. Captain Morgenson strode over to Geoffrey and prodded him in the ribs with his boot.

"I only wanted to—"

Captain Morgenson kicked Geoffrey over so he rested on his wounded shoulder. Geoffrey grunted and felt blood trickle from the raw flesh. He looked up from the floor.

"There will be no second attempt. From now on, you"—he pointed at Geoffrey—"will be locked in the pool house. The windows will be boarded shut. You will stay there until the plague is cured or you die. The rest of you are under house arrest."

The others filed out under guard supervision. Morgenson stood over Geoffrey and said, "Your little movement is done. Without you riling up the other patients, things will go back to normal."

But Captain Morgenson was wrong. It was not an isolated attempt. Geoffrey had started a wheel turning, and it was powered by the frustration and resentment of thousands of patients. Each night a few more tried to slip over the wall. Morgenson ordered the ballroom doors locked at sundown, setting chamber pots by the doors for those who couldn't wait until morning.

Attempts started at lunchtime, during breakfast, in the middle of exercise sessions. A whole group of twenty patients would simply start walking towards the gate, ignoring the guards as they went.

And it wasn't just Orcas Island. Similar events were happening at camps all over the world.

Geoffrey knew because Mr. Yi whispered the news to him through one of the boarded-up windows of the pool house. In the darkness, Geoffrey smiled. The movement had a life of its own.

Lillith watched the news as she dressed for work. An image of a containment camp made her pause with one leg in her pants.

"Last night two more camps for people with AHMS erupted in violence as patients attempted to escape. Three patients are wounded, including one woman who is listed in serious condition. This is the third such attempt since the mass exodus of April 19."

Lillith hadn't heard from Geoffrey for weeks. He hadn't returned any of her messages since their fight about his plans for April 19. That didn't surprise her. What did was the fact that Geoffrey hadn't shown up in any of the newscasts since the first night of éscape attempts. Not an interview with the press, no statement of intent, nothing. What had happened to him? Wherever he was, she hoped he was all right.

When Lillith got to work and checked her vidmail, she found a message from Dr. Lam asking her to come to his office. A large Caucasian man in a charcoal-gray suit stood when she entered the room.

Lillith shook the man's proffered hand.

"Agent Gant," he said in a rumbling bass voice. "I'm here to pick up some files."

"The president and Congress," Dr. Lam said, "have requested copies of all our material regarding the plague. We, of course, are happy to cooperate."

"Of course," Lillith said, hope welling in her chest. The administration must be taking Geoffrey seriously if they wanted information. Perhaps Geoffrey was right and Congress would repeal the AHMS Containment Act.

"I'll post the files on the secured GOVnet. Will that suffice?"

Gant inclined his head. "That would be great. May I also talk to you about some of the early cases? There are a few things I'd like your opinion on."

Lillith exchanged a look with Dr. Lam. He seemed as surprised as she by this turn of events. "George Danvers worked closely with me on this."

"Of course, we'll speak to him as well. But your insights on some of the early cases were very"—Gant grinned as he found the right word—"enlightening."

Geoffrey squinted at the bright light as the pool house door opened. A tall man stood silhouetted against the sun.

Somewhere in the main house a breaker must have been switched on, because the lights inside the pool house lit up. The door shut with a whump.

When Geoffrey's eyes adjusted to the light, he saw a tall, broad man in his early forties. There were streaks of gray at his temples. His features were unremarkable, midwestern: wide face, strong chin, and a nose that had been broken at some point in his past. He wore a crisp black suit and patent leather shoes.

"Geoffrey Allen," he said in a deep voice. "I'm Agent Gant, Homeland Security. I'd like a few words with you."

The words "Homeland Security" constricted Geoffrey's chest. He kept his voice level. "Does the government consider me a terrorist?"

Gant settled into a rattan chair opposite the gas fireplace. His business suit looked out of place against the tropical print of the cushions.

The guards had chained Geoffrey's left wrist to a ring on the mantel that held the fireplace tools, so his range of motion was limited to a ten-foot radius. He tried to move away from the man, but the chain pulled up short.

Gant raised an eyebrow at the pallet of towels Geoffrey had built on the tile floor, then the chafing manacle. "That doesn't look comfortable. I'll get those taken off."

Geoffrey ignored the comment. He settled cross-legged onto the pallet. "Why are you here?"

Gant leaned forward until his elbows rested on his knees. "To offer you a deal. A few misguided people have followed your example, trying to escape from the camps." His expression grew somber. "Some have been hurt. A woman was shot in California. We want you to make a statement asking them to stop the attempts, to be patient and wait for their release when the time is right."

"When will that be?" Geoffrey asked. "When all the people infected with AHMS are dead?"

"We can't release them now. There's too much at stake."

"Yes, the lives of thousands of people dying in the camps." Geoffrey rattled his chains. "The millions that will die if the camps produce a vaccine-resistant version of the plague. I won't stop fighting until the victims of AHMS are free."

Gant stood in a fluid movement that belied his bulk. "I had hoped you would see reason."

An icy chill ran the length of Geoffrey's back. He was suddenly aware of how large, and how lethal, Mr. Gant was. The butt of a gun peeked out of a black leather shoulder holster under the man's jacket. "What are you going to do?" Geoffrey asked. "Kill me?"

Agent Gant crouched next to Geoffrey. "No," he said softly. "Dead, you'd be a martyr, and nothing the agency did could touch you. Alive, you can be prosecuted.

"Did you think the Justice Department had forgotten about you? Your case was put on hiatus because Dr. Watkins declared you unfit to stand trial. But you're not in Dr. Watkins's care anymore, are you?"

Gant leaned closer. "Tell the other patients to cooperate with camp personnel or we'll try you for treason."

Geoffrey didn't blink. He fought to keep his voice level. "I don't respond to threats."

"It's your funeral." Gant crossed the room to the door and exited. The deadbolt shot home with a click.

Geoffrey's blood chilled. If Gant had spoken with Lillith then he had the financial proof he needed to link Geoffrey to the plague. They could try him and convict him.

Geoffrey gritted his teeth. It didn't matter; he wouldn't cooperate. Let Gant do his worst. If he had to die to fight the oppression of the changed, so be it.

GEOFFREY ALLEN: TRAITOR? Lillith stared at the headline on her screen. She skimmed the story with an increasing concern.

"Gant," she said aloud, her tone making the word a curse. His probing questions about Geoffrey as patient zero, his interest in how the plague originated . . . all were being used as ammunition against Geoffrey.

"God, I'm an idiot," Lillith shouted to her empty apartment. "The one time anyone listens to me . . . and now this."

She had to warn Geoffrey, tell him it wasn't her

fault. She hadn't meant to give Homeland Security fuel for a treason charge.

Ellie Peterson came on screen, her pink and blond face arranged in a sober expression. "The news today: The attorney general may charge Geoffrey Allen with treason for his part in the origin of AHMS. Full coverage at eleven."

"Et tu Brute?" Lillith asked the woman's image. They were all stabbing their knives in today. But where was the corpse?

Lillith speed-dialed Geoffrey's connection address. Still no answer. Was he blocking her calls?

She sat heavily on her bed. Her cat, Peekers, shifted at the mattress's rocking, then settled down in a new crescent configuration to resume sleep.

On the news at eleven, Ellie Peterson was on the streets of Seattle, interviewing people.

Ellie held a microphone into the face of a woman stepping out of a natural foods co-op. "What do you think about the news that Geoffrey Allen may be tried for treason?"

The woman, skinny with waist-length brown hair, said, "I think it's about time. The rich think they can do anything they like and leave the rest of us to clean up the mess." She tucked a long strand of hair behind her ear. "If it was illegal for him to get that treatment, he shouldn't have taken it. The laws are here to protect us. No one should be exempt."

A construction worker opined: "He ought to be shot. I lost eight members of my family to that <bleep> plague." He jabbed his forefinger at the camera, as if trying to pick a fight with the viewers at home. "If some <bleep> rich guy thinks he can do something like that and get away with it, he's got another <bleep> think coming. I say we put him up against the wall and blow the <bleep> away."

Geoffrey saw the broadcast. Captain Morgenson had given him a viewer, saying, "I wouldn't want you to miss your fifteen minutes of fame."

He watched the news, each interview a blow to his solar plexus. He remembered the protestors who had broken into the CDC facility . . . and the beating he had received at Fort Stewart.

Geoffrey heard sounds of agitation from the barracks and guessed that Morgenson had set up a special screening for the other patients. And Dr. Takawari was no longer around to intervene on his behalf.

Geoffrey lay on his pallet near the gas fire. He contemplated blowing out the flames and leaving the gas on. There was nothing else he could do to atone. His money and his influence were gone. He might as well die. There was no future for him. He'd never know love; his family was dead, killed by the virus he had commissioned. If only he hadn't tried to get well, he'd have died by now and the world would have been safe.

He heard a soft tapping at the window. Mr. Yi . . . Geoffrey hadn't expected him tonight. "Mr. Yi."

"People angry," Mr. Yi whispered, "say you traitor, should die. But Mr. Yi is not fooled. You not cause plague."

Geoffrey sighed. "The hell of it is, Mr. Yi, I did. I bribed a researcher to create the virus. I injected it. I wanted to be cured at any cost."

Mr. Yi was silent a long time. Geoffrey thought the old man had left; then he heard, "We all have fate, but what we do with fate is what makes a man."

Geoffrey wasn't sure whether this was meant as condolence or a curse. "Mr. Yi?"

The old man was gone.

"I want wings," Exeter said, striding into Idaho's lab unannounced. She wended her way through the pathways of DNA synthesizers that hummed as internal robot arms sucked fluids from tiny plastic wells. The lab was crowded. So many demands were coming in from outside, Idaho had bought more equipment to keep pace.

Exeter leaned over Idaho, her blond hair tickling his chest. She manipulated the computer touchpad and opened a file. Architectural diagrams of triangles labeled with lift ratios filled the screen. "I've worked out the physics."

Idaho put his hands around her waist and pulled her into his lap. Recent enhancements to his muscle density made her feel light in his arms. He inhaled, savoring the honey scent of her skin . . . the way Blue's skin had smelled. The endocrine changes were working.

Exeter pointed at the screen. "Well?"

Idaho sighed and closed the file. "It's a large modification. You couldn't conceal your changes in public."

The atmosphere of paranoia since the escape attempts made it harder to hide. His changelings had to be very careful now not to get caught. If word about his engineered changes got out, they'd all be locked away in containment camps . . . without the tools they needed to stay well.

"So?" Exeter put her arms around Idaho's neck. "I don't leave the ranch now; who's going to see? And I can still go out on Halloween." She pursed her soft pink lips and stroked the tips of his fingers where the subcutaneous fangs lay hidden. "I'm tired of being human."

"That you never were."

Exeter cackled the wild free laugh that was wholly her own. Blue had been quiet, introspective. This was a new, electric Blue. And the woman wanted wings.

"Besides," she said, "it's not as if anything is permanent anymore. If wings get old, you can change me back." Exeter-Blue kissed his cheek and nuzzled his earlobe. "It's just meat, Idy."

With a start, Idaho realized she was right. The implications of rewriting DNA meant whatever defined you was subject to change. He'd thought of his changes as one-way. Something not to be undertaken lightly. Exeter's statement turned that on its head.

How much could you change and still be you? If personality was hardwired into DNA, and you changed that, would you be someone entirely new, reborn with a new consciousness?

"Do I get my wings?" Exeter asked.

Idaho held her at arm's length and looked at her speculatively. "Would it make you happy?"

Exeter grinned so wide her gums showed above pearly teeth. "Yes!"

He kissed the tip of her nose. "Then you shall have them, for as long as you wish." He turned his mind from his musings. This would be his most extensive modification; it would require changes to her metabolism, bone density, and musculature, designing neurons to handle responses from appendages that would be her fifth and sixth limbs.

Idaho brought up the admin page for his search programs and changed the subject of inquiry from Geoffrey Allen to bird physiology and examples of recombinant DNA fusing avian and mammalian DNA.

Exeter doodled on her tablet PC, drawing designs for wings: rainbow feathers, bat wings, downy owl wings.

While the spider programs ran the search, Idaho slipped a pair of goggles on to read what they had gleaned earlier in the day.

The spiders had collected stolen snatches of video, hacked communiqués, information on Geoffrey Allen's whereabouts. This wasn't altruism. Geoffrey Allen was pushing to recognize the rights of the changed. And like it or not, what happened to the infected in the camps affected the future of the changelings.

One of these snippets was interesting. A big man with a nose that had once been broken said, "The attorney general signed the papers today. We're picking up Geoffry Allen on Tuesday. I'm flying out first thing tomorrow morning to make the arrest myself." He rubbed his hands together. "This collar will be a real career enhancer. Allen's trial will be the biggest since Nuremberg."

If Geoffrey Allen went down, Congress would bury

the changed forever. Idaho stood and flexed; cords of muscle as dense as steel cables writhed under his skin.

It was time for a confrontation, a real-world test of his changelings. He should have been frightened. What he had in mind was dangerous in the extreme. Instead he was eager. He'd spent too much time talking to Exeter . . . or perhaps she'd tinkered with his endocrine system.

Idaho forwarded the message to Lillith and told her to catch a plane and meet him at the ranch before dawn.

Then he placed a call to a Canadian smuggler who owned a private plane. The smuggler had caught AHMS while smuggling marijuana into the U.S. from Canada and now relied on cures from Idaho's network to stay healthy. He was a very useful contact.

Idaho pulled other useful information off the Web: blueprints from the private files of the architect who had designed the Allen estate, Captain Morgenson's reports on the camp for the last three months, and satellite footage of the current placement of guards and watchtowers.

Lillith stepped off the plane in Billings. A rental car waited for her at the Avis counter near the baggage claim. Lillith started when the agent referred to her as Harriet Tubman—was Idaho insane? But her thumbprint matched, and the rental agent handed over the keys.

My own little underground railroad, she thought. *Idaho, you count too much on the obliviousness of others.*

The drive to the ranch was peaceful. Winding country roads through the mountains. The other cars on the road were few and utilitarian: pickup trucks with sheepdogs in the back, sport utility vehicles pulling horse trailers, and a dump truck full of hay.

At last she turned into the private road that led to Idaho's 180-acre ranch. The gate was reinforced with welded iron bars. Quonset huts were erected in a semicircle around a large nineteenth-century barn. Dozens of cars were parked near the barn. A single-engine plane fitted out with pontoons squatted at the end of an dirt runway. On the side was written DEHAVILLAND DHC-2.

A five-year-old boy ran across the lawn in front of the white farmhouse. A woman with electric-blue hair scooped the boy up and hoisted him onto her hip. Idaho's ranch looked like a gathering of Deadheads. People sat on the ends of VW vans and exchanged hand-rolled cigarettes.

The reclusive Idaho had changed if he let this many people stay with him. She had hopes for his humanity.

A bulky Hispanic man stepped down from the porch. He was good-looking in the way soap opera stars are: bland perfection. When he shook her hand, there was an unnatural smoothness to his gestures, as if his joints moved on ball bearings. "I'm Dweezer," he said in a high voice at odds with his physique. "Idaho's in the barn."

"Thank you," Lillith said, conscious that the man watched her go. Her inch-high heels sank into the soft earth around the barn, and Lillith hoped the hems of her black wool slacks wouldn't be ruined.

Lillith's attention was caught by a girl with magenta hair and a familiar profile. The teenager sat cross-legged on the hood of a Ford pickup and smiled lazily at the sky.

Lillith stopped walking and stared. "Is that who I think it is?"

Dweezer grinned and nodded. "Yep. If you'll follow me."

The barn, rustic on the outside, was not what she expected inside. The room was dimly lit, and her eyes needed a moment to take in the forty DNA synthesizers, lined up in rows in the center of the barn. The room was warm with their waste heat and loud with the combined humming of tiny robot arms siphoning amino acids to create new genetic codes.

Three eight-foot by ten-foot wall screens displayed the progress of sequencing and synthesizing runs. A fourth screen showed Idaho's simulation of the genome.

Idaho's white-blond hair was backlit in the reflected glow of this last display. He stroked his fingers along an old-style touch pad. "Dweezer, she here yet?" he called without looking up from the screen.

Lillith slid her hand along the wall inside the door. Her fingers found a light switch. She flipped it on. A single incandescent bulb lit the room.

A hard slap stung Lillith's hand and the light winked off.

"Don't," Idaho said from behind her. "My eyes can't take the light."

Lillith gasped and whirled to face him. Then she looked back to the chair he had been sitting in a second ago. It was forty feet away. Impossible. He couldn't have crossed that distance so fast . . . without her even seeing. . . . Lillith stumbled away from the door, farther into the room. "Idaho?"

Idaho closed the barn door behind him. "Yes, Lillith." His voice was tired. "It is me."

In the glow from the display screens she saw his eyes. They reflected light like a cat's, and—she peered closer—had the same oval iris.

He flicked an impatient hand at his face. "A temporary setback. My first attempt at night vision, from feline physiology. In bright light, however, the slits generate diffraction patterns. Colored vertical lines surround everything." He pressed his fingertips to his temples. "I don't know how cats stand it; I get migraines."

"What's happened to you?" she whispered.

Idaho raised his palm before her, fingers splayed. With a twitch of muscles in the back of his hand, hypodermic fangs shot out from under his fingernails. Drops of clear liquid oozed out of the ends. He said, "I transformed myself."

Lillith raised the back of her hand to her mouth. Her throat was so tight she could barely speak. "How?"

Idaho's eerie eyes held hers. "I think you know."

Lillith reached to touch his hand. The fangs slid back at her approach. She took his hand in hers like a palm reader. The fangs fitted into tiny tubes growing under his fingernails. Muscles rippled beneath Idaho's blue-white skin. Lillith hefted his arm; it was twice as dense as a normal human arm. There was slight mottling of beige and white on the inside of his elbow. She looked up. "The virus? You caught it?"

Idaho took back his hand and hugged himself. "I embraced it." He stretched his arms wide. "There is so much more to AHMS than you ever imagined. In your hurry to cure it, protect against it, destroy it, you overlooked its usefulness. AHMS is the key to unlocking human potential."

He was mad, more insane than she had realized. Lillith was suddenly scared, and glad that she had already been vaccinated. "Do the others"—she pointed to the door—"know?"

Idaho cocked his head at her. "Know?" He laughed. "That is why they're here. They've come to trade their humanity for something better."

Lillith's eyes widened; she recalled turquoise irises in a black face, fangs that were not implants. "*That's* why they work for you, all the hackers. You help them change."

"Them and the infected who refuse the government's hospitality."

She was surrounded by people who had deliberately infected themselves. If she were smart, she would jump back into her car and drive the hell away from here.

"Geoffrey," she choked out. "Why do you want to help him?"

Idaho moved faster than her eyes could follow and seated himself on one of the tables, next to a DNA sequencer. "It might be sentiment. He was our Prometheus, the one who made AHMS a reality."

"I don't believe that, not from you," Lillith said. "Why?"

Idaho stared at her a long moment. The expression in his changed eyes was the hot glow of a fanatic.

"Because," he said, "Geoffrey Allen's fight for the rights of the changed affects my changelings."

Lillith shook her head. "Changelings?"

"Those who suffer in the grip of AHMS are changed. Those who embrace it are changelings. Everyone out there"—he pointed to the door—"is one . . . or wants to be. Most choose minor modifications in hair color or skin, improvements in strength and dexterity. They can pass for human. But if the government finds out what we're doing, we'll be shipped off to the camps, separated from our loved ones and the treatments that keep our genome stable.

"Geoffrey Allen's fight to protect the changed is my fight, too. He is a powerful symbol. If he fails, we will have to keep hiding."

Lillith needed Idaho's help, but his new self scared her . . . even more than when he was a ghost on the Net. The thought that occurred next horrified her. "You don't have a version of the plague that bypasses the vaccine?"

"No." Idaho smiled. "Not yet . . . give us time."

CHAPTER 18

Lillith looked at the satellite photo of Orcas Island displayed on the wall screen of Exeter's camper. "It's impossible," she said. "We don't have the resources to break Geoffrey out of a military encampment."

Idaho and Exeter lounged on a built-in couch no wider than a bench. Exeter sat sideways, her legs across Idaho's lap. The feathered nubs growing out from between her shoulders made it impossible for her to lean back.

Lillith couldn't get over the woman's resemblance to Blue, Idaho's dead sister. How much of that similarity had Idaho engineered?

"You're wrong," Idaho said. "Dweezer, would you hand Gordon your knife?"

With motions too fast for Lillith to follow, Dweezer produced a switchblade from his jeans pocket, reached across the tiny dining table, and handed it to Gordon.

Nate, who was also at the table, folded his long legs sideways to give Gordon room. Nate had long blond hair pulled up in a topknot to display a ring of short golden-white horns encircling his brow. Their color matched the implanted tusks that curled around his nostrils.

Gordon stood up and flourished the knife like a stage magician, displaying its gleaming blade. Then he stripped off his T-shirt, revealing pasty white skin over a firm muscular body. In a single motion, he reversed the knife and stabbed at his heart.

Lillith jumped to her feet. "No!" She snatched up the discarded shirt to use as a compress. Idaho's changelings were insane. She grabbed Gordon's wrist and pulled it away from the wound.

But there was no wound. Gordon's white skin was undamaged.

She touched the skin of his chest in wonder. It felt hard and smooth, like wood.

It flexed when Gordon chuckled at her. He poked his chest a couple of times with the tip of the blade, and it made a hollow tapping noise.

"My knife." Dweezer held out his hand. He examined the blade and *tsked*. "Gordon, man, you got to get your own. It's too hard on the blade." He folded it back into his pocket.

Bruno, whom Idaho had introduced as a bush pilot from Canada, clapped slowly. "Very nice. But a thick skin and fast reflexes won't stop bullets. We need a plan." He straightened from where he was leaning against the back of the driver's chair. "I can get us on the island. I transport gene therapies from Good Works International; the camp commander gave me a landing pass." He squatted next to where Idaho held the map and pointed at the airport parking lot. "There's a cargo van here that will get us to the front gate. My question is, How do we locate your friend once we're at the camp?"

Lillith said, "We could email him."

"No." Idaho leaned forward and pointed at a dot on the map. The electronic map zoomed in on the Allen estate. "His communications are sure to be monitored. We'll send a pickup location to one of the other patients, have him pass the message to Geoffrey. That old man with him in the CNN interview."

Bruno folded his arms across his wide chest. "And if he doesn't—or can't—show?"

"Improvise." Idaho's eyes bored into Bruno's and the pilot looked away. "We *must* get Geoffrey Allen out. Our future depends on it."

Bruno grunted. He combed his black hair back with

meaty fingers. "So we pick him up and fly him out—with the United States army in hot pursuit—what then?"

Idaho shrugged. "That's where your expertise comes in."

"Yeah, but I smuggle goods no one knows I'm carrying. This snatch-and-grab is a whole 'nother ball game."

Lillith checked her watch. "We've got to move soon. Gant's plane is already in the air. We have to get Geoffrey off the island before he arrives."

"All right, then." Bruno clapped his hands together. "Let's go."

Nate, Dweezer, and Gordon stood. Gordon shrugged back into his shirt.

Lillith said, "All right, let me grab my medical bag from the car."

Idaho shook his hand at her. "You're not going." He waved at Bruno, Dweezer, Nate, and Gordon.

Lillith jabbed her finger at Idaho. "You're picking up an infected man in a situation that is likely to get someone wounded. The team needs a doctor."

Idaho tapped his fingers against the armrest of the vinyl couch, a rapid staccato that sounded like rain. He looked at Bruno.

Bruno shrugged. "The plane seats six."

"Perfect," Lillith said. "That leaves one for Geoffrey." She opened the camper door. Looking back over her shoulder, she said, "Let's go."

Geoffrey woke to an urgent tapping on the pool house window. "Mr. Yi?"

"Police coming." Mr. Yi's voice was agitated. "Computer you give me, beep many times. I open. Six messages. Say police come. Take you away."

Geoffrey put his head in his hands. They were going to arrest him. He'd be put on trial for treason. It'd be a media circus.

He heard the sound of wood creaking outside the window. A beam of dim light broke through the boards Morgenson's men had nailed over the windows.

"Message also say help come soon. Take you away," Mr. Yi said. He pulled at one of the boards covering the window. It broke free. "Must hurry."

Geoffrey couldn't believe the old man was so strong. Seventy if he was a day.

Mr. Yi held a crowbar in his left hand and a newly removed board in his right. "Hurry," he urged again, "hide by gate. Until friend-van come."

Geoffrey cranked open the window and slid through the opening. "Thank—"

"No time." Mr. Yi tapped the board back into place with the crowbar. "Go!"

Geoffrey ran through the gloom. There were few guards on patrol this early in the morning. He zigzagged through the outbuildings, sticking to the shadows, working his way to the front gate.

Geoffrey tucked himself under the branches of a cedar tree near the front gate. He rubbed his hands together against the chill. He wished there'd been time to ask Mr. Yi who had sent the messages. Who would come to help? Surely not Ellie Peterson. The reporter had shown her allegiance was only to the news. Idaho? Geoffrey couldn't imagine the hacker doing anything out of altruism. Henry Paulson would only act within the law.

There was one person who might attempt such a thing: Lillith. The thought of her filled him with both hope and dread. Hope that she might rescue him, dread because he hadn't spoken to her since they'd quarreled about his escape plans.

From his hiding place, Geoffrey saw the path to the pool house. The outdoor lights illuminating the pool and its surroundings came on.

The door leading from his parents' bedroom—now Morgenson's office—opened. Captain Morgenson led Agent Gant across the deck surrounding the house and downstairs towards the pool house. Two armed guards followed.

Geoffrey's breath caught in his throat. Gant was already here. Worse, Mr. Yi still crouched in the shadow of the pool house. The lights blocked the old man from sneaking back to the barracks.

Captain Morgenson pointed at the destruction to the boarded window and shouted, "Fan out. I want Geoffrey Allen found." He pulled out a cell phone and within seconds alarms sounded and lights lit the entire estate as bright as daytime.

Guards scrambled from what had once been the servants' quarters. They were slipping into shirts and buttoning pants as they emerged. They searched the grounds.

Mr. Yi ducked under a boxwood hedge planted next to the pool house. Heavy booted feet poked the foundation plantings. In moments the old man would be discovered.

Geoffrey froze in terror. He wanted to rush to Mr. Yi's side, save the old man from discovery. But he was too far away. There was nothing he could do. Not without giving up his one chance of rescue.

A guard gave a shout and pulled a struggling Mr. Yi out of the bushes. "Found him!" the man said, dragging Mr. Yi to where Captain Morgenson and Agent Gant stood.

Agent Gant looked down. "That's not Allen. He's too old."

Patients stumbled out of the ballroom onto the deck surrounding the mansion. The sirens must have woken them.

"Am too." Mr. Yi thumped his chest. He shouted, "I Mr. Allen."

Morgenson's eyes narrowed. "Don't play games. . . ." he growled.

"Let him go," a man said from the deck. "I'm Allen."

Geoffrey stared in amazement as a man close to his own height stepped forward. He had the same mottled coloring of all the plague patients. Geoffrey recognized him as one of the patients who'd joined him in the first escape attempt.

"Bring him here," Captain Morgenson yelled.

Two guards escorted the man to the pool house.

Gant grabbed the man's chin and turned his head this way and that. After a half minute's inspection, he pushed the man away. "It's not Allen."

"They change," Morgenson said, waving at the crowd in frustration. "The patients look more alike as they exchange DNA."

Another voice from the deck shouted, "It's me! I'm Allen!" Then another.

Geoffrey, in his hiding place, realized the guards couldn't tell them apart.

"I'm Geoffrey Allen," a woman said in a soprano voice.

"No, over here." A man waved his hands over his head. "I'm Geoffrey Allen."

The cry overtook the camp as all the changed, young and old, male and female, stumbled out of the ballroom and declared themselves the real Geoffrey Allen.

Geoffrey's heart swelled with gratitude and pride. Despite the bad publicity, despite knowing he had caused the plague, the patients in the Orcas Island camp were on his side.

Morgenson scrubbed his face with his hand and then gestured at the ballroom. "Bring them all out here. We'll sort this out. We'll separate out the women and the men that are too old or too young, then we'll check the identichips of whoever's left."

Lillith and the others landed at the Orcas Island airport. A gleaming Learjet with a State Department insignia painted on its side was parked in front of the airport office. Two guards with automatic rifles paced around it.

"Shit," Lillith said when she alighted from Bruno's plane and saw the jet. "We're too late."

Bruno pulled out a set of triangular boards tethered together with rope and chocked his plane's wheels. "Maybe," he said. "Maybe not." He nodded at the jet. "It's tied down and hasn't been prepped for take-off. Gant may have other business at the camp."

Lillith shivered, thinking of the hard-eyed agent. "We've got to try."

Bruno passed her a short-range radio. "Take the speed boys"—he nodded at Dweezer and Nate—"and the van." He took a bandanna from his back pocket and scrubbed sweat off his forehead. "This is going to get hairy." He stuffed the bandanna back. "There's a dock to the east of the Allen compound. By road, it's the first right after you leave the estate. If you're pursued, they'll expect you to make for the airport, not the next house over." He cocked his head to indicate the pontoons on his plane. "I'll do a water landing and wait for you there for"—he checked his watch—"thirty minutes. Then I'm gone. You understand?"

Lillith nodded. "Won't they hear your plane land?"

Bruno wiped his face again and looked up at the half-moon. "Not if I land with the engine off and no lights."

Lillith left Gordon with Bruno. Dweezer drove while she and Nate discussed how they would locate Geoffrey in a camp housing several hundred of the changed.

"What if we grab the wrong guy?" Nate said. "After a few months of gene swapping, they'll all look alike."

"I'll know Geoffrey when we find him," Lillith said. Her traitorous mind whispered, *If you find him.*

The van was parked where Bruno had said it would be. Lillith handed Dweezer the keys. She navigated the way from a map on her palmtop. The roads twisted their way around Mount Constitution to the east side of the island.

"Something's wrong," Lillith said as they drew near the Allen estate. Through the trees they could see floodlights lighting the compound. "That can't be normal."

Dweezer pulled the van off the road and hid it in the trees, out of sight of the Allen estate. Lillith and Nate crept through the trees and underbrush to scout the situation at the camp.

They lay on a rise overlooking the compound. Lillith whispered, "What's going on?"

Nate handed her the binoculars. "I can't tell. Everyone's just standing around."

The patients were gathered outside and had been sorted into two groups: children, women, and old men in one, the rest of the men in another. Gant was there, questioning the men in the second group. She saw him strike a man and he went down. Instantly, the other patients went wild, struggling against the guards restraining them.

"If Gant is here for Geoffrey, why is he questioning the other patients?" She trained the field glasses on the group. All of the young men had light brown skin and brown hair. Some were a patchwork like she had seen in Geoffrey. There was a tendency towards epicanthic folds around the eyes. But where was Geoffrey? Was he the short one on the end? Or that man in the center? They all looked alike from months of exchanging DNA. Lillith watched Gant sort through the prisoners, rejecting one after another.

"He can't find Geoffrey," she whispered. "Gant doesn't know which one he is."

Nate pulled an parabolic microphone out of the duffel bag they'd packed for the trip. He listened a moment, then grinned. "Cool. It's like that scene in *Spartacus*."

"What?" Lillith put the receiver to her ear. She heard a chorus of people: "I'm Geoffrey Allen." "No, I'm Geoffrey Allen." "Actually, I prefer 'Jeff.'"

A guard came running with an identichip reader. Gant placed a man's hand over the device. He scowled as he read the display.

The patients didn't resist as they were scanned. But they looked defiant, each still declaring himself to be Geoffrey Allen.

Gant worked his way through the queue of patients, scanning each in turn. Lillith held her breath, waiting for Geoffrey to be caught. She had to get him out of there. But what could she do? Dweezer's and Nate's modifications might have let them succeed in a surprise attack, but they couldn't take on the whole camp.

When the last man in the queue was scanned, Gant shook the machine and rescanned him. Then he threw it at the ground. He whirled around, his eyes searching the shadows in the camp.

"Geoffrey Allen, I know you're out there." He paused. "I know you can hear me."

Lillith's heart leaped. Geoffrey had done it. He must have gotten Idaho's message. He had escaped and was hiding near the gate, waiting for the van to pick him up. She turned to say something to Nate.

"Oh shit," he breathed, looking through binoculars at the camp.

Lillith put her field glasses to her face and looked back at the scene. What she saw froze her.

An old man kneeled in the dirt in front of Gant. The agent had his handgun trained on the back of the man's head. Through the parabolic microphone, Lillith heard Gant say, "I'm not going back without you, Allen. Come out or the old man dies."

"Gant," Morgenson said. "Take it easy." He took a step towards Gant.

Gant held the gun up high. "I'm pulling back the hammer. Can you hear that, Allen? Some hero you are, letting an old man die for your sins."

"No! No! Geoffrey Allen—run away!" Mr. Yi said.

Gant's face broke into a triumphant grin. Lillith's sensitive equipment picked up his whisper: "So he *is* still here." Gant lowered the gun to sight on Mr. Yi's head.

Lillith's chest was so tight she couldn't breathe. Through the binoculars she saw Agent Gant's arm flex. She braced herself for the explosion of a gunshot.

"Wait!"

Lillith whirled the field glasses to find the source of the shout.

Geoffrey emerged from under the branches of a cedar tree. One hand was raised. "I'm here! Don't hurt him."

"No . . . Geoffrey," Lillith breathed. She swung back to see Gant release the hammer with his thumb and holster his weapon. The aural microphone picked up his aside to Captain Morgenson. "That's how the big boys get results."

Captain Morgenson spat on the ground and helped a trembling Mr. Yi to his feet.

Two guards ran out to gather Geoffrey and bring him to Agent Gant. Geoffrey walked between them, his head hung low in defeat.

Lillith had seen enough. She shoved the goggles and microphone back into the duffel, and slung it over her shoulder. "Come on," she whispered to Nate. She hurried down the slope. "We've got one chance left."

The guards cuffed Geoffrey's hands behind his back and shoved him to his knees in front of Gant.

"No," Mr. Yi said. "No."

Gant snapped, "Someone shut that old man up."

Mr. Yi was forcibly carried back into the barracks. Guards rounded up the other patients and escorted them to their beds.

Gant knelt close to Geoffrey and hissed in his ear, "Who was in this with you?"

"No one," Geoffrey said. "I broke through the window myself."

Gant clubbed Geoffrey with a closed fist.

Geoffrey's head snapped to the side. Stars bloomed in his vision. The pain of impact was intense. He tasted blood.

"Who helped you escape?"

"No one," Geoffrey mumbled through swelling lips.

Gant struck him again. "Don't lie to me."

Geoffrey shook his head, trying to clear his vision.

Behind him, Captain Morgenson said, "Gant, that's enough."

Gant looked up. "I'm taking custody of this prisoner. He is none of your business."

Captain Morgenson's voice grew louder. "Not while you're in my camp. I am the commanding officer here, and this interrogation is over."

Gant stood.

Geoffrey spit blood and bile onto the lawn. He couldn't see the looks the two men exchanged, only their shoes. Morgenson's boots were planted firmly.

Gant stepped back. "Put him in the car," he said. He bent down to whisper in Geoffrey's ear. "This isn't finished."

Morgenson's men bundled Geoffrey into the back of one of the vans they used to transport patients. They looped a chain through his cuffs and padlocked them to an eyebolt in the floor.

Gant pulled on the chain. Satisfied, he closed and locked the door.

Geoffrey's mouth throbbed as the van bounced over the deer grate at the entrance to the estate. The van picked up speed once they were on county roads.

Suddenly he was thrown forward with a lurch. Geoffrey's wrists burned as he jerked to the end of his chain.

Gant shouted in the front of the van. Two gunshots exploded, and there was the crash of breaking glass.

What the hell was going on?

The rear doors of the van crashed open, and a young man with tusks and a crown of horns poking through his blond hair stuck his head in. He leapt up and grabbed the cuffs that bound Geoffrey's wrists. He was so tall he was nearly bent double under the van's low roof. Tusks sprouted from the sides of his nose. "I'm Nate." With a grunt, he snapped the hinge joining the bracelets of Geoffrey's handcuffs. "Idaho sent me."

Nate gathered Geoffrey in his arms and ran from

the van. He rounded it in a circle, dodging erratically left and right to avoid gunfire.

Another van was parked across the road. The front wheel was jacked up, and a spare lay against it as if someone had been repairing a flat. Words painted on the side read GOOD WORKS INTERNATIONAL.

Nate dove towards the back of the van.

Over his shoulder, Geoffrey saw Gant, backlit against the headlights of the army van, taking aim. "No!" he shouted.

Nate threw Geoffrey in first. Geoffrey bounced off the metal floor with bruising force.

Nate grabbed the rim of the open door and raised his foot to step into the van.

A gunshot cracked.

Nate's body arched. Blood spurted from his chest, and he collapsed half in and half out of the van.

"Go! Go! Go!" a familiar voice shouted beside him. Lillith grabbed the collar of Nate's shirt and hauled him into the van. "Close the door!" she yelled at Geoffrey.

He complied with shock-numbed hands. Geoffrey felt like his head was full of cotton. Nothing made sense; he shivered.

"Oh shit! What happened to Nate?" asked the man in the driver's seat. His movie-star face was screwed up with concern.

"Same thing that will happen to us if you don't get us out of here!" Lillith screamed back.

The engine roared to life, and they were thrown against the closed door as the van spun out and back through the gate. Wheel rims screeched on gravel as they drove away. Shots rang out behind them, and the van began to skid uncontrollably.

"They're shooting out the tires," Gordon said in a grim voice. "Hold on."

"Press here," Lillith ordered.

Geoffrey held his hands to Nate's chest, feeling warm blood ooze out under his hands.

The van rocked and swerved as it pelted down the winding roads that encircled Mount Constitution.

"Oh man," said the driver, "they're following us."

"Shit." Lillith crawled up to the passenger's seat. To Geoffrey's horror, she pulled a gun out of the glove box and began firing.

Had the whole world gone insane?

Nate tried to say something, but all that came out was bubbling red froth.

Lillith fired another shot. "That'll slow them down." She turned back to Geoffrey. "How's he doing?"

"Not good!" Geoffrey felt Nate's body relax under his hands and smelled shit. "Get back here!"

Lillith looked out at the road. "Turn here," she shouted, gesturing right with both arms.

Dweezer cranked the wheel over hard. The van rocked on two wheels and then bounced back down after it completed the turn.

Lillith crawled back to where Nate lay. She felt his neck for a pulse. Then she pulled Geoffrey's hands away. Her dark eyes were lowered. "It's too late. He's gone."

The van jolted down a gravel road to an abandoned cottage. A red-and-white pontoon plane waited at the end of a pier.

Lillith helped Geoffrey out of the van and hurried towards the plane.

A big man with a dark beard held open the door while Lillith helped Geoffrey inside. He took in the blood spattering Geoffrey and Lillith without changing his expression.

Dweezer jogged up behind, carrying Nate's body.

"Leave the corpse," Bruno said.

"No way, man," Dweezer said, hefting Nate's body higher on his shoulder. "He's one of us. I'm not leaving him behind."

"Then stay," Bruno said, climbing into the pilot's seat. "We're about to have every coast guard chopper in the area after us. We can't carry deadweight."

Dweezer looked like he wanted to punch someone. "We can't leave him here. They'll see his changes."

Bruno cursed and held open the door so Dweezer could load Nate's body into one of the passenger seats.

When everyone was inside, Bruno closed the door and taxied the plane. Water splashed under the plane's pontoons as they built up speed to take off.

When the plane was in the air, Geoffrey asked Lillith, "Who—"

"Quiet." The pilot's voice was thick with tension. "I'm flying under five hundred feet, in the dark, only a half-moon in the sky and no running lights or radio contact. If I make a mistake, we're dead."

Everyone in the plane went silent. The pilot sweated, concentrating on flying.

Helicopters searched the area, their headlights scanning the water. Bruno took a wide path around the San Juan Islands. He flew inward, skirting the Cascade mountain range.

They went north for a half an hour, then Bruno circled a pasture that was lit only by a yellow bug light on the side of a nearby barn. Lillith looked out the side window. She could see the field in the plane's landing lights. The strip of land seemed too short for the plane. She started to say something, then noticed Bruno's intensity and remained silent.

The plane dipped towards the ground. Bruno pulled back hard on the flaps. The plane bounced once, twice. It skidded to a stop twenty feet short of the trees.

Lillith released a breath she hadn't realized she'd been holding.

Bruno turned the plane and taxied to the barn.

"Where are we?" asked Lillith.

"Canada. More than that, you don't need to know," said Bruno. "Place is owned by a business associate of mine. Likes his privacy."

When they got near the barn, Bruno cut the power and, with Dweezer and Gordon's help, pushed the plane inside. In the distance, search helicopters chuffed.

Lillith hunkered down next to Geoffrey and cleaned his split lip from the beating Gant had given him. She felt his forehead for temperature. He was shivering.

"How long since your last treatment?" she asked.

Geoffrey's teeth chattered. "Three days."

Lillith pulled her medical bag out of the duffel and handed him two aspirin. It felt like treating an amputated leg with a Band-Aid. "Hang on," she said. "Once we get to Idaho's camp, he can treat you."

"Hey, Doc," Dweezer said. "As long as you're patching people up." He held out his left arm. Shards of glass from the van's windshield had nicked his forearms.

Lillith cleaned and dressed his wounds.

When she was done, Dweezer swung his arms, stretching his shoulders. The motion was so fast it was nearly a blur.

Geoffrey watched Dweezer, transfixed. He touched his brow. "The man who found me, the one who died, he was tall and had . . . horns." Geoffrey licked his lips. "Who—what—are you two?"

Dweezer crossed the ten feet between them in less time than it took to blink. He pointed across the room at the man with the black ponytail. "Me and Gordon are changelings. You caught the plague by accident and it makes you sick. " He picked a crowbar off a wall rack of tools and bent it into a U. "We caught it on purpose and it makes us strong."

Geoffrey's brow furrowed as he took it in. "You infected yourselves . . . deliberately?"

"Yeah." Dweezer threw the ruined crowbar in a corner.

"You're using the plague as a *plaything*?" Geoffrey felt dizzy and paused to catch his breath. "Don't you realize it could mutate into a vaccine-resistant strain? Your tinkering could kill us all."

Dweezer was suddenly centimeters from Geoffrey's face. Each breath puffed into Geoffrey's eyes. "You didn't mind our changes"—he flexed his bicep and muscles like cables moved under the skin—"when they saved you from that camp. Do you think that would have been possible"—he patted his bicep—"without this?" He pointed out to the plane. "Nate's dead because of you, man. He deserves your gratitude."

Lillith pulled Geoffrey away. "Easy now, we'll have time to talk about this when we get to Idaho's ranch." She found a horse blanket and wrapped it around Geoffrey.

Geoffrey looked across the barn to Dweezer and Gordon. "It's insane. They'll be the death of us all."

"Shh," Lillith said. "Get some sleep."

Bruno pulled sleeping bags and ground pads out of the plane and settled in under one of the wings. The others unrolled their bags along the back of the hangar, farther from the wind that blew in under the wide metal doors.

Lillith slept fitfully. Twice, helicopters overhead woke her, and she worried their searchlights might pick up the plane's tire tracks in the pasture outside. But no one came to the barn.

At dawn, the smell of coffee woke her. Bruno tended a percolator set over a camp stove.

"Things have quieted down," he said. "We'll take off in fifteen minutes. Tell the others." After finishing his coffee, he refueled the plane from a set of gasoline tanks stacked up near a tractor.

The sky was lightening in the east when Bruno's plane lifted off. Lillith held her breath again as they skimmed over treetops, just barely clearing them on the way out.

Bruno flew inside Canada and dipped below the U.S. border when they were three hundred miles away from Orcas Island.

Idaho's ranch was five miles off the highway. The plane followed a series of diminishing dirt roads before it came into view. From the air, Geoffrey thought it looked like a Gypsy encampment. VW vans were parked in clusters around tents erected near the barn and outbuildings. A white farmhouse was surrounded by clotheslines filled with flapping jeans and T-shirts.

Bruno circled the DeHavilland DHC-2 to line up with the landing strip cut into the western pasture. He eased back on the power and pulled up the flaps. The plane hit the uneven ground with a bounce and rolled to a stop.

Dozens of people ran out of the house and the barn.

One woman, her hair an unnatural blue green, scanned the arrivals, growing more distressed by the moment. "Where's Nate?" she asked, her eyes wild with fear.

Dweezer went over and talked softly to her. After a moment, he showed her what was in the plane. She collapsed to the ground, crying. He gently pulled her to her feet, and she clung to him and cried.

The others crowded around the grieving woman, murmuring consolation. Two men took Nate's body out of the plane and carried it towards the rows of tents.

"Can you take us to Idaho?" Lillith asked one of the onlookers. The woman, who had feathers growing out of her scalp, pointed towards the barn.

A boy no more than five years old ran up to Geoffrey with a lancet and a capillary tube. "I need a sample," he said in a piping voice. "Idaho wants to see what variations you're carrying."

"Is this necessary?" Geoffrey asked.

Lillith nodded.

Reluctantly, he held out his hand to the boy.

The boy cradled Geoffrey's hand with care and expertly pricked the pad of his ring finger with the lancet. Then he sucked up a sample into the capillary tube.

Before he could run off, Geoffrey caught the boy's wrist. "Have you been vaccinated?"

The boy tossed him a scornful look. "Of course not." He ran to the lab.

"I've seen babies die of the plague," Geoffrey said. "Idaho is insane if he's infecting children. He must be stopped."

"Shhh," Lillith hissed.

They followed the boy to the barn. It took a few seconds for Geoffrey's eyes to adjust from the daylight outside. The room was lit by a single bulb and the reflected glow of computer monitors.

"I should warn you," Lillith whispered. "Idaho . . . practices what he preaches."

In the dim glow, Lillith spotted Idaho hunched over a DNA synthesizer, checking its readout.

"So," said Idaho, "this is our Prometheus." His cat's eyes reflected gold. In a second, he crossed the twenty feet of cluttered floor between them. Idaho offered his hand to Geoffrey.

Geoffrey sucked in a breath. He stepped back and did not shake his hand. "Thank you for rescuing me, but . . ." He gestured at Idaho's face. "This is wrong. If you have the plague, you're sick and you need treatment."

"I will live for a hundred years—perhaps longer— at full health," said Idaho. "I can lift a small car if I put my mind to it." He cocked his head. "Why on earth should I want to be cured of that?"

"Because you have ΛHMS. Without regular treatments, you'll mutate and die." Geoffrey pointed at the door. "The variants I've brought with me from Orcas Island may kill those people out there."

Lillith put a restraining hand on Geoffrey's shoulder.

Idaho grinned. "But didn't you yourself give me the equipment to treat the plague? Haven't I cut my teeth on solving the variants in the Orcas Island camp? Do not worry for my changelings; worry instead for the guards of Orcas Island. I might choose to include a few of my own designs in the next shipment of treatments. Imagine Captain Morgenson's surprise when his captives grow stronger and sprout weaponry." He slid out poison-tipped fangs from under his fingernails.

Geoffrey thought of Mr. Yi transformed into something inhuman. Outrage heated his face. "No."

"Or"—Idaho retracted the fangs—"I can simply include the regular treatments. It makes no difference to me."

"Why did you rescue me?" Geoffrey narrowed his eyes at Idaho. "You know I haven't anything to pay you with. I no longer have any influence. The world wants me dead. Why take this risk?"

"Because you gave me the tools to change the world. You think you've killed humanity. That's wrong. You helped it *evolve*." Idaho held up a finger to forestall interruption. "And I need you as a spokesman. You and I have the same goal in one respect. We both want full rights for those infected by the plague. Your changed and my changelings."

"Haven't you been listening to the news? I'm a world criminal. The State Department wants to arrest me for treason." Geoffrey pointed at his own chest. "What would make people listen to me?"

"Notoriety, if nothing else." Idaho bent and checked the display of one of the sequencers at his feet. "If you called Ellie Peterson, she would plaster your image across every display in the world in minutes."

"I won't be a spokesman for your obscenity. I won't encourage people to modify themselves with the plague."

Idaho looked up, catching Geoffrey with his eerie gaze. "I should hope not. We're already flooded with requests."

Geoffrey blinked in disbelief. "Who'd choose to become a monster?"

"Oh." Idaho stood up and stroked the top of the sequencer like a pet. "You'd be surprised. There are ten thousand changelings in New York State alone. Some were infected accidentally and hiding from discovery. Others embraced the change. The same network that feeds medicine to your precious camps keeps them healthy."

Geoffrey sat down heavily. Ten thousand people. "Are they all . . . like you?"

"Of course not. Most look as human as"—he pointed at Lillith—"her. Only a few are willing to go beyond. I have designed thousands of variations . . . but I want more." He clenched and unclenched his hands. "I rescued you, Geoffrey, to finish what you started. I want full rights for my changelings. With the current laws, they are restricted to small, easily hidden changes. Help me rewrite the law. So your changed can return to their families. So my changelings can choose more elaborate modifications without risking capture and imprisonment.

"If you deny me because you disagree with my philosophy regarding the plague, you also deny the changed their freedom."

Geoffrey shook his head. "The world will listen to me as a curiosity, as a criminal. But what makes you think the lawmakers will change anything because of me?"

Idaho's eyes glittered in the dark light. "Because I have"—his unholy face lit with the ghost of a smile— "leverage." He pulled a palmtop out of his pocket and tapped the screen. A list of names appeared. "These are some of my changelings." He pointed at one name and it highlighted. He picked out two others.

Geoffrey read the names. He recognized them from his mother's Social Register: powerful families with international influence. "I see."

"They're here, on the ranch." Idaho handed him a cell phone. "It's untraceable. Call your reporter friend."

Geoffrey took the phone. He punched in the number for Ellie Peterson's private line and then cradled it against his ear.

She answered after two rings. "Ellie Peterson for CNN."

"This is Geoffrey Allen."

There was a pause, then Ellie said, "I'm so sorry about April 19. I hope you understand it wasn't personal. I'm a reporter. Getting stories is what I do."

"Forget that," Geoffrey said, his voice coming out tighter than he'd intended. "I have a much bigger story for you."

CHAPTER 19

At Idaho's direction, Dweezer and Gordon converted the living room of the farmhouse into an impromptu studio. They hung white sheets on the walls, both to reflect light and to conceal architectural details that might give a clue to the house's location.

Geoffrey had set the interview for eight o'clock, mountain time.

At 7:55, Geoffrey placed another call from another anonymous cell phone. It was different than the last one. Geoffrey wondered where Idaho acquired them, then decided he was better off not knowing.

Ellie picked up the phone before it finished ringing. "Is everything still a go?"

"Are you receiving our signal?"

A pause, then Ellie said, "Strong and clear."

"Will this go out live, no filters?" he asked.

"You've got my word on that." She sounded solemn. "This time I promise."

Geoffrey hoped she was sincere. They needed CNN's credibility to help get their message across. Sending anonymous video out over the Net wouldn't have the same impact.

At eight o'clock sharp, the transmission was broadcast live.

Idaho had set up a portable television on the windowsill, where they could all monitor what was being transmitted.

Ellie Peterson's voice trembled with suppressed excitement as she introduced the broadcast. "We have, speaking live from an undisclosed location, Mr. Geoffrey Allen, who recently evaded arrest in an early morning flight from a containment camp in Washington State."

The feed shifted to their camera. Idaho turned off the volume on the tiny television to prevent feedback.

Ten minutes, Idaho had warned him, was all they could risk without the FBI being able to break through Idaho's encryption and layers of misdirection.

Geoffrey took a deep, centering breath. Then he said, "People of the world, I speak for those infected with AHMS. We are not a threat to your health and should be released from the camps. Keeping us together may generate new forms of the virus resistant to the vaccine."

Across the bottom of the image, Idaho added a scrolling link to a Web site with more information.

"Now," said Geoffrey, stepping back, "I have some people I'd like you to meet."

A young woman strode into the camera's field of view. Her magenta hair sprung from her head in a mass of curls. She grinned, displaying the smile her father had been famous for on the campaign trail. She wiggled her fingers at the camera. "Hi, Daddy."

Geoffrey had Dweezer zoom the camera in on her. "Lacey Johnstone, the president's daughter, is infected with the plague," Geoffrey explained. "The color changes you see are produced by her own body."

The camera focused on Lacey's eyelashes. They were bright pink, as were the downy hairs that covered her cheek.

Geoffrey continued, "She and others like her call themselves 'changelings.' They've deliberately infected themselves with the plague in order to perform body modifications."

Idaho held up five fingers. Only five minutes left.

"Others have made more drastic changes," Geoffrey said.

Lacey moved aside.

A Japanese boy stepped forward, his head held high and challenging.

"Meet Ichiro Idei," Geoffrey said, "the son of the president of Sony Inc."

Ichiro held up his hands, displaying fingernails as long and sharp as stilettos. He spoke briefly in Japanese, then in English: "Father, the plague can be a tool, not a destroyer. Would you imprison us all?"

"The last person I want to introduce is Prince Naseem bin Ahmad al-Saud, from Saudi Arabia."

A dark-skinned youth wearing a Princeton sweatshirt joined Lacey and Ichiro. In his hands he held five striped billiard balls.

"My people, I am fast." With gestures so quick they blurred in the air, Naseem threw the balls in complicated arcs. "I am strong." He let all but one fall to the ground. This last he crumpled in his hand, letting dust trail from his fingers. "Even if the rest of the world throws this gift of Allah away, we should grasp it with both hands."

Idaho cut the connection. The red "on" light on Dweezer's camera died. "Got it." He reviewed the tape, checking what had already gone out on the airwaves. "Looks good."

As they'd discussed in the planning, the CNN broadcast was just the start. From an anonymous server, Idaho transmitted an email message to addresses he had hacked from databases of the Social Security Administration and the Internal Revenue Service. It contained facts about the plague, information about changelings and their motivations, and medical data about the dangers of the containment camps.

"And now," Idaho said, wiping a lock of hair out of his slitted eyes, "things get better . . . or they get worse."

The display screen filled with Net statistics. Interactive graphs showed a flood of spider programs active on the Web, seeking Geoffrey's location. Idaho's programs monitored bandwidth utilization, reporting a spike in activity as the automated search programs scoured the Net.

Idaho filtered the display to a line graph. A red line showed an exponential increase in activity. "They're looking for us."

Lillith and Geoffrey stayed up late, monitoring the news to gauge the public's reaction to the broadcast. Lillith was too anxious to sleep. There was still a manhunt under way for Geoffrey, and she was an accomplice to his escape.

One by one, the changelings retired to sleep in tents, vans, and upstairs bedrooms. Idaho left his tablet PC with Lillith and retired with Exeter to his subterranean trailer.

Lillith turned the PC's input to broadcast video and clicked through local and national news channels, catching the headlines of emerging stories. In New York, an anonymous tip led police to a changeling lab where they arrested six changelings and confiscated millions of dollars' worth of lab equipment.

Lillith changed the channel. Video footage of the California border showed officers asking passengers to step out of their cars and take blood tests.

On an international station, the Saudi Arabian government offered a hundred-million-dollar reward for the safe return of their prince.

At ten, the president interrupted scheduled programming to address the nation and ask the public to remain calm. In the last five minutes of his speech, he asked his daughter to contact him, promising help and medical treatment.

Hours of news monitoring later, Lillith's eyelids began to droop. It had been a long day, but she was too wound up to sleep. She yawned and stretched. "You want some coffee?"

"Please," Geoffrey said, never taking his eyes from the screen.

Lacey Johnstone was in the kitchen with Ichiro. Ichiro minced green onions with his fingernail knives.

"Your father made a press announcement," Lillith told Lacey. "He mentioned you; do you want to see the video?"

Lacey shrugged, her mass of magenta hair rising and falling. "He's been sending me emails, too. 'Come home, all will be forgiven, yadda, yadda, yadda.'"

Lillith wondered what in the world would make the girl risk her health for such a trivial change. Was it to distance herself from her famous father? Or simply the young's assumption they were immortal?

"Will you go?"

Lacey blinked; her green eyes contrasted brilliantly against her magenta lashes. "Not until being a changeling is legal. It's not, you know, fair. Why should Ichiro and I get special treatment just because our parents are important?"

"Ichiro, do you feel the same?"

Ichiro's lips twitched into the ghost of a smile. "There are many changelings in Tokyo. It would be impractical to imprison them all. The laws must change."

Lillith hoped he was right.

Geoffrey checked CNN. The channel showed four black youths herded into a police van. One had tiger-striped skin; the others were either unchanged or had modifications too subtle to show up in the shot.

Geoffrey pointed at the scene. "Aren't you worried about your changelings?"

Idaho did not look up from the sequencer. "I warned them to hide, that there would be reprisals from our announcement. Any that are caught were careless."

"But what if they reveal the location of the ranch?" He watched Idaho work.

Idaho turned his head towards Geoffrey. His eyes flashed in the dim light. "Those who know the location of the ranch are here."

Geoffrey had supposed the dozens of people who

lived on the ranch were groupies who had moved here to be near Idaho. But Idaho's tone indicated otherwise. "They aren't allowed to leave?" He wondered if this prohibition extended to himself and Lillith.

"The ranch must not be compromised." Idaho stretched, and the muscles of his back rippled under his skin.

Even when he agreed with you, Idaho was intimidating. Idaho angry . . . would be enough to persuade anyone.

"And," Idaho said, flexing his fangs, "I do not think they will remain imprisoned long. After all, we broke you out of the camps. Would we do any less for our own?"

Debates raged in Congress. Internet opinion polls swung from pro to con and back again. Quotes from people on the street ranged from declaring the Changeling Plague God's punishment for the blasphemer to wistfulness about what they, themselves, would change.

Two weeks after their broadcast, *Time* magazine ran Geoffrey's image on the home page of their Web site. Above his head were the words TERRORIST OR MESSIAH?

Idaho turned off the display and loaded a new sample of his own DNA into the sequencer. He'd been feeling strange lately, more aggressive. Perhaps his testosterone levels were elevated.

Prince Naseem serviced the synthesizer, screwing reagent bottles to the ports underneath its cabinet. Everyone on the ranch, no matter their station in the outside world, maintained the machines that gave life.

Naseem kept his head bowed as he worked. "I have seen it on the television. My family offers a reward. If I go home, Idaho, you will have much money to work towards a cure."

"Yes," Idaho said, fitting the ninety-six-well plate

into the sequencer. "But I would lose my best example of speed modifications. We're not done with your work yet."

Naseem smiled a knowing smile and finished topping off the fluids. He closed the cabinet and straightened. "I understand, my friend."

Idaho, who had meant what he said and no more—he hated to leave work unfinished—was glad the prince would stay, regardless of what the boy chose to believe.

To keep the movement's momentum going, Idaho launched a campaign that included mass emailing of information about the plague, blackmailing senators with confidential material they'd been foolish enough to store on a networked computer, and transmitting additional pleas by celebrity changelings.

Today, Idaho had scheduled Lacey to contact her father.

Dweezer was behind the camera, checking the shot. An alarm on his wrist computer beeped. "The channel's clean," he said.

Lacey looked at Idaho; he nodded. She placed the video call. The time had been arranged earlier in the day.

The president answered on the first ring. He spoke from the Oval Office. It was eleven p.m. in Washington, D.C., and none of the White House staff were present.

Without his makeup, the president looked washed out. There were dark circles under his eyes. He looked less the powerful leader of one of the world's wealthiest nations, more the overwrought father of a rebellious teenager.

"Lacey, your mother and I gave you everything." He paced the floor in front of his desk. "How could you do this to yourself?"

"Daddy, this isn't about you." Lacey touched her chest with her fingertips. "It's about me, what *I* want."

"You've deliberately infected yourself with a deadly disease. Unless we find a cure—and my advisors tell me a cure is decades away, if it's even possible—you'll have to take custom-blended genetic therapies for the rest of your life." He groped for words with his hands. "Why?"

"I didn't choose the disease, Daddy. I caught it before the vaccine."

The president's face paled.

"Yes, that's why I wouldn't come home. Think what a political nightmare that would have been. Might have been a problem for the reelection campaign, huh?"

"I never—"

Lacey interrupted him. "Idaho saved me, kept me out of the containment camps and the news. These changes are just an added bonus."

"If you come home," the president said, "we'd take care of you, get the best doctors."

Lacey shook her magenta mane. "With the current laws, I'd have to live the rest of my life in a containment camp. That's not fair." She pointed her finger at the screen. "The younger generation is changing, Daddy. Not you nor all the leaders of the world can stop it. You can't legislate this away. You have to give us our rights."

The president scrubbed the five-o'clock shadow on his chin. "That's not possible. I can't tell Congress how to vote."

Lacey put her hands on her hips. "When your investment banker friends needed laws changed, you pushed that through."

"Honey, that was for the good of the country."

"So is this, Daddy. So is this."

Idaho held up a finger. One minute left.

Lacey shook her head at her father. "I won't come home until I can walk the streets as a free woman. As long as the Containment Act is in place, your daughter is a fugitive. Live with that."

They disconnected.

Lacey let out a slow breath and looked to Ichiro for support.

Ichiro gave her the thumbs-up sign, emphasized by his sheathed fingernails.

"Good work," Idaho said, patting Lacey's shoulder.

Lillith and Geoffrey sat in the dark after the others had gone upstairs. The house was filled past capacity, so she and Geoffrey had been relegated to sleeping in the living room. The camera, still attached to its tripod, was propped in the corner. It looked as tired as she felt.

Lillith unfolded the sprung couch. It flopped into a yellowed mattress that sagged in the middle. There was no bedding. She looked up at the sheets still thumbtacked to the walls. She moved to one and unpinned a corner. "Help me with these."

Geoffrey grabbed the other corner and unpinned it. "Do you think any of this"—he nodded at the camera—"will work?"

Lillith sighed. "If we sway public opinion, the lawmakers might listen . . . maybe."

Geoffrey wrapped the blanket into a ball and sat heavily on the thin mattress. He hunched over, head nearly touching his knees. "It's going to fail. I know it."

Lillith rubbed his back in a comforting gesture. "We have to try. That's all we can do."

He looked up at her with red-rimmed eyes. "My life has been one long disaster. First cystic fibrosis and now . . . now . . . I've killed everyone I loved. I set loose a plague."

The left side of Lillith's mouth contorted into a painful smile. "You're not alone in that. Fowler used my research for the basis of his virus." She held her arms out to him.

Geoffrey hesitated. Then they hugged, a long hard hug born of desperation and shared guilt.

It was like hugging one of her younger brothers. "We can't ever undo or make up for what's happened," Lillith said over his shoulder, "but we can mitigate the damage."

Geoffrey crowded into the main room of the barn to watch the Senate vote on CNN. Everyone at the ranch was here.

A projection screen covered the wall opposite the hayloft. On it were displayed the one hundred men and women who would decide the fate of the changed in the United States and set a precedent for the world.

Idaho was just inside the door, pressed against a back wall and watching the crowd.

"Are you nervous?" Geoffrey asked.

Idaho shrugged in a slow motion. "What do the opinions of a few old men and women matter? They couldn't stop the drug trade; they can't stop this. Too many people know how to synthesize changes. Knowledge cannot be suppressed."

Geoffrey thought of all the ways the government could make life hard for the changelings: imprisonment, restricting access to equipment, making DNA reagents controlled substances. He didn't voice his reservations, however; Idaho was volatile enough without provoking an argument.

Geoffrey worked through the crowd to stand next to Lillith. She reached out and grasped his hand in worry and anticipation. Lacey and Ichiro were draped around each other, his fingernail-knives protected in lacquered wooden sheaths. Exeter pressed her body against Idaho. She wore an electric-blue silk sheath that skimmed the tops of her thighs. Children were cradled in their mothers' laps, being shushed. Lovers wrapped arms around each other. Dweezer and his friends leaned against the back wall.

The air was tight with anxiety.

The bill to repeal the Containment Act had gone through dozens of revisions and endless debate.

Geoffrey had memorized the text of the bill. If passed, it would grant freedom to the changed . . . but at a price. They would each be implanted with a chip to make it possible to identify people whose DNA was in flux.

He worried the chips might be used to track the movements of the changed. But if the bill failed, the changed would remain in the camps indefinitely or until a cure was found, which was practically the same thing.

The vice president of the United States, serving as president of the Senate, called for the vote. As each senator touched one of two buttons on his or her desk, the vote was tallied. The numbers were displayed on-screen behind the vice president's dais.

Geoffrey held his breath.

The count fluctuated; first opposing was ahead, then supporting.

The vice president looked up at the gallery. The CNN cameras showed the president watching the proceedings. He nodded at the VP.

It was close. When the final numbers were in, the results were forty-nine for, forty-nine against, two abstentions. All eyes turned to the vice president. In cases where the Senate was tied, he was given the tie-breaking vote. He reached down and voted. The count updated: fifty for. The vice president's vote had been cast *for* the measure.

Geoffrey's heart felt as if it would burst. Triumph flooded his veins. He pumped his fist in the air.

A cheer raised the roof of the barn. Lillith whooped with joy and grabbed Geoffrey. He was grinning so hard his face hurt.

Exeter wrapped her body around Idaho and kissed him hard. Dweezer and his friends high-fived each other. Lacey looked pleased with herself. Ichiro grinned.

Geoffrey knew this was only the beginning for the rest of the world, but it was a start. A very good start.

He worked his way through the cheering crowd to the back of the barn, where Idaho embraced Exeter.

"Well," said Geoffrey. "You got what you wanted."

"Yes." Idaho's face was inscrutable. "I usually do."

"You're not worried about the implanted-microchip requirement?"

"Cracking the security of a microchip is a trivial problem. We'll have programmable versions on the street before the end of the month. My changelings will be able to be whoever they want to be." He kissed Exeter deeply.

Geoffrey looked away from their display of intimacy. The only woman he'd gotten close enough to kiss had died from a disease he'd given her. He wondered what June, with her aspirations to become a nurse, would have thought of this new world where amateur microbiologists rewrote their DNA at will.

The twin-engine plane buzzed like a dragonfly over Puget Sound. Geoffrey had chartered Bruno's plane to carry him and Lillith back to the Allen estate. As soon as the law had been repealed, Geoffrey had asked Henry Poulson to petition for the return of the Allen estate and reparations for the damages done during the army's occupation.

Orcas Island lay like a raw emerald in the middle of Puget Sound. Geoffrey remembered their last flight over the island, when they'd been running away in the middle of the night. He looked back at Lillith. Her eyes were on the horizon. She looked lost in thought.

The noon sun bounced off ripples in the ocean water in bright flashes. The blue sky above was cloudless. On a day like today it was easy to let go of the horror of the past two years, to pretend the plague had never happened and that he was merely returning home from an Aspen ski trip. Geoffrey allowed himself the fantasy for a few minutes.

Bruno's DeHavilland landed softly on the tarmac of the Allen family's private runway. Army privates packed the helicopters with the last personnel and equipment to leave the camp. Captain Morgenson oversaw the operation.

Geoffrey stepped out of the plane and a warm breeze riffled his multicolored hair. Lillith stepped down after him.

"Geoffrey," Morgenson said in greeting. His voice was tight.

"Where is Mr. Yi?"

Captain Morgenson said a word to his second-in-command, then turned to Geoffrey. "Follow me." He led Geoffrey and Lillith to one of the guest bedrooms the army used as an ICU.

Mr. Yi lay under an oxygen tent. Geoffrey reached under the plastic and took his gnarled hand in his own. Mr. Yi's eyes opened. They were clouded and focused shakily on Geoffrey, but when they did, Mr. Yi grinned. "You come back," he said in a whisper.

Geoffrey patted the old man's hand. "We won, Mr. Yi. The camp is being dismantled, and everyone is going home."

Mr. Yi turned his head to one side and coughed. When he turned back, Geoffrey was alarmed to see flecks of blood on the white pillow.

"No home," Mr. Yi said, "to go to."

Geoffrey wanted to crush the old man in his arms and force life back into him. He hadn't been at his parents' bedside when they were dying, and now he was glad. Mr. Yi's illness tore him apart. "Of course you have a home," he said. "Aren't we family? Don't I have your eyes? You'll stay with me."

Mr. Yi smiled, but his expression was sad. "Tell me . . . everything."

Geoffrey told Mr. Yi about the wild flight from the camp, how they found children of world leaders who had the plague and used them as leverage, about the police pulling changed and changelings off the street, how Congress had relented, how there was funding again for a cure and the changed were being allowed to go home.

Mr. Yi fell asleep during Geoffrey's monologue, the ghost of a smile on the old man's face.

*   *   *

The Allen compound on Orcas Island was quiet now that the army and most of the changed had moved out. Geoffrey had invited those who had nowhere else to go to stay with him.

Lillith had asked to live on the island, to tend the sick who remained and because she needed a quiet place to find peace in the new order of things.

On the mainland, Idaho's ranch had been opened to the public as a research station for the changed, part commune and part medical facility. Geoffrey followed their press releases. They made huge strides in controlling the disease.

Idaho had moved with Exeter to a new, undisclosed location and was working on a cure for AHMS, a way to drive the original, unstable virus out of the host's system. His changelings were too susceptible to new variations; too much time was wasted in synthesizing treatments for defects, and that limited the time that could be spent creating new designs.

No one knew where Idaho's secret lab was, not even Lillith. Geoffrey was relieved the enigmatic man was out of his life. As much as he admired the man's intelligence and ambition . . . Idaho disturbed him. Geoffrey hoped Idaho had found what he needed to feel safe.

Geoffrey didn't know if he, himself, would ever feel secure. He walked outside. The morning was cold and gray. He followed the path to the dock. Perhaps if he told his troubles to the Pacific Ocean, it would be big enough to hold them.

Lillith sat on a teak bench overlooking Puget Sound. Dawn was breaking gray and rose in the east. Morning fog clung to the water. Overhead a gull screamed.

"Mr. Yi died in his sleep last night," Geoffrey said. "He took a piece of me with him."

"They always do." She patted the bench beside her.

Geoffrey sat and looked out over the ocean. "Where do we go from here?"

Lillith watched the Pacific as she answered. "It's not up to us anymore. If the past two years have taught me anything, it's that you can't solve the problems of the world. And what's more, you don't have to—not alone." They looked out over the sea. Two humans at the dawn of a new age. The sun rose and, for the first time in years, Geoffrey looked forward to what the day might bring.

EPILOGUE

Static degraded the transmission, blurring the video and distorting sound. Multiple filters processed the signal and resolved snow into an image. A hologram wavered in midair, a glowing meter-wide ball.

In the three-dimensional image, a man with leopard-spotted skin sat, one ankle crossed over his knee, on the end of a desk. The man's head was covered with a crest of blue-green feathers. They flexed with his smile as he said, "This is Edo Gulianni with *Genemod Magazine,* bringing you the latest trends in DNA fashion."

Beside him, small and dark, sat an elderly woman in an antique wing-backed chair.

He indicated the woman with a wave of his hand. "In our studios today, we have a very special guest. A woman who was in on the ground floor of modern biomedicine, who saw it all unfold. Dr. Lillith Watkins!"

The audience responded with applause, whoops, and cheers, and from the back of the room, the ululating howl of a wolf. The camera swept over them—a panoply of furred, winged, and scaled creatures, mostly bipedal, but some not. A woman with blue skin and silver hair cheered next to a man whose flesh was the brightly colored pebbled skin of a Gila monster.

Before this mass of color and imagination, Lillith was very plain and brown. She had allowed age to settle on her, drawing her skin into loose folds and stealing the flesh from her body. Her cap of hair was yellowish white. She was like a wrinkled old apple thrown into a pile of costume jewelry.

Edo placed a well-manicured hand on her arm, and his perfectly proportioned face sobered. "Is it true, Dr. Watkins, that you've refused any sort of body modification?"

Lillith faced the camera, and her mouth worked a bit before she spoke. "I was the first person in North America to test the Japanese vaccine. I have never had the plague."

Edo's face softened with sympathy. "But there are new versions of the changeling virus that circumvent the vaccine." He winked at Lillith. "Haven't you ever considered it?"

Lillith snorted. "This old body has carried me safely through many years. I don't see any reason to change now."

"Not even for health reasons? Patients who've had age-related DNA corrections have attained life spans of one hundred and fifty years so far, with no sign of slowing down."

Lillith winced and shifted on her chair. "Young man, you weren't there in the beginning. You didn't see the things I've seen."

The talk show host leaned back and recrossed his legs, the purple silk of his pants rustling. "Yes? Why don't you tell our audience what it was like? Is it true you treated Geoffrey Allen, the infamous 'patient zero'?"

Lillith nodded. "I did. He spent seven months in quarantine with us at the CDC. And then, of course, we worked together in the Changeling Defense League for years after that."

Edo ruffled his crest. "Do you think, if he'd had the foreknowledge of the consequences of his actions, he'd have taken the cure for his cystic fibrosis?"

Lillith shook her head and said in a voice filled with emotion, "I don't know. A lot of people died in that plague, including the people close to him: his parents, a woman he wanted to marry."

"It's too bad we can't ask him ourselves," said the host, his voice somber, "with the recent assassination." The host's crest flattened, giving the impression of a crestfallen rooster. "Were you able to attend his funeral last month?"

"No." Lillith looked down at her hands. "I figure I'll see him soon enough, by and by."

"Um-hmm." The birdman's gaze flitted over the TelePrompTer. "You also knew the genius designer Idaho Blue, did you not?"

"Yes," Lillith agreed. "He designed the original treatments for AHMS."

"Please, tell the folks at home what he's like in person."

Lillith's eyes met the camera. Brown and rheumy, they stared out of the video. "Idaho was . . . a very private person, even then. He lost his sister very young, and that affected him."

The host leaned his cheek close to Lillith's and said, "And do you know where he is now?"

A gentle smile lit Lillith's face. "I have my suspicions."

"Anything you care to share with the people at home?"

The smile widened. Lillith's face shone with mischief. "No. I don't think he'd approve."

"Oh ho!" the host leaned back and clapped his hands together. "So he's still alive. So tell me, which of the sightings are real?"

Lillith's eyes took on a faraway look. "If he's where I think he is . . . none of them. But let's move on to other topics. Idaho has a right to his privacy."

"Come on, his disappearance is the biggest mystery in the modern world. He's worshipped around the world as the originator of modern molecular biology, and twenty years ago—poof—he disappears. No one's seen him since the Tokyo 2047 fashion show." Edo leaned forward in simulated intimacy and stage-whispered, "Is it true he still moves among us, so changed no one recognizes him?"

Lillith shook her head. "Idaho's location is his concern. When he wants us to know, he'll tell us."

The hologram transmission faded. The ball hung in the air, crackling static.

Idaho shut down the display with a wave of his hand. He'd learned enough. Lillith had kept his secret; he was safe. She was the only person on Earth who knew where he was. It was through her that he'd ordered the technology he needed to build his ultimate hideaway.

Idaho grinned in the reflected glow of Jupiter's gaseous clouds. Somewhere high above the cloud cover, Earth was nothing more than a glowing dot in the sky.

Jupiter roiled below him with storm fronts and wind shear. Idaho stood on the ledge of a floating platform that was all he had left of the ship he'd built to bring him to this world. It held a couple of rooms, a link to orbiting satellites, and a porch where he could absorb energy and nutrients from the atmosphere.

Idaho stretched wide and let the wind catch the membranes that ran along his body from his wrists to ankles.

His body was its own self-contained space suit. Algae in his bloodstream recycled what little oxygen his new metabolism needed, and the venting orifices of his body ensured that his internal pressure was equalized with that of the gas giant. Insulating flesh kept out the heat and cold of space.

Idaho contracted his stomach and tacked his wings, pivoting his body so he faced downwind.

Exeter was there, her joyous shout transmitted to him through the inductive network they shared. There was no sound through her sealed mouth and lungs.

She looked very much like a pterodactyl, with her shielded eyes and sleek, winged body. Muscles bunched under her gray-gold skin as she worked her way obliquely through the wind, back to him.

They tangled in midair and fell, accelerating faster and faster into the core of Jupiter's gaseous gravity well. Heat built up from the friction of their fall until, laughing, Exeter broke free and caught a convection current back to the outer atmosphere.

Idaho joined her, feeling complete and happy and free.

See what's coming in March...

THE SHADOW OF THE STORM
by Kurt R.A. Giambastiani
President George Custer is prepared to wage war against the Indian nations of the Cheyenne Alliance for possession of the unsettled frontier—unaware that his only son lives among them and fights beside them...
45916-4

PAPER MAGE
by Leah R. Cutter
In a small Chinese village during the Tang Dynasty, an unsure young woman has managed to elude the conventions of her society to become a gifted paper mage—one who creates magic with the ancient art of paper folding. Because her gifts are in demand for the protection they can offer, Xiao Yen must leave behind her beloved family and embark on a dangerous mission. Yet she has no idea that this looming adventure will shape the very woman she is to become.
45917-2

THE BEST OF DREAMS OF DECADENCE
edited by Angela Kessler
From Angela Kessler, editor and publisher of the premier vampire magazine, *Dreams of Decadence*, comes an elite selection of prose and poetry as eerie and immortal as the undead themselves. Collected for the first time in one volume, these dark dreams bring to life the irresistible lures and longings of the vampire experience—from the gothic to the modern, the fanciful to the fierce, the icy-veined to the hot-blooded.
45918-0

To order call: 1-800-788-6262